THE EARLY WORK OF
PHILIP K. DICK

VOLUME ONE:
THE VARIABLE MAN
& OTHER STORIES

THE EARLY WORK OF
PHILIP
K. DICK

VOLUME ONE:
THE VARIABLE MAN
& OTHER STORIES

SERIES EDITOR:
GREGG RICKMAN

PRIME BOOKS

THE EARLY WORK OF PHILIP K. DICK

VOLUME ONE:
THE VARIABLE MAN & OTHER STORIES

Interior design and typesetting by
Linduna [www.linduna.com]

Prime Books
www.prime-books.com

ISBN: 978-1-60701-202-3

TABLE OF CONTENTS

———

INTRODUCTION
BY GREGG RICKMAN

Philip K. Dick published his first science fiction story, "Beyond Lies the Wub," in the July 1952 issue of *Planet Stories*. It was not his first sale; "Roog" (completed in November of the previous year) had already been purchased, for the February 1953 issue of *The Magazine of Fantasy and Science Fiction,* by editor and fellow Berkeley resident Anthony Boucher. But it was the first of his stories to actually see print.

"Beyond Lies the Wub" is a darkly humorous story of cannibalism and possession. The witty, erudite wub—a 400 pound pig-like creature, found on Mars and purchased for 50 cents—resists being eaten by every means at its disposal. The wub is too fat to run away, too out of shape to fight. He instead tries to talk the ship's captain, who seems obsessed with consuming him, into sparing him, reading Captain Franco's mind and raising issues of ethics and philosophy in support of his right to life.

"Philosophy," snorts the practical captain. "It may interest you to know that we will be hard put to find something to eat for the next month."

This little story lays down certain themes Dick continued to develop for the remaining three decades of his literary career. This was not the Philip Dick who would write such science fiction classics as *The Man in the High Castle* (1962), *The Three Stigmata of Palmer Eldritch* (1965), *Ubik* (1969) or *A Scanner Darkly* (1977); this was a young author struggling to find his voice and make his way in the world. But the outlines of the artist he would become are apparent.

At the time he wrote the story, Dick wrote in 1980, "I was a fireball radical and atheist, and religion was entirely foreign to me." Yet the tale is full of religious imagery, down to the parody of the Eucharist, in which those who imbibe the wub's body and blood become him—or at least Captain Franco does. The name Franco could not have been an accident either, recalling as it does that of the dictator of Spain, a *bête noir* of Berkeley's left, with which Dick associated himself.

Further, "Beyond Lies the Wub" displays the career-long conflict in Dick's work between those with empathy and those without. "Casting about in an effort to contrast the truly human from what I was later to call the 'android or the reflex machine,'" he wrote that he was happy to hit upon the "gentle wub."

Philip K. Dick was 23 years old in July 1952. He had been born in Chicago in the last days of December, 1928. His parents separated when he was four. His mother, Dorothy, raised him, in Washington, D.C., and then in Berkeley, California. As a child he developed a difficulty in swallowing, a condition that along with agoraphobia plagued him intermittently throughout his life. The boy was a fan of the science fiction magazines that blossomed in the years just before World War II, and wrote some fantasies himself. As a teenager he found work at a Berkeley record store. He worked fulltime until he was 21, married a young woman named Kleo Apostolides, and in 1950 bought a house in the poorer southern end of the city, near Oakland.

At the age of 21 he quit full time employment. Interviewing the author in 1981, I asked him what he did then.

"I wrote fantasy and science fiction," he told me. "I worked half time and then I wrote the other half. And one day I was standing in the record store and my old bogey hit me. I thought I was choking . . .

"So I went to the boss and said, I'm sick. I have to go home. I got one of the salesmen to drive me home and I called and said I can't come back to work, I'm sick and I don't know what's wrong.

"Well what was wrong was that I didn't want to work in the store. I wanted to write. I simply stayed home and wrote and the first month I sold something to *Galaxy* and then pretty soon I was in orbit. But the phobia was designed to get me out of that store. In other words it was designed to press me to do that which I yearned to do."

Dick put this tale more succinctly to his friend Paul Williams, as related in Williams' *Only Apparently Real*: "It's as if Beethoven really wanted to work in the delicatessen, you know, and he got a phobia every time he started to chop up salami, so he became a composer."

Dick was aided in his quest to write by the presence in Berkeley of the well-regarded author and editor Anthony Boucher (1912-68). In 1949 Boucher co-founded what was, with John W. Campbell's *Astounding* and Horace Gold's *Galaxy*, one of the three major jour-nals in periodical science fiction in the early 1950s, *The Magazine of Fantasy and Science Fiction*, universally known as *F&SF*. *Astounding* specialized in hard, nuts-and-bolts science fiction, while Gold "only wanted sociological science fiction," as Dick told me in 1981. As Dick yearned to publish fantasy, *F&SF* was a natural goal for him.

Boucher was by all accounts a delightful man who gave generously of himself, offering writing workshops to all comers every Thursday evening. Dick's agoraphobia kept him from attending regularly, but he often sent Kleo to the sessions with his latest manuscript, and benefited enormously from both Boucher's enthusiasm and criticism. "I knew Tony for almost twenty years," Dick wrote after Boucher's death, "and he did for me such powerful things that I am not the person I would have been if there had been no Tony Boucher." He told Williams that his criticism was merciless but beneficial: "He was teaching me to throw away all the golden garbage that I was turning out, forcing me to do something else than I was doing."

Kleo Dick (now Kleo Mini) remembers that her husband wrote a dozen or more stories of "sad little people . . . wonderful little fantasy stories for which there was no market." Fantasy fiction was indeed Dick's first love. Kleo Mini remembers that just two of them eventu-ally sold, "Of Withered Apples" (reprinted here) and "Roog." Kleo remembers that there were "fifteen or twenty out before we sold one. One morning we went out, and seventeen of his manuscripts had been returned in one day. They were spilling out all over the front porch. I think it was one of the worst days of our lives, but we just went in and addressed new envelopes, and sent them out again."

Two of Dick's friends of the era told me they remembered a "remarkable collection of rejection slips" mounted on the wall of his office. But eventually his persistence paid off—he sold "Roog" (a dog's eye view of garbage men as aliens) to *F&SF* and began selling to the smaller markets as well. 'Beyond Lies the Wub" was, as mentioned, the first story actually published. "Reader reaction was excellent," he wrote in 1980, "and Jack O'Sullivan, editor of *Planet*, wrote to tell me that in his opinion it was a very fine little story—whereupon he paid me something like fifteen dollars. It was my introduction to pulp payment rates."

"Wub" was published in *Planet*'s July 1952 issue. July 1952 was a key month for Philip Dick in other ways, for it was that month that the Scott Meredith Literary Agency began handling his sales. For the rest of his life, almost thirty years, he was a Meredith client, the agency managing sales for his short stories, novels, and attempts to publish straight literary fiction.

Prior to that July Dick had written and sold 15 science fiction stories, which like "Beyond Lies the Wub" and "Roog" appeared on the stands over the next couple of years. Seven of these stories appear in this volume—"Beyond Lies the Wub," "The Gun" (*Planet Stories*, September 1952), "The Skull" (*If,* September), "Mr. Spaceship" (*Imagination,* January 1953), "Piper in the Woods" (*Imagination,* February), "The Variable Man" (*Space Science Fiction,* September), and "The Crystal Crypt" (*Planet Stories,* January 1954). From July 1952 on all of Dick's fiction can be dated more precisely, as the Meredith agency kept meticulous records as to when each story reached them, which magazines they tried to interest, and where each tale was eventually published. "Meddler," for example, reached the agency on July 24, and was eventually placed in *Future*, in October 1954.

The early 1950s were a boom period for science fiction, and Dick and his agents had many markets to choose from. There had been only a few science fiction magazines in the 1940s. By 1950, according to Lester del Ray in his *The World of Science Fiction*, there were 25. The field's peak year was 1953, with 36 titles, which rapidly declined to 18 titles in 1956, and then to six in 1961. (By that time Dick had switched to full-time novel writing, keeping pace with a changing industry.)

Dick rode this wave, publishing four stories in 1952, 31 in 1953, 28 in 1954—and then twelve in 1955 (and one novel), five in 1956 (and two novels). Only a small handful of these stories were placed in the top market magazines, magazines that paid as high as 3 cents a word: six in *F&SF*, seven in *Galaxy*, just one ("Imposter") in *Astounding*. These became in turn the stories that Dick's several collections of stories tended to reprint. Many others of his stories were not reprinted at all until the 1987 publication of the five-volume *The Collected Stories of Philip K. Dick*. Some of them have not been reprinted since, until this volume. It would be a mistake, however, to dismiss these "bottom market" stories, sold for a penny a word, as unimportant. Where any of Dick's stories landed was often strictly a matter of luck. Some of his best work in this period appeared in magazines like *Planet Stories* and *Imagination*. Dick never hacked out any of these short stories, and worked hard to make each of them the best that he could.

Dick usually wrote late at night, sometimes as late as 2 or 3 in the morning. As Kleo Mini recalls, "He usually worked things out in his head. Then he'd diagram the plot lines, how the characters would interact, before he actually did any writing." After several drafts "he'd make a lot of changes even to the last copy—he might change words or phrases because they felt right." He cooperated, to some degree, with editorial suggestions, accepting Boucher's suggestions without question, and cutting "The Mold of Yancy" (1955) for another editor from 9500 to 7000 words. He refused however to edit "Recall Mechanism" in 1955 for the bottom market magazine *Imagination*, preferring to wait until 1959 for its eventual publication in another magazine. He stopped writing for the well-paying Horace Gold after discovering that editor's habits of interpolating editorial changes without consulting him.

The February 1953 issue of *Imagination*, which carried his science fantasy "Piper in the Woods" (found in this volume), also carries a full page "Introducing the Author" feature on Philip Dick, accompanied by a photo of the author, chin in hand. In the feature Dick speaks of the "files and stacks of magazines, boxes of notes and data, parts of unfinished stories, a huge desk full of related material in various stages" that surrounded him as he wrote. French critic Marcel Thaon wrote in 1977

> The picture of Dick on the dust-jacket of *Imagination*, when he was in his 20s, looking at us doubtfully, bones visible in his face, eyes frightened, mouth prominent, resembles the fragile heroes that he loves . . . As with identifying with this skimpy figure, he wrote only short stories in that period.

In his later years, Philip Dick was dismissive of much of this early work. "My stories," he told me in 1981, "just appall me in that period." He claimed to have been a bad science fiction writer, largely because he had "started off as a fantasy writer. I wrote short fantasies for *F&SF*. And I only wrote science fiction because there was much more of a market (for it). And my early science fiction was *very bad*. I was a very *bad* science fiction writer, but I was a very good fantasy writer, but outside of Tony Boucher nobody existed to buy fantasy."

Many of Dick's earliest stories, as we've seen, are indeed pure fantasy, while others allude to the genre, as with "Piper in the Woods," inspired by the beautiful chapter ("The Piper at the Gates of Dawn") in Kenneth Grahame's *The Wind in the Willows* when Mole and Rat encounter the God Pan. It works perfectly as a title for a story about alien creatures whose defense against colonization is to convince humans that they would prefer life as plants. Dick will return again and again to the theme of an entity who can cast a spell on those who encounter him. (After all, what is "Beyond Lies the Wub" but a tale of alien absorption?) Nature seems benign but can be dangerous—as here, or with the butterflies of "Meddler," or the "little dried apple" that Lori Patterson consumes in "Of Withered Apples."

Dick, though, was wrong about his strengths. While some of these fantasies are excellent, they pale in significance besides his best early science fiction stories.

Science fiction was a wonderful vehicle for writers to comment on the world of the 1950s. Dick used the format to comment on civil rights ("James P. Crow"), the dangers of psychiatric medicine ("Jon's World"), or the ongoing dangers of the Cold War. Many of these short stories take place against the background of an earth destroyed by war. Philip Dick's future earths are variously described as "Ruins, vast ruins. People poking around. Ruin and death everywhere. Slag" ("Meddler"), or "a globe of ruin and ash" ("Jon's World"). One of his most optimistic stories, "The Variable Man" posits a way out of the Cold War's "mutual assured destruction" stand-off by means of a man from 1913 who does not so much think outside the box, but instead feels his way, slowly and by hand.

Dick's great overarching theme became, in the great novels of the 1960s and later, the notion that the world as we know it is but a shadow of a more intense, alternate reality. We only sometimes glimpse the truth, like poor Ed Fletcher in "Adjustment Team," seeing reality as buildings and people "fallen into grey clouds of dust" not because of atomic war but because of his sudden ability to see reality as it really is. The visionary child in "Jon's World" gives voice to this theme in a story completed in October 1952. His visions are

" . . . Like looking through a window. A window into
another world. A real world. Much more real than this.
It makes all this just a shadow world. Only dim shadows.
Shapes. Images."

From "Beyond Lies the Wub" through to "Jon's World" and
"Adjustment Team," it is Dick's science fiction stories, more so than
his fantasies, that gave the young author his best forum to explore
what really mattered to him. Good in and of themselves, they lay down
markers for what will be his most significant work in the future.

Gregg Rickman
Berkeley, California
May, 2008

Works Cited

Lester Del Ray, *The World of Science Fiction: 1926-1976 The History of a Subculture* (New York: Ballantine Books, 1979)

Philip K. Dick, "Story Notes," in Mark Hurst, ed., *The Golden Man* (New York: Berkley, 1980)

Gregg Rickman, *Philip K. Dick: In His Own Words* (Long Beach, CA: Fragments West/The Valentine Press, 1984; second ed., 1989)

Gregg Rickman, *To the High Castle, Philip K. Dick: A Life 1928-1962* (Long Beach, CA: Fragments West/The Valentine Press, 1989)

Marcel Thaon, "The Early Dick" ("Dick aux premieres ages"). Translated copy in Philip Dick papers.

Paul Williams, *Only Apparently Real* (New York: Arbor House, 1986)

BEYOND LIES THE WUB

They had almost finished with the loading. Outside stood the Optus, his arms folded, his face sunk in gloom. Captain Franco walked leisurely down the gangplank, grinning.

"What's the matter?" he said. "You're getting paid for all this."

The Optus said nothing. He turned away, collecting his robes. The Captain put his boot on the hem of the robe.

"Just a minute. Don't go off. I'm not finished."

"Oh?" The Optus turned with dignity. "I am going back to the village." He looked toward the animals and birds being driven up the gangplank into the spaceship. "I must organize new hunts."

Franco lit a cigarette. "Why not? You people can go out into the veldt and track it all down again. But when we run halfway between Mars and Earth—"

The Optus went off, wordless. Franco joined the first mate at the bottom of the gangplank.

"How's it coming?" he asked. He looked at his watch. "We got a good bargain here."

The mate glanced at him sourly. "How do you explain that?"

"What's the matter with you? We need it more than they do."

"I'll see you later, Captain." The mate threaded his way up the plank, between the long-legged Martian go-birds, into the ship.

Franco watched him disappear. He was just starting up after him, up the plank toward the port, when he saw *it*.

"My God!" He stood staring, his hands on his hips. Peterson was walking along the path, his face red, leading *it* by a string.

"I'm sorry, Captain," he said, tugging at the string. Franco walked toward him.

"What is it?"

The wub stood sagging, its great body settling slowly. It was sitting down, its eyes half shut. A few flies buzzed about its flank, and it switched its tail.

It sat. There was silence.

"It's a wub," Peterson said. "I got it from a native for fifty cents. He said it was a very unusual animal. Very respected."

"This?" Franco poked the great sloping side of the wub. "It's a pig! A huge dirty pig!"

"Yes sir, it's a pig. The natives call it a wub."

"A huge pig. It must weigh four hundred pounds." Franco grabbed a tuft of the rough hair. The wub gasped. Its eyes opened, small and moist. Then its great mouth twitched.

A tear rolled down the wub's cheek and splashed on the floor.

"Maybe it's good to eat," Peterson said nervously.

"We'll soon find out," Franco said.

❖ ❖ ❖

The wub survived the takeoff, sound asleep in the hold of the ship. When they were out in space and everything was running smoothly, Captain Franco bade his men fetch the wub upstairs so that he might perceive what manner of beast it was.

The wub grunted and wheezed, squeezing up the passageway.

"Come on," Jones grated, pulling at the rope. The wub twisted, rubbing its skin off on the smooth chrome walls. It burst into the anteroom, tumbling down in a heap. The men leaped up.

"Good Lord," French said. "What is it?"

"Peterson says it's a wub," Jones said. "It belongs to him." He kicked at the wub. The wub stood up unsteadily, panting.

"What's the matter with it?" French came over. "Is it going to be sick?"

They watched. The wub rolled its eyes mournfully. It gazed around at the men.

"I think it's thirsty," Peterson said. He went to get some water. French shook his head.

"No wonder we had so much trouble taking off. I had to reset all my ballast calculations."

Peterson came back with the water. The wub began to lap gratefully, splashing the men.

Captain Franco appeared at the door.

"Let's have a look at it." He advanced, squinting critically. "You got this for fifty cents?"

"Yes, sir," Peterson said. "It eats almost anything. I fed it on grain and it liked that. And then potatoes, and mash, and scraps from the table, and milk. It seems to enjoy eating. After it eats it lies down and goes to sleep."

"I see," Captain Franco said. "Now, as to its taste. That's the real question. I doubt if there's much point in fattening it up any more. It seems fat enough to me already. Where's the cook? I want him here. I want to find out—"

The wub stopped lapping and looked up at the Captain.

"Really, Captain," the wub said. "I suggest we talk of other matters."

The room was silent.

"What was that?" Franco said. "Just now."

"The wub, sir," Peterson said. "It spoke."

They all looked at the wub.

"What did it say? What did it say?"

"It suggested we talk about other things."

Franco walked toward the wub. He went all around it, examining it from every side. Then he came back over and stood with the men.

"I wonder if there's a native inside it," he said thoughtfully. "Maybe we should open it up and have a look."

"Oh, goodness!" the wub cried. "Is that all you people can think of, killing and cutting?"

Franco clenched his fists. "Come out of there! Whoever you are, come out!"

Nothing stirred. The men stood together, their faces blank, staring at the wub. The wub swished its tail. It belched suddenly.

"I beg your pardon," the wub said.

"I don't think there's anyone in there," Jones said in a low voice. They all looked at each other.

The cook came in.

"You wanted me, Captain?" he said. "What's this thing?"

"This is a wub," Franco said. "It's to be eaten. Will you measure it and figure out—"

"I think we should have a talk," the wub said. "I'd like to discuss this with you, Captain, if I might. I can see that you and I do not agree on some basic issues."

The Captain took a long time to answer. The wub waited good-naturedly, licking the water from its jowls.

"Come into my office," the Captain said at last. He turned and walked out of the room. The wub rose and padded after him. The men watched it go out. They heard it climbing the stairs.

"I wonder what the outcome will be," the cook said. "Well, I'll be in the kitchen. Let me know as soon as you hear."

"Sure," Jones said. "Sure."

❖ ❖ ❖

The wub eased itself down in the corner with a sigh. "You must forgive me," it said. "I'm afraid I'm addicted to various forms of relaxation. When one is as large as I—"

The Captain nodded impatiently. He sat down at his desk and folded his hands.

"All right," he said. "Let's get started. You're a wub? Is that correct?"

The wub shrugged. "I suppose so. That's what they call us, the natives, I mean. We have our own term."

"And you speak English? You've been in contact with Earthmen before?"

"No."

"Then how do you do it?"

"Speak English? Am I speaking English? I'm not conscious of speaking anything in particular. I examined your mind—"

"My mind?"

"I studied the contents, especially the semantic warehouse, as I refer to it—"

"I see," the Captain said. "Telepathy. Of course."

"We are a very old race," the wub said. "Very old and very ponderous. It is difficult for us to move around. You can appreciate anything so slow and heavy would be at the mercy of more agile forms of life. There was no use in our relying on physical defenses. How could we win? Too heavy to run, too soft to fight, too good-natured to hunt for game—"

"How do you live?"

"Plants. Vegetables. We can eat almost anything. We're very catholic. Tolerant, eclectic, catholic. We live and let live. That's how we've gotten along."

The wub eyed the Captain.

"And that's why I so violently objected to this business about having me boiled. I could see the image in your mind—most of me in the frozen food locker, some of me in the kettle, a bit for your pet cat—"

"So you read minds?" the Captain said. "How interesting. Anything else? I mean, what else can you do along those lines?"

"A few odds and ends," the wub said absently, staring around the room. "A nice apartment you have here, Captain. You keep it quite neat. I respect life-forms that are tidy. Some Martian birds are quite tidy. They throw things out of their nests and sweep them—"

"Indeed." The Captain nodded. "But to get back to the problem—"

"Quite so. You spoke of dining on me. The taste, I am told, is good. A little fatty, but tender. But how can any lasting contact be established between your people and mine if you resort to such barbaric attitudes? Eat me? Rather you should discuss questions with me, philosophy, the arts—"

The Captain stood up. "Philosophy. It might interest you to know that we will be hard put to find something to eat for the next month. An unfortunate spoilage—"

"I know." The wub nodded. "But wouldn't it be more in accord with your principles of democracy if we all drew straws, or something along that line? After all, democracy is to protect the minority from just such infringements. Now, if each of us casts one vote—"

The Captain walked to the door.

"Nuts to you," he said. He opened the door. He opened his mouth.

He stood frozen, his mouth wide, his eyes staring, his fingers still on the knob.

The wub watched him. Presently it padded out of the room, edging past the Captain. It went down the hall, deep in meditation.

❖ ❖ ❖

The room was quiet.

"So you see," the wub said, "we have a common myth. Your mind contains many familiar myth symbols. Ishtar, Odysseus—"

Peterson sat silently, staring at the floor. He shifted in his chair.

"Go on," he said. "Please go on."

"I find in your Odysseus a figure common to the mythology of most self-conscious races. As I interpret it, Odysseus wanders as an individual aware of himself as such. This is the idea of separation, of separation from family and country. The process of individuation."

"But Odysseus returns to his home." Peterson looked out the port window, at the stars, endless stars, burning intently in the empty universe. "Finally he goes home."

"As must all creatures. The moment of separation is a temporary period, a brief journey of the soul. It begins, it ends. The wanderer returns to land and race..."

The door opened. The wub stopped, turning its great head.

Captain Franco came into the room, the men behind him. They hesitated at the door.

"Are you all right?" French said.

"Do you mean me?" Peterson said, surprised. "Why me?"

Franco lowered his gun. "Come over here," he said to Peterson. "Get up and come here."

There was silence.

"Go ahead," the wub said. "It doesn't matter."

Peterson stood up. "What for?"

"It's an order."

Peterson walked to the door. French caught his arm.

"What's going on?" Peterson wrenched loose. "What's the matter with you?"

Captain Franco moved toward the wub. The wub looked up from where it lay in the corner, pressed against the wall.

"It is interesting," the wub said, "that you are obsessed with the idea of eating me. I wonder why."

"Get up," Franco said.

"If you wish." The wub rose, grunting. "Be patient. It is difficult for me." It stood, gasping, its tongue lolling foolishly.

"Shoot it now," French said.

"For God's sake!" Peterson exclaimed. Jones turned to him quickly, his eyes gray with fear.

"You didn't see him—like a statue, standing there, his mouth open. If we hadn't come down, he'd still be there."

"Who? The Captain?" Peterson stared around. "But he's all right now."

They looked at the wub, standing in the middle of the room, its great chest rising and falling.

"Come on," Franco said. "Out of the way."

The men pulled aside toward the door.

"You are quite afraid, aren't you?" the wub said. "Have I done anything to you? I am against the idea of hurting. All I have done is try to protect myself. Can you expect me to rush eagerly to my death? I am a sensible being like yourselves. I was curious to see your ship, learn about you. I suggested to the native—"

The gun jerked.

"See," Franco said. "I thought so."

The wub settled down, panting. It put its paws out, pulling its tail around it.

"It is very warm," the wub said. "I understand that we are close to the jets. Atomic power. You have done many wonderful things with it—technically. Apparently your scientific hierarchy is not equipped to solve moral, ethical—"

Franco turned to the men, crowding behind him, wide-eyed, silent.

"I'll do it. You can watch."

French nodded. "Try to hit the brain. It's no good for eating. Don't hit the chest. If the rib cage shatters, we'll have to pick bones out."

"Listen," Peterson said, licking his lips. "Has it done anything? What harm has it done? I'm asking you. And anyhow, it's still mine. You have no right to shoot it. It doesn't belong to you."

Franco raised his gun.

"I'm going out," Jones said, his face white and sick. "I don't want to see it."

"Me, too," French said. The men straggled out, murmuring. Peterson lingered at the door.

"It was talking to me about myths," he said. "It wouldn't hurt anyone."

He went outside.

Franco walked toward the wub. The wub looked up slowly. It swallowed.

"A very foolish thing," it said. "I am sorry that you want to do it. There was a parable that your Saviour related—"

It stopped, staring at the gun.

"Can you look me in the eye and do it?" the wub said. "Can you do that?"

The Captain gazed down. "I can look you in the eye," he said. "Back on the farm we had hogs, dirty razorback hogs. I can do it."

Staring down at the wub, into the gleaming, moist eyes, he pressed the trigger.

❖ ❖ ❖

The taste was excellent.

They sat glumly around the table, some of them hardly eating at all. The only one who seemed to be enjoying himself was Captain Franco.

"More?" he said, looking around. "More? And some wine, perhaps."

"Not me," French said. "I think I'll go back to the chart room."

"Me, too." Jones stood up, pushing his chair back. "I'll see you later."

The Captain watched them go. Some of the others excused themselves.

"What do you suppose the matter is?" the Captain said. He turned to Peterson. Peterson sat staring down at his plate, at the potatoes, the green peas, and at the thick slab of tender, warm meat.

He opened his mouth. No sound came.

The Captain put his hand on Peterson's shoulder.

"It is only organic matter, now," he said. "The life essence is gone." He ate, spooning up the gravy with some bread. "I, myself, love to eat. It is one of the greatest things that a living creature can enjoy. Eating, resting, meditation, discussing things."

Peterson nodded. Two more men got up and went out. The Captain drank some water and sighed.

"Well," he said. "I must say that this was a very enjoyable meal. All the reports I had heard were quite true—the taste of wub. Very fine. But I was prevented from enjoying this in times past."

He dabbed at his lips with his napkin and leaned back in his chair. Peterson stared dejectedly at the table.

The Captain watched him intently. He leaned over.

"Come, come," he said. "Cheer up! Let's discuss things."

He smiled.

"As I was saying before I was interrupted, the role of Odysseus in the myths—"

Peterson jerked up, staring.

"To go on," the Captain said. "Odysseus, as I understand him—"

THE GUN

The Captain peered into the eyepiece of the telescope. He adjusted the focus quickly.

"It was an atomic fission we saw, all right," he said presently. He sighed and pushed the eyepiece away. "Any of you who wants to look may do so. But it's not a pretty sight."

"Let me look," Tance the archeologist said. He bent down to look, squinting. "Good Lord!" He leaped violently back, knocking against Dorle, the Chief Navigator.

"Why did we come all this way, then?" Dorle asked, looking around at the other men. "There's no point even in landing. Let's go back at once."

"Perhaps he's right," the biologist murmured. "But I'd like to look for myself, if I may." He pushed past Tance and peered into the sight.

He saw a vast expanse, an endless surface of gray, stretching to the edge of the planet. At first he thought it was water but after a moment he realized that it was slag, pitted, fused slag, broken only by hills of rock jutting up at intervals. Nothing moved or stirred. Everything was silent, dead.

"I see," Fomar said, backing away from the eyepiece. "Well, I won't find any legumes there." He tried to smile, but his lips stayed unmoved. He stepped away and stood by himself, staring past the others.

"I wonder what the atmospheric sample will show," Tance said.

"I think I can guess," the Captain answered. "Most of the atmosphere is poisoned. But didn't we expect all this? I don't see why we're so surprised. A fission visible as far away as our system must be a terrible thing."

He strode off down the corridor, dignified and expressionless. They watched him disappear into the control room.

As the Captain closed the door the young woman turned. "What did the telescope show? Good or bad?"

"Bad. No life could possibly exist. Atmosphere poisoned, water vaporized, all the land fused."

"Could they have gone underground?"

The Captain slid back the port window so that the surface of the planet under them was visible. The two of them stared down, silent and disturbed. Mile after mile of unbroken ruin stretched out, blackened slag, pitted and scarred, and occasional heaps of rock.

Suddenly Nasha jumped. "Look! Over there, at the edge. Do you see it?"

They stared. Something rose up, not rock, not an accidental formation. It was round, a circle of dots, white pellets on the dead skin of the planet. A city? Buildings of some kind?

"Please turn the ship," Nasha said excitedly. She pushed her dark hair from her face. "Turn the ship and let's see what it is!"

The ship turned, changing its course. As they came over the white dots the Captain lowered the ship, dropping it down as much as he dared. "Piers," he said. "Piers of some sort of stone. Perhaps poured artificial stone. The remains of a city."

"Oh, dear," Nasha murmured. "How awful." She watched the ruins disappear behind them. In a half-circle the white squares jutted from the slag, chipped and cracked, like broken teeth.

"There's nothing alive," the Captain said at last. "I think we'll go right back; I know most of the crew want to go. Get the Government Receiving Station on the sender and tell them what we found, and that we—"

He staggered.

The first atomic shell had struck the ship, spinning it around. The Captain fell to the floor, crashing into the control table. Papers and instruments rained down on him. As he started to his feet the second shell struck. The ceiling cracked open, struts and girders twisted and bent. The ship shuddered, falling suddenly down, then righting itself as automatic controls took over.

The Captain lay on the floor by the smashed control board. In the corner Nasha struggled to free herself from the debris.

Outside the men were already sealing the gaping leaks in the side of the ship, through which the precious air was rushing, dissipating into the void beyond. "Help me!" Dorle was shouting. "Fire over here, wiring ignited." Two men came running. Tance watched helplessly, his eyeglasses broken and bent.

"So there is life here, after all," he said, half to himself. "But how could—"

"Give us a hand," Fomar said, hurrying past. "Give us a hand, we've got to land the ship!"

❖ ❖ ❖

It was night. A few stars glinted above them, winking through the drifting silt that blew across the surface of the planet.

Dorle peered out, frowning. "What a place to be stuck in." He resumed his work, hammering the bent metal hull of the ship back into place. He was wearing a pressure suit; there were still many small leaks, and radioactive particles from the atmosphere had already found their way into the ship.

Nasha and Fomar were sitting at the table in the control room, pale and solemn, studying the inventory lists.

"Low on carbohydrates," Fomar said. "We can break down the stored fats if we want to, but—"

"I wonder if we could find anything outside." Nasha went to the window. "How uninviting it looks." She paced back and forth, very slender and small, her face dark with fatigue. "What do you suppose an exploring party would find?"

Fomar shrugged. "Not much. Maybe a few weeds growing in cracks here and there. Nothing we could use. Anything that would adapt to this environment would be toxic, lethal."

Nasha paused, rubbing her cheek. There was a deep scratch there, still red and swollen. "Then how do you explain—*it*? According to your theory the inhabitants must have died in their skins, fried like yams. But who fired on us? Somebody detected us, made a decision, aimed a gun."

"And gauged distance," the Captain said feebly from the cot in the corner. He turned toward them. "That's the part that worries me. The first shell put us out of commission, the second almost destroyed us. They were well aimed, perfectly aimed. We're not such an easy target."

"True." Fomar nodded. "Well, perhaps we'll know the answer before we leave here. What a strange situation! All our reasoning tells us that no life could exist; the whole planet burned dry, the atmosphere itself gone, completely poisoned."

"The gun that fired the projectiles survived," Nasha said. "Why not people?"

"It's not the same. Metal doesn't need air to breathe. Metal doesn't get leukemia from radioactive particles. Metal doesn't need food and water."

There was silence.

"A paradox," Nasha said. "Anyhow, in the morning I think we should send out a search party. And meanwhile we should keep on trying to get the ship in condition for the trip back."

"It'll be days before we can take off," Fomar said. "We should keep every man working here. We can't afford to send out a party."

Nasha smiled a little. "We'll send you in the first party. Maybe you can discover—what was it you were so interested in?"

"Legumes. Edible legumes."

"Maybe you can find some of them. Only—"

"Only what?"

"Only watch out. They fired on us once without even knowing who we were or what we came for. Do you suppose that they fought with each other? Perhaps they couldn't imagine anyone being friendly, under any circumstances. What a strange evolutionary trait, inter-species warfare. Fighting within the race!"

"We'll know in the morning," Fomar said. "Let's get some sleep."

❖ ❖ ❖

The sun came up chill and austere. The three people, two men and a woman, stepped through the port, dropping down on the hard ground below.

"What a day," Dorle said grumpily. "I said how glad I'd be to walk on firm ground again, but—"

"Come on," Nasha said. "Up beside me. I want to say something to you. Will you excuse us, Tance?"

Tance nodded gloomily. Dorle caught up with Nasha. They walked together, their metal shoes crunching the ground underfoot. Nasha glanced at him.

"Listen. The Captain is dying. No one knows except the two of us. By the end of the day-period of this planet he'll be dead. The shock did something to his heart. He was almost sixty, you know."

Dorle nodded. "That's bad. I have a great deal of respect for him. You will be captain in his place, of course. Since you're vice-captain now—"

"No. I prefer to see someone else lead, perhaps you or Fomar. I've been thinking over the situation and it seems to me that I should declare myself mated to one of you, whichever of you wants to be captain. Then I could devolve the responsibility."

"Well, I don't want to be captain. Let Fomar do it."

Nasha studied him, tall and blond, striding along beside her in his pressure suit. "I'm rather partial to you," she said. "We might try it for a time, at least. But do as you like. Look, we're coming to something."

They stopped walking, letting Tance catch up. In front of them was some sort of a ruined building. Dorle stared around thoughtfully.

"Do you see? This whole place is a natural bowl, a huge valley. See how the rock formations rise up on all sides, protecting the floor. Maybe some of the great blast was deflected here."

They wandered around the ruins, picking up rocks and fragments. "I think this was a farm," Tance said, examining a piece of wood. "This was part of a tower windmill."

"Really?" Nasha took the stick and turned it over. "Interesting. But let's go; we don't have much time."

"Look," Dorle said suddenly. "Off there, a long way off. Isn't that something?" He pointed.

Nasha sucked in her breath. "The white stones."

"What?"

Nasha looked up at Dorle. "The white stones, the great broken teeth. We saw them, the Captain and I, from the control room." She touched Dorle's arm gently. "That's where they fired from. I didn't think we had landed so close."

"What is it?" Tance said, coming up to them. "I'm almost blind without my glasses. What do you see?"

"The city. Where they fired from."

"Oh." All three of them stood together. "Well, let's go," Tance said. "There's no telling what we'll find there." Dorle frowned at him.

"Wait. We don't know what we would be getting into. They must have patrols. They probably have seen us already, for that matter."

"They probably have seen the ship itself," Tance said. "They probably know right now where they can find it, where they can blow it up. So what difference does it make whether we go closer or not?"

"That's true," Nasha said. "If they really want to get us we haven't a chance. We have no armaments at all; you know that."

"I have a hand weapon," Dorle nodded. "Well, let's go on, then. I suppose you're right, Tance."

"But let's stay together," Tance said nervously. "Nasha, you're going too fast."

Nasha looked back. She laughed. "If we expect to get there by nightfall we must go fast."

❖ ❖ ❖

They reached the outskirts of the city at about the middle of the afternoon. The sun, cold and yellow, hung above them in the colorless sky. Dorle stopped at the top of a ridge overlooking the city.

"Well, there it is. What's left of it."

There was not much left. The huge concrete piers which they had noticed were not piers at all, but the ruined foundations of buildings. They had been baked by the searing heat, baked and charred almost to the ground. Nothing else remained, only this irregular circle of white squares, perhaps four miles in diameter.

Dorle spat in disgust. "More wasted time. A dead skeleton of a city, that's all."

"But it was from here that the firing came," Tance murmured. "Don't forget that."

"And by someone with a good eye and a great deal of experience," Nasha added. "Let's go."

They walked into the city between the ruined buildings. No one spoke. They walked in silence, listening to the echo of their footsteps.

"It's macabre," Dorle muttered. "I've seen ruined cities before but they died of old age, old age and fatigue. This was killed, seared to death. This city didn't die—it was murdered."

"I wonder what the city was called," Nasha said. She turned aside, going up the remains of a stairway from one of the foundations. "Do you think we might find a signpost? Some kind of plaque?"

She peered into the ruins.

"There's nothing there," Dorle said impatiently. "Come on."

"Wait." Nasha bent down, touching a concrete stone. "There's something inscribed on this."

"What is it?" Tance hurried up. He squatted in the dust, running his gloved fingers over the surface of the stone. "Letters, all right." He took a writing stick from the pocket of his pressure suit and copied the inscription on a bit of paper. Dorle glanced over his shoulder. The inscription was:

FRANKLIN APARTMENTS

"That's this city," Nasha said softly. "That was its name."

Tance put the paper in his pocket and they went on. After a time Dorle said, "Nasha, you know, I think we're being watched. But don't look around."

The woman stiffened. "Oh? Why do you say that? Did you see something?"

"No. I can feel it, though. Don't you?"

Nasha smiled a little. "I feel nothing, but perhaps I'm more used to being stared at." She turned her head slightly. "Oh!"

Dorle reached for his hand weapon. "What is it? What do you see?" Tance had stopped dead in his tracks, his mouth half open.

"The gun," Nasha said. "It's the gun."

"Look at the size of it. The size of the thing." Dorle unfastened his hand weapon slowly. "That's it, all right."

The gun was huge. Stark and immense it pointed up at the sky, a mass of steel and glass, set in a huge slab of concrete. Even as they watched the gun moved on its swivel base, whirring underneath. A slim vane turned with the wind, a network of rods atop a high pole.

"It's alive," Nasha whispered. "It's listening to us, watching us."

The gun moved again, this time clockwise. It was mounted so that it could make a full circle. The barrel lowered a trifle, then resumed its original position.

"But who fires it?" Tance said.

Dorle laughed. "No one. No one fires it."

They stared at him. "What do you mean?"

"It fires itself."

They couldn't believe him. Nasha came close to him, frowning, looking up at him. "I don't understand. What do you mean, it fires itself?"

"Watch, I'll show you. Don't move." Dorle picked up a rock from the ground. He hesitated a moment and the tossed the rock high in the air. The rock passed in front of the gun. Instantly the great barrel moved, the vanes contracted.

The rock fell to the ground. The gun paused, then resumed its calm swivel, its slow circling.

"You see," Dorle said, "it noticed the rock, as soon as I threw it up in the air. It's alert to anything that flies or moves above the ground level. Probably it detected us as soon as we entered the gravitational field of the planet. It probably had a bead on us from the start. We don't have a chance. It knows all about the ship. It's just waiting for us to take off again."

"I understand about the rock," Nasha said, nodding. "The gun noticed it, but not us, since we're on the ground, not above. It's only designed to combat objects in the sky. The ship is safe until it takes off again, then the end will come."

"But what's this gun for?" Tance put in. "There's no one alive here. Everyone is dead."

"It's a machine," Dorle said. "A machine that was made to do a job. And it's doing the job. How it survived the blast I don't know. On it goes, waiting for the enemy. Probably they came by air in some sort of projectiles."

"The enemy," Nasha said. "Their own race. It is hard to believe that they really bombed themselves, fired at themselves."

"Well, it's over with. Except right here, where we're standing. This one gun, still alert, ready to kill. It'll go on until it wears out."

"And by that time we'll be dead," Nasha said bitterly.

"There must have been hundreds of guns like this," Dorle murmured. "They must have been used to the sight, guns, weapons, uniforms. Probably they accepted it as a natural thing, part of their lives, like eating and sleeping. An institution, like the church and the state. Men trained to fight, to lead armies, a regular profession. Honored, respected."

Tance was walking slowly toward the gun, peering nearsightedly up at it. "Quite complex, isn't it? All those vanes and tubes. I suppose this is some sort of a telescopic sight." His gloved hand touched the end of a long tube.

Instantly the gun shifted, the barrel retracting. It swung—

"Don't move!" Dorle cried. The barrel swung past them as they stood, rigid and still. For one terrible moment it hesitated over their heads, clicking and whirring, settling into position. Then the sounds died out and the gun became silent.

Tance smiled foolishly inside his helmet. "I must have put my finger over the lens. I'll be more careful." He made his way up onto the circular slab, stepping gingerly behind the body of the gun. He disappeared from view.

"Where did he go?" Nasha said irritably. "He'll get us all killed."

"Tance, come back!" Dorle shouted. "What's the matter with you?"

"In a minute." There was a long silence. At last the archeologist appeared. "I think I've found something. Come up and I'll show you."

"What is it?"

"Dorle, you said the gun was here to keep the enemy off. I think I know why they wanted to keep the enemy off."

They were puzzled.

"I think I've found what the gun is supposed to guard. Come and give me a hand."

"All right," Dorle said abruptly. "Let's go." He seized Nasha's hand. "Come on. Let's see what he's found. I thought something like this might happen when I saw that the gun was—"

"Like what?" Nasha pulled her hand away. "What are you talking about? You act as if you knew what he's found."

"I do." Dorle smiled down at her. "Do you remember the legend that all races have, the myth of the buried treasure, and the dragon, the serpent that watches it, guards it, keeping everyone away?"

She nodded. "Well?"

Dorle pointed up at the gun.

"That," he said, "is the dragon. Come on."

❖ ❖ ❖

Between the three of them they managed to pull up the steel cover and lay it to one side. Dorle was wet with perspiration when they finished.

"It isn't worth it," he grunted. He stared into the dark yawning hold. "Or is it?"

Nasha clicked on her hand lamp, shining the beam down the stairs. The steps were thick with dusk and rubble. At the bottom was a steel door.

"Come on," Tance said excitedly. He started down the stairs. They watched him reach the door and pull hopefully on it without success. "Give a hand!"

"All right." They came gingerly after him. Dorle examined the door. It was bolted shut, locked. There was an inscription on the door but he could not read it.

"Now what?" Nasha said.

Dorle took out his hand weapon. "Stand back. I can't think of any other way." He pressed the switch. The bottom of the door glowed red. Presently it began to crumble. Dorle clicked the weapon off. "I think we can get through. Let's try."

The door came apart easily. In a few minutes they had carried it away in pieces and stacked the pieces on the first step. Then they went on, flashing the light ahead of them.

They were in a vault. Dust lay everywhere, on everything, inches thick. Wood crates lined the walls, huge boxes and crates, packages and containers. Tance looked around curiously, his eyes bright.

"What exactly are all these?" he murmured. "Something valuable, I would think." He picked up a round drum and opened it. A spool fell to the floor, unwinding a black ribbon. He examined it, holding it up to the light.

"Look at this!"

They came around him. "Pictures," Nasha said. "Tiny pictures."

"Records of some kind." Tance closed the spool up in the drum again. "Look, hundreds of drums." He flashed the light around. "And those crates. Let's open one."

Dorle was already prying at the wood. The wood had turned brittle and dry. He managed to pull a section away.

It was a picture. A boy in a blue garment, smiling pleasantly, staring ahead, young and handsome. He seemed almost alive, ready to move toward them in the light of the hand lamp. It was one of them, one of the ruined race, the race that had perished.

For a long time they stared at the picture. At last Dorle replaced the board.

"All these other crates," Nasha said. "More pictures. And these drums. What are in the boxes?"

"This is their treasure," Tance said, almost to himself. "Here are their pictures, their records. Probably all their literature is here, their stories, their myths, their ideas about the universe."

"And their history," Nasha said. "We'll be able to trace their development and find out what it was that made them become what they were."

Dorle was wandering around the vault. "Odd," he murmured. "Even at the end, even after they had begun to fight they still knew, someplace down inside them, that their real treasure was this, their books and pictures, their myths. Even after their big cities and buildings and industries were destroyed they probably hoped to come back and find this. After everything else was gone."

"When we get back home we can agitate for a mission to come here," Tance said. "All this can be loaded up and taken back. We'll be leaving about—"

He stopped.

"Yes," Dorle said dryly. "We'll be leaving about three day-periods from now. We'll fix the ship, then take off. Soon we'll be home, that is, if nothing happens. Like being shot down by that—"

"Oh, stop it," Nasha said impatiently. "Leave him alone. He's right: all this must be taken back home, sooner or later. We'll have to solve the problem of the gun. We have no choice."

Dorle nodded. "What's your solution, then? As soon as we leave the ground we'll be shot down." His face twisted bitterly. "They've guarded their treasure too well. Instead of being preserved it will lie here until it rots. It serves them right."

"How?"

"Don't you see? This was the only way they knew, building a gun and setting it up to shoot anything that came along. They were so certain that everything was hostile, the enemy, coming to take their possessions away from them. Well, they can keep them."

Nasha was deep in thought, her mind far away. Suddenly she gasped. "Dorle," she said. "What's the matter with us? We have no problem. The gun is no menace at all."

The two men stared at her.

"No menace?" Dorle said. "It's already shot us down once. And as soon as we take off again—"

"Don't you see?" Nasha began to laugh. "The poor foolish gun, it's completely harmless. Even I could deal with it."

"You?"

Her eyes were flashing. "With a crowbar. With a hammer or a stick of wood. Let's go back to the ship and load up. Of course we're at its mercy in the air: that's the way it was made. It can fire into the sky, shoot down anything that flies. But that's all. Against something on the ground it has no defenses. Isn't that right?"

Dorle nodded slowly. "The soft underbelly of the dragon. In the legend, the dragon's armor doesn't cover its stomach." He began to laugh. "That's right. That's perfectly right."

"Let's go, then," Nasha said. "Let's get back to the ship. We have work to do here."

❖ ❖ ❖

It was early the next morning when they reached the ship. During the night the Captain had died, and the crew had ignited his body, according to custom. They had stood solemnly around it until the last ember died. As they were going back to their work the woman and the two men appeared, dirty and tired, still excited.

And presently, from the ship, a line of people came, each carrying something in his hands. The line marched across the gray slag, the eternal expanse of fused metal. When they reached the weapon they all fell on the gun at once, with crowbars, hammers, anything that was heavy and hard.

The telescopic sights shattered into bits. The wiring was pulled out, torn to shreds. The delicate gears were smashed, dented.

Finally the warheads themselves were carried off and the firing pins removed.

The gun was smashed, the great weapon destroyed. The people went down into the vault and examined the treasure. With its metal-armored guardian dead there was no danger any longer. They studied the pictures, the films, the crates of books, the jeweled crowns, the cups, the statues.

At last, as the sun was dipping into the gray mists that drifted across the planet they came back up the stairs again. For a moment they stood around the wrecked gun looking at the unmoving outline of it.

Then they started back to the ship. There was still much work to be done. The ship had been badly hurt, much had been damaged and lost. The important thing was to repair it as quickly as possible, to get it into the air.

With all of them working together it took just five more days to make it spaceworthy.

❖ ❖ ❖

Nasha stood in the control room, watching the planet fall away behind them. She folded her arms, sitting down on the edge of the table.

"What are you thinking?" Dorle said.

"I? Nothing."

"Are you sure?"

"I was thinking that there must have been a time when this planet was quite different, when there was life on it."

"I suppose there was. It's unfortunate that no ships from our system came this far, but then we had no reason to suspect intelligent life until we saw the fission glow in the sky."

"And then it was too late."

"Not quite too late. After all, their possessions, their music, books, their pictures, all of that will survive. We'll take them home and study them, and they'll change us. We won't be the same afterwards. Their sculpturing, especially. Did you see the one of the great winged creature, without a head or arms? Broken off, I suppose. But those wings— It looked very old. It will change us a great deal."

"When we come back we won't find the gun waiting for us," Nasha said. "Next time it won't be there to shoot us down. We can land and take the treasure, as you call it." She smiled up at Dorle. "You'll lead us back there, as a good captain should."

"Captain?" Dorle grinned. "Then you've decided."

Nasha shrugged. "Fomar argues with me too much. I think, all in all, I really prefer you."

"Then let's go," Dorle said. "Let's go back home."

The ship roared up, flying over the ruins of the city. It turned in a huge arc and then shot off beyond the horizon, heading into outer space.

❖ ❖ ❖

Down below, in the center of the ruined city, a single half-broken detector vane moved slightly, catching the roar of the ship. The base of the great gun throbbed painfully, straining to turn. After a moment, a red warning light flashed on down inside its destroyed works.

And a long way off, a hundred miles from the city, another warning light flashed on, far underground. Automatic relays flew into action. Gears turned, belts whined. On the ground above a section of metal slag slipped back. A ramp appeared.

A moment later a small cart rushed to the surface.

The cart turned toward the city. A second cart appeared behind it. It was loaded with wiring cables. Behind it a third cart came, loaded with telescopic tube sights. And behind came more carts, some with relays, some with firing controls, some with tools and parts, screws and bolts, pins and nuts. The final one contained atomic warheads.

The carts lined up behind the first one, the lead cart. The lead cart started off, across the frozen ground, bumping calmly along, followed by the others. Moving toward the city.

To the damaged gun.

THE SKULL

"What is this opportunity?" Conger asked. "Go on. I'm interested."

The room was silent; all faces were fixed on Conger—still in the drab prison uniform. The Speaker leaned forward slowly.

"Before you went to prison your trading business was paying well—all illegal—all very profitable. Now you have nothing, except the prospect of another six years in a cell."

Conger scowled.

"There is a certain situation, very important to this Council, that requires your peculiar abilities. Also, it is a situation you might find interesting. You were a hunter, were you not? You've done a great deal of trapping, hiding in the bushes, waiting at night for the game? I imagine hunting must be a source of satisfaction to you, the chase, the stalking—"

Conger sighed. His lips twisted. "All right," he said. "Leave that out. Get to the point. Who do you want me to kill?"

The Speaker smiled. "All in proper sequence," he said softly.

❖ ❖ ❖

The car slid to a stop. It was night; there was no light anywhere along the street. Conger looked out. "Where are we? What is this place?"

The hand of the guard pressed into his arm. "Come. Through that door."

Conger stepped down, onto the damp sidewalk. The guard came swiftly after him, and then the Speaker. Conger took a deep breath of the cold air. He studied the dim outline of the building rising up before them.

"I know this place. I've seen it before." He squinted, his eyes growing accustomed to the dark. Suddenly he became alert. "This is—"

"Yes. The First Church." The Speaker walked toward the steps. "We're expected."

"Expected? *Here?*"

"Yes." The Speaker mounted the stairs.

"You know we're not allowed in their Churches, especially with guns!" He stopped. Two armed soldiers loomed up ahead, one on each side.

"All right?" The Speaker looked up at them. They nodded. The door of the Church was open. Conger could see other soldiers inside, standing about, young soldiers with large eyes, gazing at the icons and holy images.

"I see," he said.

"It was necessary," the Speaker said. "As you know, we have been singularly unfortunate in the past in our relations with the First Church."

"This won't help."

"But it's worth it. You will see."

❖ ❖ ❖

They passed through the hall and into the main chamber where the altar piece was, and the kneeling places. The Speaker scarcely glanced at the altar as they passed by. He pushed open a small side door and beckoned Conger through.

"In here. We have to hurry. The faithful will be flocking in soon."

Conger entered, blinking. They were in a small chamber, low-ceilinged, with dark panels of old wood. There was a smell of ashes and smoldering spices in the room. He sniffed. "What's that? The smell."

"Cups on the wall. I don't know." The Speaker crossed impatiently to the far side. "According to our information, it is hidden here by this—"

Conger looked around the room. He saw books and papers, holy signs and images. A strange low shiver went through him.

"Does my job involve anyone of the Church? If it does—"

The Speaker turned, astonished. "Can it be that you believe in the Founder? Is it possible, a hunter, a killer—"

"No. Of course not. All their business about resignation to death, non-violence—"

"What is it, then?"

Conger shrugged. "I've been taught not to mix with such as these. They have strange abilities. And you can't reason with them."

The Speaker studied Conger thoughtfully. "You have the wrong idea. It is no one here that we have in mind. We've found that killing them only tends to increase their numbers."

"Then why come here? Let's leave."

"No. We came for something important. Something you will need to identify your man. Without it you won't be able to find him." A trace of a smile crossed the Speaker's face. "We don't want you to kill the wrong person. It's too important."

"I don't make mistakes." Conger's chest rose. "Listen, Speaker—"

"This is an unusual situation," the Speaker said. "You see, the person you are after—the person that we are sending you to find—is known only by certain objects here. They are the only traces, the only means of identification. Without them—"

"What are they?"

He came toward the Speaker. The Speaker moved to one side. "Look," he said. He drew a sliding wall away, showing a dark square hole. "In there."

Conger squatted down, staring in. He frowned. "A skull! A skeleton!"

"The man you are after has been dead for two centuries," the Speaker said. "This is all that remains of him. And this is all you have with which to find him."

For a long time Conger said nothing. He stared down at the bones, dimly visible in the recess of the wall. How could a man dead centuries be killed? How could he be stalked, brought down?

Conger was a hunter, a man who had lived as he pleased, where he pleased. He had kept himself alive by trading, bringing furs and pelts in from the Provinces on his own ship, riding at high speed, slipping through the customs line around Earth.

He had hunted in the great mountains of the moon. He had stalked through empty Martian cities. He had explored—

The Speaker said, "Soldier, take these objects and have them carried to the car. Don't lose any part of them."

The soldier went into the cupboard, reaching gingerly, squatting on his heels.

"It is my hope," the Speaker continued softly, to Conger, "that you will demonstrate your loyalty to us, now. There are always ways for citizens to restore themselves, to show their devotion to their society. For you I think this would be a very good chance. I seriously doubt that a better one will come. And for your efforts there will be quite a restitution, of course."

The two men looked at each other; Conger, thin, unkempt, the Speaker immaculate in his uniform.

"I understand you," Conger said. "I mean, I understand this part, about the chance. But how can a man who has been dead two centuries be—"

"I'll explain later," the Speaker said. "Right now we have to hurry." The soldier had gone out with the bones, wrapped in a blanket held carefully in his arms. The Speaker walked to the door. "Come. They've already discovered that we've broken in here, and they'll be coming at any moment."

They hurried down the damp steps to the waiting car. A second later the driver lifted the car up into the air, above the house-tops.

❖ ❖ ❖

The Speaker settled back in the seat.

"The First Church has an interesting past," he said. "I suppose you are familiar with it, but I'd like to speak of a few points that are of relevancy to us.

"It was in the twentieth century that the Movement began—during one of the periodic wars. The Movement developed rapidly, feeding on the general sense of futility, the realization that each war was breeding greater war, with no end in sight. The Movement posed a simple answer to the problem: Without military preparations—weapons—there could be no war. And without machinery and complex scientific technocracy there could be no weapons.

"The Movement preached that you couldn't stop war by planning for it. They preached that man was losing to his machinery and science, that it was getting away from him, pushing him into greater and greater wars. Down with society, they shouted. Down with factories and science! A few more wars and there wouldn't be much left of the world.

"The Founder was an obscure person from a small town in the American Middle West. We don't even know his name. All we know is that one day he appeared, preaching a doctrine of non-violence, non-resistance; no fighting, no paying taxes for guns, no research except for medicine. Live out your life quietly, tending your garden, staying out of public affairs; mind your own business. Be obscure, unknown, poor. Give away most of your possessions, leave the city. At least that was what developed from what he told the people."

The car dropped down and landed on a roof.

"The Founder preached this doctrine, or the germ of it; there's no telling how much the faithful have added themselves. The local authorities picked him up at once, of course. Apparently they were convinced that he meant it; he was never released. He was put to death, and his body buried secretly. It seemed that the cult was finished."

The Speaker smiled. "Unfortunately, some of his disciples reported seeing him after the date of his death. The rumor spread; he had conquered death, he was divine. It took hold, grew. And here we are today, with a First Church, obstructing all social progress, destroying society, sowing the seeds of anarchy—"

"But the wars," Conger said. "About them?"

"The wars? Well, there were no more wars. It must be acknowledged that the elimination of war was the direct result of non-violence practiced on a general scale. But we can take a more objective view of war today. What was so terrible about it? War had a profound selective value, perfectly in accord with the teachings of Darwin and Mendel and others. Without war the mass of useless, incompetent mankind, without training or intelligence, is permitted to grow and expand unchecked. War acted to reduce their numbers; like storms and earthquakes and droughts, it was nature's way of eliminating the unfit.

"Without war the lower elements of mankind have increased all out of proportion. They threaten the educated few, those with scientific knowledge and training, the ones equipped to direct society. They have no regard for science or a scientific society, based on reason. And this Movement seeks to aid and abet them. Only when scientists are in full control can the—"

He looked at his watch and then kicked the car door open. "I'll tell you the rest as we walk."

They crossed the dark roof. "Doubtless you now know whom those bones belonged to, who it is that we are after. He has been dead just two centuries, now, this ignorant man from the Middle West, this Founder. The tragedy is that the authorities of the time acted too slowly. They allowed him to speak, to get his message across. He was allowed to preach, to start his cult. And once such a thing is under way, there's no stopping it.

"But what if he had died before he preached? What if none of his doctrines had ever been spoken? It took only a moment for him to utter them, that we know. They say he spoke just once, just one time. *Then* the authorities came, taking him away. He offered no resistance; the incident was small."

The Speaker turned to Conger.

"Small, but we're reaping the consequences of it today."

They went inside the building. Inside, the soldiers had already laid out the skeleton on a table. The soldiers stood around it, their young faces intense.

Conger went over to the table, pushing past them. He bent down, staring at the bones. "So these are his remains," he murmured. "The Founder. The Church has hidden them for two centuries."

"Quite so," the Speaker said. "But now we have them. Come along down the hall."

They went across the room to a door. The Speaker pushed it open. Technicians looked up. Conger saw machinery, whirring and turning; benches and retorts. In the center of the room was a gleaming crystal cage.

The Speaker handed a Slem-gun to Conger. "The important thing to remember is that the skull must be saved and brought back—for comparison and proof. Aim low—at the chest."

Conger weighed the gun in his hands. "It feels good," he said. "I know this gun—that is, I've seen them before, but I never used one."

The Speaker nodded. "You will be instructed on the use of the gun and the operation of the cage. You will be given all data we have on the time and location. The exact spot was a place called Hudson's field. About 1960 in a small community outside Denver, Colorado. And don't forget—the only means of identification you will have will be the skull. There are visible characteristics of the front teeth, especially the left incisor—"

Conger listened absently. He was watching two men in white carefully wrapping the skull in a plastic bag. They tied it and carried it into the crystal cage. "And if I should make a mistake?"

"Pick the wrong man? Then find the right one. Don't come back until you succeed in reaching this Founder. And you can't wait for him to start speaking; that's what we must avoid! You must act in advance. Take chances; shoot as soon as you think you've found him. He'll be someone unusual, probably a stranger in the area. Apparently he wasn't known."

Conger listened dimly.

"Do you think you have it all now?" the Speaker asked.

"Yes. I think so." Conger entered the crystal cage and sat down, placing his hands on the wheel.

"Good luck," the Speaker said. "We'll be awaiting the outcome. There's some philosophical doubt as to whether one can alter the past. This should answer the question once and for all."

Conger fingered the controls of the cage.

"By the way," the Speaker said. "Don't try to use this cage for purposes not anticipated in your job. We have a constant trace on it. If we want it back, we can get it back. Good luck."

Conger said nothing. The cage was sealed. He raised his finger and touched the wheel control. He turned the wheel carefully.

He was still staring at the plastic bag when the room outside vanished.

For a long time there was nothing at all. Nothing beyond the crystal mesh of the cage. Thoughts rushed through Conger's mind, helter-skelter. How would he know the man? How could he be certain, in advance? What had he looked like? What was his name? How had he acted, before he spoke? Would he be an ordinary person, or some strange outlandish crank?

Conger picked up the Slem-gun and held it against his cheek. The metal of the gun was cool and smooth. He practiced moving the sight. It was a beautiful gun, the kind of gun he could fall in love with. If he had owned such a gun in the Martian desert—on the long nights when he had lain, cramped and numbed with cold, waiting for things that moved through the darkness—

He put the gun down and adjusted the meter readings of the cage. The spiraling mist was beginning to condense and settle. All at once forms wavered and fluttered around him.

Colors, sounds, movements filtered through the crystal wire. He clamped the controls off and stood up.

He was on a ridge overlooking a small town. It was high noon. The air was crisp and bright. A few automobiles moved along a road. Off in the distance were some level fields. Conger went to the door and stepped outside. He sniffed the air. Then he went back into the cage.

He stood before the mirror over the shelf, examining his features. He had trimmed his beard—they had not got him to cut it off—and his hair was neat. He was dressed in the clothing of the middle-twentieth century, the odd collar and coat, the shoes of animal hide. In his pocket was money of the times. That was important. Nothing more was needed.

Nothing, except his ability, his special cunning. But he had never used it in such a way before.

He walked down the road toward the town.

The first things he noticed, were the newspapers on the stands. April 5, 1961. He was not too far off. He looked around him. There was a filling station, a garage, some taverns and a ten-cent store. Down the street was a grocery store and some public buildings.

A few minutes later he mounted the stairs of the little public library and passed through the doors into the warm interior.

The librarian looked up, smiling.

"Good afternoon," she said.

He smiled, not speaking because his words would not be correct; accented and strange, probably. He went over to a table and sat down by a heap of magazines. For a moment he glanced through them. Then he was on his feet again. He crossed the room to a wide rack against the wall. His heart began to beat heavily.

Newspapers—weeks on end. He took a roll of them over to the

table and began to scan them quickly. The print was odd, the letters strange. Some of the words were unfamiliar.

He set the papers aside and searched farther. At last he found what he wanted. He carried the *Cherrywood Gazette* to the table and opened it to the first page. He found what he wanted:

PRISONER HANGS SELF

An unidentified man, held by the county sheriff's office for suspicion of criminal syndicalism, was found dead this morning, by—

He finished the item. It was vague, uninforming. He needed more. He carried the *Gazette* back to the racks and then, after a moment's hesitation, approached the librarian.

"More?" he asked. "More papers. Old ones?"

She frowned. "How old? Which papers?"

"Months old. And—before."

"Of the *Gazette*? This is all we have. What did you want? What are you looking for? Maybe I can help you."

He was silent.

"You might find older issues at the *Gazette* office," the woman said, taking off her glasses. "Why don't you try there? But if you'd tell me, maybe I could help you—"

He went out.

The *Gazette* office was down a side street; the sidewalk was broken and cracked. He went inside. A heater glowed in the corner of the small office. A heavy-set man stood up and came slowly over to the counter.

"What did you want, mister?" he said.

"Old papers. A month. Or more."

"To buy? You want to buy them?"

"Yes." He held out some of the money he had. The man stared.

"Sure," he said. "Sure. Wait a minute." He went quickly out of the room. When he came back he was staggering under the weight of his armload, his face red. "Here are some," he grunted. "Took what I could find. Covers the whole year. And if you want more—"

Conger carried the papers outside. He sat down by the road and began to go through them.

What he wanted was four months back, in December. It was a tiny item, so small that he almost missed it. His hands trembled as he scanned it, using the small dictionary for some of the archaic terms.

MAN ARRESTED FOR
UNLICENSED DEMONSTRATION

An unidentified man who refused to give his name was picked up in Cooper Creek by special agents of the sheriff's office, according to Sheriff Duff. It was said the man was recently noticed in this area and had been watched continually. It was—

Cooper Creek. December, 1960. His heart pounded. That was all he needed to know. He stood up, shaking himself, stamping his feet on the cold ground. The sun had moved across the sky to the very edge of the hills. He smiled. Already he had discovered the exact time and place. Now he needed only to go back, perhaps to November, to Cooper Creek—

He walked back through the main section of town, past the library, past the grocery store. It would not be hard; the hard part was over. He would go there; rent a room, prepare to wait until the man appeared.

He turned the corner. A woman was coming out of a doorway loaded down with packages. Conger stepped aside to let her pass. The woman glanced at him. Suddenly her face turned white. She stared, her mouth open.

Conger hurried on. He looked back. What was wrong with her? The woman was still staring; she had dropped the packages to the ground. He increased his speed. He turned a second corner and went up a side street. When he looked back again the woman had come to the entrance of the street and was starting after him. A man joined her, and the two of them began to run toward him.

He lost them and left town, striding quickly, easily, up into the hills at the edge of town. When he reached the cage he stopped. What had happened? Was it something about his clothing? His dress?

He pondered. Then, as the sun set, he stepped into the cage.

Conger sat before the wheel. For a moment he waited, his hands resting lightly on the control. Then he turned the wheel, just a little, following the control readings carefully.

The grayness settled down around him.

But not for very long.

❖ ❖ ❖

The man looked him over critically. "You better come inside," he said. "Out of the cold."

"Thanks." Conger went gratefully through the open door, into the living room. It was warm and close from the heat of the little kerosene heater in the corner. A woman, large and shapeless in her flowered dress, came from the kitchen. She and the man studied him critically.

"It's a good room," the woman said. "I'm Mrs. Appleton. It's got heat. You need that this time of year."

"Yes." He nodded, looking around.

"You want to eat with us?"

"What?"

"You want to eat with us?" The man's brows knitted. "You're not a foreigner, are you, mister?"

"No." He smiled. "I was born in this country. Quite far west, though."

"California?"

"No." He hesitated. "Oregon."

"What's it like up there?" Mrs. Appleton asked. "I hear there's a lot of trees and green. It's so barren here. I come from Chicago, myself."

"That's the Middle West," the man said to her. "You ain't no foreigner."

"Oregon isn't foreign, either," Conger said. "It's part of the United States."

The man nodded absently. He was staring at Conger's clothing.

"That's a funny suit you got on, mister," he said. "Where'd you get that?"

Conger was lost. He shifted uneasily. "It's a good suit," he said. "Maybe I better go some other place, if you don't want me here."

They both raised their hands protestingly. The woman smiled at him. "We just have to look out for those Reds. You know, the government is always warning us about them."

"The Reds?" He was puzzled.

"The government says they're all around. We're supposed to report anything strange or unusual, anybody doesn't act normal."

"Like me?"

They looked embarrassed. "Well, you don't look like a Red to me," the man said. "But we have to be careful. The Tribune says—"

Conger half listened. It was going to be easier than he had thought. Clearly, he would know as soon as the Founder appeared. These people, so suspicious of anything different, would be buzzing and gossiping and spreading the story. All he had to do was lie low and listen, down at the general store, perhaps. Or even here, in Mrs. Appleton's boarding house.

"Can I see the room?" he said.

"Certainly." Mrs. Appleton went to the stairs. "I'll be glad to show it to you."

They went upstairs. It was colder upstairs, but not nearly as cold as outside. Nor as cold as nights on the Martian deserts. For that he was grateful.

❖❖❖

He was walking slowly around the store, looking at the cans of vegetables, the frozen packages of fish and meats shining and clean in the open refrigerator counters.

Ed Davies came toward him. "Can I help you?" he said. The man was a little oddly dressed, and with a beard! Ed couldn't help smiling.

"Nothing," the man said in a funny voice. "Just looking."

"Sure," Ed said. He walked back behind the counter. Mrs. Hacket was wheeling her cart up.

"Who's he?" she whispered, her sharp face turned, her nose moving, as if it were sniffing. "I never seen him before."

"I don't know."

"Looks funny to me. Why does he wear a beard? No one else wears a beard. Must be something the matter with him."

"Maybe he likes to wear a beard. I had an uncle who—"

"Wait." Mrs. Hacket stiffened. "Didn't that—what was his name? The Red—that old one. Didn't he have a beard? Marx. He had a beard."

Ed laughed. "This ain't Karl Marx. I saw a photograph of him once."

Mrs. Hacket was staring at him. "You did?"

"Sure." He flushed a little. "What's the matter with that?"

"I'd sure like to know more about him," Mrs. Hacket said. "I think we ought to know more, for our own good."

❖ ❖ ❖

"Hey, mister! Want a ride?"

Conger turned quickly, dropping his hand to his belt. He relaxed. Two young kids in a car, a girl and a boy. He smiled at them. "A ride? Sure."

Conger got into the car and closed the door. Bill Willet pushed the gas and the car roared down the highway.

"I appreciate a ride," Conger said carefully. "I was taking a walk between towns, but it was farther than I thought."

"Where are you from?" Lora Hunt asked. She was pretty, small and dark, in her yellow sweater and blue skirt.

"From Cooper Creek."

"Cooper Creek?" Bill said. He frowned. "That's funny. I don't remember seeing you before."

"Why, do you come from there?"

"I was born there. I know everybody there."

"I just moved in. From Oregon."

"From Oregon? I didn't know Oregon people had accents."

"Do I have an accent?"

"You use words funny."

"How?"

"I don't know. Doesn't he, Lora?"

"You slur them," Lora said, smiling. "Talk some more. I'm interested in dialects." She glanced at him, white-teethed. Conger felt his heart constrict.

"I have a speech impediment."

"Oh." Her eyes widened. "I'm sorry."

They looked at him curiously as the car purred along. Conger for his part was struggling to find some way of asking them questions without seeming curious. "I guess people from out of town don't come here much," he said. "Strangers."

"No." Bill shook his head. "Not very much."

"I'll bet I'm the first outsider for a long time."

"I guess so."

Conger hesitated. "A friend of mine—someone I know, might be coming through here. Where do you suppose I might—" He stopped. "Would there be anyone certain to see him? Someone I could ask, make sure I don't miss him if he comes?"

They were puzzled. "Just keep your eyes open. Cooper Creek isn't very big."

"No. That's right."

They drove in silence. Conger studied the outline of the girl. Probably she was the boy's mistress. Perhaps she was his trial wife. Or had they developed trial marriage back so far? He could not remember. But surely such an attractive girl would be someone's mistress by this time; she would be sixteen or so, by her looks. He might ask her sometime, if they ever met again.

❖ ❖ ❖

The next day Conger went walking along the one main street of Cooper Creek, He passed the general store, the two filling stations, and then the post office. At the corner was the soda fountain.

He stopped. Lora was sitting inside, talking to the clerk. She was laughing, rocking back and forth.

Conger pushed the door open. Warm air rushed around him. Lora was drinking hot chocolate, with whipped cream. She looked up in surprise as he slid into the seat beside her.

"I beg your pardon," he said. "Am I intruding?"

"No." She shook her head. Her eyes were large and dark. "Not at all."

The clerk came over. "What do you want?"

Conger looked at the chocolate. "Same as she has."

Lora was watching Conger, her arms folded, elbows on the counter. She smiled at him. "By the way. You don't know my name. Lora Hunt."

She was holding out her hand. He took it awkwardly, not knowing what to do with it. "Conger is my name," he murmured.

"Conger? Is that your last or first name?"

"Last or first?" He hesitated. "Last. Omar Conger."

"Omar?" She laughed. "That's like the poet, Omar Khayyam."

"I don't know of him. I know very little of poets. We restored very few works of art. Usually only the Church has been interested enough—" He broke off. She was staring. He flushed. "Where I come from," he finished.

"The Church? Which church do you mean?"

"The Church." He was confused. The chocolate came and he began to sip it gratefully. Lora was still watching him.

"You're an unusual person," she said. "Bill didn't like you, but he never likes anything different. He's so—so prosaic. Don't you think that when a person gets older he should become—broadened in his outlook?"

Conger nodded.

"He says foreign people ought to stay where they belong, not come here. But you're not so foreign. He means orientals; you know."

Conger nodded.

The screen door opened behind them. Bill came into the room. He stared at them. "Well," he said.

Conger turned. "Hello."

"Well." Bill sat down. "Hello, Lora." He was looking at Conger. "I didn't expect to see you here."

Conger tensed. He could feel the hostility of the boy. "Something wrong with that?"

"No. Nothing wrong with it."

There was silence. Suddenly Bill turned to Lora. "Come on. Let's go."

"Go?" She was astonished. "Why?"

"Just go!" He grabbed her hand. "Come on! The car's outside."

"Why, Bill Willet," Lora said. "You're jealous!"

"Who is this guy?" Bill said. "Do you know anything about him? Look at him, his beard—"

She flared. "So what? Just because he doesn't drive a Packard and go to Cooper High!"

Conger sized the boy up. He was big—big and strong. Probably he was part of some civil control organization.

"Sorry," Conger said. "I'll go."

"What's your business in town?" Bill asked. "What are you doing here? Why are you hanging around Lora?"

Conger looked at the girl. He shrugged. "No reason. I'll see you later."

He turned away. And froze. Bill had moved. Conger's fingers went to his belt. *Half pressure*, he whispered to himself. *No more. Half pressure.*

He squeezed. The room leaped around him. He himself was protected by the lining of his clothing, the plastic sheathing inside.

"My God—" Lora put her hands up. Conger cursed. He hadn't meant any of it for her. But it would wear off. There was only a half-amp to it. It would tingle.

Tingle, and paralyze.

He walked out the door without looking back. He was almost to the corner when Bill came slowly out, holding onto the wall like a drunken man. Conger went on.

❖ ❖ ❖

As Conger walked, restless, in the night, a form loomed in front of him. He stopped, holding his breath.

"Who is it?" a man's voice came. Conger waited, tense.

"Who is it?" the man said again. He clicked something in his hand. A light flashed. Conger moved.

"It's me," he said.

"Who is 'me'?"

"Conger is my name. I'm staying at the Appleton's place. Who are you?"

The man came slowly up to him. He was wearing a leather jacket. There was a gun at his waist.

"I'm Sheriff Duff. I think you're the person I want to talk to. You were in Bloom's today, about three o'clock?"

"Bloom's?"

"The fountain. Where the kids hang out." Duff came up beside him, shining his light into Conger's face. Conger blinked.

"Turn that thing away," he said.

A pause. "All right." The light flickered to the ground. "You were there. Some trouble broke out between you and the Willet boy. Is that right? You had a beef over his girl—"

"We had a discussion," Conger said carefully.

"Then what happened?"

"Why?"

"I'm just curious. They say you did something."

"Did something? Did what?"

"I don't know. That's what I'm wondering. They saw a flash, and something seemed to happen. They all blacked out. Couldn't move."

"How are they now?"

"All right."

There was silence.

"Well?" Duff said. "What was it? A bomb?"

"A bomb?" Conger laughed. "No. My cigarette lighter caught fire. There was a leak, and the fluid ignited."

"Why did they all pass out?"

"Fumes."

Silence. Conger shifted, waiting. His fingers moved slowly toward his belt. The Sheriff glanced down. He grunted.

"If you say so," he said. "Anyhow, there wasn't any real harm done." He stepped back from Conger. "And that Willet is a trouble-maker."

"Good night, then," Conger said. He started past the Sheriff.

"One more thing, Mr. Conger. Before you go. You don't mind if I look at your identification, do you?"

"No. Not at all." Conger reached into his pocket. He held his wallet out. The Sheriff took it and shined his flashlight on it. Conger watched, breathing shallowly. They had worked hard on the wallet, studying historic documents, relics of the times, all the papers they felt would be relevant.

Duff handed it back. "Okay. Sorry to bother you." The light winked off.

When Conger reached the house he found the Appletons sitting around the television set. They did not look up as he came in. He lingered at the door.

"Can I ask you something?" he said. Mrs. Appleton turned slowly. "Can I ask you—what's the date?"

"The date?" She studied him. "The first of December."

"December first! Why, it was just November!"

They were all looking at him. Suddenly he remembered. In the twentieth century they still used the old twelve month system. November fed directly into December; there was no Quartember between them.

He gasped. Then it was tomorrow! The second of December! Tomorrow!

"Thanks," he said. "Thanks."

He went up the stairs. What a fool he was, forgetting. The Founder had been taken into captivity on the second of December, according to the newspaper records. Tomorrow, only twelve hours hence, the Founder would appear to speak to the people and then be dragged away.

The day was warm and bright. Conger's shoes crunched the melting crust of snow. On he went, through the trees heavy with white. He climbed a hill and strode down the other side, sliding as he went.

He stopped to look around. Everything was silent. There was no one in sight. He brought out a thin rod from his waist and turned the handle of it. For a moment nothing happened. Then there was a shimmering in the air.

The crystal cage appeared and settled slowly down. Conger sighed. It was good to see it again. After all, it was his only way back.

He walked up on the ridge. He looked around with some satisfaction, his hands on his hips. Hudson's field was spread out, all the way to the beginning of town. It was bare and flat, covered with a thin layer of snow.

Here, the Founder would come. Here, he would speak to them. And here the authorities would take him.

Only he would be dead before they came. He would be dead before he even spoke.

Conger returned to the crystal globe. He pushed through the door and stepped inside. He took the Slem-gun from the shelf and screwed the bolt into place. It was ready to go, ready to fire. For a moment he considered. Should he have it with him?

No. It might be hours before the Founder came, and suppose someone approached him in the meantime? When he saw the Founder coming toward the field, then he could go and get the gun.

Conger looked toward the shelf. There was the neat package. He took it down and unwrapped it.

He held the skull in his hands, turning it over. In spite of himself, a cold feeling rushed through him. This was the man's skull, the skull of the Founder, who was still alive, who would come here, this day, who would stand on the field not fifty yards away.

What if *he* could see this, his own skull, yellow and corroded? Two centuries old. Would he still speak? Would he speak, if he could see it, the grinning, aged skull? What would there be for him to say, to tell the people? What message could he bring?

What action would not be futile, when a man could look upon his own aged, yellowed skull? Better they should enjoy their temporary lives, while they still had them to enjoy.

A man who could hold his own skull in his hands would believe in few causes, few movements. Rather, he would preach the opposite—

A sound. Conger dropped the skull back on the shelf and took up the gun. Outside something was moving. He went quickly to the door, his heart beating. Was it *he*? Was it the Founder, wandering by himself in the cold, looking for a place to speak? Was he meditating over his words, choosing his sentences?

What if he could see what Conger had held!

He pushed the door open, the gun raised.

Lora!

He stared at her. She was dressed in a wool jacket and boots, her hands in her pockets. A cloud of steam came from her mouth and nostrils. Her breast was rising and falling.

Silently, they looked at each other. At last Conger lowered the gun.

"What is it?" he said. "What are you doing here?"

She pointed. She did not seem able to speak. He frowned; what was wrong with her?

"What is it?" he said. "What do you want?" He looked in the direction she had pointed. "I don't see anything."

"They're coming."

"They? Who? Who are coming?"

"They are. The police. During the night the Sheriff had the state police send cars. All around, everywhere. Blocking the roads. There's about sixty of them coming. Some from town, some around behind." She stopped, gasping. "They said—they said—"

"What?"

"They said you were some kind of Communist. They said—"

Conger went into the cage. He put the gun down on the shelf and came back out. He leaped down and went to the girl.

"Thanks. You came here to tell me? You don't believe it?"

"I don't know."

"Did you come alone?"

"No. Joe brought me in his truck. From town."

"Joe? Who's he?"

"Joe French. The plumber. He's a friend of Dad's."

"Let's go." They crossed the snow, up the ridge and onto the field. The little panel truck was parked half way across the field. A heavy short man was sitting behind the wheel, smoking his pipe. He sat up as he saw the two of them coming toward him.

"Are you the one?" he said to Conger.

"Yes. Thanks for warning me."

The plumber shrugged. "I don't know anything about this. Lora says you're all right." He turned around. "It might interest you to know some more of them are coming. Not to warn you— Just curious."

"More of them?" Conger looked toward the town. Black shapes were picking their way across the snow.

"People from the town. You can't keep this sort of thing quiet, not in a small town. We all listen to the police radio; they heard the same way Lora did. Someone tuned in, spread it around—"

The shapes were getting closer. Conger could make out a couple of them. Bill Willet was there, with some boys from the high school. The Appletons were along, hanging back in the rear.

"Even Ed Davies," Conger murmured.

The storekeeper was toiling onto the field, with three or four other men from the town.

"All curious as hell," French said. "Well, I guess I'm going back to town. I don't want my truck shot full of holes. Come on, Lora."

She was looking up at Conger, wide-eyed.

"Come on," French said again. "Let's go. You sure as hell can't stay here, you know."

"Why?"

"There may be shooting. That's what they all came to see. You know that don't you, Conger?"

"Yes."

"You have a gun? Or don't you care?" French smiled a little. "They've picked up a lot of people in their time, you know. You won't be lonely."

He cared, all right! He had to stay here, on the field. He couldn't afford to let them take him away. Any minute the Founder would appear, would step onto the field. Would he be one of the townsmen, standing silently at the foot of the field, waiting, watching?

Or maybe he was Joe French. Or maybe one of the cops. Anyone of them might find himself moved to speak. And the few words spoken this day were going to be important for a long time.

And Conger had to be there, ready when the first word was uttered!

"I care," he said. "You go on back to town. Take the girl with you."

Lora got stiffly in beside Joe French. The plumber started up the motor. "Look at them, standing there," he said. "Like vultures. Waiting to see someone get killed."

❖ ❖ ❖

The truck drove away, Lora sitting stiff and silent, frightened now. Conger watched for a moment. Then he dashed back into the woods, between the trees, toward the ridge.

He could get away, of course. Anytime he wanted to he could get away. All he had to do was to leap into the crystal cage and turn the handles. But he had a job, an important job. He had to be here, here at this place, at this time.

He reached the cage and opened the door. He went inside and picked up the gun from the shelf. The Slem-gun would take care of them. He notched it up to full count. The chain reaction from it would flatten them all, the police, the curious, sadistic people—

They wouldn't take him! Before they got him, all of them would be dead. *He* would get away. He would escape. By the end of the day they would all be dead, if that was what they wanted, and he—

He saw the skull.

Suddenly he put the gun down. He picked up the skull. He turned the skull over. He looked at the teeth. Then he went to the mirror.

He held the skull up, looking in the mirror. He pressed the skull against his cheek. Beside his own face the grinning skull leered back at him, beside *his* skull, against his living flesh.

He bared his teeth. And he knew.

It was his own skull that he held. He was the one who would die. He was the Founder.

After a time he put the skull down. For a few minutes he stood at the controls, playing with them idly. He could hear the sound of motors outside, the muffled noise of men. Should he go back to the present, where the Speaker waited? He could escape, of course—

Escape?

He turned toward the skull. There it was, his skull, yellow with age. Escape? Escape, when he had held it in his own hands?

What did it matter if he put it off a month, a year, ten years, even fifty? Time was nothing. He had sipped chocolate with a girl born a hundred and fifty years before his time. Escape? For a little while, perhaps.

But he could not *really* escape, no more so than anyone else had ever escaped, or ever would.

Only, he had held it in his hands, his own bones, his own death's-head. *They* had not.

He went out the door and across the field, empty handed. There were a lot of them standing around, gathered together, waiting. They expected a good fight; they knew he had something. They had heard about the incident at the fountain.

And there were plenty of police—police with guns and tear gas, creeping across the hills and ridges, between the trees, closer and closer. It was an old story, in this century.

One of the men tossed something at him. It fell in the snow by his feet, and he looked down. It was a rock. He smiled.

"Come on!" one of them called. "Don't you have any bombs?"

"Throw a bomb! You with the beard! Throw a bomb!"

"Let 'em have it!"

"Toss a few A Bombs!"

They began to laugh. He smiled. He put his hands to his hips. They suddenly turned silent, seeing that he was going to speak.

"I'm sorry," he said simply. "I don't have any bombs. You're mistaken."

There was a flurry of murmuring.

"I have a gun," he went on. "A very good one. Made by science even more advanced than your own. But I'm not going to use that, either."

They were puzzled.

"Why not?" someone called. At the edge of the group an older woman was watching. He felt a sudden shock. He had seen her before. Where?

He remembered. The day at the library. As he had turned the corner he had seen her. She had noticed him and been astounded. At the time, he did not understand why.

Conger grinned. So he *would* escape death, the man who right now was voluntarily accepting it. They were laughing, laughing at a man who had a gun but didn't use it. But by a strange twist of science he would appear again, a few months later, after his bones had been buried under the floor of a jail.

And so, in a fashion, he would escape death. He would die, but then, after a period of months, he would live again, briefly, for an afternoon.

An afternoon. Yet long enough for them to see him, to understand that he was still alive. To know that somehow he had returned to life.

And then, finally, he would appear once more, after two hundred years had passed. Two centuries later.

He would be born again, born, as a matter of fact, in a small trading village on Mars. He would grow up, learning to hunt and trade—

A police car came on the edge of the field and stopped. The people retreated a little. Conger raised his hands.

"I have an odd paradox for you," he said. "Those who take lives will lose their own. Those who kill, will die. But he who gives his own life away will live again!"

They laughed, faintly, nervously. The police were coming out, walking toward him. He smiled. He had said everything he intended to say. It was a good little paradox he had coined. They would puzzle over it, remember it.

Smiling, Conger awaited a death foreordained.

MR. SPACESHIP

Kramer leaned back. "You can see the situation. How can we deal with a factor like this? The perfect variable."

"Perfect? Prediction should still be possible. A living thing still acts from necessity, the same as inanimate material. But the cause-effect chain is more subtle; there are more factors to be considered. The difference is quantitative, I think. The reaction of the living organism parallels natural causation, but with greater complexity."

Gross and Kramer looked up at the board plates, suspended on the wall, still dripping, the images hardening into place. Kramer traced a line with his pencil.

"See that? It's a pseudopodium. They're alive, and so far, a weapon we can't beat. No mechanical system can compete with that, simple or intricate. We'll have to scrap the Johnson Control and find something else."

"Meanwhile the war continues as it is. Stalemate. Checkmate. They can't get to us, and we can't get through their living minefield."

Kramer nodded. "It's a perfect defense, for them. But there still might be one answer."

"What's that?"

"Wait a minute." Kramer turned to his rocket expert, sitting with the charts and files. "The heavy cruiser that returned this week. It didn't actually touch, did it? It came close but there was no contact."

"Correct." The expert nodded. "The mine was twenty miles off. The cruiser was in space-drive, moving directly toward Proxima, line-straight, using the Johnson Control, of course. It had deflected a quarter of an hour earlier for reasons unknown. Later it resumed its course. That was when they got it."

"It shifted," Kramer said. "But not enough. The mine was coming along after it, trailing it. It's the same old story, but I wonder about the contact."

"Here's our theory," the expert said. "We keep looking for contact, a trigger in the pseudopodium. But more likely we're witnessing a psychological phenomena, a decision without any physical correlative. We're watching for something that isn't there. The mine *decides* to blow up. It sees our ship, approaches, and then decides."

"Thanks." Kramer turned to Gross. "Well, that confirms what I'm saying. How can a ship guided by automatic relays escape a mine that decides to explode? The whole theory of mine penetration is that you must avoid tripping the trigger. But here the trigger is a state of mind in a complicated, developed life-form."

"The belt is fifty thousand miles deep," Gross added. "It solves another problem for them, repair and maintenance. The damn things reproduce, fill up the spaces by spawning into them. I wonder what they feed on?"

"Probably the remains of our first-line. The big cruisers must be a delicacy. It's a game of wits, between a living creature and a ship piloted by automatic relays. The ship always loses." Kramer opened a folder. "I'll tell you what I suggest."

"Go on," Gross said. "I've already heard ten solutions today. What's yours?"

"Mine is very simple. These creatures are superior to any mechanical system, but only because they're alive. Almost any other life-form could compete with them, any higher life-form. If the yuks can put out living mines to protect their planets, we ought to be able to harness some of our own life-forms in a similar way. Let's make use of the same weapon ourselves."

"Which life-form do you propose to use?"

"I think the human brain is the most agile of known living forms. Do you know of any better?"

"But no human being can withstand outspace travel. A human pilot would be dead of heart failure long before the ship got anywhere near Proxima."

"But we don't need the whole body," Kramer said. "We need only the brain."

"What?"

"The problem is to find a person of high intelligence who would contribute, in the same manner that eyes and arms are volunteered."

"But a brain . . . "

"Technically, it could be done. Brains have been transferred several times, when body destruction made it necessary. Of course, to a spaceship, to a heavy outspace cruiser, instead of an artificial body, that's new."

The room was silent.

"It's quite an idea," Gross said slowly. His heavy square face twisted. "But even supposing it might work, the big question is *whose* brain?"

❖ ❖ ❖

It was all very confusing, the reasons for the war, the nature of the enemy. The Yucconae had been contacted on one of the outlying planets of Proxima Centauri. At the approach of the Terran ship, a host of dark slim pencils had lifted abruptly and shot off into the distance. The first real encounter came between three of the yuk pencils and a single exploration ship from Terra. No terrans survived. After that it was all out war, with no holds barred.

Both sides feverishly constructed defense rings around their systems. Of the two, the Yucconae belt was the better. The ring around Proxima was a living ring, superior to anything Terra could throw against it. The standard equipment by which Terran ships were guided in outspace, the Johnson Control, was not adequate. Something more was needed. Automatic relays were not good enough.

—Not good at all, Kramer thought to himself, as he stood looking down the hillside at the work going on below him. A warm wind blew along the hill, rustling the weeds and grass. At the bottom, in the valley, the mechanics had almost finished; the last elements of the reflex system had been removed from the ship and crated up.

All that was needed now was the new core, the new central key that would take the place of the mechanical system. A human brain, the brain of an intelligent, wary human being. But would the human being part with it? That was the problem.

Kramer turned. Two people were approaching him along the road, a man and a woman. The man was Gross, expressionless, heavy-set, walking with dignity. The woman was— He stared in surprise and growing annoyance. It was Dolores, his wife. Since they'd separated he had seen little of her . . .

"Kramer," Gross said. "Look who I ran into. Came back down with us. We're going into town."

"Hello, Phil," Dolores said. "Well, aren't you glad to see me?"

He nodded. "How have you been? You're looking fine." She was still pretty and slender in her uniform, the blue-gray of Internal Security, Gross's organization.

"Thanks." She smiled. "You seem to be doing all right, too. Commander Gross tells me that you're responsible for this project, Operation Head, as they call it. Whose head have you decided on?"

"That's the problem." Kramer lit a cigarette. "This ship is to be equipped with a human brain instead of the Johnson system. We've constructed special draining baths for the brain, electronic relays to catch the impulses and magnify them, a continual feeding duct that supplies the living cells with everything they need. But—"

"But we still haven't got the brain itself," Gross finished. They began to walk back toward the car. "If we can get that we'll be ready for the tests."

"Will the brain remain alive?" Dolores asked. "Is it actually going to live as part of the ship?"

"It will be alive, but not conscious. Very little life is actually conscious. Animals, trees, insects are quick in their responses, but they aren't conscious. In this process of ours the individual personality, the ego, will cease. We only need the response ability, nothing more."

Dolores shuddered. "How terrible!"

"In time of war everything must be tried," Kramer said absently. "If one life sacrificed will end the war it's worth it. This ship might get through. A couple more like it and there wouldn't be any more war."

❖ ❖ ❖

They got into the car. As they drove down the road, Gross said, "Have you thought of anyone yet?"

Kramer shook his head. "That's out of my line."

"What do you mean?"

"I'm an engineer. It's not in my department."

"But all this was your idea."

"My work ends there."

Gross was staring at him oddly. Kramer shifted uneasily.

"Then who is supposed to do it?" Gross said. "I can have my organization prepare examinations of various kinds, to determine fitness, that kind of thing—"

"Listen, Phil," Dolores said suddenly.

"What?"

She turned toward him. "I have an idea. Do you remember that professor we had in college? Michael Thomas?"

Kramer nodded.

"I wonder if he's still alive." Dolores frowned. "If he is he must be awfully old."

"Why, Dolores?" Gross asked.

"Perhaps an old person who didn't have much time left, but whose mind was still clear and sharp—"

"Professor Thomas," Kramer rubbed his jaw. "He certainly was a wise old duck. But could he still be alive? He must have been seventy, then."

"We could find that out," Gross said. "I could make a routine check."

"What do you think?" Dolores said. "If any human mind could outwit those creatures—"

"I don't like the idea," Kramer said. In his mind an image had appeared, the image of an old man sitting being a desk, his bright gentle eyes moving about the classroom. The old man leaning forward, a thin hand raised—

"Keep him out of this," Kramer said.

"What's wrong?" Gross looked at him curiously.

"It's because *I* suggested it," Dolores said.

"No." Kramer shook his head. "It's not that. I didn't expect anything like this, somebody I knew, a man I studied under. I remember him very clearly. He was a very distinct personality."

"Good," Gross said. "He sounds fine."

"We can't do it. We're asking his death!"

"This is war," Gross said, "and war doesn't wait on the needs of the individual. You said that yourself. Surely he'll volunteer; we can keep it on that basis."

"He may already be dead," Dolores murmured.

"We'll find that out," Gross said, speeding up the car. They drove the rest of the way in silence.

❖❖❖

For a long time the two of them stood studying the small wood house, overgrown with ivy, set back on the lot behind the enormous oak. The little town was silent and sleepy; once in a while a car moved slowly along the distant highway, but that was all.

"This is the place," Gross said to Kramer. He folded his arms. "Quite a quaint little house."

Kramer said nothing. The two Security Agents behind them were expressionless.

Gross started toward the gate. "Let's go. According to the check he's still alive, but very sick. His mind is agile, however. That seems to be certain. It's said he doesn't leave the house. A woman takes care of his needs. He's very frail."

They went down the stone walk and up onto the porch. Gross rang the bell. They waited. After a time they heard slow footsteps. The door opened. An elderly woman in a shapeless wrapper studied them impassively.

"Security," Gross said, showing his card. "We wish to see Professor Thomas."

"Why?"

"Government business." He glanced at Kramer.

Kramer stepped forward. "I was a pupil of the Professor's," he said. "I'm sure he won't mind seeing us."

The woman hesitated uncertainly. Gross stepped into the doorway. "All right, mother. This is war time. We can't stand out here."

The two Security Agents followed him, and Kramer came reluctantly behind, closing the door. Gross stalked down the hall until he came to an open door. He stopped, looking in. Kramer could see the white corner of a bed, a wooden post and the edge of a dresser.

He joined Gross.

In the dark room a withered old man lay, propped up on endless pillows. At first it seemed as if he were asleep; there was no motion or sign of life. But after a time Kramer saw with a faint shock that the old man was watching them, intently, his eyes fixed on them, unmoving, unwinking.

"Professor Thomas?" Gross said. "I'm Commander Gross of Security. This man with me is perhaps known to you—"

The faded eyes fixed on Kramer.

"I know him. Philip Kramer . . . You've grown heavier, boy." The voice was feeble, the rustle of dry ashes. "Is it true you're married now?"

"Yes. I married Dolores French. You remember her." Kramer came toward the bed. "But we're separated. It didn't work out very well. Our careers—"

"What we came here about, Professor," Gross began, but Kramer cut him off with an impatient wave.

"Let me talk. Can't you and your men get out of here long enough to let me talk to him?"

Gross swallowed. "All right, Kramer." He nodded to the two men. The three of them left the room, going out into the hall and closing the door after them.

The old man in the bed watched Kramer silently. "I don't think much of him," he said at last. "I've seen his type before. What's he want?"

"Nothing. He just came along. Can I sit down?" Kramer found a stiff upright chair beside the bed. "If I'm bothering you—"

"No. I'm glad to see you again, Philip. After so long. I'm sorry your marriage didn't work out."

"How have you been?"

"I've been very ill. I'm afraid that my moment on the world's stage has almost ended." The ancient eyes studied the younger man reflectively. "You look as if you have been doing well. Like everyone else I thought highly of. You've gone to the top in this society."

Kramer smiled. Then he became serious. "Professor, there's a project we're working on that I want to talk to you about. It's the first ray of hope we've had in this whole war. If it works, we may be able to crack the yuk defenses, get some ships into their system. If we can do that the war might be brought to an end."

"Go on. Tell me about it, if you wish."

"It's a long shot, this project. It may not work at all, but we have to give it a try."

"It's obvious that you came here because of it," Professor Thomas murmured. "I'm becoming curious. Go on."

❖ ❖ ❖

After Kramer finished the old man lay back in the bed without speaking. At last he sighed.

"I understand. A human mind, taken out of a human body." He sat up a little, looking at Kramer. "I suppose you're thinking of me."

Kramer said nothing.

"Before I make my decision, I want to see the papers on this, the theory and outline of construction. I'm not sure I like it. For reasons of my own, I mean. But I want to look at the material. If you'll do that—"

"Certainly." Kramer stood up and went to the door. Gross and the two Security Agents were standing outside, waiting tensely. "Gross, come inside."

They filed into the room.

"Give the Professor the papers," Kramer said. "He wants to study them before deciding."

Gross brought the file out of his coat pocket, a manila envelope. He handed it to the old man on the bed. "Here it is, Professor. You're welcome to examine it. Will you give us your answer as soon as possible? We're very anxious to begin, of course."

"I'll give you my answer when I've decided." He took the envelope with a thin, trembling hand. "My decision depends on what I find out from these papers. If I don't like what I find, then I will not become involved with this work in any shape or form." He opened the envelope with shaking hands. "I'm looking for one thing."

"What is it?" Gross said.

"That's my affair. Leave me a number by which I can reach you when I've decided."

Silently, Gross put his card down on the dresser. As they went out Professor Thomas was already reading the first of the papers, the outline of the theory.

❖ ❖ ❖

Kramer sat across from Dale Winter, his second in line. "What then?" Winter said.

"He's going to contact us." Kramer scratched with a drawing pen on some paper. "I don't know what to think."

"What do you mean?" Winter's good-natured face was puzzled.

"Look." Kramer stood up, pacing back and forth, his hands in his uniform pockets. "He was my teacher in college. I respected him as a man, as well as a teacher. He was more than a voice, a talking book. He was a person, a calm, kindly person I could look up to. I always wanted to be like him, someday. Now look at me."

"So?"

"Look at what I'm asking. I'm asking for his life, as if he were some kind of laboratory animal kept around in a cage, not a man, a teacher at all."

"Do you think he'll do it?"

"I don't know." Kramer went to the window. He stood looking out. "In a way, I hope not."

"But if he doesn't—"

"Then we'll have to find somebody else, I know. There would be somebody else. Why did Dolores have to—"

The vidphone rang. Kramer pressed the button.

"This is Gross." The heavy features formed. "The old man called me. Professor Thomas."

"What did he say?" He knew; he could tell already, by the sound of Gross's voice.

"He said he'd do it. I was a little surprised myself, but apparently he means it. We've already made arrangements for his admission to the hospital. His lawyer is drawing up the statement of liability."

Kramer only half heard. He nodded wearily. "All right. I'm glad. I suppose we can go ahead, then."

"You don't sound very glad."

"I wonder why he decided to go ahead with it."

"He was very certain about it." Gross sounded pleased. "He called me quite early. I was still in bed. You know, this calls for a celebration."

"Sure," Kramer said. "It sure does."

❖ ❖ ❖

Toward the middle of August, the project neared completion. They stood outside in the hot autumn heat, looking up at the sleek metal sides of the ship.

Gross thumped the metal with his hand. "Well, it won't be long. We can begin the test any time."

"Tell us more about this," an officer in gold braid said. "It's such an unusual concept."

"Is there really a human brain inside the ship?" a dignitary asked, a small man in a rumpled suit. "And the brain is actually alive?"

"Gentlemen, this ship is guided by a living brain instead of the usual Johnson relay-control system. But the brain is not conscious. It will function by reflex only. The practical difference between it and the Johnson system is this: a human brain is far more intricate than any man-made structure, and its ability to adapt itself to a situation, to respond to danger, is far beyond anything that could be artificially built."

Gross paused, cocking his ear. The turbines of the ship were beginning to rumble, shaking the ground under them with a deep vibration. Kramer was standing a short distance away from the others, his arms folded, watching silently. At the sound of the turbines he walked quickly around the ship to the other side. A few workmen were clearing away the last of the waste, the scraps of wiring and scaffolding. They glanced up at him and went on hurriedly with their work. Kramer mounted the ramp and entered the control cabin of the ship. Winter was sitting at the controls with a Pilot from Space-transport.

"How's it look?" Kramer asked.

"All right." Winter got up. "He tells me that it would be best to take off manually. The robot controls—" Winter hesitated. "I mean, the built-in controls, can take over later on in space."

"That's right," the Pilot said. "It's customary with the Johnson system, and so in this case we should—"

"Can you tell anything yet?" Kramer asked.

"No," the Pilot said slowly. "I don't think so. I've been going over everything. It seems to be in good order. There's only one thing I wanted to ask you about." He put his hand on the control board. "There are some changes here I don't understand."

"Changes?"

"Alterations from the original design. I wonder what the purpose is."

Kramer took a set of the plans from his coat. "Let me look." He turned the pages over. The Pilot watched carefully over his shoulder.

"The changes aren't indicated on your copy," the Pilot said. "I wonder—" He stopped. Commander Gross had entered the control cabin.

"Gross, who authorized alterations?" Kramer said. "Some of the wiring has been changed."

"Why, your old friend." Gross signaled to the field tower through the window.

"My old friend?"

"The Professor. He took quite an active interest." Gross turned to the Pilot. "Let's get going. We have to take this out past gravity for the test, they tell me. Well, perhaps it's for the best. Are you ready?"

"Sure." The Pilot sat down and moved some of the controls around. "Any time."

"Go ahead, then," Gross said.

"The Professor—" Kramer began, but at that moment there was a tremendous roar and the ship leaped under him. He grasped one of the wall holds and hung on as best he could. The cabin was filling with a steady throbbing, the raging of the jet turbines underneath them.

The ship leaped. Kramer closed his eyes and held his breath. They were moving out into space, gaining speed each moment.

❖ ❖ ❖

"Well, what do you think?" Winter said nervously. "Is it time yet?"

"A little longer," Kramer said. He was sitting on the floor of the cabin, down by the control wiring. He had removed the metal covering-plate, exposing the complicated maze of relay wiring. He was studying it, comparing it to the wiring diagrams.

"What's the matter?" Gross said.

"These changes. I can't figure out what they're for. The only pattern I can make out is that for some reason—"

"Let me look," the Pilot said. He squatted down beside Kramer. "You were saying?"

"See this lead here? Originally it was switch controlled. It closed and opened automatically, according to temperature change. Now it's wired so that the central control system operates it. The same with the others. A lot of this was still mechanical, worked by pressure, temperature stress. Now it's under the central master."

"The brain?" Gross said. "You mean it's been altered so that the brain manipulates it?"

Kramer nodded. "Maybe Professor Thomas felt that no mechanical relays could be trusted. Maybe he thought that things would be happening too fast. But some of these could close in a split second. The brake rockets could go on as quickly as—"

"Hey," Winter said from the control seat. "We're getting near the moon stations. What'll I do?"

They looked out the port. The corroded surface of the moon gleamed up at them, a corrupt and sickening sight. They were moving swiftly toward it.

"I'll take it," the Pilot said. He eased Winter out of the way and strapped himself in place. The ship began to move away from the moon as he manipulated the controls. Down below them they could see the observation stations dotting the surface, and the tiny squares that were the openings of the underground factories and hangars. A red blinker winked up at them and the Pilot's fingers moved on the board in answer.

"We're past the moon," the Pilot said, after a time. The moon had fallen behind them; the ship was heading into outer space. "Well, we can go ahead with it."

Kramer did not answer.

"Mr. Kramer, we can go ahead any time."

Kramer started. "Sorry. I was thinking. All right, thanks." He frowned, deep in thought.

"What is it?" Gross asked.

"The wiring changes. Did you understand the reason for them when you gave the okay to the workmen?"

Gross flushed. "You know I know nothing about technical material. I'm in Security."

"Then you should have consulted me."

"What does it matter?" Gross grinned wryly. "We're going to have to start putting our faith in the old man sooner or later."

The Pilot stepped back from the board. His face was pale and set. "Well, it's done," he said. "That's it."

"What's done?" Kramer said.

"We're on automatic. The brain. I turned the board over to it—to him, I mean. The Old Man." The Pilot lit a cigarette and puffed nervously. "Let's keep our fingers crossed."

❖ ❖ ❖

The ship was coasting evenly, in the hands of its invisible pilot. Far down inside the ship, carefully armored and protected, a soft human brain lay in a tank of liquid, a thousand minute electric charges playing over its surface. As the charges rose they were picked up and amplified, fed into relay systems, advanced, carried on through the entire ship—

Gross wiped his forehead nervously. "So *he* is running it, now. I hope he knows what he's doing."

Kramer nodded enigmatically. "I think he does."

"What do you mean?"

"Nothing." Kramer walked to the port. "I see we're still moving in a straight line." He picked up the microphone. "We can instruct the brain orally, through this." He blew against the microphone experimentally.

"Go on," Winter said.

"Bring the ship around half-right," Kramer said. "Decrease speed."

They waited. Time passed. Gross looked at Kramer. "No change. Nothing."

"Wait."

Slowly the ship was beginning to turn. The turbines missed, reducing their steady beat. The ship was taking up its new course, adjusting itself. Nearby some space debris rushed past, incinerating in the blasts of the turbine jets.

"So far so good," Gross said.

They began to breathe more easily. The invisible pilot had taken control smoothly, calmly. The ship was in good hands. Kramer spoke

"No—listen!"

The sputter came again. Then, mixed with the sputter, almost lost in it, a voice came, toneless, without inflection, a mechanical, lifeless voice from the metal speaker in the wall, above their heads.

" . . . Is it you, Philip? I can't make you out. Darkness . . . Who's there? With you . . . "

"It's me, Kramer." His fingers tightened against the microphone handle. "You must release the controls, Professor. We have to get back to Terra. You must."

Silence. Then the faint, faltering voice came again, a little stronger than before. "Kramer. Everything so strange. I was right, though. Consciousness result of thinking. Necessary result. Cogito ergo sum. Retain conceptual ability. Can you hear me?"

"Yes, Professor—"

"I altered the wiring. Control. I was fairly certain . . . I wonder if I can do it. Try . . . "

Suddenly the air-conditioning snapped into operation. It snapped abruptly off again. Down the corridor a door slammed. Something thudded. The men stood listening. Sounds came from all sides of them, switches shutting, opening. The lights blinked off; they were in darkness. The lights came back on, and at the same time the heating coils dimmed and faded.

"Good God!" Winter said.

Water poured down on them, the emergency fire-fighting system. There was a screaming rush of air. One of the escape hatches had slid back, and the air was roaring frantically out into space.

The hatch banged closed. The ship subsided into silence. The heating coils glowed into life. As suddenly as it had begun the weird exhibition ceased.

"I can do—everything," the dry, toneless voice came from the wall speaker. "It is all controlled. Kramer, I wish to talk to you. I've been—been thinking. I haven't seen you in many years. A lot to discuss. You've changed, boy. We have much to discuss. Your wife—"

"We can't. We've lost control."

"Lost control?"

"This is an experimental ship."

Gross took the radio. "This is Commander Gross, Security. We're being carried into outer space. There's nothing we can do. Is there any way that we can be removed from this ship?"

A hesitation. "We have some fast pursuit ships that could pick you up if you wanted to jump. The chances are good that they'd find you. Do you have space flares?"

"We do," the Pilot said. "Let's try it."

"Abandon ship?" Kramer said. "If we leave now we'll never see it again."

"What else can we do? We're gaining speed all the time. Do you propose that we stay here?"

"No." Kramer shook his head. "Damn it, there ought to be a better solution."

"Could you contact *him*?" Winter asked. "The Old Man? Try to reason with him?"

"It's worth a chance," Gross said. "Try it."

"All right." Kramer took the microphone. He paused a moment. "Listen! Can you hear me? This is Phil Kramer. Can you hear me, Professor? Can you hear me? I want you to release the controls."

There was silence.

"This is Kramer, Professor. Can you hear me? Do you remember who I am? Do you understand who this is?"

Above the control panel the wall speaker made a sound, a sputtering static. They looked up.

"Can you hear me, Professor? This is Philip Kramer. I want you to give the ship back to us. If you can hear me, release the controls! Let go, Professor. Let go!"

Static. A rushing sound, like the wind. They gazed at each other. There was silence for a moment.

"It's a waste of time," Gross said.

No one spoke.

"You can see what has happened," Kramer said calmly. "The old man won't let go of it, now that he has it. I was afraid of this when I saw the wiring changes. Everything in this ship is centrally controlled, even the cooling system, the hatches, the garbage release. We're helpless."

"Nonsense." Gross strode to the board. He took hold of the wheel and turned it. The ship continued on its course, moving away from the moon, leaving it behind.

"Release!" Kramer said into the microphone. "Let go of the controls! We'll take it back. Release."

"No good," the Pilot said. "Nothing." He spun the useless wheel. "It's dead, completely dead."

"And we're still heading out," Winter said, grinning foolishly. "We'll be going through the first-line defense belt in a few minutes. If they don't shoot us down—"

"We better radio back." The Pilot clicked the radio to *send*. "I'll contact the main bases, one of the observation stations."

"Better get the defense belt, at the speed we're going. We'll be into it in a minute."

"And after that," Kramer said, "we'll be in outer space. He's moving us toward outspace velocity. Is this ship equipped with baths?"

"Baths?" Gross said.

"The sleep tanks. For space-drive. We may need them if we go much faster."

"But good God, where are we going?" Gross said. "Where—where's he taking us?"

❖ ❖ ❖

The Pilot obtained contact. "This is Dwight, on ship," he said. "We're entering the defense zone at high velocity. Don't fire on us."

"Turn back," the impersonal voice came through the speaker. "You're not allowed in the defense zone."

a few more words into the microphone, and they swung again. Now they were moving back the way they had come, toward the moon.

"Let's see what he does when we enter the moon's pull," Kramer said. "He was a good mathematician, the old man. He could handle any kind of problem."

The ship veered, turning away from the moon. The great eaten-away globe fell behind them.

Gross breathed a sigh of relief. "That's that."

"One more thing." Kramer picked up the microphone. "Return to the moon and land the ship at the first space field," he said into it.

"Good Lord," Winter murmured. "Why are you—"

"Be quiet." Kramer stood, listening. The turbines gasped and roared as the ship swung full around, gaining speed. They were moving back, back toward the moon again. The ship dipped down, heading toward the great globe.

"We're going a little fast," the Pilot said. "I don't see how he can put down at this velocity."

❖ ❖ ❖

The port filled up, as the globe swelled rapidly. The Pilot hurried toward the board, reaching for the controls. All at once the ship jerked. The nose lifted and the ship shot out into space, away from the moon, turning at an oblique angle. The men were thrown to the floor by the sudden change in course. They got to their feet again, speechless, staring at each other.

The Pilot gazed down at the board. "It wasn't me! I didn't touch a thing. I didn't even get to it."

The ship was gaining speed each moment. Kramer hesitated. "Maybe you better switch it back to manual."

The Pilot closed the switch. He took hold of the steering controls and moved them experimentally. "Nothing." He turned around. "Nothing. It doesn't respond."

The Pilot grabbed Kramer's arm. "There's a ship standing off our bow. Look."

❖❖❖

They ran to the port. A slender pale craft was moving along with them, keeping pace with them. It was signal blinking.

"A Terran pursuit ship," the Pilot said. "Let's jump. They'll pick us up. Suits—"

He ran to a supply cupboard and turned the handle. The door opened and he pulled the suits out onto the floor.

"Hurry," Gross said. A panic seized them. They dressed frantically, pulling the heavy garments over them. Winter staggered to the escape hatch and stood by it, waiting for the others. They joined him, one by one.

"Let's go!" Gross said. "Open the hatch."

Winter tugged at the hatch. "Help me."

They grabbed hold, tugging together. Nothing happened. The hatch refused to budge.

"Get a crowbar," the Pilot said.

"Hasn't anyone got a blaster?" Gross looked frantically around. "Damn it, blast it open!"

"Pull," Kramer grated. "Pull together."

"Are you at the hatch?" The toneless voice came, drifting and eddying through the corridors of the ship. They looked up, staring around them. "I sense something nearby, outside. A ship? You are leaving, all of you? Kramer, you are leaving, too? Very unfortunate. I had hoped we could talk. Perhaps at some other time you might be induced to remain."

"Open the hatch!" Kramer said, staring up at the impersonal walls of the ship. "For God's sake, open it!"

There was silence, an endless pause. Then, very slowly, the hatch slid back. The air screamed out, rushing past them into space.

One by one they leaped, one after the other, propelled away by the repulsive material of the suits. A few minutes later they were being hauled aboard the pursuit ship. As the last one of them was lifted through the port, their own ship pointed itself suddenly upward and shot off at tremendous speed. It disappeared.

Kramer removed his helmet, gasping. Two sailors held onto him and began to wrap him in blankets. Gross sipped a mug of coffee, shivering.

"It's gone," Kramer murmured.

"I'll have an alarm sent out," Gross said.

"What's happened to your ship?" a sailor asked curiously. "It sure took off in a hurry. Who's on it?"

"We'll have to have it destroyed," Gross went on, his face grim. "It's got to be destroyed. There's no telling what it—what *he* has in mind." Gross sat down weakly on a metal bench. "What a close call for us. We were so damn trusting."

"What could he be planning," Kramer said, half to himself. "It doesn't make sense. I don't get it."

❖ ❖ ❖

As the ship sped back toward the moon base they sat around the table in the dining room, sipping hot coffee and thinking, not saying very much.

"Look here," Gross said at last. "What kind of man was Professor Thomas? What do you remember about him?"

Kramer put his coffee mug down. "It was ten years ago. I don't remember much. It's vague."

He let his mind run back over the years. He and Dolores had been at Hunt College together, in physics and the life sciences. The College was small and set back away from the momentum of modern life. He had gone there because it was his home town, and his father had gone there before him.

Professor Thomas had been at the College a long time, as long as anyone could remember. He was a strange old man, keeping to himself most of the time. There were many things that he disapproved of, but he seldom said what they were.

"Do you recall anything that might help us?" Gross asked. "Anything that would give us a clue as to what he might have in mind?"

Kramer nodded slowly. "I remember one thing . . . "

One day he and the Professor had been sitting together in the school chapel, talking leisurely.

"Well, you'll be out of school, soon," the Professor had said. "What are you going to do?"

"Do? Work at one of the Government Research Projects, I suppose."

"And eventually? What's your ultimate goal?"

Kramer had smiled. "The question is unscientific. It presupposes such things as ultimate ends."

"Suppose instead along these lines, then: What if there were no war and no Government Research Projects? What would you do, then?"

"I don't know. But how can I imagine a hypothetical situation like that? There's been war as long as I can remember. We're geared for war. I don't know what I'd do. I suppose I'd adjust, get used to it."

The Professor had stared at him. "Oh, you do think you'd get accustomed to it, eh? Well, I'm glad of that. And you think you could find something to do?"

Gross listened intently. "What do you infer from this, Kramer?"

"Not much. Except that he was against war."

"We're all against war," Gross pointed out.

"True. But he was withdrawn, set apart. He lived very simply, cooking his own meals. His wife died many years ago. He was born in Europe, in Italy. He changed his name when he came to the United States. He used to read Dante and Milton. He even had a Bible."

"Very anachronistic, don't you think?"

"Yes, he lived quite a lot in the past. He found an old phonograph and records and he listened to the old music. You saw his house, how old-fashioned it was."

"Did he have a file?" Winter asked Gross.

"With Security? No, none at all. As far as we could tell he never engaged in political work, never joined anything or even seemed to have strong political convictions."

"No," Kramer agreed. "About all he ever did was walk through the hills. He liked nature."

"Nature can be of great use to a scientist," Gross said. "There wouldn't be any science without it."

"Kramer, what do you think his plan is, taking control of the ship and disappearing?" Winter said.

"Maybe the transfer made him insane," the Pilot said. "Maybe there's no plan, nothing rational at all."

"But he had the ship rewired, and he had made sure that he would retain consciousness and memory before he even agreed to the operation. He must have had something planned from the start. But what?"

"Perhaps he just wanted to stay alive longer," Kramer said. "He was old and about to die. Or—"

"Or what?"

"Nothing." Kramer stood up. "I think as soon as we get to the moon base I'll make a vidcall to earth. I want to talk to somebody about this."

"Who's that?" Gross asked.

"Dolores. Maybe she remembers something."

"That's a good idea," Gross said.

❖ ❖ ❖

"Where are you calling from?" Dolores asked, when he succeeded in reaching her.

"From a moon base."

"All kinds of rumors are running around. Why didn't the ship come back? What happened?"

"I'm afraid he ran off with it."

"He?"

"The Old Man. Professor Thomas." Kramer explained what had happened.

Dolores listened intently. "How strange. And you think he planned it all in advance, from the start?"

"I'm certain. He asked for the plans of construction and the theoretical diagrams at once."

"But why? What for?"

"I don't know. Look, Dolores. What do you remember about him? Is there anything that might give a clue to all this?"

"Like what?"

"I don't know. That's the trouble."

On the vidscreen Dolores knitted her brow. "I remember he raised chickens in his back yard and once he had a goat." She smiled. "Do you remember the day the goat got loose and wandered down the main street of town? Nobody could figure out where it came from."

"Anything else?"

"No." He watched her struggling, trying to remember. "He wanted to have a farm, sometime, I know."

"All right. Thanks." Kramer touched the switch. "When I get back to Terra maybe I'll stop and see you."

"Let me know how it works out."

He cut the line and the picture dimmed and faded. He walked slowly back to where Gross and some officers of the Military were sitting at a chart table, talking.

"Any luck?" Gross said, looking up.

"No. All she remembers is that he kept a goat."

"Come over and look at this detail chart." Gross motioned him around to his side. "Watch!"

Kramer saw the record tabs moving furiously, the little white dots racing back and forth.

"What's happening?" he asked.

"A squadron outside the defense zone has finally managed to contact the ship. They're maneuvering now, for position. Watch."

The white counters were forming a barrel formation around a black dot that was moving steadily across the board, away from the central position. As they watched, the white dots constructed around it.

"They're ready to open fire," a technician at the board said. "Commander, what shall we tell them to do?"

Gross hesitated. "I hate to be the one who makes the decision. When it comes right down to it—"

"It's not just a ship," Kramer said. "It's a man, a living person. A human being is up there, moving through space. I wish we knew what—"

"But the order has to be given. We can't take any chances. Suppose he went over to them, to the yuks."

Kramer's jaw dropped. "My God, he wouldn't do that."

"Are you sure? Do you know what he'll do?"

"He wouldn't do that."

Gross turned to the technician. "Tell them to go ahead."

"I'm sorry, sir, but now the ship has gotten away. Look down at the board."

Gross stared down, Kramer over his shoulder. The black dot had slipped through the white dots and had moved off at an abrupt angle. The white dots were broken up, dispersing in confusion.

"He's an unusual strategist," one of the officers said. He traced the line. "It's an ancient maneuver, an old Prussian device, but it worked."

The white dots were turning back. "Too many yuk ships out that far," Gross said. "Well, that's what you get when you don't act quickly." He looked up coldly at Kramer. "We should have done it when we had him. Look at him go!" He jabbed a finger at the rapidly moving black dot. The dot came to the edge of the board and stopped. It had reached the limit of the charted area. "See?"

—Now what? Kramer thought, watching. So the Old Man had escaped the cruisers and gotten away. He was alert, all right; there was nothing wrong with his mind. Or with ability to control his new body.

Body— The ship was a new body for him. He had traded in the old dying body, withered and frail, for this hulking frame of metal and plastic, turbines and rocket jets. He was strong, now. Strong and big. The new body was more powerful than a thousand human bodies. But how long would it last him? The average life of a cruiser was only ten years. With careful handling he might get twenty out of it, before some essential part failed and there was no way to replace it.

And then, what then? What would he do, when something failed and there was no one to fix it for him? That would be the end. Someplace, far out in the cold darkness of space, the ship would slow down, silent and lifeless, to exhaust its last heat into the eternal time-lessness of outer space. Or perhaps it would crash on some barren asteroid, burst into a million fragments.

It was only a question of time.

"Your wife didn't remember anything?" Gross said.

"I told you. Only that he kept a goat, once."

"A hell of a lot of help that is."

Kramer shrugged. "It's not my fault."

"I wonder if we'll ever see him again." Gross stared down at the indicator dot, still hanging at the edge of the board. "I wonder if he'll ever move back this way."

"I wonder, too," Kramer said.

❖ ❖ ❖

That night Kramer lay in bed, tossing from side to side, unable to sleep. The moon gravity, even artificially increased, was unfamiliar to him and it made him uncomfortable. A thousand thoughts wandered loose in his head as he lay, fully awake.

What did it all mean? What was the Professor's plan? Maybe they would never know. Maybe the ship was gone for good: the Old Man had left forever, shooting into outer space. They might never find out why he had done it, what purpose—if any—had been in his mind.

Kramer sat up in bed. He turned on the light and lit a cigarette. His quarters were small, a metal-lined bunk room, part of the moon station base.

The Old Man had wanted to talk to him. He had wanted to discuss things, hold a conversation, but in the hysteria and confusion all they had been able to think of was getting away. The ship was rushing off with them, carrying them into outer space. Kramer set his jaw. Could they be blamed for jumping? They had no idea where they were being taken, or why. They were helpless, caught in their own ship, and the pursuit ship standing by waiting to pick them up was their only chance. Another half hour and it would have been too late.

But what had the Old Man wanted to say? What had he intended to tell him, in those first confusing moments when the ship around them had come alive, each metal strut and wire suddenly animate, the body of a living creature, a vast metal organism?

It was weird, unnerving. He could not forget it, even now. He looked around the small room uneasily. What did it signify, the coming to life of metal and plastic? All at once they had found themselves inside a *living* creature, in its stomach, like Jonah inside the whale.

It had been alive, and it had talked to them, talked calmly and rationally, as it rushed them off, faster and faster into outer space. The wall speaker and circuit had become the vocal cords and mouth, the wiring the spinal cord and nerves, the hatches and relays and circuit breakers the muscles.

They had been helpless, completely helpless. The ship had, in a brief second, stolen their power away from them and left them defenseless, practically at its mercy. It was not right; it made him uneasy. All his life he had controlled machines, bent nature and the forces of nature to man and man's needs. The human race had slowly evolved until it was in a position to operate things, run them as it saw fit. Now all at once it had been plunged back down the ladder again, prostrate before a Power against which they were children.

Kramer got out of bed. He put on his bathrobe and began to search for a cigarette. While he was searching, the vidscreen rang.

He snapped the vidphone on. "Yes?"

The face of the immediate monitor appeared. "A call from Terra, Mr. Kramer. An emergency call."

"Emergency call? For me? Put it through." Kramer came awake, brushing his hair back out of his eyes. Alarm plucked at him.

From the speaker a strange voice came. "Philip Kramer? Is this Kramer?"

"Yes. Go on."

"This is General Hospital. New York City, Terra. Mr. Kramer, your wife is here. She has been critically injured in an accident. Your name was given to us to call. Is it possible for you to—"

"How badly?" Kramer gripped the vidphone stand. "Is it serious?"

"Yes, it's serious, Mr. Kramer. Are you able to come here? The quicker you can come the better."

"Yes." Kramer nodded. "I'll come. Thanks."

The screen died as the connection was broken. Kramer waited a moment. Then he tapped the button. The screen relit again. "Yes, sir," the monitor said.

"Can I get a ship to Terra at once? It's an emergency. My wife—"

"There's no ship leaving the moon for eight hours. You'll have to wait until the next period."

"Isn't there anything I can do?"

"We can broadcast a general request to all ships passing through this area. Sometimes cruisers pass by here returning to Terra for repairs."

"Will you broadcast that for me? I'll come down to the field."

"Yes, sir. But there may be no ship in the area for a while. It's a gamble." The screen died.

Kramer dressed quickly. He put on his coat and hurried out the lift. A moment later he was running across the general receiving lobby, past the rows of vacant desks and conference tables. At the door the sentries stepped aside and he went outside, onto the great concrete steps.

The face of the moon was in shadow. Below him the field stretched out in total darkness, a black void, endless, without form. He made his way carefully down the steps and along the ramp along the side of the field, to the control tower. A faint row of red lights showed him the way.

Two soldiers challenged him at the foot of the tower, standing in the shadows, their guns ready.

"Kramer?"

"Yes." A light was flashed in his face.

"Your call has been sent out already."

"Any luck?" Kramer asked.

"There's a cruiser nearby that has made contact with us. It has an injured jet and is moving slowly back toward Terra, away from the line."

"Good." Kramer nodded, a flood of relief rushing through him. He lit a cigarette and gave one to each of the soldiers. The soldiers lit up.

"Sir," one of them asked, "is it true about the experimental ship?"

"What do you mean?"

"It came to life and ran off?'

"No, not exactly," Kramer said. "It had a new type of control system instead of the Johnson units. It wasn't properly tested."

"But sir, one of the cruisers that was there got up close to it, and a buddy of mine says this ship acted funny. He never saw anything like it. It was like when he was fishing once on Terra, in Washington

State, fishing for bass. The fish were smart, going this way and that—"

"Here's your cruiser," the other soldier said. "Look!"

An enormous vague shape was settling slowly down onto the field. They could make nothing out but its row of tiny green blinkers. Kramer stared at the shape.

"Better hurry, sir," the soldiers said. "They don't stick around here very long."

"Thanks." Kramer loped across the field, toward the black shape that rose above him, extended across the width of the field. The ramp was down from the side of the cruiser and he caught hold of it. The ramp rose, and a moment later Kramer was inside the hold of the ship. The hatch slid shut behind him.

As he made his way up the stairs to the main deck the turbines roared up from the moon, out into space.

Kramer opened the door to the main deck. He stopped suddenly, staring around him in surprise. There was nobody in sight. The ship was deserted.

"Good God," he said. Realization swept over him, numbing him. He sat down on a bench, his head swimming. "Good God."

The ship roared out into space leaving the moon and Terra farther behind each moment.

And there was nothing he could do.

❖ ❖ ❖

"So it was you who put the call through," he said at last. "It was you who called me on the vidphone, not any hospital on Terra. It was all part of the plan." He looked up and around him. "And Dolores is really—"

"Your wife is fine," the wall speaker above him said tonelessly. "It was a fraud. I'm sorry to trick you that way, Philip, but it was all I could think of. Another day and you would have been back on Terra.

I don't want to remain in this area any longer than necessary. They have been so certain of finding me out in deep space that I have been able to stay here without too much danger. But even the purloined letter was found eventually."

Kramer smoked his cigarette nervously. "What are you going to do? Where are we going?'

"First, I want to talk to you. I have many things to discuss. I was very disappointed when you left me, along with the others. I had hoped that you would remain." The dry voice chuckled. "Remember how we used to talk in the old days, you and I? That was a long time ago."

The ship was gaining speed. It plunged through space at tremendous speed, rushing through the last of the defense zone and out beyond. A rush of nausea made Kramer bend over for a moment.

When he straightened up the voice from the wall went on. "I'm sorry to step it up so quickly, but we are still in danger. Another few moments and we'll be free."

"How about yuk ships? Aren't they out here?'

"I've already slipped away from several of them. They're quite curious about me."

"Curious?"

"They sense that I'm different, more like their own organic mines. They don't like it. I believe they will begin to withdraw from this area, soon. Apparently they don't want to get involved with me. They're an odd race, Philip. I would have liked to study them closely, try to learn something about them. I'm of the opinion that they use no inert material. All their equipment and instruments are alive, in some form or other. They don't construct or build at all. The idea of *making* is foreign to them. They utilize existing forms. Even their ships—"

"Where are we going?" Kramer said. "I want to know where you are taking me."

"Frankly, I'm not certain."

"You're not certain?"

"I haven't worked some details out. There are a few vague spots in my program, still. But I think that in a short while I'll have them ironed out."

"What is your program?" Kramer said.

"It's really very simple. But don't you want to come into the control room and sit? The seats are much more comfortable than that metal bench."

Kramer went into the control room and sat down at the control board. Looking at the useless apparatus made him feel strange.

"What's the matter?" the speaker above the board rasped.

Kramer gestured helplessly. "I'm powerless. I can't do anything. And I don't like it. Do you blame me?"

"No. No, I don't blame you. But you'll get your control back, soon. Don't worry. This is only a temporary expedient, taking you off this way. It was something I didn't contemplate. I forgot that orders would be given out to shoot me on sight."

"It was Gross's idea."

"I don't doubt that. My conception, my plan, came to me as soon as you began to describe your project, that day at my house. I saw at once that you were wrong; you people have no understanding of the mind at all. I realized that the transfer of a human brain from an organic body to a complex artificial spaceship would not involve the loss of the intellectualization faculty of the mind. When a man thinks, he *is*.

"When I realized that, I saw the possibility of an age-old dream becoming real. I was quite elderly when I first met you, Philip. Even then my life-span had come pretty much to its end. I could look ahead to nothing but death, and with it the extinction of all my ideas. I had made no mark on the world, none at all. My students, one by one, passed from me into the world, to take up jobs in the great Research Project, the search for better and bigger weapons of war.

"The world has been fighting for a long time, first with itself, then with the Martians, then with these beings from Proxima Centauri, whom we know nothing about. The human society has evolved war as a cultural institution, like the science of astronomy, or mathematics. War is a part of our lives, a career, a respected vocation. Bright, alert young men and women move into it, putting their shoulders to the wheel as they did in the time of Nebuchadnezzar. It has always been so.

"But is it innate in mankind? I don't think so. No social custom is innate. There were many human groups that did not go to war; the Eskimos never grasped the idea at all, and the American Indians never took to it well.

"But these dissenters were wiped out, and a cultural pattern was established that became the standard for the whole planet. Now it has become ingrained in us.

"But if someplace along the line some other way of settling problems had arisen and taken hold, something different than the massing of men and to—"

"What's your plan?" Kramer said. "I know the theory. It was part of one of your lectures."

"Yes, buried in a lecture on plant selection, as I recall. When you came to me with this proposition I realized that perhaps my conception could be brought to life, after all. If my theory were right that war is only a habit, not an instinct, a society built up apart from Terra with a minimum of cultural roots might develop differently. If it failed to absorb our outlook, if it could start out on another foot, it might not arrive at the same point to which we have come: a dead end, with nothing but greater and greater wars in sight, until nothing is left but ruin and destruction everywhere.

"Of course, there would have to be a Watcher to guide the experiment, at first. A crisis would undoubtedly come very quickly, probably in the second generation. Cain would arise almost at once.

"You see, Kramer, I estimate that if I remain at rest most of the time, on some small planet or moon, I may be able to keep functioning for almost a hundred years. That would be time enough, sufficient to see the direction of the new colony. After that— Well, after that it would be up to the colony itself.

"Which is just as well, of course. Man must take control eventually, on his own. One hundred years, and after that they will have control of their destiny. Perhaps I am wrong, perhaps war is more than a habit. Perhaps it is a law of the universe, that things can only survive as groups by group violence.

"But I'm going ahead and taking the chance that it is only a habit, that I'm right, that war is something we're so accustomed to that we don't realize it is a very unnatural thing. Now as to the place! I'm still a little vague about that. We must find the place, still.

"That's what we're doing now. You and I are going to inspect a few systems off the beaten path, planets where the trading prospects are low enough to keep Terran ships away. I know of one planet that might be a good place. It was reported by the Fairchild expedition in their original manuscript. We may look into that, for a start."

The ship was silent.

❖ ❖ ❖

Kramer sat for a time, staring down at the metal floor under him. The floor throbbed dully with the motion of the turbines. At last he looked up.

"You might be right. Maybe our outlook is only a habit." Kramer got to his feet. "But I wonder if something has occurred to you?"

"What is that?"

"If it's such a deeply ingrained habit, going back thousands of years, how are you going to get your colonists to make the break, leave Terra and Terran customs? How about *this* generation, the first ones, the people who found the colony? I think you're right that the next generation would be free of all this, if there were an—" He grinned. "—An Old Man Above to teach them something else instead."

Kramer looked up at the wall speaker. "How are you going to get the people to leave Terra and come with you, if by your own theory, this generation can't be saved, it all has to start with the next?"

The wall speaker was silent. Then it made a sound, the faint dry chuckle.

"I'm surprised at you, Philip. Settlers can be found. We won't need many, just a few." The speaker chuckled again. "I'll acquaint you with my solution."

At the far end of the corridor a door slid open. There was sound, a hesitant sound. Kramer turned.

"Dolores!"

Dolores Kramer stood uncertainly, looking into the control room. She blinked in amazement. "Phil! What are you doing here? What's going on?"

They stared at each other.

"What's happening?" Dolores said. "I received a vidcall that you had been hurt in a lunar explosion—"

The wall speaker rasped into life. "You see, Philip, that problem is already solved. We don't need so many people; even a single couple might do."

Kramer nodded slowly. "I see," he murmured thickly. "Just one couple. One man and woman."

"They might make it all right, if there were someone to watch and see that things went as they should. There will be quite a few things I can help you with, Philip. Quite a few. We'll get along very well, I think."

Kramer grinned wryly. "You could even help us name the animals," he said. "I understand that's the first step."

"I'll be glad to," the toneless, impersonal voice said. "As I recall, my part will be to bring them to you, one by one. Then you can do the actual naming."

"I don't understand," Dolores faltered. "What does he mean, Phil? Naming animals. What kind of animals? Where are we going?"

Kramer walked slowly over to the port and stood staring silently out, his arms folded. Beyond the ship myriad fragments of light gleamed, countless coals glowing in the dark void. Stars, suns, systems. Endless, without number. A universe of worlds. An infinity of planets, waiting for them, gleaming and winking from the darkness.

He turned back, away from the port. "Where are we going?" He smiled at his wife, standing nervous and frightened, her large eyes full of alarm. "I don't know where we are going," he said. "But somehow that doesn't seem important right now . . . I'm beginning to see the Professor's point, it's the result that counts."

And for the first time in many months he put his arm around Dolores. At first she stiffened, the fright and nervousness still in her eyes. But then suddenly she relaxed against him and there were tears wetting her cheeks.

"Phil . . . do you really think we can start over again—you and I?"

He kissed her tenderly, then passionately.

And the spaceship shot swiftly through the endless, trackless eternity of the void . . .

PIPER IN THE WOODS

"Well, Corporal Westerburg," Doctor Henry Harris said gently, "just why do you think you're a plant?"

As he spoke, Harris glanced down again at the card on his desk. It was from the Base Commander himself, made out in Cox's heavy scrawl: *Doc, this is the lad I told you about. Talk to him and try to find out how he got this delusion. He's from the new Garrison, the new check station on Asteroid Y-3, and we don't want anything to go wrong there. Especially a silly damn thing like this!*

Harris pushed the card aside and stared back up at the youth across the desk from him. The young man seemed ill at ease and appeared to be avoiding answering the question Harris had put to him. Harris frowned. Westerburg was a good looking chap, actually handsome in his Patrol uniform, a shock of blond hair over one eye. He was tall, almost six feet, a fine healthy lad, just two years out of Training, according to the card. Born in Detroit. Had measles when he was nine. Interested in jet engines, tennis, and girls. Twenty-six years old.

"Well, Corporal Westerburg," Doctor Harris said again. "Why do you think you're a plant?"

The Corporal looked up shyly. He cleared his throat. "Sir, I *am* a plant, I don't just think so. I've been a plant for several days now."

"I see." The Doctor nodded. "You mean that you weren't always a plant?"

"No sir. I just became a plant recently."

"And what were you before you became a plant?"

"Well, sir, I was just like the rest of you."

There was silence. Doctor Harris took up his pen and scratched a few lines, but nothing of importance came. A plant? And such a healthy-looking lad! Harris removed his steel-rimmed glasses and polished them with his handkerchief. He put them on again and leaned back in his chair. "Care for a cigarette, Corporal?"

"No, sir."

The Doctor lit one for himself, resting his arm on the edge of the chair. "Corporal, you must realize that there are very few men who become plants, especially on such short notice. I have to admit you are the first person who has ever told me such a thing."

"Yes, sir, I realize it's quite rare."

"You can understand why I'm interested, then. When you say you're a plant, you mean you're not capable of mobility? Or do you mean you're a vegetable, as opposed to an animal? Or just what?"

The Corporal looked away. "I can't tell you any more," he murmured. "I'm sorry, sir."

"Well, would you mind telling me *how* you became a plant?"

Corporal Westerburg hesitated. He stared down at the floor, then out the window at the spaceport, then at a fly on the desk. At last he stood up, getting slowly to his feet. "I can't even tell you that, sir," he said.

"You can't? Why not?"

"Because—because I promised not to."

The room was silent. Doctor Harris rose, too, and they both stood facing each other. Harris frowned, rubbing his jaw. "Corporal, just *who* did you promise?"

"I can't even tell you that, sir. I'm sorry."

The Doctor considered this. At last he went to the door and opened it. "All right, Corporal. You may go now. And thanks for your time."

"I'm sorry I'm not more helpful." The Corporal went slowly out and Harris closed the door after him. Then he went across his office to the vidphone. He rang Commander Cox's letter. A moment later the beefy good-natured face of the Base Commander appeared.

"Cox, this is Harris. I talked to him, all right. All I could get is the statement that he's a plant. What else is there? What kind of behavior pattern?"

"Well," Cox said, "the first thing they noticed was that he wouldn't do any work. The Garrison Chief reported that this Westerburg would wander off outside the Garrison and just sit, all day long. Just sit."

"In the sun?"

"Yes. Just sit in the sun. Then at nightfall he would come back in. When they asked why he wasn't working in the jet repair building he told them he had to be out in the sun. Then he said—" Cox hesitated.

"Yes? Said what?"

"He said that work was unnatural. That it was a waste of time. That the only worthwhile thing was to sit and contemplate—outside."

"What then?"

"Then they asked him how he got that idea, and then he revealed to them that he had become a plant."

"I'm going to have to talk to him again, I can see," Harris said. "And he's applied for a permanent discharge from the Patrol? What reason did he give?"

"The same, that he's a plant now, and has no more interest in being a Patrolman. All he wants to do is sit in the sun. It's the damnedest thing I ever heard."

"All right. I think I'll visit him in his quarters." Harris looked at his watch. "I'll go over after dinner."

"Good luck," Cox said gloomily. "But who ever heard of a man turning into a plant? We told him it wasn't possible, but he just smiled at us."

"I'll let you know how I make out," Harris said.

❖❖❖

Harris walked slowly down the hall. It was after six; the evening meal was over. A dim concept was coming into his mind, but it was much too soon to be sure. He increased his pace, turning right at the end of the hall. Two nurses passed, hurrying by. Westerburg was quartered with a buddy, a man who had been injured in a jet blast and who was now almost recovered. Harris came to the dorm wing and stopped, checking the numbers on the doors.

"Can I help you, sir?" the robot attendant said, gliding up.

"I'm looking for Corporal Westerburg's room."

"Three doors to the right."

Harris went on. Asteroid Y-3 had only recently been garrisoned and staffed. It had become the primary check-point to halt and examine ships entering the system from outer space. The Garrison made sure that no dangerous bacteria, fungus, or what-not arrived to infect the system. A nice asteroid it was, warm, well-watered, with trees and lakes and lots of sunshine. And the most modern Garrison in the nine planets. He shook his head, coming to the third door. He stopped, raising his hand and knocking.

"Who's there?" sounded through the door.

"I want to see Corporal Westerburg."

The door opened. A bovine youth with horn-rimmed glasses looked out, a book in his hand. "Who are you?"

"Doctor Harris."

"I'm sorry, sir. Corporal Westerburg is asleep."

"Would he mind if I woke him up? I want very much to talk to him." Harris peered inside. He could see a neat room, with a desk, a rug and lamp, and two bunks. On one of the bunks was Westerburg, lying face up, his arms folded across his chest, his eyes tightly closed.

"Sir," the bovine youth said, "I'm afraid I can't wake him up for you, much as I'd like to."

"You can't? Why not?"

"Sir, Corporal Westerburg won't wake up, not after the sun sets. He just won't. He can't be awakened."

"Cataleptic? Really?"

"But in the morning, as soon as the sun comes up, he leaps out of bed and goes outside. Stays the whole day."

"I see," the Doctor said. "Well, thanks anyhow." He went back out into the hall and the door shut after him. "There's more to this than I realized," he murmured. He went on back the way he had come.

It was a warm sunny day. The sky was almost free of clouds and a gentle wind moved through the cedars along the bank of the stream. There was a path leading from the hospital building down the slope to the stream. At the stream a small bridge led over to the other side, and a few patients were standing on the bridge, wrapped in their bathrobes, looking aimlessly down at the water.

It took Harris several minutes to find Westerburg. The youth was not with the other patients, near or around the bridge. He had gone farther down, past the cedar trees and out onto a strip of bright meadow, where poppies and grass grew everywhere. He was sitting on the stream bank, on a flat gray stone, leaning back and staring up, his mouth open a little. He did not notice the Doctor until Harris was almost beside him.

"Hello," Harris said softly.

Westerburg opened his eyes, looking up. He smiled and got slowly to his feet, a graceful, flowing motion that was rather surprising for a man of his size. "Hello, Doctor. What brings you out here?"

"Nothing. Thought I'd get some sun."

"Here, you can share my rock," Westerburg moved over and Harris sat down gingerly, being careful not to catch his trousers on the sharp edges of the rock. He lit a cigarette and gazed silently down at the water. Beside him, Westerburg had resumed his strange position, leaning back, resting on his hands, staring up with his eyes shut tight.

"Nice day," the Doctor said.

"Yes."

"Do you come here every day?"

"You like it better out here than inside."

"I can't stay inside," Westerburg said.

"You can't? How do you mean, 'can't'?"

"You would die without *air*, wouldn't you?" the Corporal said.

"And you'd die without sunlight?"

Westerburg nodded.

"Corporal, may I ask you something? Do you plan to do this the rest of your life, sit out in the sun on a flat rock? Nothing else?"

Westerburg nodded.

"How about your job? You went to school for years to become a Patrolman. You wanted to enter the Patrol very badly. You were given a fine rating and a first-class position. How do you feel, giving all that up? You know, it won't be easy to get back in again. Do you realize that?"

"I realize it."

"And you're really going to give it all up?"

"That's right."

Harris was silent for a while. At last he put his cigarette out and turned toward the youth. "All right, let's say you give up your job and sit in the sun. Well, what happens, then? Someone else has to do the job instead of you. Isn't that true? The job has to be done, *your* job has to be done. And if you don't do it someone else has to."

"I suppose so."

"Westerburg, suppose everyone felt the way you do? Suppose everyone wanted to sit in the sun all day? What would happen? No one would check ships coming from outer space. Bacteria and toxic crystals would enter the system and cause mass death and suffering. Isn't that right?"

"If everyone felt the way I do they wouldn't be going into outer space."

"But they have to. They have to trade, they have to get minerals and products and new plants."

"Why?"

"To keep society going."

"Why?"

"Well—" Harris gestured. "People couldn't live without society."

Westerburg said nothing to that. Harris watched him, but the youth did not answer.

"Isn't that right?" Harris said.

"Perhaps. It's a peculiar business, Doctor. You know, I struggled for years to get through Training. I had to work and pay my own way. Washed dishes, worked in kitchens. Studied at night, learned, crammed, worked on and on. And you know what I think, now?"

"What?"

"I wish I'd become a plant earlier."

Doctor Harris stood up. "Westerburg, when you come inside, will you stop off at my office? I want to give you a few tests, if you don't mind."

"The shock box?" Westerburg smiled. "I knew that would be coming around. Sure, I don't mind."

Nettled, Harris left the rock, walking back up the bank a short distance. "About three, Corporal?"

The Corporal nodded.

Harris made his way up the hill, to the path, toward the hospital building. The whole thing was beginning to become more clear to him. A boy who had struggled all his life. Financial insecurity. Idealized goal, getting a Patrol assignment. Finally reached it, found the load too great. And on Asteroid Y-3 there was too much vegetation to look at all day. Primitive identification and projection on the flora of the asteroid. Concept of security involved in immobility and permanence. Unchanging forest.

He entered the building. A robot orderly stopped him almost at once. "Sir, Commander Cox wants you urgently, on the vidphone."

"Thanks." Harris strode to the office. He dialed Cox's letter and the Commander's face came presently into focus. "Cox? This is Harris. I've been out talking to the boy. I'm beginning to get this lined up, now. I can see the pattern, too much load too long. Finally gets what he wants and the idealization shatters under the—"

"Harris!" Cox barked. "Shut up and listen. I just got a report from Y-3. They're sending an express rocket here. It's on the way."

"An express rocket?"

"Five more cases like Westerburg. All say they're plants! The Garrison Chief is worried as hell. Says we *must* find out what it is or the Garrison will fall apart, right away. Do you get me, Harris? Find out what it is!"

"Yes, sir," Harris murmured. "Yes, sir."

By the end of the week there were twenty cases, and all, of course, were from Asteroid Y-3.

Commander Cox and Harris stood together at the top of the hill, looking gloomily down at the stream below. Sixteen men and four women sat in the sun along the bank, none of them moving, none speaking. An hour had gone by since Cox and Harris appeared, and in all that time the twenty people below had not stirred.

"I don't get it," Cox said, shaking his head. "I just absolutely don't get it. Harris, is this the beginning of the end? Is everything going to start cracking around us? It gives me a hell of a strange feeling to see those people down there basking away in the sun, just sitting and basking."

"Who's that man there with the red hair?"

"That's Ulrich Deutsch. He was Second in Command at the Garrison. Now look at him! Sits and dozes with his mouth open and his eyes shut. A week ago that man was climbing, going right up to the top. When the Garrison Chief retires he was supposed to take over. Maybe another year, at the most. All his life he's been climbing to get up there."

"And now he sits in the sun," Harris finished.

"That woman. The brunette, with the short hair. Career woman. Head of the entire office staff of the Garrison. And the man beside her. Janitor. And that cute little gal there, with the bosom. Secretary, just out of school. All kinds. And I got a note this morning, three more coming in sometime today."

Harris nodded. "The strange thing is—they really *want* to sit down there. They're completely rational; they could do something else, but they just don't care to."

"Well?" Cox said. "What are you going to do? Have you found anything? We're counting on you. Let's hear it."

"I couldn't get anything out of them directly," Harris said, "but I've had some interesting results with the shock box. Let's go inside and I'll show you."

"Fine," Cox turned and started toward the hospital. "Show me anything you've got. This is serious. Now I know how Tiberius felt when Christianity showed up in high places."

❖ ❖ ❖

Harris snapped off the light. The room was pitch black. "I'll run this first reel for you. The subject is one of the best biologists stationed at the Garrison. Robert Bradshaw. He came in yesterday. I got a good run from the shock box because Bradshaw's mind is so highly differentiated. There's a lot of repressed material of a non-rational nature, more than usual."

He pressed a switch. The projector whirred, and on the far wall a three-dimensional image appeared in color, so real that it might have been the man himself. Robert Bradshaw was a man of fifty, heavy-set, with iron-gray hair and a square jaw. He sat in the chair calmly, his hands resting on the arms, oblivious to the electrodes attached to his neck and wrist. "There I go," Harris said. "Watch."

His film-image appeared, approaching Bradshaw. "Now, Mr. Bradshaw," his image said, "this won't hurt you at all, and it'll help us a lot." The image rotated the controls on the shock box, Bradshaw stiffened, and his jaw set, but otherwise he gave no sign. The image of Harris regarded him for a time and then stepped away from the controls.

"Can you hear me, Mr. Bradshaw?" the image asked.

"Yes."

"What is your name?"

"Robert C. Bradshaw."

"What is your position?"

"Chief Biologist at the check station on Y-3."

"Are you there now?"

"No, I'm back on Terra. In a hospital."

"Why?"

"Because I admitted to the Garrison Chief that I had become a plant."

"Is that true? That you are a plant."

"Yes, in a non-biological sense. I retain the physiology of a human being, of course."

"What do you mean, then, that you're a plant?"

"The reference is to attitudinal response, to Weltanschauung."

"Go on."

"It is possible for a warm-blooded animal, an upper primate, to adopt the psychology of a plant, to some extent."

"Yes?"

"I refer to this."

"And the others? They refer to this also?"

"Yes."

"How did this occur, your adopting this attitude?

Bradshaw's image hesitated, the lips twisting. "See?" Harris said to Cox. "Strong conflict. He wouldn't have gone on, if he had been fully conscious."

"I—"

"Yes?"

"I was taught to become a plant."

The image of Harris showed surprise and interest. "What do you mean, you were *taught* to become a plant?"

"They realized my problems and taught me to become a plant. Now I'm free from them, the problems."

"Who? Who taught you?"

"The Pipers."

"Who? The Pipers? Who are the Pipers?"

There was no answer.

"Mr. Bradshaw, who are the Pipers?"

After a long, agonized pause, the heavy lips parted. "They live in the woods . . . "

Harris snapped off the projector, and the lights came on. He and Cox blinked. "That was all I could get," Harris said. "But I was lucky to get that. He wasn't supposed to tell, not at all. That was the thing they all promised not to do, tell who taught them to become plants. The Pipers who live in the woods on Asteroid Y-3."

"You got this story from all twenty?"

"No." Harris grimaced. "Most of them put up too much fight. I couldn't even get *this* much from them."

Cox reflected. "The Pipers. Well? What do you propose to do? Just wait around until you can get the full story? Is that your program?"

"No." Harris said. "Not at all. I'm going to Y-3 and find out who the Pipers are, myself."

❖ ❖ ❖

The small patrol ship made its landing with care and precision, its jets choking into final silence. The hatch slid back and Doctor Henry Harris found himself staring out at a field, a brown, sun-baked landing field. At the end of the field was a tall signal tower. Around the field on all sides were long gray buildings, the Garrison check station itself. Not far off a huge Venusian cruiser was parked, a vast green hulk, like an enormous lime. The technicians from the station were swarming all over it, checking and examining each inch of it for lethal life-forms and poisons that might have attached themselves to the hull.

"All out, sir," the pilot said.

Harris nodded. He took hold of his two suitcases and stepped carefully down. The ground was hot underfoot, and he blinked in the bright sunlight. Jupiter was in the sky, and the vast planet reflected considerable sunlight down onto the asteroid.

Harris started across the field, carrying his suitcase. A field attendant was already busy opening the storage compartment of the Patrol ship, extracting his trunk. The attendant lowered the trunk into a waiting dolly and came after him, manipulating the little truck with bored skill.

As Harris came to the entrance of the signal tower the gate slid back and a man came forward, an older man, large and robust, with white hair and a steady walk.

"How are you, Doctor?" he said, holding his hand out. "I'm Lawrence Watts, the Garrison Chief."

They shook hands. Watts smiled down at Harris. He was a huge old man, still regal and straight in his dark blue uniform, with his gold epaulets sparkling on his shoulders.

"Have a good trip?" Watts asked. "Come on inside and I'll have a drink fixed for you. It gets hot around here, with the Big Mirror up there."

"Jupiter?" Harris followed him inside the building. The signal tower was cool and dark, a welcome relief. "Why is the gravity so near Terra's? I expected to go flying off like a kangaroo. Is it artificial?"

"No. There's a dense core of some kind to the asteroid, some kind of metallic deposit. That's why we picked this asteroid out of all the others. It made the construction problem much simpler, and it also explains why the asteroid has natural air and water. Did you see the hills?"

"The hills?"

"When we get up higher in the tower we'll be able to see over the buildings. There's quite a natural park here, a regular little forest, complete with everything you'd want. Come in here, Harris. This is my office." The old man strode at quite a clip, around the corner and into a large, well-furnished apartment. "Isn't this pleasant? I intend to make my last year here as amiable as possible." He frowned. "Off course, with Deutsch gone, I may be here forever. Oh, well." He shrugged. "Sit down, Harris."

"Thanks." Harris took a chair, stretching his legs out. He watched Watts as he closed the door to the hall. "By the way, any more cases come up?"

"Two more today." Watts was grim. "Makes almost thirty, in all. We have three hundred men in this station. At the rate it's going—"

"Chief, you spoke about a forest on the asteroid. Do you allow the crew to go into the forest at will? Or do you restrict them to the buildings and grounds?"

Watts rubbed his jaw. "Well, it's a difficult situation, Harris. I have to let the men leave the grounds sometimes. They can *see* the forest from the buildings, and as long as you can see a nice place to stretch out and relax that does it. Once every ten days they have a full period of rest. Then they go out and fool around."

"And then it happens?"

"Yes, I suppose so. But as long as they can see the forest, they'll want to go. I can't help it."

"I know. I'm not censuring you. Well, what's your theory? What happens to them out there? What do they do?"

"What happens? Once they get out there and take it easy for a while they don't want to come back and work. It's boondoggling. Playing hookey. They don't want to work, so off they go."

"How about this business of their delusions?"

Watts laughed good-naturedly. "Listen, Harris. You know as well as I do that's a lot of poppycock. They're no more plants than you or I.

They just don't want to work, that's all. When I was a cadet we had a few ways to make people work. I wish we could lay a few on their backs, like we used to."

"You think this is simple goldbricking, then?"

"Don't you think it is?"

"No," Harris said. "They really believe they're plants. I put them through the high-frequency shock treatment, the shock box. The whole nervous system is paralyzed, all inhibitions stopped cold. They tell the truth, then. And they said the same thing—and more."

Watts paced back and forth, his hands clasped behind his back. "Harris, you're a doctor, and I suppose you know what you're talking about. But look at the situation here. We have a garrison, a good modern garrison. We're probably the most modern outfit in the system. Every new device and gadget is here that science can produce. Harris, this garrison is one vast machine. The men are parts, and each has his job, the Maintenance Crew, the Biologists, the Office Crew, the Managerial Staff.

"Look what happens when one person steps away from his job. Everything else begins to creak. We can't service the bugs if no one services the machines. We can't order food to feed the crews if no one makes out reports, takes inventories. We can't direct any kind of activity if the Second in Command decides to go out and sit in the sun all day.

"Thirty people, one tenth of the Garrison. But we can't run without them. The Garrison is built that way. If you take the supports out the whole building falls. No one can leave. We're all tied here and these people know it. They know they have no right to do that, run off on their own. No one has that right anymore. We're all too tightly inter-woven to suddenly start doing what we want. It's unfair to the rest, the majority."

Harris nodded. "Chief, can I ask you something?"

"What is it?"

"Are there any inhabitants on the asteroid? Any natives?"

"Natives?" Watts considered. "Yes, there's some kind of aborigines living out there." He waved vaguely toward the window.

"What are they like? Have you seen them?"

"Yes, I've seen them. At least, I saw them when we first came here. They hung around for a while, watching us, then after a time they disappeared."

"Did they die off? Diseases of some kind?"

"No. They just—just disappeared. Into their forest. They're still there, someplace."

"What kind of people are they?"

"Well, the story is that they're originally from Mars. They don't look much like Martians, though. They're dark, a kind of coppery color. Thin. Very agile, in their own way. They hunt and fish. No written language. We don't pay much attention to them."

"I see." Harris paused. "Chief, have you ever heard of anything called—The Pipers?"

"The Pipers?" Watts frowned. "No. Why?"

"The patients mentioned something called The Pipers. According to Bradshaw, the Pipers taught him to become a plant. He learned it from them, a kind of teaching."

"The Pipers. What are they?"

"I don't know," Harris admitted. "I thought maybe you might know. My first assumption, of course, was that they're the natives. But now I'm not so sure, after hearing your description of them."

"The natives are primitive savages. They don't have anything to teach anybody, especially a top-flight biologist."

Harris hesitated. "Chief, I'd like to go into the woods and look around. Is that possible?"

"Certainly. I can arrange it for you. I'll give you one of the men to show you around."

"I'd rather go alone. Is there any danger?"

"No, none that I know of. Except—"

"Except the Pipers," Harris finished. "I know. Well, there's only one way to find them, and that's it. I'll have to take my chances."

"If you walk in a straight line," Chief Watts said, "you'll find your-self back at the Garrison in about six hours. It's a damn small asteroid. There's a couple of streams and lakes, so don't fall in."

"How about snakes or poisonous insects?"

"Nothing like that reported. We did a lot of tramping around at first, but it's grown back now, the way it was. We never encountered anything dangerous."

"Thanks, Chief," Harris said. They shook hands. "I'll see you before nightfall."

"Good luck." The Chief and his two armed escorts turned and went back across the rise, down the other side toward the Garrison. Harris watched them go until they disappeared inside the building. Then he turned and started into the grove of trees.

The woods were very silent around him as he walked. Trees towered up on all sides of him, huge dark-green trees like eucalyptus. The ground underfoot was soft with endless leaves that had fallen and rotted into the soil. After awhile the grove of high trees fell behind and he found himself crossing a dry meadow, the grass and weeds burned brown in the sun. Insects buzzed around him, rising up from the dry weed-stalks. Something scuttled ahead, hurrying through the under-growth. He caught sight of a gray ball with many legs, scampering furiously, its antennae weaving.

The meadow ended at the bottom of a hill. He was going up, now, going higher and higher. Ahead of him an endless expanse of green rose, acres of wild growth. He scrambled to the top finally, blowing and panting, catching his breath.

He went on. Now he was going down again, plunging into a deep gully. Tall ferns grew, as large as trees. He was entering a living Jurassic forest, ferns that stretched out endlessly ahead of him. Down he went, walking carefully. The air began to turn cold around him. The floor of the gully was damp and silent; underfoot the ground was almost wet.

He came out on a level table. It was dark, with the ferns growing up on all sides, dense growths of ferns, silent and unmoving. He came upon a natural path, an old stream bed, rough and rocky, but easy to follow. The air was thick and oppressive. Beyond the ferns he could see the side of the next hill, a green field rising up.

Something gray was ahead. Rocks, piled-up boulders, scattered and stacked here and there. The stream led directly to them. Apparently this had been a pool of some kind, a stream emptying from it. He climbed the first of the boulders awkwardly, feeling his way up. At the top he paused, resting again.

As yet he had had no luck. So far he had not met any of the natives. It would be through them that he would find the mysterious Pipers that were stealing the men away, if such really existed. If he could find the natives, talk to them, perhaps he could find out something. But as yet he had been unsuccessful. He looked around. The woods were very silent. A slight breeze moved through the ferns rustling them, but that was all. Where were the natives? Probably they had a settlement of some sort, huts, a clearing. The asteroid was small, he should be able to find them by nightfall.

❖ ❖ ❖

He started down the rocks. More rocks rose up ahead and he climbed them. Suddenly he stopped, listening. Far off, he could hear a sound, the sound of water. Was he approaching a pool of some kind? He went on again, trying to locate the sound. He scrambled down rocks and up rocks, and all around him there was silence, except for the splashing of distant water. Maybe a waterfall, water in motion. A stream. If he found the stream he might find the natives.

The rocks ended and the stream bed began again, but this time it was wet, the bottom muddy and overgrown with moss. He was on the right track; not too long ago this stream had flowed, probably during the rainy season. He went up on the side of the stream, pushing through the ferns and vines. A golden snake slid expertly out of his path. Something glinted ahead, something sparkling through the ferns. Water. A pool. He hurried, pushing the vines aside and stepping out, leaving them behind.

He was standing on the edge of a pool, a deep pool sunk in a hollow of gray rocks, surrounded by ferns and vines. The water was clear and bright, and in motion, flowing in a waterfall at the far end. It was beautiful, and he stood watching, marveling at it, the undisturbed quality of it. Untouched, it was. Just as it had always been, probably. As long as the asteroid existed. Was he the first to see it? Perhaps. It was so hidden, so concealed by the ferns. It gave him a strange feeling, a feeling almost of ownership. He stepped down a little toward the water.

And it was then he noticed her.

The girl was sitting on the far edge of the pool, staring down into the water, resting her head on one drawn-up knee. She had been bathing; he could see that at once. Her coppery body was still wet and glistening with moisture, sparkling in the sun. She had not seen him. He stopped, holding his breath, watching her.

She was lovely, very lovely, with long dark hair that wound around her shoulders and arms. Her body was slim, very slender, with a supple grace to it that made him stare, accustomed as he was to various forms of anatomy. How silent she was! Silent and unmoving, staring down at the water. Time passed, strange, unchanging time, as he watched the girl. Time might even have ceased, with the girl sitting on the rock staring into the water, and the rows of great ferns behind her, as rigid as if they had been painted there.

All at once the girl looked up. Harris shifted, suddenly conscious of himself as an intruder. He stepped back. "I'm sorry," he murmured. "I'm from the Garrison. I didn't mean to come poking around."

She nodded without speaking.

"You don't mind?" Harris asked presently.

"No."

So she spoke Terran! He moved a little toward her, around the side of the pool. "I hope you don't mind my bothering you. I won't be on the asteroid very long. This is my first day here. I just arrived from Terra."

She smiled faintly.

"I'm a doctor. Henry Harris." He looked down at her, at the slim coppery body gleaming in the sunlight, a faint sheen of moisture on her arms and thighs. "You might be interested in why I'm here." He paused. "Maybe you can even help me."

She looked up a little. "Oh?"

"Would you like to help me?"

She smiled. "Yes. Of course."

"That's good. Mind if I sit down?" He looked around and found himself a flat rock. He sat down slowly, facing her. "Cigarette?"

"No."

"Well, I'll have one." He lit up, taking a deep breath. "You see, we have a problem at the Garrison. Something has been happening to some of the men, and it seems to be spreading. We have to find out what causes it or we won't be able to run the Garrison."

He waited for a moment. She nodded slightly. How silent she was! Silent and unmoving. Like the ferns.

"Well, I've been able to find out a few things from them, and one very interesting fact stands out. They keep saying that something called—called The Pipers are responsible for their condition. They say the Pipers taught them—" He stopped. A strange look had flitted across her dark, small face. "Do you know the Pipers?"

She nodded.

Acute satisfaction flooded over Harris. "You do? I was sure the natives would know." He stood up again. "I was sure they would, if the Pipers really existed. Then they do exist, do they?"

"They exist."

Harris frowned. "And they're here, in the woods?"

"Yes."

"I see." He ground his cigarette out impatiently. "You don't suppose there's any chance you could take me to them, do you?"

"Take you?"

"Yes. I have this problem and I have to solve it. You see, the Base Commander on Terra has assigned this to me, this business about the Pipers. It has to be solved. And I'm the one assigned to the job. So it's important to me to find them. Do you see? Do you understand?"

She nodded.

"Well, will you take me to them?"

The girl was silent. For a long time she sat, staring down into the water, resting her head against her knee. Harris began to become impatient. He fidgeted back and forth, resting first on one leg and then on the other.

"Well, will you?" he said again. "It's important to the whole Garrison. What do you say?" He felt around in his pockets. "Maybe I could give you something. What do I have . . . " He brought out his lighter. "I could give you my lighter."

The girl stood up, rising slowly, gracefully, without motion or effort. Harris' mouth fell open. How supple she was, gliding to her feet in a single motion! He blinked. Without effort she had stood, seemingly without *change*. All at once she was standing instead of sitting, standing and looking calmly at him, her small face expressionless.

"Will you?" he said.

"Yes. Come along." She turned away, moving toward the row of ferns.

Harris followed quickly, stumbling across the rocks. "Fine," he said. "Thanks a lot. I'm very interested to meet these Pipers. Where are you taking me, to your village? How much time do we have before nightfall?"

The girl did not answer. She had entered the ferns already, and Harris quickened his pace to keep from losing her. How silently she glided!

"Wait," he called. "Wait for me."

The girl paused, waiting for him, slim and lovely, looking silently back.

He entered the ferns, hurrying after her.

❖ ❖ ❖

"Well I'll be damned!" Commander Cox said. "It sure didn't take you long." He leaped down the steps two at a time. "Let me give you a hand."

Harris grinned, lugging his heavy suitcases. He set them down and breathed a sigh of relief. "It isn't worth it," he said. "I'm going to give up taking so much."

"Come on inside. Soldier, give him a hand." A Patrolman hurried over and took one of the suitcases. The three men went inside and down the corridor to Harris' quarters. Harris unlocked the door and the Patrolman deposited his suitcase inside.

"Thanks," Harris said. He set the other down beside it. "It's good to be back, even for a little while."

"A little while?"

"I just came back to settle my affairs. I have to return to Y-3 tomorrow morning."

"Then you didn't solve the problem?"

"I solved it, but I haven't *cured* it. I'm going back and get to work right away. There's a lot to be done."

"But you found out what it is?"

"Yes. It was just what the men said. The Pipers."

"The Pipers do exist?"

"Yes." Harris nodded. "They do exist." He removed his coat and put it over the back of the chair. Then he went to the window and let it down. Warm spring air rushed into the room. He settled himself on the bed, leaning back.

"The Pipers exist, all right—in the minds of the Garrison crew! To the crew, the Pipers are real. The crew created them. It's a mass hypnosis, a group projection, and all the men there have it, to some degree."

"How did it start?"

"Those men on Y-3 were sent because they were skilled, highly-trained men with exceptional ability. All their lives they've been schooled by complex modern society, fast tempo and high integration between people. Constant pressure toward some goal, some job to be done.

"Those men are put down suddenly on an asteroid where there are natives living the most primitive of existence, completely vegetable lives. No concept of goal, no concept of purpose, and hence no ability to plan. The natives live the way the animals live, from day to day, sleeping, picking food from the trees. A kind of Garden-of-Eden existence, without struggle or conflict."

"So? But—"

"Each of the Garrison crew sees the natives and *unconsciously* thinks of his own early life, when he was a child, when *he* had no worries, no responsibilities, before he joined modern society. A baby lying in the sun.

"But he can't admit this to himself! He can't admit that he might *want* to live like the natives, to lie and sleep all day. So he invents The Pipers, the idea of a mysterious group living in the woods who trap him, lead him into their kind of life. Then he can blame *them*, not himself. They 'teach' him to become a part of the woods."

"What are you going to do? Have the woods burned?"

"No." Harris shook his head. "That's not the answer; the woods are harmless. The answer is psycho-therapy for the men. That's why I'm going right back, so I can begin work. They've got to be made to see that the Pipers are inside them, their own unconscious voices calling to them to give up their responsibilities. They've got to be made to realize that there are no Pipers, at least, not outside themselves. The woods are harmless and the natives have nothing to teach anyone. They're primitive savages, without even a written language. We're seeing a psychological projection by a whole Garrison of men who want to lay down their work and take it easy for a while."

The room was silent.

"I see," Cox said presently. "Well, it makes sense." He got to his feet. "I hope you can do something with the men you get back."

"I hope so, too," Harris agreed. "And I think I can. After all, it's just a question of increasing their self-awareness. When they have that the Pipers will vanish."

Cox nodded. "Well, you go ahead with your unpacking, Doc. I'll see you at dinner. And maybe before you leave, tomorrow."

"Fine."

Harris opened the door and the Commander went out into the hall. Harris closed the door after him and then went back across the room. He looked out the window for a moment, his hands in his pockets.

It was becoming evening, the air was turning cool. The sun was just setting as he watched, disappearing behind the buildings of the city surrounding the hospital. He watched it go down.

Then he went over to his two suitcases. He was tired, very tired from his trip. A great weariness was beginning to descend over him. There were so many things to do, so terribly many. How could he hope to do them all? Back to the asteroid. And then what?"

He yawned, his eyes closing. How sleepy he was! He looked over at the bed. Then he sat down on the edge of it and took his shoes off. So much to do, the next day.

He put his shoes in the corner of the room. Then he bent over, unsnapping one of the suitcases. He opened the suitcase. From it he took a bulging gunny-sack. Carefully, he emptied the contents of the sack out on the floor. Dirt, rich soft dirt. Dirt he had collected during his last hours there, dirt he had carefully gathered up.

When the dirt was spread out on the floor he sat down in the middle of it. He stretched himself out, leaning back. When he was fully comfortable he folded his hands across his chest and closed his eyes. So much work to do— But later on, of course. Tomorrow. How warm the dirt was . . .

He was sound asleep in a moment.

THE VARIABLE MAN

I

Security Commissioner Reinhart rapidly climbed the front steps and entered the Council building. Council guards stepped quickly aside and he entered the familiar place of great whirring machines. His thin face rapt, eyes alight with emotion, Reinhart gazed intently up at the central SRB computer, studying its reading.

"Straight gain for the last quarter," observed Kaplan, the lab organizer. He grinned proudly as if personally responsible. "Not bad, Commissioner."

"We're catching up to them," Reinhart retorted. "But too damn slowly. We must finally go over—and soon."

Kaplan was in a talkative mood. "We design new offensive weapons, they counter with improved defenses. And nothing is actually made! Continual improvement, but neither we nor Centaurus can stop designing long enough to stabilize for production."

"It will end," Reinhart stated coldly, "as soon as Terra turns out a weapon for which Centaurus can build no defense."

"Every weapon has a defense. Design and discord. Immediate obsolescence. Nothing lasts long enough to—"

"What we count on is the *lag*," Reinhart broke in, annoyed. His hard gray eyes bored into the lab organizer and Kaplan slunk back.

"The time lag between our offensive design and their counter development. The lag varies." He waved impatiently toward the massed banks of SRB machines. "As you well know."

At this moment, 9:30 AM, May 7, 2136, the statistical ratio on the SRB machines stood at 21-17 on the Centauran side of the ledger. All facts considered, the odds favored a successful repulsion by Proxima Centaurus of a Terran military attack. The ratio was based on the total information known to the SRB machines, on a gestalt of the vast flow of data that poured in endlessly from all sectors of the Sol and Centaurus systems.

21-17 on the Centauran side. But a month ago it had been 24-18 in the enemy's favor. Things were improving, slowly but steadily. Centaurus, older and less virile than Terra, was unable to match Terra's rate of technocratic advance. Terra was pulling ahead.

"If we went to war now," Reinhart said thoughtfully, "we would lose. We're not far enough along to risk an overt attack." A harsh, ruthless glow twisted across his handsome features, distorting them into a stern mask. "But the odds are moving in our favor. Our offensive designs are gradually gaining on their defenses."

"Let's hope the war comes soon," Kaplan agreed. "We're all on edge. This damn waiting . . ."

The war would come soon. Reinhart knew it intuitively. The air was full of tension, the *élan*. He left the SRB rooms and hurried down the corridor to his own elaborately guarded office in the Security wing. It wouldn't be long. He could practically feel the hot breath of destiny on his neck—for him a pleasant feeling. His thin lips set in a humorless smile, showing an even line of white teeth against his tanned skin. It made him feel good, all right. He'd been working at it a long time.

First contact, a hundred years earlier, had ignited instant conflict between Proxima Centauran outposts and exploring Terran raiders. Flash fights, sudden eruptions of fire and energy beams.

And then the long, dreary years of inaction between enemies where contact required years of travel, even at nearly the speed of light. The two systems were evenly matched. Screen against screen. Warship against power station. The Centauran Empire surrounded Terra, an iron ring that couldn't be broken, rusty and corroded as it was. New weapons had to be conceived, if Terra was to break out.

Through the windows of his office, Reinhart could see endless buildings and streets. Terrans hurrying back and forth. Bright specks that were commute ships, little eggs that carried businessmen and white-collar workers around. The huge transport tubes that shot masses of workmen to factories and labor camps from their housing units. All these people, waiting to break out. Waiting for the day.

Reinhart snapped on his vidscreen, the confidential channel. "Give me Military Designs," he ordered sharply.

He sat tense, his wiry body taut, as the vidscreen warmed into life. Abruptly he was facing the hulking image of Peter Sherikov, director of the vast network of labs under the Ural Mountains.

Sherikov's great bearded features hardened as he recognized Reinhart. His bushy black eyebrows pulled up in a sullen line. "What do you want? You know I'm busy. We have too much work to do, as it is. Without being bothered by—politicians."

"I'm dropping over your way," Reinhart answered lazily. He adjusted the cuff of his immaculate gray cloak. "I want a full description of your work and whatever progress you've made."

"You'll find a regular departmental report plate filed in the usual way, around your office someplace. If you'll refer to that you'll know exactly what we—"

"I'm not interested in that. I want to *see* what you're doing. And I expect you to be prepared to describe your work fully. I'll be there shortly. Half an hour."

Reinhart cut the circuit. Sherikov's heavy features dwindled and faded. Reinhart relaxed, letting his breath out. Too bad he had to work with Sherikov. He had never liked the man. The big Polish scientist was an individualist, refusing to integrate himself with society. Independent, atomistic in outlook. He held concepts of the individual as an end, diametrically contrary to the accepted organic state Weltansicht.

But Sherikov was the leading research scientist, in charge of the Military Designs Department. And on Designs the whole future of Terra depended. Victory over Centaurus—or more waiting, bottled up in the Sol system, surrounded by a rotting, hostile Empire, now sinking into ruin and decay, yet still strong.

Reinhart got quickly to his feet and left the office. He hurried down the hall and out of the Council building.

A few minutes later he was heading across the mid-morning sky in his highspeed cruiser, toward the Asiatic landmass, the vast Ural mountain range. Toward the Military Designs labs.

Sherikov met him at the entrance. "Look here, Reinhart. Don't think you're going to order me around. I'm not going to—"

"Take it easy." Reinhart fell into step beside the bigger man. They passed through the check and into the auxiliary labs. "No immediate coercion will be exerted over you or your staff. You're free to continue your work as you see fit—for the present. Let's get this straight. My concern is to integrate your work with our total social needs. As long as your work is sufficiently productive—"

Reinhart stopped in his tracks.

"Pretty, isn't he?" Sherikov said ironically.

"What the hell is it?"

"Icarus, we call him. Remember the Greek myth? The legend of Icarus. Icarus flew . . . This Icarus is going to fly, one of these days." Sherikov shrugged. "You can examine him, if you want. I suppose this is what you came here to see."

Reinhart advanced slowly. "This is the weapon you've been working on?"

"How does he look?"

Rising up in the center of the chamber was a squat metal cylinder, a great ugly cone of dark gray. Technicians circled around it, wiring up the exposed relay banks. Reinhart caught a glimpse of endless tubes and filaments, a maze of wires and terminals and parts criss-crossing each other, layer on layer.

"What is it?" Reinhart perched on the edge of a workbench, leaning his big shoulders against the wall.

"An idea of Jamison Hedge—the same man who developed our instantaneous interstellar vidcasts forty years ago. He was trying to find a method of faster than light travel when he was killed, destroyed along with most of his work. After that ftl research was abandoned. It looked as if there were no future in it."

"Wasn't it shown that nothing could travel faster than light?"

"The interstellar vidcasts do! No, Hedge developed a valid ftl drive. He managed to propel an object at fifty times the speed of light. But as the object gained speed, its length began to diminish and its mass increased. This was in line with familiar twentieth-century concepts of mass-energy transformation. We conjectured that as Hedge's object gained velocity it would continue to lose length and gain mass until its length became nil and its mass infinite. Nobody can imagine such an object."

"Go on."

"But what actually occurred is this. Hedge's object continued to lose length and gain mass until it reached the theoretical limit of velocity, the speed of light. At that point the object, still gaining speed, simply ceased to exist. Having no length, it ceased to occupy space. It disappeared. However, the object had not been *destroyed*. It continued on its way, gaining momentum each moment, moving in an arc across the galaxy, away from the Sol system. Hedge's object entered some other realm of being, beyond our powers of conception. The next phase of Hedge's experiment consisted in a search for some way to slow the ftl object down, back to a sub-ftl speed, hence back into our universe. This counterprinciple was eventually worked out."

"With what result?"

"The death of Hedge and destruction of most of his equipment. His experimental object, in re-entering the space-time universe, came into being in space already occupied by matter. Possessing an incredible mass, just below infinity level, Hedge's object exploded in a titanic cataclysm. It was obvious that no space travel was possible with such a drive. Virtually all space contains *some* matter. To re-enter space would bring automatic destruction. Hedge had found his ftl drive and his counterprinciple, but no one before this has been able to put them to any use."

Reinhart walked over toward the great metal cylinder. Sherikov jumped down and followed him. "I don't get it," Reinhart said. "You said the principle is no good for space travel."

"That's right."

"What's this for, then? If the ship explodes as soon as it returns to our universe—"

"This is not a ship." Sherikov grinned slyly. "Icarus is the first practical application of Hedge's principles. Icarus is a bomb."

"So this is our weapon," Reinhart said. "A bomb. An immense bomb."

"A bomb, moving at a velocity greater than light. A bomb which will not exist in our universe. The Centaurans won't be able to detect or stop it. How could they? As soon as it passes the speed of light it will cease to exist—beyond all detection."

"But—"

"Icarus will be launched outside the lab, on the surface. He will align himself with Proxima Centaurus, gaining speed rapidly. By the time he reaches his destination he will be traveling at ftl-100. Icarus will be brought back to this universe within Centaurus itself. The explosion should destroy the star and wash away most of its planets—including their central hub-planet, Armun. There is no way they can halt Icarus, once he has been launched. No defense is possible. Nothing can stop him. It is a real fact."

"When will it be ready?"

Sherikov's eyes flickered. "Soon."

"Exactly how soon?"

The big Pole hesitated. "As a matter of fact, there's only one thing holding us back."

Sherikov led Reinhart around to the other side of the lab. He pushed a lab guard out of the way.

"See this?" He tapped a round globe, open at one end, the size of a grapefruit. "This is holding us up."

"What is it?"

"The central control turret. This thing brings Icarus back to sub-ftl flight at the correct moment. It must be absolutely accurate. Icarus will be within the star only a matter of a microsecond. If the turret does not function exactly, Icarus will pass out the other side and shoot beyond the Centauran system."

"How near completed is this turret?"

Sherikov hedged uncertainly, spreading out his big hands. "Who can say? It must be wired with infinitely minute equipment—microscope grapples and wires invisible to the naked eye."

"Can you name any completion date?"

Sherikov reached into his coat and brought out a manila folder. "I've drawn up the data for the SRB machines, giving a date of completion. You can go ahead and feed it. I entered ten days as the maximum period. The machines can work from that."

Reinhart accepted the folder cautiously. "You're sure about the date? I'm not convinced I can trust you, Sherikov."

Sherikov's features darkened. "You'll have to take a chance, Commissioner. I don't trust you any more than you trust me. I know how much you'd like an excuse to get me out of here and one of your puppets in."

Reinhart studied the huge scientist thoughtfully. Sherikov was going to be a hard nut to crack. Designs was responsible to Security, not the Council. Sherikov was losing ground—but he was still a potential danger. Stubborn, individualistic, refusing to subordinate his welfare to the general good.

"All right." Reinhart put the folder slowly away in his coat. "I'll feed it. But you better be able to come through. There can't be any slip-ups. Too much hangs on the next few days."

"If the odds change in our favor are you going to give the mobilization order?"

"Yes," Reinhart stated. "I'll give the order the moment I see the odds change."

❖ ❖ ❖

Standing in front of the machines, Reinhart waited nervously for the results. It was two o'clock in the afternoon. The day was warm, a pleasant May afternoon. Outside the building the daily life of the planet went on as usual.

As usual? Not exactly. The feeling was in the air, an expanding excitement growing every day. Terra had waited a long time. The attack on Proxima Centaurus had to come—and the sooner the better. The ancient Centauran Empire hemmed in Terra, bottled the human race up in its one system. A vast, suffocating net draped across the heavens, cutting Terra off from the bright diamonds beyond . . . And it had to end.

The SRB machines whirred, the visible combination disappearing. For a time no ratio showed. Reinhart tensed, his body rigid. He waited.

The new ratio appeared.

Reinhart gasped. 7-6. Toward Terra!

Within five minutes the emergency mobilization alert had been flashed to all Government departments. The Council and President Duffe had been called to immediate session. Everything was happening fast.

But there was no doubt. 7-6. In Terra's favor. Reinhart hurried frantically to get his papers in order, in time for the Council session.

❖ ❖ ❖

At histo-research the message plate was quickly pulled from the confidential slot and rushed across the central lab to the chief official.

"Look at this!" Fredman dropped the plate on his superior's desk. "Look at it!"

Harper picked up the plate, scanning it rapidly. "Sounds like the real thing. I didn't think we'd live to see it."

Fredman left the room, hurrying down the hall. He entered the time bubble office. "Where's the bubble?" he demanded, looking around.

One of the technicians looked slowly up. "Back about two hundred years. We're coming up with interesting data on the War of 1914. According to material the bubble has already brought up—"

"Cut it. We're through with routine work. Get the bubble back to the present. From now on all equipment has to be free for Military work."

"But—the bubble is regulated automatically."

"You can bring it back manually."

"It's risky." The technician hedged. "If the emergency requires it, I suppose we could take a chance and cut the automatic."

"The emergency requires *everything*," Fredman said feelingly.

❖ ❖ ❖

"But the odds might change back," Margaret Duffe, President of the Council, said nervously. "Any minute they can revert."

"This is our chance!" Reinhart snapped, his temper rising. "What the hell's the matter with you? We've waited years for this."

The Council buzzed with excitement. Margaret Duffe hesitated uncertainly, her blue eyes clouded with worry. "I realize the opportunity is here. At least, statistically. But the new odds have just appeared. How do we know they'll last? They stand on the basis of a single weapon."

"You're wrong. You don't grasp the situation." Reinhart held himself in check with great effort. "Sherikov's weapon tipped the ratio in our favor. But the odds have been moving in our direction for months. It was only a question of time. The new balance was inevitable, sooner or later. It's not just Sherikov. He's only one factor in this. It's all nine planets of the Sol system—not a single man."

One of the Councilmen stood up. "The President must be aware the entire planet is eager to end this waiting. All our activities for the past eighty years have been directed toward—"

Reinhart moved close to the slender President of the Council. "If you don't approve the war, there probably will be mass rioting. Public reaction will be strong. Damn strong. And you know it."

Margaret Duffe shot him a cold glance. "You sent out the emergency order to force my hand. You were fully aware of what you were doing. You knew once the order was out there'd be no stopping things."

A murmur rushed through the Council, gaining volume. "We have to approve the war! . . . We're committed! . . . It's too late to turn back!"

Shouts, angry voices, insistent waves of sound lapped around Margaret Duffe. "I'm as much for the war as anybody," she said sharply. "I'm only urging moderation. An inter-system war is a big thing. We're going to war because a machine says we have a statistical chance of winning."

"There's no use starting the war unless we can win it," Reinhart said. "The SRB machines tell us whether we can win."

"They tell us our *chance* of winning. They don't guarantee anything."

"What more can we ask, besides a good chance of winning?"

Margaret Duffe clamped her jaw together tightly. "All right. I hear all the clamor. I won't stand in the way of Council approval. The vote can go ahead." Her cold, alert eyes appraised Reinhart. "Especially since the emergency order has already been sent out to all Government departments."

"Good." Reinhart stepped away with relief. "Then it's settled. We can finally go ahead with full mobilization."

Mobilization proceeded rapidly. The next forty-eight hours were alive with activity.

Reinhart attended a policy-level Military briefing in the Council rooms, conducted by Fleet Commander Carleton.

"You can see our strategy," Carleton said. He traced a diagram on the blackboard with a wave of his hand. "Sherikov states it'll take eight more days to complete the ftl bomb. During that time the fleet we have near the Centauran system will take up positions. As the bomb goes off the fleet will begin operations against the remaining Centauran ships. Many will no doubt survive the blast, but with Armun gone we should be able to handle them."

Reinhart took Commander Carleton's place. "I can report on the economic situation. Every factory on Terra is converted to arms production. With Armun out of the way we should be able to promote mass insurrection among the Centauran colonies. An inter-system Empire is hard to maintain, even with ships that approach light speed. Local warlords should pop up all over the place. We want to have weapons available for them and ships starting *now* to reach them in time. Eventually we hope to provide a unifying principle around which the colonies can all collect. Our interest is more economic than political. They can have any kind of government they want, as long as they act as supply areas for us. As our eight system planets act now."

Carleton resumed his report. "Once the Centauran fleet has been scattered we can begin the crucial stage of the war. The landing of men and supplies from the ships we have waiting in all key areas throughout the Centauran system. In this stage—"

Reinhart moved away. It was hard to believe only two days had passed since the mobilization order had been sent out. The whole system was alive, functioning with feverish activity. Countless problems were being solved—but much remained.

He entered the lift and ascended to the SRB room, curious to see if there had been any change in the machines' reading. He found it the same. So far so good. Did the Centaurans know about Icarus? No doubt; but there wasn't anything they could do about it. At least, not in eight days.

Kaplan came over to Reinhart, sorting a new batch of data that had come in. The lab organizer searched through his data. "An amusing item came in. It might interest you." He handed a message plate to Reinhart.

It was from histo-research:

> **May 9, 2136**
>
> This is to report that in bringing the research time bubble up to the present the manual return was used for the first time. Therefore a clean break was not made and a quantity of material from the past was brought forward. This material included an individual from the early twentieth century who escaped from the lab immediately. He has not yet been taken into protective custody. Histo-research regrets this incident, but attributes it to the emergency.
>
> **E. Fredman**

Reinhart handed the plate back to Kaplan. "Interesting. A man from the past—hauled into the middle of the biggest war the universe has seen."

"Strange things happen. I wonder what the machines will think."

"Hard to say. Probably nothing." Reinhart left the room and hurried along the corridor to his own office.

As soon as he was inside he called Sherikov on the vidscreen, using the confidential line.

The Pole's heavy features appeared. "Good day, Commissioner. How's the war effort?"

"Fine. How's the turret wiring proceeding?"

A faint frown flickered across Sherikov's face. "As a matter of fact, Commissioner—"

"What's the matter?" Reinhart said sharply.

Sherikov floundered. "You know how these things are. I've taken my crew off it and tried robot workers. They have greater dexterity, but they can't make decisions. This calls for more than mere dexterity. This calls for—" He searched for the word. "—for an *artist*."

Reinhart's face hardened. "Listen, Sherikov. You have eight days left to complete the bomb. The data given to the SRB machines contained that information. The 7-6 ratio is based on that estimate. If you don't come through—"

Sherikov twisted in embarrassment. "Don't get excited, Commissioner. We'll complete it."

"I hope so. Call me as soon as it's done." Reinhart snapped off the connection. If Sherikov let them down he'd have him taken out and shot. The whole war depended on the ftl bomb.

The vidscreen glowed again. Reinhart snapped it on. Kaplan's face formed on it. The lab organizer's face was pale and frozen. "Commissioner, you better come up to the SRB office. Something's happened."

"What is it?"

"I'll show you."

Alarmed, Reinhart hurried out of his office and down the corridor. He found Kaplan standing in front of the SRB machines. "What's the story?" Reinhart demanded. He glanced down at the reading. It was unchanged.

Kaplan held up a message plate nervously. "A moment ago I fed this into the machines. After I saw the results I quickly removed it. It's that item I showed you. From histo-research. About the man from the past."

"What happened when you fed it?"

Kaplan swallowed unhappily. "I'll show you. I'll do it again. Exactly as before." He fed the plate into a moving intake belt. "Watch the visible figures," Kaplan muttered.

Reinhart watched, tense and rigid. For a moment nothing happened. 7-6 continued to show. Then—The figures disappeared. The machines faltered. New figures showed briefly. 4-24 for Centaurus. Reinhart gasped, suddenly sick with apprehension. But the figures vanished. New figures appeared. 16-38 for Centaurus. Then 48-86. 79-15 in Terra's favor. Then nothing. The machines whirred, but nothing happened.

Nothing at all. No figures. Only a blank.

"What's it mean?" Reinhart muttered, dazed.

"It's fantastic. We didn't think this could—"

"*What's happened?*"

"The machines aren't able to handle the item. No reading can come. It's data they can't integrate. They can't use it for prediction material, and it throws off all their other figures."

"Why?"

"It's—it's a variable." Kaplan was shaking, white-lipped and pale. "Something from which no inference can be made. The man from the past. The machines can't deal with him. The variable man!"

II

Thomas Cole was sharpening a knife with his whetstone when the tornado hit.

The knife belonged to the lady in the big green house. Every time Cole came by with his Fixit cart the lady had something to be sharpened. Once in a while she gave him a cup of coffee, hot black coffee from an old bent pot. He liked that fine; he enjoyed good coffee.

The day was drizzly and overcast. Business had been bad. An automobile had scared his two horses. On bad days less people were outside and he had to get down from the cart and go to ring doorbells.

But the man in the yellow house had given him a dollar for fixing his electric refrigerator. Nobody else had been able to fix it, not even the factory man. The dollar would go a long way. A dollar was a lot.

He knew it was a tornado even before it hit him. Everything was silent. He was bent over his whetstone, the reins between his knees, absorbed in his work.

He had done a good job on the knife; he was almost finished. He spat on the blade and was holding it up to see—and then the tornado came.

All at once it was there, completely around him. Nothing but grayness. He and the cart and horses seemed to be in a calm spot in the center of the tornado. They were moving in a great silence, gray mist everywhere.

And while he was wondering what to do, and how to get the old lady's knife back to her, all at once there was a bump and the tornado tipped him over, sprawled out on the ground. The horses screamed in fear, struggling to pick themselves up. Cole got quickly to his feet.

Where was he?

The grayness was gone. White walls stuck up on all sides. A deep light gleamed down, not daylight but something like it. The team was pulling the cart on its side, dragging it along, tools and equipment falling out. Cole righted the cart, leaping up onto the seat.

And for the first time saw the people.

Men, with astonished white faces, in some sort of uniforms. And a feeling of danger!

Cole headed the team toward the door. Hoofs thundered steel against steel as they pounded through the doorway, scattering the astonished men in all directions. He was out in a wide hall. A building, like a hospital.

The hall divided. More men were coming, spilling from all sides.

Shouting and milling in excitement, like white ants. Something cut past him, a beam of dark violet. It seared off a corner of the cart, leaving the wood smoking.

Cole felt fear. He kicked at the terrified horses. They reached a big door, crashing wildly against it. The door gave—and they were outside, bright sunlight blinking down on them. For a sickening second the cart tilted, almost turning over. Then the horses gained speed, racing across an open field, toward a distant line of green, Cole holding tightly to the reins.

Behind him the little white-faced men had come out and were standing in a group, gesturing frantically. He could hear their faint shrill shouts.

But he had got away. He was safe. He slowed the horses down and began to breathe again.

The woods were artificial. Some kind of park. But the park was wild and overgrown. A dense jungle of twisted plants. Everything growing in confusion.

The park was empty. No one was there. By the position of the sun he could tell it was either early morning or late afternoon. The smell of the flowers and grass, the dampness of the leaves, indicated morning. It had been late afternoon when the tornado had picked him up. And the sky had been overcast and cloudy.

Cole considered. Clearly, he had been carried a long way. The hospital, the men with white faces, the odd lighting, the accented words he had caught—everything indicated he was no longer in Nebraska—maybe not even in the United States.

Some of his tools had fallen out and gotten lost along the way. Cole collected everything that remained, sorting them, running his fingers over each tool with affection. Some of the little chisels and wood gouges were gone. The bit box had opened, and most of the smaller bits had been lost. He gathered up those that remained and replaced them tenderly in the box. He took a keyhole saw down, and with an oil rag wiped it carefully and replaced it.

Above the cart the sun rose slowly in the sky. Cole peered up, his horny hand over his eyes. A big man, stoop-shouldered, his chin gray and stubbled. His clothes wrinkled and dirty. But his eyes were clear, a pale blue, and his hands were finely made.

He could not stay in the park. They had seen him ride that way; they would be looking for him.

Far above something shot rapidly across the sky. A tiny black dot moving with incredible haste. A second dot followed. The two dots were gone almost before he saw them. They were utterly silent.

Cole frowned, perturbed. The dots made him uneasy. He would have to keep moving—and looking for food. His stomach was already beginning to rumble and groan.

Work. There was plenty he could do: gardening, sharpening, grinding, repair work on machines and clocks, fixing all kinds of household things. Even painting and odd jobs and carpentry and chores.

He could do anything. Anything people wanted done. For a meal and pocket money.

Thomas Cole urged the team into life, moving forward. He sat hunched over in the seat, watching intently, as the Fixit cart rolled slowly across the tangled grass, through the jungle of trees and flowers.

❖ ❖ ❖

Reinhart hurried, racing his cruiser at top speed, followed by a second ship, a military escort. The ground sped by below him, a blur of gray and green.

The remains of New York lay spread out, a twisted, blunted ruin overgrown with weeds and grass. The great atomic wars of the twentieth century had turned virtually the whole seaboard area into an endless waste of slag.

Slag and weeds below him. And then the sudden tangle that had been Central Park.

Histo-research came into sight. Reinhart swooped down, bringing his cruiser to rest at the small supply field behind the main buildings.

Harper, the chief official of the department, came over quickly as soon as Reinhart's ship landed.

"Frankly, we don't understand why you consider this matter important," Harper said uneasily.

Reinhart shot him a cold glance. "I'll be the judge of what's important. Are you the one who gave the order to bring the bubble back manually?"

"Fredman gave the actual order. In line with your directive to have all facilities ready for—"

Reinhart headed toward the entrance of the research building. "Where is Fredman?"

"Inside."

"I want to see him. Let's go."

Fredman met them inside. He greeted Reinhart calmly, showing no emotion. "Sorry to cause you trouble, Commissioner. We were trying to get the station in order for the war. We wanted the bubble back as quickly as possible." He eyed Reinhart curiously. "No doubt the man and his cart will soon be picked up by your police."

"I want to know everything that happened, in exact detail."

Fredman shifted uncomfortably. "There's not much to tell. I gave the order to have the automatic setting canceled and the bubble brought back manually. At the moment the signal reached it, the bubble was passing through the spring of 1913. As it broke loose, it tore off a piece of ground on which this person and his cart were located. The person naturally was brought up to the present, inside the bubble."

"Didn't any of your instruments tell you the bubble was loaded?"

"We were too excited to take any readings. Half an hour after the manual control was thrown, the bubble materialized in the observation room. It was de-energized before anyone noticed what was inside. We tried to stop him but he drove the cart out into the hall, bowling us out of the way. The horses were in a panic."

"What kind of cart was it?"

"There was some kind of sign on it. Painted in black letters on both sides. No one saw what it was."

"Go ahead. What happened then?"

"Somebody fired a Slem-ray after him, but it missed. The horses carried him out of the building and onto the grounds. By the time we reached the exit the cart was halfway to the park."

Reinhart reflected. "If he's still in the park we should have him shortly. But we must be careful." He was already starting back toward his ship, leaving Fredman behind. Harper fell in beside him.

Reinhart halted by his ship. He beckoned some Government guards over. "Put the executive staff of this department under arrest. I'll have them tried on a treason count, later on." He smiled ironically as Harper's face blanched sickly pale. "There's a war going on. You'll be lucky if you get off alive."

Reinhart entered his ship and left the surface, rising rapidly into the sky. A second ship followed after him, a military escort. Reinhart flew high above the sea of gray slag, the unrecovered waste area. He passed over a sudden square of green set in the ocean of gray. Reinhart gazed back at it until it was gone.

Central Park. He could see police ships racing through the sky, ships and transports loaded with troops, heading toward the square of green. On the ground some heavy guns and surface cars rumbled along, lines of black approaching the park from all sides.

They would have the man soon. But meanwhile, the SRB machines were blank. And on the SRB machines' readings the whole war depended.

About noon the cart reached the edge of the park. Cole rested for a moment, allowing the horses time to crop at the thick grass. The silent expanse of slag amazed him. What had happened? Nothing stirred. No buildings, no sign of life. Grass and weeds poked up occasionally through it, breaking the flat surface here and there, but even so, the sight gave him an uneasy chill.

Cole drove the cart slowly out onto the slag, studying the sky above him. There was nothing to hide him, now that he was out of the park. The slag was bare and uniform, like the ocean. If he were spotted—

A horde of tiny black dots raced across the sky, coming rapidly closer. Presently they veered to the right and disappeared. More planes, wingless metal planes. He watched them go, driving slowly on.

Half an hour later something appeared ahead. Cole slowed the cart down, peering to see. The slag came to an end. He had reached

its limits. Ground appeared, dark soil and grass. Weeds grew everywhere. Ahead of him, beyond the end of the slag, was a line of buildings, houses of some sort. Or sheds.

Houses, probably. But not like any he had ever seen.

The houses were uniform, all exactly the same. Like little green
shells, rows of them, several hundred. There was a little lawn in front
of each. Lawn, a path, a front porch, bushes in a meager row around
each house. But the houses were all alike and very small.

Little green shells in precise, even rows. He urged the cart
cautiously forward, toward the houses.

No one seemed to be around. He entered a street between two
rows of houses, the hoofs of his two horses sounding loudly in the
silence. He was in some kind of town. But there were no dogs or children. Everything was neat and silent. Like a model. An exhibit. It
made him uncomfortable.

A young man walking along the pavement gaped at him in wonder.
An oddly-dressed youth, in a toga-like cloak that hung down to his
knees. A single piece of fabric. And sandals.

Or what looked like sandals. Both the cloak and the sandals were
of some strange half-luminous material. It glowed faintly in the
sunlight. Metallic, rather than cloth.

A woman was watering flowers at the edge of a lawn. She straightened up as his team of horses came near. Her eyes widened in astonishment—and then fear. Her mouth fell open in a soundless O and
her sprinkling can slipped from her fingers and rolled silently onto
the lawn.

Cole blushed and turned his head quickly away. The woman was
scarcely dressed! He flicked the reins and urged the horses to hurry.

Behind him, the woman still stood. He stole a brief, hasty look
back—and then shouted hoarsely to his team, ears scarlet. He had
seen right. She wore only a pair of translucent shorts. Nothing else. A
mere fragment of the same half-luminous material that glowed and
sparkled. The rest of her small body was utterly naked.

He slowed the team down. She had been pretty. Brown hair and eyes, deep red lips. Quite a good figure. Slender waist, downy legs, bare and supple, full breasts—He clamped the thought furiously off. He had to get to work. Business.

Cole halted the Fixit cart and leaped down onto the pavement. He selected a house at random and approached it cautiously. The house was attractive. It had a certain simple beauty. But it looked frail—and exactly like the others.

He stepped up on the porch. There was no bell. He searched for it, running his hand uneasily over the surface of the door. All at once there was a click, a sharp snap on a level with his eyes. Cole glanced up, startled. A lens was vanishing as the door section slid over it. He had been photographed.

While he was wondering what it meant, the door swung suddenly open. A man filled up the entrance, a big man in a tan uniform, blocking the way ominously.

"What do you want?" the man demanded.

"I'm looking for work," Cole murmured. "Any kind of work. I can do anything, fix any kind of thing. I repair broken objects. Things that need mending." His voice trailed off uncertainly. "Anything at all."

"Apply to the Placement Department of the Federal Activities Control Board," the man said crisply. "You know all occupational therapy is handled through them." He eyed Cole curiously. "Why have you got on those ancient clothes?"

"Ancient? Why, I—"

The man gazed past him at the Fixit cart and the two dozing horses. "What's that? What are those two animals? *Horses?*" The man rubbed his jaw, studying Cole intently. "That's strange," he said.

"Strange?" Cole murmured uneasily. "Why?"

"There haven't been any horses for over a century. All the horses were wiped out during the Fifth Atomic War. That's why it's strange."

Cole tensed, suddenly alert. There was something in the man's eyes, a hardness, a piercing look. Cole moved back off the porch, onto the path. He had to be careful. Something was wrong.

"I'll be going," he murmured.

"There haven't been any horses for over a hundred years." The man came toward Cole. "Who are you? Why are you dressed up like that? Where did you get that vehicle and pair of horses?"

"I'll be going," Cole repeated, moving away.

The man whipped something from his belt, a thin metal tube. He stuck it toward Cole.

It was a rolled-up paper, a thin sheet of metal in the form of a tube. Words, some kind of script. He could not make any of them out. The man's picture, rows of numbers, figures—

❖ ❖ ❖

"I'm Director Winslow," the man said. "Federal Stockpile Conservation. You better talk fast, or there'll be a Security car here in five minutes."

Cole moved—fast. He raced, head down, back along the path to the cart, toward the street.

Something hit him. A wall of force, throwing him down on his face. He sprawled in a heap, numb and dazed. His body ached, vibrating wildly, out of control. Waves of shock rolled over him, gradually diminishing.

He got shakily to his feet. His head spun. He was weak, shattered, trembling violently. The man was coming down the walk after him. Cole pulled himself onto the cart, gasping and retching. The horses jumped into life. Cole rolled over against the seat, sick with the motion of the swaying cart.

He caught hold of the reins and managed to drag himself up in a sitting position. The cart gained speed, turning a corner. Houses flew past. Cole urged the team weakly, drawing great shuddering breaths.

Houses and streets, a blur of motion, as the cart flew faster and faster along.

Then he was leaving the town, leaving the neat little houses behind. He was on some sort of highway. Big buildings, factories, on both sides of the highway. Figures, men watching in astonishment.

After a while the factories fell behind. Cole slowed the team down. What had the man meant? Fifth Atomic War. Horses destroyed. It didn't make sense. And they had things he knew nothing about. Force fields. Planes without wings—soundless.

Cole reached around in his pockets. He found the identification tube the man had handed him. In the excitement he had carried it off. He unrolled the tube slowly and began to study it. The writing was strange to him.

For a long time he studied the tube. Then, gradually, he became aware of something. Something in the top right-hand corner.

A date. October 6, 2128.

Cole's vision blurred. Everything spun and wavered around him. October, 2128. Could it be?

But he held the paper in his hand. Thin, metal paper. Like foil. And it had to be. It said so, right in the corner, printed on the paper itself.

Cole rolled the tube up slowly, numbed with shock. Two hundred years. It didn't seem possible. But things were beginning to make sense. He was in the future, two hundred years in the future.

While he was mulling this over, the swift black Security ship appeared overhead, diving rapidly toward the horse-drawn cart, as it moved slowly along the road.

❖ ❖ ❖

Reinhart's vidscreen buzzed. He snapped it quickly on. "Yes?"

"Report from Security."

"Put it through." Reinhart waited tensely as the lines locked in place. The screen re-lit.

"This is Dixon. Western Regional Command." The officer cleared his throat, shuffling his message plates. "The man from the past has been reported, moving away from the New York area."

"Which side of your net?"

"Outside. He evaded the net around Central Park by entering one of the small towns at the rim of the slag area."

"*Evaded?*"

"We assumed he would avoid the towns. Naturally the net failed to encompass any of the towns."

Reinhart's jaw stiffened. "Go on."

"He entered the town of Petersville a few minutes before the net closed around the park. We burned the park level, but naturally found nothing. He had already gone. An hour later we received a report from a resident in Petersville, an official of the Stockpile Conservation Department. The man from the past had come to his door, looking for work. Winslow, the official, engaged him in conversation, trying to hold onto him, but he escaped, driving his cart off. Winslow called Security right away, but by then it was too late."

"Report to me as soon as anything more comes in. We must have him—and damn soon." Reinhart snapped the screen off. It died quickly.

He sat back in his chair, waiting.

❖ ❖ ❖

Cole saw the shadow of the Security ship. He reacted at once. A second after the shadow passed over him, Cole was out of the cart, running and falling. He rolled, twisting and turning, pulling his body as far away from the cart as possible.

There was a blinding roar and flash of white light. A hot wind rolled over Cole, picking him up and tossing him like a leaf. He shut his eyes, letting his body relax. He bounced, falling and striking the ground. Gravel and stones tore into his face, his knees, the palms of his hands.

Cole cried out, shrieking in pain. His body was on fire. He was being consumed, incinerated by the blinding white orb of fire. The orb expanded, growing in size, swelling like some monstrous sun, twisted and bloated. The end had come. There was no hope. He gritted his teeth—

The greedy orb faded, dying down. It sputtered and winked out, blackening into ash. The air reeked, a bitter acrid smell. His clothes were burning and smoking. The ground under him was hot, baked dry, seared by the blast. But he was alive. At least, for a while.

Cole opened his eyes slowly. The cart was gone. A great hole gaped where it had been, a shattered sore in the center of the highway. An ugly cloud hung above the hole, black and ominous. Far above, the wingless plane circled, watching for any signs of life.

Cole lay, breathing shallowly, slowly. Time passed. The sun moved across the sky with agonizing slowness. It was perhaps four in the afternoon. Cole calculated mentally. In three hours it would be dark. If he could stay alive until then—

Had the plane seen him leap from the cart?

He lay without moving. The late afternoon sun beat down on him. He felt sick, nauseated and feverish. His mouth was dry.

Some ants ran over his outstretched hand. Gradually, the immense black cloud was beginning to drift away, dispersing into a formless blob.

The cart was gone. The thought lashed against him, pounding at his brain, mixing with his labored pulsebeat. *Gone*. Destroyed. Nothing but ashes and debris remained. The realization dazed him.

Finally the plane finished its circling, winging its way toward the horizon. At last it vanished. The sky was clear.

Cole got unsteadily to his feet. He wiped his face shakily. His body ached and trembled. He spat a couple of times, trying to clear his mouth. The plane would probably send in a report. People would be coming to look for him. Where could he go?

To his right a line of hills rose up, a distant green mass. Maybe he could reach them. He began to walk slowly. He had to be very careful.

They were looking for him—and they had weapons. Incredible weapons.

He would be lucky to still be alive when the sun set. His team and Fixit cart were gone—and all his tools. Cole reached into his pockets, searching through them hopefully. He brought out some small screwdrivers, a little pair of cutting pliers, some wire, some solder, the whetstone, and finally the lady's knife.

Only a few small tools remained. He had lost everything else. But without the cart he was safer, harder to spot. They would have more trouble finding him, on foot.

Cole hurried along, crossing the level fields toward the distant range of hills.

The call came through to Reinhart almost at once. Dixon's features formed on the vidscreen. "I have a further report, Commissioner." Dixon scanned the plate. "Good news. The man from the past was sighted moving away from Petersville, along highway 13, at about ten miles an hour, on his horse-drawn cart. Our ship bombed him immediately."

"Did—did you get him?"

"The pilot reports no sign of life after the blast."

Reinhart's pulse almost stopped. He sank back in his chair. "Then he's dead!"

"Actually, we won't know for certain until we can examine the debris. A surface car is speeding toward the spot. We should have the complete report in a short time. We'll notify you as soon as the information comes in."

Reinhart reached out and cut the screen. It faded into darkness. Had they got the man from the past? Or had he escaped again? Weren't they ever going to get him? Couldn't he be captured? And meanwhile, the SRB machines were silent, showing nothing at all.

Reinhart sat brooding, waiting impatiently for the report of the surface car to come.

❖ ❖ ❖

It was evening.

"Come on!" Steven shouted, running frantically after his brother. "Come on back!"

"Catch me." Earl ran and ran, down the side of the hill, over behind a military storage depot, along a neotex fence, jumping finally down into Mrs. Norris' back yard.

Steven hurried after his brother, sobbing for breath, shouting and gasping as he ran. "Come back! You come back with that!"

"What's he got?" Sally Tate demanded, stepping out suddenly to block Steven's way.

Steven halted, his chest rising and falling. "He's got my inter-system vidsender." His small face twisted with rage and misery. "He better give it back!"

Earl came circling around from the right. In the warm gloom of evening he was almost invisible. "Here I am," he announced. "What are you going to do?"

Steven glared at him hotly. His eyes made out the square box in Earl's hands. "You give that back! Or—or I'll tell Dad."

Earl laughed. "Make me."

"Dad'll make you."

"You better give it to him," Sally said.

"Catch me." Earl started off. Steven pushed Sally out of the way, lashing wildly at his brother. He collided with him, throwing him sprawling. The box fell from Earl's hands. It skidded to the pavement, crashing into the side of a guide-light post.

Earl and Steven picked themselves up slowly. They gazed down at the broken box.

"See?" Steven shrilled, tears filling his eyes. "See what you did?"

"You did it. You pushed into me."

"You did it!" Steven bent down and picked up the box. He carried it over to the guide-light, sitting down on the curb to examine it.

Earl came slowly over. "If you hadn't pushed me it wouldn't have got broken."

Night was descending rapidly. The line of hills rising above the town were already lost in darkness. A few lights had come on here and there. The evening was warm. A surface car slammed its doors, some place off in the distance. In the sky ships droned back and forth, weary commuters coming home from work in the big underground factory units.

Thomas Cole came slowly toward the three children grouped around the guide-light. He moved with difficulty, his body sore and bent with fatigue. Night had come, but he was not safe yet.

He was tired, exhausted and hungry. He had walked a long way. And he had to have something to eat—soon.

A few feet from the children Cole stopped. They were all intent and absorbed by the box on Steven's knees. Suddenly a hush fell over the children. Earl looked up slowly.

In the dim light the big stooped figure of Thomas Cole seemed extra menacing. His long arms hung down loosely at his sides. His face was lost in shadow. His body was shapeless, indistinct. A big unformed statue, standing silently a few feet away, unmoving in the half-darkness.

"Who are you?" Earl demanded, his voice low.

"What do you want?" Sally said. The children edged away nervously. "Get away."

Cole came toward them. He bent down a little. The beam from the guide-light crossed his features. Lean, prominent nose, beak-like, faded blue eyes—

Steven scrambled to his feet, clutching the vidsender box. "You get out of here!"

"Wait." Cole smiled crookedly at them. His voice was dry and raspy. "What do you have there?" He pointed with his long, slender fingers. "The box you're holding."

The children were silent. Finally Steven stirred. "It's my inter-system vidsender."

"Only it doesn't work," Sally said.

"Earl broke it." Steven glared at his brother bitterly. "Earl threw it down and broke it."

Cole smiled a little. He sank down wearily on the edge of the curb, sighing with relief. He had been walking too long. His body ached with fatigue. He was hungry and tired. For a long time he sat, wiping perspiration from his neck and face, too exhausted to speak.

"Who are you?" Sally demanded, at last. "Why do you have on those funny clothes? Where did you come from?"

"Where?" Cole looked around at the children. "From a long way off. A long way." He shook his head slowly from side to side, trying to clear it.

"What's your therapy?" Earl said.

"My therapy?"

"What do you do? Where do you work?"

Cole took a deep breath and let it out again slowly. "I fix things. All kinds of things. Any kind."

Earl sneered. "Nobody fixes things. When they break you throw them away."

Cole didn't hear him. Sudden need had roused him, getting him suddenly to his feet. "You know any work I can find?" he demanded. "Things I could do? I can fix anything. Clocks, typewriters, refrigerators, pots and pans. Leaks in the roof. I can fix anything there is."

Steven held out his inter-system vidsender. "Fix this."

There was silence. Slowly, Cole's eyes focused on the box. "That?"

"My sender. Earl broke it."

Cole took the box slowly. He turned it over, holding it up to the light. He frowned, concentrating on it. His long, slender fingers moved carefully over the surface, exploring it.

"He'll steal it!" Earl said suddenly.

"No." Cole shook his head vaguely. "I'm reliable." His sensitive fingers found the studs that held the box together. He depressed the studs, pushing them expertly in. The box opened, revealing its complex interior.

"He got it open," Sally whispered.

"Give it back!" Steven demanded, a little frightened. He held out his hand. "I want it back."

The three children watched Cole apprehensively. Cole fumbled in his pocket. Slowly he brought out his tiny screwdrivers and pliers. He laid them in a row beside him. He made no move to return the box.

"I want it back," Steven said feebly.

Cole looked up. His faded blue eyes took in the sight of the three children standing before him in the gloom. "I'll fix it for you. You said you wanted it fixed."

"I want it back." Steven stood on one foot, then the other, torn by doubt and indecision. "Can you really fix it? Can you make it work again?"

"Yes."

"All right. Fix it for me, then."

A sly smile flickered across Cole's tired face. "Now, wait a minute. If I fix it, will you bring me something to eat? I'm not fixing it for nothing."

"Something to eat?"

"Food. I need hot food. Maybe some coffee."

Steven nodded. "Yes. I'll get it for you."

Cole relaxed. "Fine. That's fine." He turned his attention back to the box resting between his knees. "Then I'll fix it for you. I'll fix it for you good."

His fingers flew, working and twisting, tracing down wires and relays, exploring and examining. Finding out about the inter-system vidsender. Discovering how it worked.

Steven slipped into the house through the emergency door. He made his way to the kitchen with great care, walking on tip-toe. He punched the kitchen controls at random, his heart beating excitedly. The stove began to whirr, purring into life. Meter readings came on, crossing toward the completion marks.

Presently the stove opened, sliding out a tray of steaming dishes.

The mechanism clicked off, dying into silence. Steven grabbed up the contents of the tray, filling his arms. He carried everything down the hall, out the emergency door and into the yard. The yard was dark. Steven felt his way carefully along.

He managed to reach the guide-light without dropping anything at all.

Thomas Cole got slowly to his feet as Steven came into view. "Here," Steven said. He dumped the food onto the curb, gasping for breath. "Here's the food. Is it finished?"

Cole held out the inter-system vidsender. "It's finished. It was pretty badly smashed."

Earl and Sally gazed up, wide-eyed. "Does it work?" Sally asked.

"Of course not," Earl stated. "How could it work? He couldn't—"

"Turn it on!" Sally nudged Steven eagerly. "See if it works."

Steven was holding the box under the light, examining the switches. He flicked the main switch on. The indicator light gleamed. "It lights up," Steven said.

"Say something into it."

Steven spoke into the box. "Hello! Hello! This is operator 6-Z75 calling. Can you hear me? This is operator 6-Z75. Can you hear me?"

In the darkness, away from the beam of the guide-light, Thomas Cole sat crouched over the food. He ate gratefully, silently. It was good food, well cooked and seasoned. He drank a container of orange juice and then a sweet drink he didn't recognize. Most of the food was strange to him, but he didn't care. He had walked a long way and he still had a long way to go, before morning. He had to be deep in the hills before the sun came up. Instinct told him that he would be safe among the trees and tangled growth—at least, as safe as he could hope for.

He ate rapidly, intent on the food. He did not look up until he was finished. Then he got slowly to his feet, wiping his mouth with the back of his hand.

The three children were standing around in a circle, operating the inter-system vidsender. He watched them for a few minutes. None of them looked up from the small box. They were intent, absorbed in what they were doing.

"Well?" Cole said, at last. "Does it work all right?"

After a moment Steven looked up at him. There was a strange expression on his face. He nodded slowly. "Yes. Yes, it works. It works fine."

Cole grunted. "All right." He turned and moved away from the light. "That's fine."

The children watched silently until the figure of Thomas Cole had completely disappeared. Slowly, they turned and looked at each other. Then down at the box in Steven's hands. They gazed at the box in growing awe. Awe mixed with dawning fear.

Steven turned and edged toward his house. "I've got to show it to my Dad," he murmured, dazed. "He's got to know. *Somebody's* got to know!"

III

Eric Reinhart examined the vidsender box carefully, turning it around and around.

"Then he did escape from the blast," Dixon admitted reluctantly. "He must have leaped from the cart just before the concussion."

Reinhart nodded. "He escaped. He got away from you—twice." He pushed the vidsender box away and leaned abruptly toward the man standing uneasily in front of his desk. "What's your name again?"

"Elliot. Richard Elliot."

"And your son's name?"

"Steven."

"It was last night this happened?"

"About eight o'clock."

"Go on."

"Steven came into the house. He acted queerly. He was carrying his inter-system vidsender." Elliot pointed at the box on Reinhart's desk. "That. He was nervous and excited. I asked what was wrong. For a while he couldn't tell me. He was quite upset. Then he showed me the vidsender." Elliot took a deep, shaky breath. "I could see right away it was different. You see I'm an electrical engineer. I had opened it once before, to put in a new battery. I had a fairly good idea how it should look." Elliot hesitated. "Commissioner, it had been *changed*. A lot of the wiring was different. Moved around. Relays connected differently. Some parts were missing. New parts had been jury rigged out of old. Then I discovered the thing that made me call Security. The vidsender—it really *worked*."

"Worked?"

"You see, it never was anything more than a toy. With a range of a few city blocks. So the kids could call back and forth from their rooms. Like a sort of portable vidscreen. Commissioner, I tried out the vidsender, pushing the call button and speaking into the microphone. I—I got a ship of the line. A battleship operating beyond Proxima Centaurus—over eight light years away. As far out as the actual vidsenders operate. Then I called Security. Right away."

For a time Reinhart was silent. Finally he tapped the box lying on the desk. "You got a ship of the line—with *this?*"

"That's right."

"How big are the regular vidsenders?"

Dixon supplied the information. "As big as a twenty-ton safe."

"That's what I thought." Reinhart waved his hand impatiently. "All right, Elliot. Thanks for turning the information over to us. That's all."

Security police led Elliot outside the office.

Reinhart and Dixon looked at each other. "This is bad," Reinhart said harshly. "He has some ability, some kind of mechanical ability. Genius, perhaps, to do a thing like this. Look at the period he came from, Dixon. The early part of the twentieth century. Before the wars began. That was a unique period. There was a certain vitality, a certain ability. It was a period of incredible growth and discovery. Edison. Pasteur. Burbank. The Wright brothers. Inventions and machines.

People had an uncanny ability with machines. A kind of intuition about machines—which we don't have."

"You mean—"

"I mean a person like this coming into our own time is bad in itself, war or no war. He's too different. He's oriented along different lines. He has abilities we lack. This fixing skill of his. It throws us off, out of kilter. And with the war . . .

"Now I'm beginning to understand why the SRB machines couldn't factor him. It's impossible for us to understand this kind of person. Winslow says he asked for work, any kind of work. The man said he could do anything, fix anything. Do you understand what that means?"

"No," Dixon said. "What does it mean?"

"Can any of us fix anything? No. None of us can do that. We're specialized. Each of us has his own line, his own work. I understand my work, you understand yours. The tendency in evolution is toward greater and greater specialization. Man's society is an ecology that forces adaptation to it. Continual complexity makes it impossible for any of us to know anything outside our own personal field—I can't follow the work of the man sitting at the next desk over from me. Too much knowledge has piled up in each field. And there are too many fields.

"This man is different. He can fix anything, do anything. He doesn't work with knowledge, with science—the classified accumulation of facts. He *knows* nothing. It's not in his head, a form of learning. He works by intuition—his power is in his hands, not his head. Jack-of-all-trades. His hands! Like a painter, an artist. In his hands—and he cuts across our lives like a knife-blade."

"And the other problem?"

"The other problem is that this man, this variable man, has escaped into the Albertine Mountain Range. Now we'll have one hell of a time finding him. He's clever—in a strange kind of way. Like some sort of animal. He's going to be hard to catch."

Reinhart sent Dixon out. After a moment he gathered up the handful of reports on his desk and carried them up to the SRB room. The SRB room was closed up, sealed off by a ring of armed Security police. Standing angrily before the ring of police was Peter Sherikov, his beard waggling angrily, his immense hands on his hips.

"What's going on?" Sherikov demanded. "Why can't I go in and peep at the odds?"

"Sorry." Reinhart cleared the police aside. "Come inside with me. I'll explain." The doors opened for them and they entered. Behind them the doors shut and the ring of police formed outside. "What brings you away from your lab?" Reinhart asked.

Sherikov shrugged. "Several things. I wanted to see you. I called you on the vidphone and they said you weren't available. I thought maybe something had happened. What's up?"

"I'll tell you in a few minutes." Reinhart called Kaplan over. "Here are some new items. Feed them in right away. I want to see if the machines can total them."

"Certainly, Commissioner." Kaplan took the message plates and placed them on an intake belt. The machines hummed into life.

"We'll know soon," Reinhart said, half aloud.

Sherikov shot him a keen glance. "We'll know what? Let me in on it. What's taking place?"

"We're in trouble. For twenty-four hours the machines haven't given any reading at all. Nothing but a blank. A total blank."

Sherikov's features registered disbelief. "But that isn't possible. *Some* odds exist at all times."

"The odds exist, but the machines aren't able to calculate them."

"Why not?"

"Because a variable factor has been introduced. A factor which the machines can't handle. They can't make any predictions from it."

"Can't they reject it?" Sherikov said slyly. "Can't they just—just *ignore* it?"

"No. It exists, as real data. Therefore it affects the balance of the material, the sum total of all other available data. To reject it would be to give a false reading. The machines can't reject any data that's known to be true."

Sherikov pulled moodily at his black beard. "I would be interested in knowing what sort of factor the machines can't handle. I thought they could take in all data pertaining to contemporary reality."

"They can. This factor has nothing to do with contemporary reality. That's the trouble. Histo-research in bringing its time bubble back from the past got overzealous and cut the circuit too quickly. The bubble came back loaded—with a man from the twentieth century. A man from the past."

"I see. A man from two centuries ago." The big Pole frowned. "And with a radically different Weltanschauung. No connection with our present society. Not integrated along our lines at all. Therefore the SRB machines are perplexed."

Reinhart grinned. "Perplexed? I suppose so. In any case, they can't do anything with the data about this man. The variable man. No statistics at all have been thrown up—no predictions have been made. And it knocks everything else out of phase. We're dependent on the constant showing of these odds. The whole war effort is geared around them."

"The horse-shoe nail. Remember the old poem? 'For want of a nail the shoe was lost. For want of the shoe the horse was lost. For want of the horse the rider was lost. For want—'"

"Exactly. A single factor coming along like this, one single individual, can throw everything off. It doesn't seem possible that one person could knock an entire society out of balance—but apparently it is."

"What are you doing about this man?"

"The Security police are organized in a mass search for him."

"Results?"

"He escaped into the Albertine Mountain Range last night. It'll be hard to find him. We must expect him to be loose for another forty-eight hours. It'll take that long for us to arrange the annihilation of the range area. Perhaps a trifle longer. And meanwhile—"

"Ready, Commissioner," Kaplan interrupted. "The new totals."

The SRB machines had finished factoring the new data. Reinhart and Sherikov hurried to take their places before the view windows.

For a moment nothing happened. Then odds were put up, locking in place.

Sherikov gasped. 99-2. In favor of Terra. "That's wonderful! Now we—"

The odds vanished. New odds took their places. 97-4. In favor of Centaurus. Sherikov groaned in astonished dismay. "Wait," Reinhart said to him. "I don't think they'll last."

The odds vanished. A rapid series of odds shot across the screen, a violent stream of numbers, changing almost instantly. At last the machines became silent.

Nothing showed. No odds. No totals at all. The view windows were blank.

"You see?" Reinhart murmured. "The same damn thing!"

Sherikov pondered. "Reinhart, you're too Anglo-Saxon, too impulsive. Be more Slavic. This man will be captured and destroyed within two days. You said so yourself. Meanwhile, we're all working night and day on the war effort. The warfleet is waiting near Proxima, taking up positions for the attack on the Centaurans. All our war plants are going full blast. By the time the attack date comes we'll have a full-sized invasion army ready to take off for the long trip to the Centauran colonies. The whole Terran population has been mobilized. The eight supply planets are pouring in material. All this is going on day and night, even without odds showing. Long before the attack comes this man will certainly be dead, and the machines will be able to show odds again."

Reinhart considered. "But it worries me, a man like that out in the open. Loose. A man who can't be predicted. It goes against science. We've been making statistical reports on society for two centuries. We have immense files of data. The machines are able to predict what each person and group will do at a given time, in a given situation. But this man is beyond all prediction. He's a variable. It's contrary to science."

"The indeterminate particle."

"What's that?"

"The particle that moves in such a way that we can't predict what position it will occupy at a given second. Random. The random particle."

"Exactly. It's—it's *unnatural*."

Sherikov laughed sarcastically. "Don't worry about it, Commissioner. The man will be captured and things will return to their natural state. You'll be able to predict people again, like laboratory rats in a maze. By the way—why is this room guarded?"

"I don't want anyone to know the machines show no totals. It's dangerous to the war effort."

"Margaret Duffe, for example?"

Reinhart nodded reluctantly. "They're too timid, these parliamentarians. If they discover we have no SRB odds they'll want to shut down the war planning and go back to waiting."

"Too slow for you, Commissioner? Laws, debates, council meetings, discussions . . . Saves a lot of time if one man has all the power. One man to tell people what to do, think for them, lead them around."

Reinhart eyed the big Pole critically. "That reminds me. How is Icarus coming? Have you continued to make progress on the control turret?"

A scowl crossed Sherikov's broad features. "The control turret?" He waved his big hand vaguely. "I would say it's coming along all right. We'll catch up in time."

Instantly Reinhart became alert. "Catch up? You mean you're still behind?"

"Somewhat. A little. But we'll catch up." Sherikov retreated toward the door. "Let's go down to the cafeteria and have a cup of coffee. You worry too much, Commissioner. Take things more in your stride."

"I suppose you're right." The two men walked out into the hall. "I'm on edge. This variable man. I can't get him out of my mind."

"Has he done anything yet?"

"Nothing important. Rewired a child's toy. A toy vidsender."

"Oh?" Sherikov showed interest. "What do you mean? What did he do?"

"I'll show you." Reinhart led Sherikov down the hall to his office. They entered and Reinhart locked the door. He handed Sherikov the toy and roughed in what Cole had done. A strange look crossed Sherikov's face. He found the studs on the box and depressed them. The box opened. The big Pole sat down at the desk and began to study the interior of the box. "You're sure it was the man from the past who rewired this?"

"Of course. On the spot. The boy damaged it playing. The variable man came along and the boy asked him to fix it. He fixed it, all right."

"Incredible." Sherikov's eyes were only an inch from the wiring. "Such tiny relays. How could he—"

"What?"

"Nothing." Sherikov got abruptly to his feet, closing the box carefully. "Can I take this along? To my lab? I'd like to analyze it more fully."

"Of course. But why?"

"No special reason. Let's go get our coffee." Sherikov headed toward the door. "You say you expect to capture this man in a day or so?"

"*Kill* him, not capture him. We've got to eliminate him as a piece of data. We're assembling the attack formations right now. No slip-ups, this time. We're in the process of setting up a cross-bombing pattern to level the entire Albertine Range. He must be destroyed, within the next forty-eight hours."

Sherikov nodded absently. "Of course," he murmured. A preoccupied expression still remained on his broad features. "I understand perfectly."

❖ ❖ ❖

Thomas Cole crouched over the fire he had built, warming his hands. It was almost morning. The sky was turning violet gray. The mountain air was crisp and chilly. Cole shivered and pulled himself closer to the fire.

The heat felt good against his hands. *His hands.* He gazed down at them, glowing yellow-red in the firelight. The nails were black and chipped. Warts and endless calluses on each finger, and the palms. But they were good hands, the fingers were long and tapered. He respected them, although in some ways he didn't understand them.

Cole was deep in thought, meditating over his situation.

He had been in the mountains two nights and a day. The first night had been the worst. Stumbling and falling, making his way uncertainly up the steep slopes, through the tangled brush and undergrowth—

But when the sun came up he was safe, deep in the mountains, between two great peaks. And by the time the sun had set again he had fixed himself a shelter and a means of making a fire. Now he had a neat little box trap, operated by a plaited grass rope and pit, a notched stake. One rabbit already hung by his hind legs and the trap was waiting for another.

The sky turned from violet gray to a deep cold gray, a metallic color. The mountains were silent and empty. Far off someplace a bird sang, its voice echoing across the vast slopes and ravines. Other birds began to sing. Off to his right something crashed through the brush, an animal pushing its way along.

Day was coming. His second day. Cole got to his feet and began to unfasten the rabbit. Time to eat. And then? After that he had no plans. He knew instinctively that he could keep himself alive indefinitely with the tools he had retained, and the genius of his hands. He could kill game and skin it. Eventually he could build himself a permanent shelter, even make clothes out of hides. In winter—

But he was not thinking that far ahead. Cole stood by the fire, staring up at the sky, his hands on his hips. He squinted, suddenly tense. Something was moving. Something in the sky, drifting slowly through the grayness. A black dot.

He stamped out the fire quickly. What was it? He strained, trying to see. A bird?

A second dot joined the first. Two dots. Then three. Four. Five. A fleet of them, moving rapidly across the early morning sky. Toward the mountains.

Toward him.

Cole hurried away from the fire. He snatched up the rabbit and carried it along with him, into the tangled shelter he had built. He was invisible, inside the shelter. No one could find him. But if they had seen the fire—

He crouched in the shelter, watching the dots grow larger. They were planes, all right. Black wingless planes, coming closer each moment. Now he could hear them, a faint dull buzz, increasing until the ground shook under him.

The first plane dived. It dropped like a stone, swelling into a great black shape. Cole gasped, sinking down. The plane roared in an arch, swooping low over the ground. Suddenly bundles tumbled out, white bundles falling and scattering like seeds.

The bundles drifted rapidly to the ground. They landed. They were men. Men in uniform.

Now the second plane was diving. It roared overhead, releasing its load. More bundles tumbled out, filling the sky. The third plane dived, then the fourth. The air was thick with drifting bundles of white, a blanket of descending weed spores, settling to earth.

On the ground the soldiers were forming into groups. Their shouts carried to Cole, crouched in his shelter. Fear leaped through him. They were landing on all sides of him. He was cut off. The last two planes had dropped men behind him.

He got to his feet, pushing out of the shelter. Some of the soldiers had found the fire, the ashes and coals. One dropped down, feeling the coals with his hand. He waved to the others. They were circling all around, shouting and gesturing. One of them began to set up some kind of gun. Others were unrolling coils of tubing, locking a collection of strange pipes and machinery in place.

Cole ran. He rolled down a slope, sliding and falling. At the bottom he leaped to his feet and plunged into the brush. Vines and leaves tore at his face, slashing and cutting him. He fell again, tangled in a mass of twisted shrubbery. He fought desperately, trying to free himself. If he could reach the knife in his pocket—

Voices. Footsteps. Men were behind him, running down the slope. Cole struggled frantically, gasping and twisting, trying to pull loose. He strained, breaking the vines, clawing at them with his hands.

A soldier dropped to his knee, leveling his gun. More soldiers arrived, bringing their rifles and aiming.

Cole cried out. He closed his eyes, his body suddenly went limp. He waited, his teeth locked together, sweat dripping down his neck, into his shirt, sagging against the mesh of vines and branches coiled around him.

Silence.

Cole opened his eyes slowly. The soldiers had regrouped. A huge man was striding down the slope toward them, barking orders as he came.

Two soldiers stepped into the brush. One of them grabbed Cole by the shoulder.

"Don't let go of him." The huge man came over, his black beard jutting out. "Hold on."

Cole gasped for breath. He was caught. There was nothing he could do. More soldiers were pouring down into the gully, surrounding him on all sides. They studied him curiously, murmuring together. Cole shook his head wearily and said nothing.

The huge man with the beard stood directly in front of him, his hands on his hips, looking him up and down. "Don't try to get away," the man said. "You can't get away. Do you understood?"

Cole nodded.

"All right. Good." The man waved. Soldiers clamped metal bands around Cole's arms and wrists. The metal dug into his flesh, making him gasp with pain. More clamps locked around his legs. "Those stay there until we're out of here. A long way out."

"Where—where are you taking me?"

Peter Sherikov studied the variable man for a moment before he answered. "Where? I'm taking you to my labs. Under the Urals." He glanced suddenly up at the sky. "We better hurry. The Security police will be starting their demolition attack in a few hours. We want to be a long way from here when that begins."

❖ ❖ ❖

Sherikov settled down in his comfortable reinforced chair with a sigh. "It's good to be back." He signaled to one of his guards. "All right. You can unfasten him."

The metal clamps were removed from Cole's arms and legs. He sagged, sinking down in a heap. Sherikov watched him silently.

Cole sat on the floor, rubbing his wrists and legs, saying nothing.

"What do you want?" Sherikov demanded. "Food? Are you hungry?"

"No."

"Medicine? Are you sick? Injured?"

"No."

Sherikov wrinkled his nose. "A bath wouldn't hurt you any. We'll arrange that later." He lit a cigar, blowing a cloud of gray smoke around him. At the door of the room two lab guards stood with guns ready. No one else was in the room beside Sherikov and Cole.

Thomas Cole sat huddled in a heap on the floor, his head sunk down against his chest. He did not stir. His bent body seemed more elongated and stooped than ever, his hair tousled and unkempt, his chin and jowls a rough stubbled gray. His clothes were dirty and torn from crawling through the brush. His skin was cut and scratched; open sores dotted his neck and cheeks and forehead. He said nothing. His chest rose and fell. His faded blue eyes were almost closed. He looked quite old, a withered, dried-up old man.

Sherikov waved one of the guards over. "Have a doctor brought up here. I want this man checked over. He may need intravenous injections. He may not have had anything to eat for a while."

The guard departed.

"I don't want anything to happen to you," Sherikov said. "Before we go on I'll have you checked over. And deloused at the same time."

Cole said nothing.

Sherikov laughed. "Buck up! You have no reason to feel bad." He leaned toward Cole, jabbing an immense finger at him. "Another two hours and you'd have been dead, out there in the mountains. You know that?"

Cole nodded.

"You don't believe me. Look." Sherikov leaned over and snapped on the vidscreen mounted in the wall. "Watch this. The operation should still be going on."

The screen lit up. A scene gained form.

"This is a confidential Security channel. I had it tapped several years ago—for my own protection. What we're seeing now is being piped in to Eric Reinhart." Sherikov grinned. "Reinhart arranged what you're seeing on the screen. Pay close attention. You were there, two hours ago."

Cole turned toward the screen. At first he could not make out what was happening. The screen showed a vast foaming cloud, a vortex of motion. From the speaker came a low rumble, a deep-throated roar. After a time the screen shifted, showing a slightly different view. Suddenly Cole stiffened.

He was seeing the destruction of a whole mountain range.

The picture was coming from a ship, flying above what had once been the Albertine Mountain Range. Now there was nothing but swirling clouds of gray and columns of particles and debris, a surging tide of restless material gradually sweeping off and dissipating in all directions.

The Albertine Mountains had been disintegrated. Nothing remained but these vast clouds of debris. Below, on the ground, a ragged plain stretched out, swept by fire and rain. Gaping wounds yawned, immense holes without bottoms, craters side by side as far as the eye could see. Craters and debris. Like the blasted, pitted surface of the moon. Two hours ago it had been rolling peaks and gulleys, brush and green bushes and trees.

Cole turned away.

"You see?" Sherikov snapped the screen off. "You were down there, not so long ago. All that noise and smoke—all for you. All for you, Mr. Variable Man from the past. Reinhart arranged that, to finish you off. I want you to understand that. It's very important that you realize that."

Cole said nothing.

Sherikov reached into a drawer of the table before him. He carefully brought out a small square box and held it out to Cole. "You wired this, didn't you?"

Cole took the box in his hands and held it. For a time his tired mind failed to focus. What did he have? He concentrated on it. The box was the children's toy. The inter-system vidsender, they had called it.

"Yes. I fixed this." He passed it back to Sherikov. "I repaired that. It was broken."

Sherikov gazed down at him intently, his large eyes bright. He nodded, his black beard and cigar rising and falling. "Good. That's all I wanted to know." He got suddenly to his feet, pushing his chair back. "I see the doctor's here. He'll fix you up. Everything you need. Later on I'll talk to you again."

Unprotesting, Cole got to his feet, allowing the doctor to take hold of his arm and help him up.

After Cole had been released by the medical department, Sherikov joined him in his private dining room, a floor above the actual laboratory.

The Pole gulped down a hasty meal, talking as he ate. Cole sat silently across from him, not eating or speaking. His old clothing had been taken away and new clothing given to him. He was shaved and rubbed down. His sores and cuts were healed, his body and hair washed. He looked much healthier and younger, now. But he was still stooped and tired, his blue eyes worn and faded. He listened to Sherikov's account of the world of 2136 AD without comment.

"You can see," Sherikov said finally, waving a chicken leg, "that your appearance here has been very upsetting to our program. Now that you know more about us you can see why Commissioner Reinhart was so interested in destroying you."

Cole nodded.

"Reinhart, you realize, believes that the failure of the SRB machines is the chief danger to the war effort. But that is nothing!" Sherikov pushed his plate away noisily, draining his coffee mug. "After all, wars *can* be fought without statistical forecasts. The SRB machines only describe. They're nothing more than mechanical onlookers. In themselves, they don't affect the course of the war. *We* make the war. They only analyze."

Cole nodded.

"More coffee?" Sherikov asked. He pushed the plastic container toward Cole. "Have some."

Cole accepted another cupful. "Thank you."

"You can see that our real problem is another thing entirely. The machines only do figuring for us in a few minutes that eventually we could do for our own selves. They're our servants, tools. Not some sort of gods in a temple which we go and pray to. Not oracles who can see into the future for us. They don't see into the future. They only make statistical predictions—not prophecies. There's a big difference there, but Reinhart and his kind have made such things as the SRB machines into gods. But I have no gods. At least, not any I can see."

Cole nodded, sipping his coffee.

"I'm telling you all these things because you must understand what we're up against. Terra is hemmed in on all sides by the ancient Centauran Empire. It's been out there for centuries, thousands of years. No one knows how long. It's old—crumbling and rotting. Corrupt and venal. But it holds most of the galaxy around us, and we can't break out of the Sol system. I told you about Icarus, and Hedge's work in ftl flight. We must win the war against Centaurus. We've waited and worked a long time for this, the moment when we can break out and get room among the stars for ourselves. Icarus is the deciding weapon. The data on Icarus tipped the SRB odds in our favor—for the first time in history. Success in the war against Centaurus will depend on Icarus, not on the SRB machines. You see?"

Cole nodded.

"However, there is a problem. The data on Icarus which I turned over to the machines specified that Icarus would be completed in ten days. More than half that time has already passed. Yet, we are no closer to wiring up the control turret than we were then. The turret baffles us." Sherikov grinned ironically. "Even *I* have tried my hand on the wiring, but with no success. It's intricate—and small. Too many technical buts not worked out. We are building only once, you understand. If we had many experimental models worked out before—"

"'But this is the experimental model," Cole said.

"And built from the designs of a man dead four years—who isn't here to correct us. We've made Icarus with our own hands down here in the labs. And he's giving us plenty of trouble." All at once Sherikov got to his feet. "Let's go down to the lab and look at him."

They descended to the floor below, Sherikov leading the way. Cole stopped short at the lab door.

"Quite a sight," Sherikov agreed. "We keep him down here at the bottom for safety's sake. He's well protected. Come on in. We have work to do."

In the center of the lab Icarus rose up, the gray squat cylinder that someday would flash through space at a speed of thousands of times that of light, toward the heart of Proxima Centaurus, over four light years away. Around the cylinder groups of men in uniform were laboring feverishly to finish the remaining work.

"Over here. The turret." Sherikov led Cole over to one side of the room. "It's guarded. Centauran spies are swarming everywhere on Terra. They see into everything. But so do we. That's how we get information for the SRB machines. Spies in both systems."

The translucent globe that was the control turret reposed in the center of a metal stand, an armed guard standing at each side. They lowered their guns as Sherikov approached.

"We don't want anything to happen to this," Sherikov said. "Everything depends on it." He put out his hand for the globe. Halfway to it his hand stopped, striking against an invisible presence in the air.

Sherikov laughed. "The wall. Shut it off. It's still on."

One of the guards pressed a stud at his wrist. Around the globe the air shimmered and faded.

"Now." Sherikov's hand closed over the globe. He lifted it carefully from its mount and brought it out for Cole to see. "This is the control turret for our enormous friend here. This is what will slow him down when he's inside Centaurus. He slows down and re-enters this universe. Right in the heart of the star. Then—no more Centaurus." Sherikov beamed. "And no more Armun."

But Cole was not listening. He had taken the globe from Sherikov and was turning it over and over, running his hands over it, his face close to its surface. He peered down into its interior, his face rapt and intent.

"You can't see the wiring. Not without lenses." Sherikov signalled for a pair of micro-lenses to be brought. He fitted them on Cole's nose, hooking them behind his ears. "Now try it. You can control the magnification. It's set for 1000X right now. You can increase or decrease it."

Cole gasped, swaying back and forth. Sherikov caught hold of him. Cole gazed down into the globe, moving his head slightly, focusing the glasses.

"It takes practice. But you can do a lot with them. Permits you to do microscopic wiring. There are tools to go along, you understand." Sherikov paused, licking his lip. "We can't get it done correctly. Only a few men can wire circuits using the micro-lenses and the little tools. We've tried robots, but there are too many decisions to be made. Robots can't make decisions. They just react."

Cole said nothing. He continued to gaze into the interior of the globe, his lips tight, his body taut and rigid. It made Sherikov feel strangely uneasy.

"You look like one of those old fortunetellers," Sherikov said jokingly, but a cold shiver crawled up his spine. "Better hand it back to me." He held out his hand.

Slowly, Cole returned the globe. After a time he removed the micro-lenses, still deep in thought.

"Well?" Sherikov demanded. "You know what I want. I want you to wire this damn thing up." Sherikov came close to Cole, his big face hard. "You can do it, I think. I could tell by the way you held it—and the job you did on the children's toy, of course. You could wire it up right, and in five days. Nobody else can. And if it's not wired up Centaurus will keep on running the galaxy and Terra will have to sweat it out here in the Sol system. One tiny mediocre sun, one dust mote out of a whole galaxy."

Cole did not answer.

Sherikov became impatient. "Well? What do you say?"

"What happens if I don't wire this control for you? I mean, what happens to *me*?"

"Then I turn you over to Reinhart. Reinhart will kill you instantly. He thinks you're dead, killed when the Albertine Range was annihilated. If he had any idea I had saved you—"

"I see."

"I brought you down here for one thing. If you wire it up I'll have you sent back to your own time continuum. If you don't—"

Cole considered, his face dark and brooding.

"What do you have to lose? You'd already be dead, if we hadn't pulled you out of those hills."

"Can you really return me to my own time?"

"Of course!"

"Reinhart won't interfere?"

Sherikov laughed. "What can he do? How can he stop me? I have my own men. You saw them. They landed all around you. You'll be returned."

"Yes. I saw your men."

"Then you agree?"

"I agree," Thomas Cole said. "I'll wire it for you. I'll complete the control turret—within the next five days."

IV

Three days later Joseph Dixon slid a closed-circuit message plate across the desk to his boss.

"Here. You might be interested in this."

Reinhart picked the plate up slowly. "What is it? You came all the way here to show me this?"

"That's right."

"Why didn't you vidscreen it?"

Dixon smiled grimly. "You'll understand when you decode it. It's from Proxima Centaurus."

"Centaurus!"

"Our counter-intelligence service. They sent it direct to me. Here, I'll decode it for you. Save you the trouble."

Dixon came around behind Reinhart's desk. He leaned over the Commissioner's shoulder, taking hold of the plate and breaking the seal with his thumb nail.

"Hang on," Dixon said. "This is going to hit you hard. According to our agents on Armun, the Centauran High Council has called an emergency session to deal with the problem of Terra's impending attack. Centauran replay couriers have reported to the High Council that the Terran bomb Icarus is virtually complete. Work on the bomb has been rushed through final stages in the underground laboratories under the Ural Range, directed by the Terran physicist Peter Sherikov."

"So I understand from Sherikov himself. Are you surprised the Centaurans know about the bomb? They have spies swarming over Terra. That's no news."

"There's more." Dixon traced the message plate grimly, with an unsteady finger. "The Centauran replay couriers reported that Peter Sherikov brought an expert mechanic out of a previous time continuum to complete the wiring of the turret!"

Reinhart staggered, holding on tight to the desk. He closed his eyes, gasping.

"The variable man is still alive," Dixon murmured. "I don't know how. Or why. There's nothing left of the Albertines. And how the hell did the man get halfway around the world?"

Reinhart opened his eyes slowly, his face twisting. "Sherikov! He must have removed him before the attack was forthcoming. I gave him the exact hour. He had to get help—from the variable man. He couldn't meet his promise otherwise."

Reinhart leaped up and began to pace back and forth. "I've already informed the SRB machines that the variable man has been destroyed. The machines now show the original 7-6 ratio in our favor. But the ratio is based on false information."

"Then you'll have to withdraw the false data and restore the original situation."

"No." Reinhart shook his head. "I can't do that. The machines must be kept functioning. We can't allow them to jam again. It's too dangerous. If Duffe should become aware that—"

"What are you going to do, then?" Dixon picked up the message plate. "You can't leave the machines with false data. That's treason."

"The data can't be withdrawn! Not unless equivalent data exists to take its place." Reinhart paced angrily back and forth. "Damn it, I was *certain* the man was dead. This is an incredible situation. He must be eliminated—at any cost."

Suddenly Reinhart stopped pacing. "The turret. It's probably finished by this time. Correct?"

Dixon nodded slowly in agreement. "With the variable man helping, Sherikov has undoubtedly completed work well ahead of schedule."

Reinhart's gray eyes flickered. "Then he's no longer of any use- even to Sherikov. We could take a chance . . . Even if there were active opposition . . . "

"What's this?" Dixon demanded. "What are you thinking about?"

"How many units are ready for immediate action? How large a force can we raise without notice?"

"Because of the war we're mobilized on a twenty-four hour basis. There are seventy air units and about two hundred surface units. The balance of the Security forces have been transferred to the line, under military control."

"Men?"

"We have about five thousand men ready to go, still on Terra. Most of them in the process of being transferred to military transports. I can hold it up at any time."

"Missiles?"

"Fortunately, the launching tubes have not yet been disassembled. They're still here on Terra. In another few days they'll be moving out for the Colonial fracas."

"Then they're available for immediate use?"

"Yes."

"Good." Reinhart locked his hands, knotting his fingers harshly together in sudden decision. "That will do exactly. Unless I am completely wrong, Sherikov has only a half-dozen air units and no surface cars. And only about two hundred men. Some defense shields, of course—"

"What are you planning?"

Reinhart's face was gray and hard, like stone. "Send out orders for all available Security units to be unified under your immediate command. Have them ready to move by four o'clock this afternoon. We're going to pay a visit," Reinhart stated grimly. "A surprise visit. On Peter Sherikov."

❖ ❖ ❖

"Stop here," Reinhart ordered.

The surface car slowed to a halt. Reinhart peered cautiously out, studying the horizon ahead.

On all sides a desert of scrub grass and sand stretched out. Nothing moved or stirred. To the right the grass and sand rose up to form immense peaks, a range of mountains without end, disappearing finally into the distance. The Urals.

"Over there," Reinhart said to Dixon, pointing. "See?"

"No."

"Look hard. It's difficult to spot unless you know what to look for. Vertical pipes. Some kind of vent. Or periscopes."

Dixon saw them finally. "I would have driven past without noticing."

"It's well concealed. The main labs are a mile down. Under the range itself. It's virtually impregnable. Sherikov had it built years ago, to withstand any attack. From the air, by surface cars, bombs, missiles—"

"He must feel safe down there."

"No doubt." Reinhart gazed up at the sky. A few faint black dots could be seen, moving lazily about, in broad circles. "Those aren't ours, are they? I gave orders—"

"No. They're not ours. All our units are out of sight. Those belong to Sherikov. His patrol."

Reinhart relaxed. "Good." He reached over and flicked on the vidscreen over the board of the car. "This screen is shielded? It can't be traced?"

"There's no way they can spot it back to us. It's nondirectional."

The screen glowed into life. Reinhart punched the combination keys and sat back to wait.

After a time an image formed on the screen. A heavy face, bushy black beard and large eyes.

Peter Sherikov gazed at Reinhart with surprised curiosity. "Commissioner! Where are you calling from? What—"

"How's the work progressing?" Reinhart broke in coldly. "Is Icarus almost complete?"

Sherikov beamed with expansive pride. "He's done, Commissioner. Two days ahead of time. Icarus is ready to be launched into space. I tried to call your office, but they told me—"

"I'm not at my office." Reinhart leaned toward the screen. "Open your entrance tunnel at the surface. You're about to receive visitors."

Sherikov blinked. "Visitors?"

"I'm coming down to see you. About Icarus. Have the tunnel opened for me at once."

"Exactly where are you, Commissioner?"

"On the surface."

Sherikov's eyes flickered. "Oh? But—"

"Open up!" Reinhart snapped. He glanced at his wristwatch. "I'll be at the entrance in five minutes. I expect to find it ready for me."

"Of course." Sherikov nodded in bewilderment. "I'm always glad to see you, Commissioner. But I—"

"Five minutes, then." Reinhart cut the circuit. The screen died. He turned quickly to Dixon. "You stay up here, as we arranged. I'll go down with one company of police. You understand the necessity of exact timing on this?"

"We won't slip up. Everything's ready. All units are in their places."

"Good." Reinhart pushed the door open for him. "You join your directional staff. I'll proceed toward the entrance tunnel."

"Good luck." Dixon leaped out of the car, onto the sandy ground. A gust of dry air swirled into the car around Reinhart. "I'll see you later."

Reinhart slammed the door. He turned to the group of police crouched in the rear of the car, their guns held tightly. "Here we go," Reinhart murmured. "Hold on."

The car raced across the sandy ground, toward the entrance tunnel to Sherikov's underground fortress.

Sherikov met Reinhart at the bottom end of the tunnel, where the tunnel opened up onto the main floor of the lab.

The big Pole approached, his hand out, beaming with pride and satisfaction. "It's a pleasure to see you, Commissioner."

Reinhart got out of the car, with his group of armed Security police. "Calls for a celebration, doesn't it?" he said.

"That's a good idea! We're two days ahead, Commissioner. The SRB machines will be interested. The odds should change abruptly at the news."

"Let's go down to the lab. I want to see the control turret myself."

A shadow crossed Sherikov's face. "I'd rather not bother the workmen right now, Commissioner. They've been under a great load, trying to complete the turret in time. I believe they're putting a few last finishes on it at this moment."

"We can view them by vidscreen. I'm curious to see them at work. It must be difficult to wire such minute relays."

Sherikov shook his head. "Sorry, Commissioner. No vidscreen

on them. I won't allow it. This is too important. Our whole future depends on it."

Reinhart snapped a signal to his company of police. "Put this man under arrest."

Sherikov blanched. His mouth fell open. The police moved quickly around him, their gun-tubes up, jabbing into him. He was searched rapidly, efficiently. His gun belt and concealed energy screen were yanked off.

"What's going on?" Sherikov demanded, some color returning to his face. "What are you doing?"

"You're under arrest for the duration of the war. You're relieved of all authority. From now on one of my men will operate Designs. When the war is over you'll be tried before the Council and President Duffe."

Sherikov shook his head, dazed. "I don't understand. What's this all about? Explain it to me, Commissioner. What's happened?"

Reinhart signalled to his police. "Get ready. We're going into the lab. We may have to shoot our way in. The variable man should be in the area of the bomb, working on the control turret."

Instantly Sherikov's face hardened. His black eyes glittered, alert and hostile.

Reinhart laughed harshly. "We received a counter-intelligence report from Centaurus. I'm surprised at you, Sherikov. You know the Centaurans are everywhere with their relay couriers. You should have known—"

Sherikov moved. Fast. All at once he broke away from the police, throwing his massive body against them. They fell, scattering. Sherikov ran—directly at the wall. The police fired wildly. Reinhart fumbled frantically for his gun tube, pulling it up.

Sherikov reached the wall, running head down, energy beams flashing around him. He struck against the wall—and vanished.

"Down!" Reinhart shouted. He dropped to his hands and knees. All around him his police dived for the floor. Reinhart cursed

wildly, dragging himself quickly toward the door. They had to get
out, and right away. Sherikov had escaped. A false wall, an energy
barrier set to respond to his pressure. He had dashed through it to
safety. He—

From all sides an inferno burst, a flaming roar of death surging
over them, around them, on every side. The room was alive with
blazing masses of destruction, bouncing from wall to wall. They
were caught between four banks of power, all of them open to full
discharge. A trap—a death trap.

Reinhart reached the hall gasping for breath. He leaped to his feet.
A few Security police followed him. Behind them, in the flaming
room, the rest of the company screamed and struggled, blasted out of
existence by the leaping bursts of power.

Reinhart assembled his remaining men. Already, Sherikov's guards
were forming. At one end of the corridor a snub-barreled robot gun
was maneuvering into position. A siren wailed. Guards were running
on all sides, hurrying to battle stations.

The robot gun opened fire. Part of the corridor exploded, bursting
into fragments. Clouds of choking debris and particles swept around
them. Reinhart and his police retched, moving back along the
corridor.

They reached a junction. A second robot gun was rumbling toward
them, hurrying to get within range. Reinhart fired carefully, aiming
at its delicate control. Abruptly the gun spun convulsively. It lashed
against the wall, smashing itself into the unyielding metal. Then it
collapsed in a heap, gears still whining and spinning.

"Come on." Reinhart moved away, crouching and running. He
glanced at his watch. *Almost time.* A few more minutes. A group
of lab guards appeared ahead of them. Reinhart fired. Behind him
his police fired past him, violet shafts of energy catching the group
of guards as they entered the corridor. The guards spilled apart,
falling and twisting. Part of them settled into dust, drifting down
the corridor. Reinhart made his way toward the lab, crouching and

leaping, pushing past heaps of debris and remains, followed by his men. "Come on! Don't stop!"

Suddenly from around them the booming, enlarged voice of Sherikov thundered, magnified by rows of wall speakers along the corridor. Reinhart halted, glancing around.

"Reinhart! You haven't got a chance. You'll never get back to the surface. Throw down your guns and give up. You're surrounded on all sides. You're a mile under the surface."

Reinhart threw himself into motion, pushing into billowing clouds of particles drifting along the corridor. "Are you sure, Sherikov?" he grunted.

Sherikov laughed, his harsh, metallic peals rolling in waves against Reinhart's eardrums. "I don't want to have to kill you, Commissioner. You're vital to the war. I'm sorry you found out about the variable man. I admit we overlooked the Centauran espionage as a factor in this. But now that you know about him—"

Suddenly Sherikov's voice broke off. A deep rumble had shaken the floor, a lapping vibration that shuddered through the corridor.

Reinhart sagged with relief. He peered through the clouds of debris, making out the figures on his watch. Right on time. Not a second late.

The first of the hydrogen missiles, launched from the Council buildings on the other side of the world, were beginning to arrive. The attack had begun.

❖ ❖ ❖

At exactly six o'clock Joseph Dixon, standing on the surface four miles from the entrance tunnel, gave the sign to the waiting units.

The first job was to break down Sherikov's defense screens. The missiles had to penetrate without interference. At Dixon's signal a fleet of thirty Security ships dived from a height of ten miles, swooping above the mountains, directly over the underground laboratories. Within five minutes the defense screens had been smashed, and all the tower projectors leveled flat. Now the mountains were virtually unprotected.

"So far so good," Dixon murmured, as he watched from his secure position. The fleet of Security ships roared back, their work done. Across the face of the desert the police surface cars were crawling rapidly toward the entrance tunnel, snaking from side to side.

Meanwhile, Sherikov's counter-attack had begun to go into operation.

Guns mounted among the hills opened fire. Vast columns of flames burst up in the path of the advancing cars. The cars hesitated and retreated, as the plain was churned up by a howling vortex, a thundering chaos of explosions. Here and there a car vanished in a cloud of particles. A group of cars moving away suddenly scattered, caught up by a giant wind that lashed across them and swept them up into the air.

Dixon gave orders to have the cannon silenced. The police air arm again swept overhead, a sullen roar of jets that shook the ground below. The police ships divided expertly and hurtled down on the cannon protecting the hills.

The cannon forgot the surface cars and lifted their snouts to meet the attack. Again and again the airships came, rocking the mountains with titanic blasts.

The guns became silent. Their echoing boom diminished, died away reluctantly, as bombs took critical toll of them.

Dixon watched with satisfaction as the bombing came to an end. The airships rose in a thick swarm, black gnats shooting up in triumph from a dead carcass. They hurried back as emergency anti-aircraft robot guns swung into position and saturated the sky with blazing puffs of energy.

Dixon checked his wristwatch. The missiles were already on the way from North America. Only a few minutes remained.

The surface cars, freed by the successful bombing, began to regroup for a new frontal attack. Again they crawled forward, across the burning plain, bearing down cautiously on the battered wall of mountains, heading toward the twisted wrecks that had been the ring of defense guns. Toward the entrance tunnel.

An occasional cannon fired feebly at them. The cars came grimly on. Now, in the hollows of the hills, Sherikov's troops were hurrying to the surface to meet the attack. The first car reached the shadow of the mountains . . .

A deafening hail of fire burst loose. Small robot guns appeared everywhere, needle barrels emerging from behind hidden screens, trees, shrubs, rocks, and stones. The police cars were caught in a withering cross-fire, trapped at the base of the hills.

Down the slopes Sherikov's guards raced, toward the stalled cars. Clouds of heat rose up and boiled across the plain as the cars fired up at the running men. A robot gun dropped like a slug onto the plain and screamed toward the cars, firing as it came.

Dixon twisted nervously. Only a few minutes. Any time, now. He shaded his eyes and peered up at the sky. No sign of them yet. He wondered about Reinhart. No signal had come from below. Clearly, Reinhart had run into trouble. No doubt there was desperate fighting going on in the maze of underground tunnels, the intricate web of passages that honeycombed the earth below the mountains.

In the air, Sherikov's few defense ships darted rapidly, wildly, putting up a futile fight.

Sherikov's guards streamed out onto the plain. Crouching and running, they advanced toward the stalled cars. The police airships screeched down at them, guns thundering.

Dixon held his breath. When the missiles arrived—

The first missile struck. A section of the mountain vanished, turned to smoke and foaming gases. The wave of heat slapped Dixon across the face, spinning him around. Quickly he re-entered his ship and took off, shooting rapidly away from the scene. He glanced back. A second and third missile had arrived. Great gaping pits yawned among the mountains, vast sections missing like broken teeth. Now the missiles could penetrate to the underground laboratories below.

On the ground, the surface cars halted beyond the danger area, waiting for the missile attack to finish. When the eighth missile had struck, the cars again moved forward. No more missiles fell.

Dixon swung his ship around, heading back toward the scene. The laboratory was exposed. The top sections of it had been ripped open. The laboratory lay like a tin can, torn apart by mighty explosions, its first floors visible from the air. Men and cars were pouring down into it, fighting with the guards swarming to the surface.

❖ ❖ ❖

Dixon watched intently. Sherikov's men were bringing up heavy guns, big robot artillery. But the police ships were diving again. Sherikov's defensive patrols had been cleaned from the sky. The police ships whined down, arcing over the exposed laboratory. Small bombs fell, whistling down, pinpointing the artillery rising to the surface on the remaining lift stages.

Abruptly Dixon's vidscreen clicked. Dixon turned toward it.

Reinhart's features formed. "Call off the attack." His uniform was torn. A deep bloody gash crossed his cheek. He grinned sourly at Dixon, pushing his tangled hair back out of his face. "Quite a fight."

"Sherikov—"

"He's called off his guards. We've agreed to a truce. It's all over. No more needed." Reinhart gasped for breath, wiping grime and sweat from his neck. "Land your ship and come down here at once."

"The variable man?"

"That comes next," Reinhart said grimly. He adjusted his gun tube. "I want you down here, for that part. I want you to be in on the kill."

Reinhart turned away from the vidscreen. In the corner of the room Sherikov stood silently, saying nothing. "Well?" Reinhart barked. "Where is he? Where will I find him?"

Sherikov licked his lips nervously, glancing up at Reinhart. "Commissioner, are you sure—"

"The attack has been called off. Your labs are safe. So is your life. Now it's your turn to come through." Reinhart gripped his gun, moving toward Sherikov. "*Where is he?*"

For a moment Sherikov hesitated. Then slowly his huge body sagged, defeated. He shook his head wearily. "All right. I'll show you where he is." His voice was hardly audible, a dry whisper. "Down this way. Come on."

Reinhart followed Sherikov out of the room, into the corridor. Police and guards were working rapidly, clearing the debris and ruins away, putting out the hydrogen fires that burned everywhere. "No tricks, Sherikov."

"No tricks." Sherikov nodded resignedly. "Thomas Cole is by himself. In a wing lab off the main rooms."

"Cole?"

"The variable man. That's his name." The Pole turned his massive head a little. "He has a name."

Reinhart waved his gun. "Hurry up. I don't want anything to go wrong. This is the part I came for."

"You must remember something, Commissioner."

"What is it?"

Sherikov stopped walking. "Commissioner, nothing must happen to the globe. The control turret. Everything depends on it, the war, our whole—"

"I know. Nothing will happen to the damn thing. Let's go."

"If it should get damaged—"

"I'm not after the globe. I'm interested only in—in Thomas Cole."

They came to the end of the corridor and stopped before a metal door. Sherikov nodded at the door. "In there."

Reinhart moved back. "Open the door."

"Open it yourself. I don't want to have anything to do with it."

Reinhart shrugged. He stepped up to the door. Holding his gun level he raised his hand, passing it in front of the eye circuit. Nothing happened.

Reinhart frowned. He pushed the door with his hand. The door slid open. Reinhart was looking into a small laboratory. He glimpsed a workbench, tools, heaps of equipment, measuring devices, and in the center of the bench the transparent globe, the control turret.

"Cole?" Reinhart advanced quickly into the room. He glanced around him, suddenly alarmed. "Where—"

The room was empty. Thomas Cole was gone.

❖ ❖ ❖

When the first missile struck, Cole stopped work and sat listening.

Far off, a distant rumble rolled through the earth, shaking the floor under him. On the bench, tools and equipment danced up and down. A pair of pliers fell crashing to the floor. A box of screws tipped over, spilling its minute contents out.

Cole listened for a time. Presently he lifted the transparent globe from the bench. With carefully controlled hands he held the globe up, running his fingers gently over the surface, his faded blue eyes thoughtful. Then, after a time, he placed the globe back on the bench, in its mount.

The globe was finished. A faint glow of pride moved through the variable man. The globe was the finest job he had ever done.

The deep rumblings ceased. Cole became instantly alert. He jumped down from his stool, hurrying across the room to the door. For a moment he stood by the door listening intently. He could hear noise on the other side, shouts, guards rushing past, dragging heavy equipment, working frantically.

A rolling crash echoed down the corridor and lapped against his door. The concussion spun him around. Again a tide of energy shook the walls and floor and sent him down on his knees.

The lights flickered and winked out.

Cole fumbled in the dark until he found a flashlight. Power failure. He could hear crackling flames. Abruptly the lights came on again, an ugly yellow, then faded back out. Cole bent down and examined the door with his flashlight. A magnetic lock. Dependent on an externally induced electric flux. He grabbed a screwdriver and pried at the door. For a moment it held. Then it fell open.

Cole stepped warily out into the corridor. Everything was in shambles. Guards wandered everywhere, burned and half blinded. Two lay groaning under a pile of wrecked equipment. Fused guns, reeking metal. The air was heavy with the smell of burning wiring and plastic. A thick cloud that choked him and made him bend double as he advanced.

"Halt," a guard gasped feebly, struggling to rise. Cole pushed past him and down the corridor. Two small robot guns, still functioning, glided past him hurriedly toward the drumming chaos of battle. He followed.

At a major intersection the fight was in full swing. Sherikov's guards fought Security police, crouched behind pillars and barricades, firing wildly, desperately. Again the whole structure shuddered as a great booming blast ignited some place above. Bombs? Shells?

Cole threw himself down as a violet beam cut past his ear and disintegrated the wall behind him. A Security policeman, wild-eyed, firing erratically. One of Sherikov's guards winged him and his gun skidded to the floor.

A robot cannon turned toward him as he made his way past the intersection. He began to run. The cannon rolled along behind him, aiming itself uncertainly. Cole hunched over as he shambled rapidly along, gasping for breath. In the flickering yellow light he saw a handful of Security police advancing, firing expertly, intent on a line of defense Sherikov's guards had hastily set up.

The robot cannon altered its course to take them on, and Cole escaped around a corner.

He was in the main lab, the big chamber where Icarus himself rose, the vast squat column.

Icarus! A solid wall of guards surrounded him, grim-faced, hugging guns and protection shields. But the Security police were leaving Icarus alone. Nobody wanted to damage him. Cole evaded a lone guard tracking him and reached the far side of the lab.

It took him only a few seconds to find the force field generator. There was no switch. For a moment that puzzled him—and then he remembered. The guard had controlled it from his wrist.

Too late to worry about that. With his screwdriver he unfastened the plate over the generator and ripped out the wiring in handfuls. The generator came loose and he dragged it away from the wall. The screen was off, thank God. He managed to carry the generator into a side corridor.

Crouched in a heap, Cole bent over the generator, deft fingers flying. He pulled the wiring to him and laid it out on the floor, tracing the circuits with feverish haste.

The adaptation was easier than he had expected. The screen flowed at right angles to the wiring, for a distance of six feet. Each lead was shielded on one side; the field radiated outward, leaving a hollow cone in the center. He ran the wiring through his belt, down his trouser legs, under his shirt, all the way to his wrists and ankles.

He was just snatching up the heavy generator when two Security police appeared. They raised their blasters and fired point-blank.

Cole clicked on the screen. A vibration leaped through him that snapped his jaw and danced up his body. He staggered away, half-stupefied by the surging force that radiated out from him. The violet rays struck the field and deflected harmlessly.

He was safe.

He hurried on down the corridor, past a ruined gun and sprawled bodies still clutching blasters. Great drifting clouds of radioactive particles billowed around him. He edged by one cloud nervously. Guards lay everywhere, dying and dead, partly destroyed, eaten and corroded by the hot metallic salts in the air. He had to get out—and fast.

At the end of the corridor a whole section of the fortress was in ruins. Towering flames leaped on all sides. One of the missiles had penetrated below ground level.

Cole found a lift that still functioned. A load of wounded guards was being raised to the surface. None of them paid any attention to him. Flames surged around the lift, licking at the wounded. Workmen were desperately trying to get the lift into action. Cole leaped onto the lift. A moment later it began to rise, leaving the shouts and the flames behind.

The lift emerged on the surface and Cole jumped off. A guard spotted him and gave chase. Crouching, Cole dodged into a tangled mass of twisted metal, still white-hot and smoking. He ran for a distance, leaping from the side of a ruined defense-screen tower, onto the fused ground and down the side of a hill. The ground was hot underfoot. He hurried as fast as he could, gasping for breath. He came to a long slope and scrambled up the side.

The guard who had followed was gone, lost behind in the rolling clouds of ash that drifted from the ruins of Sherikov's underground fortress.

Cole reached the top of the hill. For a brief moment he halted to get his breath and figure where he was. It was almost evening. The sun was beginning to set. In the darkening sky a few dots still twisted and rolled, black specks that abruptly burst into flame and fused out again.

Cole stood up cautiously, peering around him. Ruins stretched out below, on all sides, the furnace from which he had escaped. A chaos of incandescent metal and debris, gutted and wrecked beyond repair. Miles of tangled rubbish and half-vaporized equipment.

He considered. Everyone was busy putting out the fires and pulling the wounded to safety. It would be a while before he was missed. But as soon as they realized he was gone they'd be after him. Most of the laboratory had been destroyed. Nothing lay back that way.

Beyond the ruins lay the great Ural peaks, the endless mountains, stretching out as far as the eye could see.

Mountains and green forests. A wilderness. They'd never find him there.

Cole started along the side of the hill, walking slowly and carefully, his screen generator under his arm. Probably in the confusion he could find enough food and equipment to last him indefinitely. He could wait until early morning then circle back toward the ruins and load up. With a few tools and his own innate skill he would get along fine. A screwdriver, hammer, nails, odds and ends—

A great hum sounded in his ears. It swelled to a deafening roar. Startled, Cole whirled around. A vast shape filled the sky behind him, growing each moment. Cole stood frozen, utterly transfixed. The shape thundered over him, above his head, as he stood stupidly, rooted to the spot.

Then, awkwardly, uncertainly, he began to run. He stumbled and fell and rolled a short distance down the side of the hill. Desperately, he struggled to hold onto the ground. His hands dug wildly, futilely, into the soft soil, trying to keep the generator under his arm at the same time.

A flash, and a blinding spark of light around him.

The spark picked him up and tossed him like a dry leaf. He grunted in agony as searing fire crackled about him, a blazing inferno that gnawed and ate hungrily through his screen. He spun dizzily and fell through the cloud of fire, down into a pit of darkness, a vast gulf between two hills. His wiring ripped off. The generator tore out of his grip and was lost behind. Abruptly, his force field ceased.

Cole lay in the darkness at the bottom of the hill. His whole body shrieked in agony as the unholy fire played over him. He was a blazing cinder, a half-consumed ash flaming in a universe of darkness. The pain made him twist and crawl like an insect, trying to burrow into the ground. He screamed and shrieked and struggled to escape, to get away from the hideous fire. To reach the curtain of darkness beyond, where it was cool and silent, where the flames couldn't crackle and eat at him.

He reached imploringly out, into the darkness, groping feebly toward it, trying to pull himself into it. Gradually, the glowing orb that was his own body faded. The impenetrable chaos of night descended. He allowed the tide to sweep over him, to extinguish the searing fire.

Dixon landed his ship expertly, bringing it to a halt in front of an overturned defense tower. He leaped out and hurried across the smoking ground.

From a lift Reinhart appeared, surrounded by his Security police. "He got away from us! He escaped!"

"He didn't escape," Dixon answered. "I got him myself."

Reinhart quivered violently. "What do you mean?"

"Come along with me. Over in this direction." He and Reinhart climbed the side of a demolished hill, both of them panting for breath. "I was landing. I saw a figure emerge from a lift and run toward the mountains, like some sort of animal. When he came out in the open I dived on him and released a phosphorous bomb."

"Then he's—*dead*?"

"I don't see how anyone could have lived through a phosphorous bomb." They reached the top of the hill. Dixon halted, then pointed excitedly down into the pit beyond the hill. "There!"

They descended cautiously. The ground was singed and burned clean. Clouds of smoke hung heavily in the air. Occasional fires still flickered here and there. Reinhart coughed and bent over to see. Dixon flashed on a pocket flare and set it beside the body.

The body was charred, half destroyed by the burning phosphorous. It lay motionless, one arm over its face, mouth open, legs sprawled grotesquely. Like some abandoned rag doll, tossed in an incinerator and consumed almost beyond recognition.

"He's alive!" Dixon muttered. He felt around curiously. "Must have had some kind of protection screen. Amazing that a man could—"

"It's him? It's really him?"

"Fits the description." Dixon tore away a handful of burned clothing. "This is the variable man. What's left of him, at least."

Reinhart sagged with relief. "Then we've finally got him. The data is accurate. He's no longer a factor."

Dixon got out his blaster and released the safety catch thoughtfully. "If you want, I can finish the job right now."

At that moment Sherikov appeared, accompanied by two armed Security police. He strode grimly down the hillside, black eyes snapping. "Did Cole—" He broke off. "Good God."

"Dixon got him with a phosphorous bomb," Reinhart said noncommittally. "He had reached the surface and was trying to get into the mountains."

Sherikov turned wearily away. "He was an amazing person. During the attack he managed to force the lock on his door and escape. The guards fired at him, but nothing happened. He had rigged up some kind of force field around him. Something he adapted."

"Anyhow, it's over with," Reinhart answered. "Did you have SRB plates made up on him?"

Sherikov reached slowly into his coat. He drew out a manila envelope. "Here's all the information I collected about him, while he was with me."

"Is it complete? Everything previous has been merely fragmentary."

"As near complete as I could make it. It includes photographs and diagrams of the interior of the globe. The turret wiring he did for me. I haven't had a chance even to look at them." Sherikov fingered the envelope. "What are you going to do with Cole?"

"Have him loaded up, taken back to the city—and officially put to sleep by the Euthanasia Ministry."

"Legal murder?" Sherikov's lips twisted. "Why don't you simply do it right here and get it over with?"

Reinhart grabbed the envelope and stuck it in his right pocket. "I'll turn this right over to the machines." He motioned to Dixon.

"Let's go. Now we can notify the fleet to prepare for the attack on Centaurus." He turned briefly back to Sherikov. "When can Icarus be launched?"

"In an hour or so, I suppose. They're locking the control turret in place. Assuming it functions correctly, that's all that's needed."

"Good. I'll notify Duffe to send out the signal to the warfleet." Reinhart nodded to the police to take Sherikov to the waiting Security ship. Sherikov moved off dully, his face gray and haggard. Cole's inert body was picked up and tossed onto a freight cart. The cart rumbled into the hold of the Security ship and the lock slid shut after it.

"It'll be interesting to see how the machines respond to the additional data," Dixon said.

"It should make quite an improvement in the odds," Reinhart agreed. He patted the envelope bulging in his inside pocket. "We're two days ahead of time."

Margaret Duffe got up slowly from her desk. She pushed her chair automatically back. "Let me get all this straight. You mean the bomb is finished? Ready to go?"

Reinhart nodded impatiently. "That's what I said. The Technicians are checking the turret locks to make sure it's properly attached. The launching will take place in half an hour."

"Thirty minutes! Then—"

"Then the attack can begin at once. I assume the fleet is ready for action."

"Of course. It's been ready for several days. But I can't believe the bomb is ready so soon." Margaret Duffe moved numbly toward the door of her office. "This is a great day, Commissioner. An old era lies behind us. This time tomorrow Centaurus will be gone. And eventually the colonies will be ours."

"It's been a long climb," Reinhart murmured.

"One thing. Your charge against Sherikov. It seems incredible that a person of his caliber could ever—"

"We'll discuss that later," Reinhart interrupted coldly. He pulled the manila envelope from his coat. "I haven't had an opportunity to feed the additional data to the SRB machines. If you'll excuse me, I'll do that now."

For a moment Margaret Duffe stood at the door. The two of them faced each other silently, neither speaking, a faint smile on Reinhart's thin lips, hostility in the woman's blue eyes.

"Reinhart, sometimes I think perhaps you'll go too far. And sometimes I think you've *already* gone too far . . . "

"I'll inform you of any change in the odds showing." Reinhart strode past her, out of the office and down the hall. He headed toward the SRB room, an intense thalamic excitement rising up inside him.

A few moments later he entered the SRB room. He made his way to the machines. The odds 7-6 showed in the view windows. Reinhart smiled a little. 7-6. False odds, based on incorrect information. Now they could be removed.

Kaplan hurried over. Reinhart handed him the envelope, and moved over to the window, gazing down at the scene below. Men and cars scurried frantically everywhere. Officials coming and going like ants, hurrying in all directions.

The war was on. The signal had been sent out to the warfleet that had waited so long near Proxima Centaurus. A feeling of triumph raced through Reinhart. He had won. He had destroyed the man from the past and broken Peter Sherikov. The war had begun as planned. Terra was breaking out. Reinhart smiled thinly. He had been completely successful.

"Commissioner."

Reinhart turned slowly. "All right."

Kaplan was standing in front of the machines, gazing down at the reading. "Commissioner—"

Sudden alarm plucked at Reinhart. There was something in Kaplan's voice. He hurried quickly over. "What is it?"

Kaplan looked up at him, his face white, his eyes wide with terror. His mouth opened and closed, but no sound came.

"*What is it?*" Reinhart demanded, chilled. He bent toward the machines, studying the reading.

And sickened with horror.

100-1. *Against* Terra!

He could not tear his gaze away from the figures. He was numb, shocked with disbelief. 100-1. *What had happened?* What had gone wrong? The turret was finished, Icarus was ready, the fleet had been notified—

There was a sudden deep buzz from outside the building. Shouts drifted up from below. Reinhart turned his head slowly toward the window, his heart frozen with fear.

Across the evening sky a trail moved, rising each moment. A thin line of white. Something climbed, gaining speed each moment. On the ground, all eyes were turned toward it, awed faces peering up.

The object gained speed. Faster and faster. Then it vanished. Icarus was on his way. The attack had begun; it was too late to stop, now.

And on the machines the odds read a hundred to one—for failure.

At eight o'clock in the evening of May 15, 2136, Icarus was launched toward the star Centaurus. A day later, while all Terra waited, Icarus entered the star, traveling at thousands of times the speed of light.

Nothing happened. Icarus disappeared into the star. There was no explosion. The bomb failed to go off.

At the same time the Terran warfleet engaged the Centauran outer fleet, sweeping down in a concentrated attack. Twenty major ships were seized. A good part of the Centauran fleet was destroyed. Many of the captive systems began to revolt, in the hope of throwing off the Imperial bonds.

Two hours later the massed Centauran warfleet from Armun abruptly appeared and joined battle. The great struggle illuminated half the Centauran system. Ship after ship flashed briefly and then faded to ash. For a whole day the two fleets fought, strung out over millions of miles of space. Innumerable fighting men died—on both sides.

At last the remains of the battered Terran fleet turned and limped toward Armun—defeated. Little of the once impressive armada remained. A few blackened hulks, making their way uncertainly toward captivity.

Icarus had not functioned. Centaurus had not exploded. The attack was a failure.

The war was over.

"We've lost the war," Margaret Duffe said in a small voice, wondering and awed. "It's over. Finished."

The Council members sat in their places around the conference table, gray-haired elderly men, none of them speaking or moving. All gazed up mutely at the great stellar maps that covered two walls of the chamber.

"I have already empowered negotiators to arrange a truce," Margaret Duffe murmured. "Orders have been sent out to Vice-Commander Jessup to give up the battle. There's no hope. Fleet Commander Carleton destroyed himself and his flagship a few minutes ago. The Centauran High Council has agreed to end the fighting. Their whole Empire is rotten to the core. Ready to topple of its own weight."

Reinhart was slumped over at the table, his head in his hands. "I don't understand . . . *Why?* Why didn't the bomb explode?" He mopped his forehead shakily. All his poise was gone. He was trembling and broken. "*What went wrong?*"

Gray-faced, Dixon mumbled an answer. "The variable man must have sabotaged the turret. The SRB machines knew . . . They analyzed the data. *They knew!* But it was too late."

Reinhart's eyes were bleak with despair as he raised his head a little. "I knew he'd destroy us. We're finished. A century of work and planning." His body knotted in a spasm of furious agony. "All because of Sherikov!"

Margaret Duffe eyed Reinhart coldly. "Why because of Sherikov?"

"He kept Cole alive! I wanted him killed from the start." Suddenly Reinhart jumped from his chair. His hand clutched convulsively at his gun. "And he's *still* alive! Even if we've lost I'm going to have the pleasure of putting a blast beam through Cole's chest!"

"Sit down!" Margaret Duffe ordered.

Reinhart was halfway to the door. "He's still at the Euthanasia Ministry, waiting for the official—"

"No, he's not," Margaret Duffe said.

Reinhart froze. He turned slowly, as if unable to believe his sense. "*What?*"

"Cole isn't at the Ministry. I ordered him transferred and your instructions cancelled."

"Where—where is he?"

There was unusual hardness in Margaret Duffe's voice as she answered. "With Peter Sherikov. In the Urals. I had Sherikov's full authority restored. I then had Cole transferred there, put in Sherikov's safekeeping. I want to make sure Cole recovers, so we can keep our promise to him—our promise to return him to his own time."

Reinhart's mouth opened and closed. All the color had drained from his face. His cheek muscles twitched spasmodically. At last he managed to speak. "You've gone insane! The traitor responsible for Earth's greatest defeat—"

"We have lost the war," Margaret Duffe stated quietly. "But this is not a day of defeat. It is a day of victory. The most incredible victory Terra has ever had."

Reinhart and Dixon were dumbfounded. "What—" Reinhart gasped. "What do you—" The whole room was in an uproar. All the Council members were on their feet. Reinhart's words were drowned out.

"Sherikov will explain when he gets here," Margaret Duffe's calm voice came. "He's the one who discovered it." She looked around the chamber at the incredulous Council members. "Everyone stay in his seat. You are all to remain here until Sherikov arrives. It's vital you hear what he has to say. His news transforms this whole situation."

❖❖❖

Peter Sherikov accepted the briefcase of papers from his armed technician. "Thanks." He pushed his chair back and glanced thoughtfully around the Council chamber. "Is everybody ready to hear what I have to say?"

"We're ready," Margaret Duffe answered. The Council members sat alertly around the table. At the far end, Reinhart and Dixon watched uneasily as the big Pole removed papers from his briefcase and carefully examined them.

"To begin, I recall to you the original work behind the ftl bomb. Jamison Hedge was the first human to propel an object at a speed greater than light. As you know, that object diminished in length and gained in mass as it moved toward light speed. When it reached that speed it vanished. It ceased to exist in our terms. Having no length it could not occupy space. It rose to a different order of existence.

"When Hedge tried to bring the object back, an explosion occurred. Hedge was killed, and all his equipment was destroyed. The force of the blast was beyond calculation. Hedge had placed his observation ship many millions of miles away. It was not far enough, however. Originally, he had hoped his drive might be used for space travel. But after his death the principle was abandoned.

"That is—until Icarus. I saw the possibilities of a bomb, an incredibly powerful bomb to destroy Centaurus and all the Empire's forces. The reappearance of Icarus would mean the annihilation of their System. As Hedge had shown, the object would re-enter space already occupied by matter, and the cataclysm would be beyond belief."

"But Icarus never came back," Reinhart cried. "Cole altered the wiring so the bomb kept on going. It's probably still going."

"Wrong," Sherikov boomed. "The bomb *did* reappear. But it didn't explode."

Reinhart reacted violently. "You mean—"

"The bomb came back, dropping below the ftl speed as soon as it entered the star Proxima. But it did not explode. There was no cataclysm. It reappeared and was absorbed by the sun, turned into gas at once."

"Why didn't it explode?" Dixon demanded.

"Because Thomas Cole solved Hedge's problem. He found a way to bring the ftl object back into this universe without collision. Without an explosion. The variable man found what Hedge was after . . . "

The whole Council was on its feet. A growing murmur filled the chamber, a rising pandemonium breaking out on all sides.

"I don't believe it!" Reinhart gasped. "It isn't possible. If Cole solved Hedge's problem that would mean—" He broke off, staggered.

"Faster than light drive can now be used for space travel," Sherikov continued, waving the noise down. "As Hedge intended. My men have studied the photographs of the control turret. They don't know *how* or *why*, yet. But we have complete records of the turret. We can duplicate the wiring, as soon as the laboratories have been repaired."

Comprehension was gradually beginning to settle over the room. "Then it'll be possible to build ftl ships," Margaret Duffe murmured, dazed. "And if we can do that—"

"When I showed him the control turret, Cole understood its purpose. Not *my* purpose, but the original purpose Hedge had been working toward. Cole realized Icarus was actually an incomplete spaceship, not a bomb at all. He saw what Hedge had seen, an ftl space drive. He set out to make Icarus work."

"We can go *beyond* Centaurus," Dixon murmured. His lips twisted. "Then the war was trivial. We can leave the Empire completely behind. We can go beyond the galaxy."

"The whole universe is open to us," Sherikov agreed. "Instead of taking over an antiquated Empire, we have the entire cosmos to map and explore, God's total creation."

Margaret Duffe got to her feet and moved slowly toward the great stellar maps that towered above them at the far end of the chamber. She stood for a long time, gazing up at the myriad suns, the legions of systems, awed by what she saw.

"Do you suppose he realized all this?" she asked suddenly. "What we can see, here on these maps?"

"Thomas Cole is a strange person," Sherikov said, half to himself. "Apparently he has a kind of intuition about machines, the way things are supposed to work. An intuition more in his hands than in his head. A kind of genius, such as a painter or a pianist has. Not a scientist. He has no verbal knowledge about things, no semantic references. He deals with the things themselves. Directly.

"I doubt very much if Thomas Cole understood what would come about. He looked into the globe, the control turret. He saw unfinished wiring and relays. He saw a job half done. An incomplete machine."

"Something to be fixed," Margaret Duffe put in.

"Something to be fixed. Like an artist, he saw his work ahead of him. He was interested in only one thing: turning out the best job he could, with the skill he possessed. For us, that skill has opened up a whole universe, endless galaxies and systems to explore. Worlds without end. Unlimited, *untouched* worlds."

Reinhart got unsteadily to his feet. "We better get to work. Start organizing construction teams. Exploration crews. We'll have to reconvert from war production to ship designing. Begin the manufacture of mining and scientific instruments for survey work."

"That's right," Margaret Duffe said. She looked reflectively up at him. "But you're not going to have anything to do with it."

Reinhart saw the expression on her face. His hands flew to his gun and he backed quickly toward the door. Dixon leaped up and joined him. "Get back!" Reinhart shouted.

Margaret Duffe signaled and a phalanx of Government troops closed in around the two men. Grim-faced, efficient soldiers with magnetic grapples ready.

Reinhart's blaster wavered—toward the Council members sitting shocked in their seats, and toward Margaret Duffe, straight at her blue eyes. Reinhart's features were distorted with insane fear. "Get back! Don't anybody come near me or she'll be the first to get it!"

Peter Sherikov slid from the table and with one great stride swept his immense bulk in front of Reinhart. His huge black-furred fist rose in a smashing arc. Reinhart sailed against the wall, struck with ringing force and then slid slowly to the floor.

The Government troops threw their grapples quickly around him and jerked him to his feet. His body was frozen rigid. Blood dripped from his mouth. He spat bits of tooth, his eyes glazed over. Dixon stood dazed, mouth open, uncomprehending, as the grapples closed around his arms and legs.

Reinhart's gun skidded to the floor as he was yanked toward the door. One of the elderly Council members picked the gun up and examined it curiously. He laid it carefully on the table. "Fully loaded," he murmured. "Ready to fire."

Reinhart's battered face was dark with hate. "I should have killed all of you. *All* of you!" An ugly sneer twisted across his shredded lips. "If I could get my hands loose—"

"You won't," Margaret Duffe said. "You might as well not even bother to think about it." She signaled to the troops and they pulled Reinhart and Dixon roughly out of the room, two dazed figures, snarling and resentful.

For a moment the room was silent. Then the Council members shuffled nervously in their seats, beginning to breathe again.

Sherikov came over and put his big paw on Margaret Duffe's shoulder. "Are you all right, Margaret?"

She smiled faintly. "I'm fine. Thanks . . . "

Sherikov touched her soft hair briefly. Then he broke away and began to pack up his briefcase busily. "I have to go. I'll get in touch with you later."

"Where are you going?" she asked hesitantly. "Can't you stay and—"

"I have to get back to the Urals." Sherikov grinned at her over his bushy black beard as he headed out of the room. "Some very important business to attend to."

❖❖❖

Thomas Cole was sitting up in bed when Sherikov came to the door. Most of his awkward, hunched-over body was sealed in a thin envelope of transparent air-proof plastic. Two robot attendants whirred ceaselessly at his side, their leads contacting his pulse, blood-pressure, respiration, and body temperature.

Cole turned a little as the huge Pole tossed down his briefcase and seated himself on the window ledge.

"How are you feeling?" Sherikov asked him.

"Better."

"You see we've quite advanced therapy. Your burns should be healed in a few months."

"How is the war coming?"

"The war is over."

Cole's lips moved. "Icarus—"

"Icarus went as expected. As *you* expected." Sherikov leaned toward the bed. "Cole, I promised you something, I mean to keep my promise—as soon as you're well enough."

"To return me to my own time?"

"That's right. It's a relatively simple matter, now that Reinhart has been removed from power. You'll be back home again, back in your own time, your own world. We can supply you with some discs of platinum or something of the kind to finance your business. You need a new Fixit truck. Tools. And clothes. A few thousand dollars ought to do it."

Cole was silent.

"I've already contacted histo-research," Sherikov continued. "The time bubble is ready as soon as you are. We're somewhat beholden to you, as you probably realize. You've made it possible for us to actualize our greatest dream. The whole planet is seething with excitement. We're changing our economy over from war to—"

"They don't resent what happened? The dud must have made an awful lot of people feel downright bad."

"At first. But they got over it—as soon as they understood what was ahead. Too bad you won't be here to see it, Cole. A whole world breaking loose. Bursting out into the universe. They want me to have an ftl ship ready by the end of the week! Thousands of applications are already on file, men and women wanting to get in on the initial flight."

Cole smiled a little. "There won't be any band, there. No parade or welcoming committee waiting for them."

"Maybe not. Maybe the first ship will wind up on some dead world, nothing but sand and dried salt. But everyone wants to go. It's almost like a holiday. People running around and shouting and throwing things in the streets."

"Afraid I must get back to the labs. Lots of reconstruction work being started." Sherikov dug into his bulging briefcase. "By the way . . . One little thing. While you're recovering here, you might like to look at these." He tossed a handful of schematics on the bed.

Cole picked them up slowly. "What's this?"

"Just a little thing I designed." Sherikov arose and lumbered toward the door. "We're realigning our political structure to eliminate any recurrence of the Reinhart affair. This will block any more one-man power grabs." He jabbed a thick finger at the schematics. "It'll turn power over to all of us, not to just a limited number one person could dominate—the way Reinhart dominated the Council.

"This gimmick makes it possible for citizens to raise and decide issues directly. They won't have to wait for the Council to verbalize a measure. Any citizen can transmit his will with one of these, make his needs register on a central control that automatically responds. When a large enough segment of the population wants a certain thing done, these little gadgets set up an active field that touches all the others. An issue won't have to go through a formal Council. The citizens can express their will long before any bunch of gray-haired old men could get around to it."

Sherikov broke off, frowning. "Of course," he continued slowly, "there's one little detail . . . "

"What's that?"

"I haven't been able to get a model to function. A few bugs . . . Such intricate work never was in my line." He paused at the door. "Well, I hope I'll see you again before you go. Maybe if you feel well enough later on we could get together for one last talk. Maybe have dinner sometime. Eh?"

But Thomas Cole wasn't listening. He was bent over the schematics, an intense frown on his weathered face. His long fingers moved restlessly over the schematics, tracing wiring and terminals. His lips moved as he calculated.

Sherikov waited a moment. Then he stepped out into the hall and softly closed the door after him.

He whistled merrily as he strode off down the corridor.

THE CRYSTAL CRYPT

"Attention Inner-Flight ship! Attention! You are ordered to land at the Control Station on Deimos for inspection. Attention! You are to land at once!"

The metallic rasp of the speaker echoed through the corridors of the great ship. The passengers glanced at each other uneasily, murmuring and peering out the port windows at the small speck below, the dot of rock that was the Martian checkpoint, Deimos.

"What's up?" an anxious passenger asked one of the pilots, hurrying through the ship to check the escape lock.

"We have to land. Keep seated." The pilot went on.

"Land? But why?" They all looked at each other. Hovering above the bulging Inner-Flight ship were three slender Martian pursuit craft, poised and alert for any emergency. As the Inner-Flight ship prepared to land the pursuit ships dropped lower, carefully maintaining themselves a short distance away.

"There's something going on," a woman passenger said nervously. "Lord, I thought we were finally through with those Martians. Now what?"

"I don't blame them for giving us one last going over," a heavy set business man said to his companion. "After all, we're the last ship leaving Mars for Terra. We're damn lucky they let us go at all."

"You think there really will be war?" a young man said to the girl sitting in the seat next to him. "Those Martians won't dare fight, not with our weapons and ability to produce. We could take care of Mars in a month. It's all talk."

The girl glanced at him. "Don't be so sure. Mars is desperate. They'll fight tooth and nail. I've been on Mars three years." She shuddered. "Thank goodness I'm getting away. If—"

"Prepare to land!" the pilot's voice came. The ship began to settle slowly, dropping down toward the tiny emergency field on the seldom visited moon. Down, down the ship dropped. There was a grinding sound, a sickening jolt. Then silence.

"We've landed," the heavy set business man said. "They better not do anything to us! Terra will rip them apart if they violate one Space Article."

"Please keep your seats," the pilot's voice came. "No one is to leave the ship, according to the Martian authorities. We are to remain here."

A restless stir filled the ship. Some of the passengers began to read uneasily, others stared out at the deserted field, nervous and on edge, watching the three Martian pursuit ships land and disgorge groups of armed men.

The Martian soldiers were crossing the field quickly, moving toward them, running double time.

This Inner-Flight spaceship was the last passenger vessel to leave Mars for Terra. All other ships had long since left, returning to safety before the outbreak of hostilities. The passengers were the very last to go, the final group of Terrans to leave the grim red planet, business men, expatriates, tourists, any and all Terrans who had not already gone home.

"What do you suppose they want?" the young man said to the girl. "It's hard to figure Martians out, isn't it? First they give the ship clearance, let us take off, and now they radio us to set down again. By the way, my name's Thacher, Bob Thacher. Since we're going to be here awhile—"

The port lock opened. Talking ceased abruptly, as everyone turned. A black-clad Martian official, a Province Leiter, stood framed against the bleak sunlight, staring around the ship. Behind him a handful of Martian soldiers stood waiting, their guns ready.

"This will not take long," the Leiter said, stepping into the ship, the soldiers following him. "You will be allowed to continue your trip shortly."

An audible sigh of relief went through the passengers.

"Look at him," the girl whispered to Thacher. "How I hate those black uniforms!"

"He's just a Provincial Leiter," Thacher said. "Don't worry."

The Leiter stood for a moment, his hands on his hips, looking around at them without expression. "I have ordered your ship grounded so that an inspection can be made of all persons aboard," he said. "You Terrans are the last to leave our planet. Most of you are ordinary and harmless—I am not interested in you. I am interested in finding three saboteurs, three Terrans, two men and a woman, who have committed an incredible act of destruction and violence. They are said to have fled to this ship."

Murmurs of surprise and indignation broke out on all sides. The Leiter motioned the soldiers to follow him up the aisle.

"Two hours ago a Martian city was destroyed. Nothing remains, only a depression in the sand where the city was. The city and all its people have completely vanished. An entire city destroyed in a second! Mars will never rest until the saboteurs are captured. And we know they are aboard this ship."

"It's impossible," the heavy set business man said. "There aren't any saboteurs here."

"We'll begin with you," the Leiter said to him, stepping up beside the man's seat. One of the soldiers passed the Leiter a square metal box. "This will soon tell us if you're speaking the truth. Stand up. Get on your feet."

The man rose slowly, flushing. "See here—"

"Are you involved in the destruction of the city? Answer!"

The man swallowed angrily. "I know nothing about any destruction of any city. And furthermore—"

"He is telling the truth," the metal box said tonelessly.

"Next person." The Leiter moved down the aisle.

A thin bald headed man stood up nervously. "No sir," he said. "I don't know a thing about it."

"He is telling the truth," the box affirmed.

"Next person! Stand up!"

One person after another stood, answered, and sat down again in relief. At last there were only a few people left who had not been questioned. The Leiter paused, studying them intently.

"Only five left. The three must be among you. We have narrowed it down." His hand moved to his belt. Something flashed, a rod of pale fire. He raised the rod, pointing it steadily at the five people. "All right, the first one of you. What do you know about this destruction? Are you involved with the destruction of our city?"

"No, not at all," the man murmured.

"Yes, he's telling the truth," the box intoned.

"Next!"

"Nothing—I know nothing. I had nothing to do with it."

"True," the box said.

The ship was silent. Three people remained, a middle-aged man and his wife and their son, a boy of about twelve. They stood in the corner, staring white-faced at the Leiter, at the rod in his dark fingers.

"It must be you," the Leiter grated, moving toward them. The Martian soldiers raised their guns. "It *must* be you. You there, the boy. What do you know about the destruction of our city? Answer!"

The boy shook his head. "Nothing," he whispered.

The box was silent for a moment. "He is telling the truth," it said reluctantly.

"Next!"

"Nothing," the woman muttered. "Nothing."

"The truth."

"Next!"

"I had nothing to do with blowing up your city," the man said. "You're wasting your time."

"It is the truth," the box said.

For a long time the Leiter stood, toying with his rod. At last he pushed it back in his belt and signalled the soldiers toward the exit lock.

"You may proceed on your trip," he said. He walked after the soldiers. At the hatch he stopped, looking back at the passengers, his face grim. "You may go—But Mars will not allow her enemies to escape. The three saboteurs will be caught, I promise you." He rubbed his dark jaw thoughtfully. "It is strange. I was certain they were on this ship."

Again he looked coldly around at the Terrans.

"Perhaps I was wrong. All right, proceed! But remember: the three will be caught, even if it takes endless years. Mars will catch them and punish them! I swear it!"

❖ ❖ ❖

For a long time no one spoke. The ship lumbered through space again, its jets firing evenly, calmly, moving the passengers toward their own planet, toward home. Behind them Deimos and the red ball that was Mars dropped farther and farther away each moment, disappearing and fading into the distance.

A sigh of relief passed through the passengers. "What a lot of hot air that was," one grumbled.

"Barbarians!" a woman said.

A few of them stood up, moving out into the aisle, toward the lounge and the cocktail bar. Beside Thacher the girl got to her feet, pulling her jacket around her shoulders.

"Pardon me," she said, stepping past him.

"Going to the bar?" Thacher said. "Mind if I come along?"

"I suppose not."

They followed the others into the lounge, walking together up the aisle. "You know," Thacher said, "I don't even know your name, yet."

"My name is Mara Gordon."

"Mara? That's a nice name. What part of Terra are you from? North America? New York?"

"I've been in New York," Mara said. "New York is very lovely." She was slender and pretty, with a cloud of dark hair tumbling down her neck, against her leather jacket.

They entered the lounge and stood undecided.

"Let's sit at a table," Mara said, looking around at the people at the bar, mostly men. "Perhaps over there."

"But someone's there already," Thacher said. The heavy set business man had sat down at the table and deposited his sample case on the floor. "Do we want to sit with *him*?"

"Oh, it's all right," Mara said, crossing to the table. "May we sit here?" she said to the man.

The man looked up, half-rising. "It's a pleasure," he murmured. He studied Thacher intently. "However, a friend of mine will be joining me in a moment."

"I'm sure there's room enough for us all," Mara said. She seated herself and Thacher helped her with her chair. He sat down, too, glancing up suddenly at Mara and the business man. They were looking at each other almost as if something had passed between them. The man was middle-aged, with a florid face and tired, grey eyes. His hands were mottled with the veins showing thickly. At the moment he was tapping nervously.

"My name's Thacher," Thacher said to him, holding out his hand. "Bob Thacher. Since we're going to be together for a while we might as well get to know each other."

The man studied him. Slowly his hand came out. "Why not? My name's Erickson. Ralf Erickson."

"Erickson?" Thacher smiled. "You look like a commercial man, to me." He nodded toward the sample case on the floor. "Am I right?"

The man named Erickson started to answer, but at that moment there was a stir. A thin man of about thirty had come up to the table, his eyes bright, staring down at them warmly. "Well, we're on our way," he said to Erickson.

"Hello, Mara." He pulled out a chair and sat down quickly, folding his hands on the table before him. He noticed Thacher and drew back a little. "Pardon me," he murmured.

"Bob Thacher is my name," Thacher said. "I hope I'm not intruding here." He glanced around at the three of them, Mara, alert, watching him intently, heavyset Erickson, his face blank, and this person. "Say, do you three know each other?" he asked suddenly.

There was silence.

The robot attendant slid over soundlessly, poised to take their orders. Erickson roused himself. "Let's see," he murmured. "What will we have? Mara?"

"Whiskey and water."

"You, Jan?"

The bright slim man smiled. "The same."

"Thacher?"

"Gin and tonic."

"Whiskey and water for me, also," Erickson said. The robot attendant went off. It returned at once with the drinks, setting on the table. Each took his own. "Well," Erickson said, holding his glass up. "To our mutual success."

All drank, Thacher and the three of them, heavy set Erickson, Mara, her eyes nervous and alert, Jan, who had just come. Again a look passed between Mara and Erickson, a look so swift that he would have not caught it had he not been looking directly at her.

"What line do you represent, Mr. Erickson?" Thacher asked.

Erickson glanced at him, then down at the sample case on the floor. He grunted. "Well, as you can see, I'm a salesman."

Thacher smiled. "I knew it! You get so you can always spot a salesman right off by his sample case. A salesman always has to carry something to show. What are you in, sir?"

Erickson paused. He licked his thick lips, his eyes blank and lidded, like a toad's. At last he rubbed his mouth with his hand and reached down, lifting up the sample case. He set it on the table in front of him.

"Well?" he said. "Perhaps we might even show Mr. Thacher."

They all stared down at the sample case. It seemed to be an ordinary leather case, with a metal handle and a snap lock. "I'm getting curious," Thacher said. "What's in there? You're all so tense. Diamonds? Stolen jewels?"

Jan laughed harshly, mirthlessly. "Erick, put it down. We're not far enough away, yet."

"Nonsense," Erick rumbled. "We're away, Jan."

"Please," Mara whispered. "Wait, Erick."

"Wait? Why? What for? You're so accustomed to—"

"Erick," Mara said. She nodded toward Thacher. "We don't know him, Erick. Please!"

"He's a Terran, isn't he?" Erickson said. "All Terrans are together in these times." He fumbled suddenly at the catch lock on the case. "Yes, Mr. Thacher. I'm a salesman. We're all salesmen, the three of us."

"Then you do know each other."

"Yes." Erickson nodded. His two companions sat rigidly, staring down. "Yes, we do. Here, I'll show you our line."

He opened the case. From it he took a letter-knife, a pencil sharpener, a glass globe paperweight, a box of thumb tacks, a stapler, some clips, a plastic ashtray, and some things Thacher could not identify. He placed the objects in a row in front of him on the table top. Then he closed the sample case.

"I gather you're in office supplies," Thacher said. He touched the letter knife with his finger. "Nice quality steel. Looks like Swedish steel, to me."

Erickson nodded, looking into Thacher's face. "Not really an impressive business, is it? Office supplies. Ashtrays, paper clips." He smiled.

"Oh—" Thacher shrugged. "Why not? They're a necessity in modern business. The only thing I wonder—"

"What's that?"

"Well, I wonder how you'd ever find enough customers on Mars to make it worth your while." He paused, examining the glass paperweight. He lifted it, holding it to the light, staring at the scene within until Erickson took it out of his hand and put it back in the sample case. "And another thing. If you three know each other, why did you sit apart when you got on?"

They looked at him quickly.

"And why didn't you speak to each other until we left Deimos?" He leaned toward Erickson, smiling at him. "Two men and a woman. Three of you. Sitting apart in the ship. Not speaking, not until the check-station was past. I find myself thinking over what the Martian said. Three saboteurs. A woman and two men."

Erickson put the things back in the sample case. He was smiling, but his face had gone chalk white. Mara stared down, playing with a drop of water on the edge of her glass. Jan clenched his hands together nervously, blinking rapidly.

"You three are the ones the Leiter was after," Thacher said softly. "You are the destroyers, the saboteurs. But their lie detector— Why didn't it trap you? How did you get by that? And now you're safe, outside the check-station." He grinned, staring around at them. "I'll be damned! And I really thought you were a salesman, Erickson. You really fooled me."

Erickson relaxed a little. "Well, Mr. Thacher, it's in a good cause. I'm sure you have no love for Mars, either. No Terran does. And I see you're leaving with the rest of us."

"True," Thacher said. "You must certainly have an interesting account to give, the three of you." He looked around the table.

"We still have an hour or so of travel. Sometimes it gets dull, this Mars-Terra run. Nothing to see, nothing to do but sit and drink in the lounge." He raised his eyes slowly. "Any chance you'd like to spin a story to keep us awake?"

Jan and Mara looked at Erickson. "Go on," Jan said. "He knows who we are. Tell him the rest of the story."

"You might as well," Mara said.

Jan let out a sigh suddenly, a sigh of relief. "Let's put the cards on the table, get this weight off us. I'm tired of sneaking around, slipping—"

"Sure," Erickson said expansively. "Why not?" He settled back in his chair, unbuttoning his vest. "Certainly, Mr. Thacher. I'll be glad to spin you a story. And I'm sure it will be interesting enough to keep you awake."

❖ ❖ ❖

They ran through the groves of dead trees, leaping across the sun-baked Martian soil, running silently together. They went up a little rise, across a narrow ridge. Suddenly Erick stopped, throwing himself down flat on the ground. The others did the same, pressing themselves against the soil, gasping for breath.

"Be silent," Erick muttered. He raised himself a little. "No noise. There'll be Leiters nearby, from now on. We don't dare take any chances."

Between the three people lying in the grove of dead trees and the City was a barren, level waste of desert, over a mile of blasted sand. No trees or bushes marred the smooth, parched surface. Only an occasional wind, a dry wind eddying and twisting, blew the sand up into little rills. A faint odor came to them, a bitter smell of heat and sand, carried by the wind.

Erick pointed. "Look. The City— There it is."

They stared, still breathing deeply from their race through the trees. The City was close, closer than they had ever seen it before.

Never had they gotten so close to it in times past. Terrans were never allowed near the great Martian cities, the centers of Martian life. Even in ordinary times, when there was no threat of approaching war, the Martians shrewdly kept all Terrans away from their citadels, partly from fear, partly from a deep, innate sense of hostility toward the white-skinned visitors whose commercial ventures had earned them the respect, and the dislike, of the whole system.

"How does it look to you?" Erick said.

The City was huge, much larger than they had imagined from the drawings and models they had studied so carefully back in New York, in the War Ministry Office. Huge it was, huge and stark, black towers rising up against the sky, incredibly thin columns of ancient metal, columns that had stood wind and sun for centuries. Around the City was a wall of stone, red stone, immense bricks that had been lugged there and fitted into place by slaves of the early Martian dynasties, under the whiplash of the first great Kings of Mars.

An ancient, sun-baked City, a City set in the middle of a wasted plain, beyond groves of dead trees, a City seldom seen by Terrans—but a City studied on maps and charts in every War Office on Terra. A City that contained, for all its ancient stone and archaic towers, the ruling group of all Mars, the Council of Senior Leiters, black-clad men who governed and ruled with an iron hand.

The Senior Leiters, twelve fanatic and devoted men, black priests, but priests with flashing rods of fire, lie detectors, rocket ships, intra-space cannon, many more things the Terran Senate could only conjecture about. The Senior Leiters and their subordinate Province Leiters—Erick and the two behind him suppressed a shudder.

"We've got to be careful," Erick said again. "We'll be passing among them, soon. If they guess who we are, or what we're here for—"

He snapped open the case he carried, glancing inside for a second. Then he closed it again, grasping the handle firmly. "Let's go," he said. He stood up slowly. "You two come up beside me. I want to make sure you look the way you should."

Mara and Jan stepped quickly ahead. Erick studied them critically as the three of them walked slowly down the slope, onto the plain, toward the towering black spires of the City.

"Jan," Erick said. "Take hold of her hand! Remember, you're going to marry her; she's your bride. And Martian peasants think a lot of their brides."

Jan was dressed in the short trousers and coat of the Martian farmer, a knotted rope tied around his waist, a hat on his head to keep off the sun. His skin was dark, colored by dye until it was almost bronze.

"You look fine," Erick said to him. He glanced at Mara. Her black hair was tied in a knot, looped through a hollowed-out yuke bone. Her face was dark, too, dark and lined with colored ceremonial pigment, green and orange stripes across her cheeks. Earrings were strung through her ears. On her feet were tiny slippers of perruh hide, laced around her ankles, and she wore long translucent Martian trousers with a bright sash tied around her waist. Between her small breasts a chain of stone beads rested, good-luck charms for the coming marriage.

"All right," Erick said. He, himself, wore the flowing gray robe of a Martian priest, dirty robes that were supposed to remain on him all his life, to be buried around him when he died. "I think we'll get past the guards. There should be heavy traffic on the road."

They walked on, the hard sand crunching under their feet. Against the horizon they could see specks moving, other persons going toward the City, farmers and peasants and merchants, bringing their crops and goods to market.

"See the cart!" Mara exclaimed.

They were nearing a narrow road, two ruts worn into the sand. A Martian hufa was pulling the cart, its great sides wet with perspiration, its tongue hanging out. The cart was piled high with bales of cloth, rough country cloth, hand dipped. A bent farmer urged the hufa on.

"And there." She pointed, smiling.

A group of merchants riding small animals were moving along behind the cart, Martians in long robes, their faces hidden by sand masks. On each animal was a pack, carefully tied on with rope. And beyond the merchants, plodding dully along, were peasants and farmers in an endless procession, some riding carts or animals, but mostly on foot.

Mara and Jan and Erick joined the line of people, melting in behind the merchants. No one noticed them; no one looked up or gave any sign. The march continued as before. Neither Jan nor Mara said anything to each other. They walked a little behind Erick, who paced with a certain dignity, a certain bearing becoming his position.

Once he slowed down, pointing up at the sky. "Look," he murmured, in the Martian hill dialect. "See that?"

Two black dots circled lazily. Martian patrol craft, the military on the outlook for any sign of unusual activity. War was almost ready to break out with Terra. Any day, almost any moment.

"We'll be just in time," Erick said. "Tomorrow will be too late. The last ship will have left Mars."

"I hope nothing stops us," Mara said. "I want to get back home when we're through."

❖ ❖ ❖

Half an hour passed. They neared the City, the wall growing as they walked, rising higher and higher until it seemed to blot out the sky itself. A vast wall, a wall of eternal stone that had felt the wind and sun for centuries. A group of Martian soldiers were standing at the entrance, the single passage-gate hewn into the rock, leading to the City. As each person went through the soldiers examined him, poking his garments, looking into his load.

Erick tensed. The line had slowed almost to a halt. "It'll be our turn, soon," he murmured. "Be prepared."

"Let's hope no Leiters come around," Jan said. "The soldiers aren't so bad."

Mara was staring up at the wall and the towers beyond. Under their feet the ground trembled, vibrating and shaking. She could see tongues of flame rising from the towers, from the deep underground factories and forges of the City. The air was thick and dense with particles of soot. Mara rubbed her mouth, coughing.

"Here they come," Erick said softly.

The merchants had been examined and allowed to pass through the dark gate, the entrance through the wall into the City. They and their silent animals had already disappeared inside. The leader of the group of soldiers was beckoning impatiently to Erick, waving him on.

"Come along!" he said. "Hurry up there, old man."

Erick advanced slowly, his arms wrapped around his body, looking down at the ground.

"Who are you and what's your business here?" the soldier demanded, his hands on his hips, his gun hanging idly at his waist. Most of the soldiers were lounging lazily, leaning against the wall, some even squatting in the shade. Flies crawled on the face of one who had fallen asleep, his gun on the ground beside him.

"My business?" Erick murmured. "I am a village priest."

"Why do you want to enter the City?"

"I must bring these two people before the magistrate to marry them." He indicated Mara and Jan, standing a little behind him. "That is the Law the Leiters have made."

The soldier laughed. He circled around Erick. "What do you have in that bag you carry?"

"Laundry. We stay the night."

"What village are you from?"

"Kranos."

"Kranos?" The soldier looked to a companion. "Ever heard of Kranos?"

"A backward pig sty. I saw it once on a hunting trip."

The leader of the soldiers nodded to Jan and Mara. The two of them advanced, their hands clasped, standing close together. One of the soldiers put his hand on Mara's bare shoulder, turning her around.

"Nice little wife you're getting," he said. "Good and firm looking." He winked, grinning lewdly.

Jan glanced at him in sullen resentment. The soldiers guffawed. "All right," the leader said to Erick. "You people can pass."

Erick took a small purse from his robes and gave the soldier a coin. Then the three of them went into the dark tunnel that was the entrance, passing through the wall of stones, into the City beyond.

They were within the City!

"Now," Erick whispered. "Hurry."

Around them the City roared and cracked, the sound of a thousand vents and machines, shaking the stones under their feet. Erick led Mara and Jan into a corner, by a row of brick warehouses. People were everywhere, hurrying back and forth, shouting above the din, merchants, peddlers, soldiers, street women. Erick bent down and opened the case he carried. From the case he quickly took three small coils of fine metal, intricate meshed wires and vanes worked together into a small cone. Jan took one and Mara took one. Erick put the remaining cone into his robe and snapped the case shut again.

"Now remember, the coils must be buried in such a way that the line runs through the center of the City. We must trisect the main section, where the largest concentration of buildings is. Remember the maps! Watch the alleys and streets carefully. Talk to no one if you can help it. Each of you has enough Martian money to buy your way out of trouble. Watch especially for cut-purses, and for heaven's sake, don't get lost."

Erick broke off. Two black-clad Leiters were coming along the inside of the wall, strolling together with their hands behind their backs. They noticed the three who stood in the corner by the warehouses and stopped.

"Go," Erick muttered. "And be back here at sundown." He smiled grimly. "Or never come back."

Each went off in a different way, walking quickly without looking back. The Leiters watched them go. "The little bride was quite lovely," one Leiter said. "Those hill people have the stamp of nobility in their blood, from the old times."

"A very lucky young peasant to possess her," the other said. They went on. Erick looked after them, still smiling a little. Then he joined the surging mass of people that milled eternally through the streets of the City.

At dusk they met outside the gate. The sun was soon to set, and the air had turned thin and frigid. It cut through their clothing like knives.

Mara huddled against Jan, trembling and rubbing her bare arms.

"Well?" Erick said. "Did you both succeed?"

Around them peasants and merchants were pouring from the entrance, leaving the City to return to their farms and villages, starting the long trip back across the plain toward the hills beyond. None of them noticed the shivering girl and the young man and the old priest standing by the wall.

"Mine's in place," Jan said. "On the other side of the City, on the extreme edge. Buried by a well."

"Mine's in the industrial section," Mara whispered, her teeth chattering. "Jan, give me something to put over me! I'm freezing."

"Good," Erick said. "Then the three coils should trisect dead center, if the models were correct." He looked up at the darkening sky. Already, stars were beginning to show. Two dots, the evening patrol, moved slowly toward the horizon. "Let's hurry. It won't be long."

They joined the line of Martians moving along the road, away from the City. Behind them the City was losing itself in the somber tones of night, its black spires disappearing into darkness.

They walked silently with the country people until the flat ridge of dead trees became visible on the horizon. Then they left the road and turned off, walking toward the trees.

"Almost time!" Erick said. He increased his pace, looking back at Jan and Mara impatiently.

"Come on!"

They hurried, making their way through the twilight, stumbling over rocks and dead branches, up the side of the ridge. At the top Erick halted, standing with his hands on his hips, looking back.

"See," he murmured. "The City. The last time we'll ever see it this way."

"Can I sit down," Mara said. "My feet hurt me."

Jan pulled at Erick's sleeve. "Hurry, Erick! Not much time left." He laughed nervously. "If everything goes right we'll be able to look at it—forever."

"But not like this," Erick murmured. He squatted down, snapping his case open. He took some tubes and wiring out and assembled them together on the ground, at the peak of the ridge. A small pyramid of wire and plastic grew, shaped by his expert hands.

At last he grunted, standing up. "All right."

"Is it pointed directly at the City?" Mara asked anxiously, looking down at the pyramid.

Erick nodded. "Yes, it's placed according—" He stopped, suddenly stiffening. "Get back! It's time! *Hurry!*"

Jan ran, down the far side of the slope, away from the City, pulling Mara with him. Erick came quickly after, still looking back at the distant spires, almost lost in the night sky.

"Down."

Jan sprawled out, Mara beside him, her trembling body pressed against his. Erick settled down into the sand and dead branches, still trying to see. "I want to see it," he murmured. "A miracle. I want to see—"

A flash, a blinding burst of violet light, lit up the sky. Erick clapped his hands over his eyes. The flash whitened, growing larger, expanding. Suddenly there was a roar, and a furious hot wind rushed past him, throwing him on his face in the sand. The hot dry wind licked and seared at them, crackling the bits of branches into flame. Mara and Jan shut their eyes, pressed tightly together.

"God—" Erick muttered.

The storm passed. They opened their eyes slowly. The sky was still alive with fire, a drifting cloud of sparks that was beginning to dissipate with the night wind. Erick stood up unsteadily, helping Jan and Mara to their feet. The three of them stood, staring silently across the dark waste, the black plain, none of them speaking.

The City was gone.

At last Erick turned away. "That part's done," he said. "Now the rest! Give me a hand, Jan. There'll be a thousand patrol ships around here in a minute."

"I see one already," Mara said, pointing up. A spot winked in the sky, a rapidly moving spot. "They're coming, Erick." There was a throb of chill fear in her voice.

"I know." Erick and Jan squatted on the ground around the pyramid of tubes and plastic, pulling the pyramid apart. The pyramid was fused, fused together like molten glass. Erick tore the pieces away with trembling fingers. From the remains of the pyramid he pulled something forth, something he held up high, trying to make it out in the darkness. Jan and Mara came close to see, both staring up intently, almost without breath.

"There it is," Erick said. "There!"

In his hand was a globe, a small transparent globe of glass. Within the glass something moved, something minute and fragile, spires almost too small to be seen, microscopic, a complex web swimming within the hollow glass globe. A web of spires. A city.

Erick put the globe into the case and snapped it shut. "Let's go," he said. They began to lope back through the trees, back the way they had come before. "We'll change in the car," he said as they ran. "I think we should keep these clothes on until we're actually inside the car. We still might encounter someone."

"I'll be glad to get my own clothing on again," Jan said. "I feel funny in these little pants."

"How do you think I feel?" Mara gasped. "I'm freezing in this, what there is of it."

"All young Martian brides dress that way," Erick said. He clutched the case tightly as they ran. "I think it looks fine."

"Thank you," Mara said. "But it is cold."

"What do you suppose they'll think?" Jan asked. "They'll assume the City was destroyed, won't they? That's certain."

"Yes," Erick said. "They'll be sure it was blown up. We can count on that. And it will be damn important to us that they think so!"

"The car should be around here, someplace," Mara said, slowing down.

"No. Farther on," Erick said. "Past that little hill over there. In the ravine, by the trees. It's so hard to see where we are."

"Shall I light something?" Jan said.

"No. There may be patrols around who—"

He halted abruptly. Jan and Mara stopped beside him. "What—" Mara begin.

A light glimmered. Something stirred in the darkness. There was a sound.

"Quick!" Erick rasped. He dropped, throwing the case far away from him into the bushes. He straightened up tensely.

A figure loomed up, moving through the darkness, and behind it came more figures, men, soldiers in uniform. The light flashed up brightly, blinding them. Erick closed his eyes. The light left him, touching Mara and Jan, standing silently together, clasping hands. Then it flicked down to the ground and around in a circle.

A Leiter stepped forward, a tall figure in black, with his soldiers close behind him, their guns ready. "You three," the Leiter said. "Who are you? Don't move. Stand where you are."

He came up to Erick, peering at him intently, his hard Martian face without expression. He went all around Erick, examining his robes, his sleeves.

"Please—" Erick began in a quavering voice, but the Leiter cut him off.

"I'll do the talking. Who are you three? What are you doing here? Speak up."

"We—we are going back to our village," Erick muttered, staring down, his hands folded. "We were in the City, and now we are going home."

One of the soldiers spoke into a mouthpiece. He clicked it off and put it away.

"Come with me," the Leiter said. "We're taking you in. Hurry along."

"In? Back to the City?"

One of the soldiers laughed. "The City is gone," he said. "All that's left of it you can put in the palm of your hand."

"But what happened?" Mara said.

"No one knows. Come on, hurry it up!"

There was a sound. A soldier came quickly out of the darkness. "A Senior Leiter," he said. "Coming this way." He disappeared again.

❖ ❖ ❖

"A Senior Leiter." The soldiers stood waiting, standing at a respectful attention. A moment later the Senior Leiter stepped into the light, a black-clad old man, his ancient face thin and hard, like a bird's, eyes bright and alert. He looked from Erick to Jan.

"Who are these people?" he demanded.

"Villagers going back home."

"No they're not. They don't stand like villagers. Villagers slump— diet poor food. These people are not villagers. I myself came from the hills, and I know."

He stepped close to Erick, looking keenly into his face. "Who are you? Look at his chin—he never shaved with a sharpened stone! Something is wrong here."

In his hand a rod of pale fire flashed. "The City is gone, and with it at least half the Leiter Council. It is very strange, a flash, then heat, and a wind. But it was not fission. I am puzzled. All at once the City has vanished. Nothing is left but a depression in the sand."

"We'll take them in," the other Leiter said. "Soldiers, surround them. Make certain that—"

"Run!" Erick cried. He struck out, knocking the rod from the Senior Leiter's hand. They were all running, soldiers shouting, flashing their lights, stumbling against each other in the darkness. Erick dropped to his knees, groping frantically in the bushes. His fingers closed over the handle of the case and he leaped up. In Terran he shouted to Mara and Jan.

"Hurry! To the car! Run!" He set off, down the slope, stumbling through the darkness. He could hear soldiers behind him, soldiers running and falling. A body collided against him and he struck out. Someplace behind him there was a hiss, and a section of the slope went up in flames. The Leiter's rod—

"Erick," Mara cried from the darkness. He ran toward her. Suddenly he slipped, falling on a stone. Confusion and firing. The sound of excited voices.

"Erick, is that you?" Jan caught hold of him, helping him up. "The car. It's over here. Where's Mara?"

"I'm here," Mara's voice came. "Over here, by the car."

A light flashed. A tree went up in a puff of fire, and Erick felt the singe of the heat against his face. He and Jan made their way toward the girl. Mara's hand caught his in the darkness.

"Now the car," Erick said. "If they haven't got to it." He slid down the slope into the ravine, fumbling in the darkness, reaching and holding onto the handle of the case. Reaching, reaching—

He touched something cold and smooth. Metal, a metal door handle. Relief flooded through him. "I've found it! Jan, get inside.

Mara, come on." He pushed Jan past him, into the car. Mara slipped in after Jan, her small agile body crowding in beside him.

"Stop!" a voice shouted from above. "There's no use hiding in that ravine. We'll get you! Come up and—"

The sound of voices was drowned out by the roar of the car's motor. A moment later they shot into the darkness, the car rising into the air. Treetops broke and cracked under them as Erick turned the car from side to side, avoiding the groping shafts of pale light from below, the last furious thrusts from the two Leiters and their soldiers.

Then they were away, above the trees, high in the air, gaining speed each moment, leaving the knot of Martians far behind.

"Toward Marsport," Jan said to Erick. "Right?"

Erick nodded. "Yes. We'll land outside the field, in the hills. We can change back to our regular clothing there, our commercial clothing. Damn it—we'll be lucky if we can get there in time for the ship."

"The last ship," Mara whispered, her chest rising and falling. "What if we don't get there in time?"

Erick looked down at the leather case in his lap. "We'll have to get there," he murmured. "We must!"

❖ ❖ ❖

For a long time there was silence. Thacher stared at Erickson. The older man was leaning back in his chair, sipping a little of his drink. Mara and Jan were silent.

"So you didn't destroy the City," Thacher said. "You didn't destroy it at all. You shrank it down and put it in a glass globe, in a paperweight. And now you're salesmen again, with a sample case of office supplies!"

Erickson smiled. He opened the briefcase and reaching into it he brought out the glass globe paperweight. He held it up, looking into it. "Yes, we stole the City from the Martians. That's how we got by the lie detector. It was true that we knew nothing about a *destroyed* City."

"But why?" Thacher said. "Why steal a City? Why not merely bomb it?"

"Ransom," Mara said fervently, gazing into the globe, her dark eyes bright. "Their biggest City, half of the Council—in Erick's hand!"

"Mars will have to do what Terra asks," Erickson said. "Now Terra will be able to make her commercial demands felt. Maybe there won't even be a war. Perhaps Terra will get her way without fighting." Still smiling, he put the globe back into the briefcase and locked it.

"Quite a story," Thacher said. "What an amazing process, reduction of size— A whole City reduced to microscopic dimensions. Amazing. No wonder you were able to escape. With such daring as that, no one could hope to stop you."

He looked down at the briefcase on the floor. Underneath them the jets murmured and vibrated evenly, as the ship moved through space toward distant Terra.

"We still have quite a way to go," Jan said. "You've heard our story, Thacher. Why not tell us yours? What sort of line are you in? What's your business?"

"Yes," Mara said. "What do you do?"

"What do I do?" Thacher said. "Well, if you like, I'll show you." He reached into his coat and brought out something. Something that flashed and glinted, something slender. A rod of pale fire.

The three stared at it. Sickened shock settled over them slowly.

Thacher held the rod loosely, calmly, pointing it at Erickson. "We knew you three were on this ship," he said. "There was not doubt of that. But we did not know what had become of the City. My theory was that the City had not been destroyed at all, that something else had happened to it. Council instruments measured a sudden loss of mass in that area, a decrease equal to the mass of the City. Somehow the City had been spirited away, not destroyed. But I could not convince the other Council Leiters of it. I had to follow you alone."

Thacher turned a little, nodding to the men sitting at the bar. The men rose at once, coming toward the table.

"A very interesting process you have. Mars will benefit a great deal from it. Perhaps it will even turn the tide in our favor. When we return to Marsport I wish to begin work on it at once. And now, if you will please pass me the briefcase—"

MEDDLER

They entered the great chamber. At the far end, technicians hovered around an immense illuminated board, following a complex pattern of lights that shifted rapidly, flashing through seemingly endless combinations. At long tables machines whirred—computers, human-operated and robot. Wall-charts covered every inch of vertical space. Hasten gazed around him in amazement.

Wood laughed. "Come over here and I'll really show you something. You recognize *this*, don't you?" He pointed to a hulking machine surrounded by silent men and women in white lab robes.

"I recognize it," Hasten said slowly. "It's something like our own Dip, but perhaps twenty times larger. What do you haul up? And *when* do you haul?" He fingered the surface-plate of the Dip, then squatted down, peering into the maw. The maw was locked shut; the Dip was in operation. "You know, if we had any idea this existed, Histo-Research would have—"

"You know now." Wood bent down beside him. "Listen. Hasten, you're the first man from outside the Department ever to get into this room. You saw the guards. No one gets in here unauthorized; the guards have orders to kill anyone trying to enter illegally."

"To hide this? A machine? You'd shoot to—"

They stood, Wood facing him, his jaw hard. "*Your* Dip digs back into antiquity. Rome. Greece. Dust and old volumes." Wood touched the big Dip beside them. "This Dip is different. We guard it with our lives, and anyone else's lives; do you know why?"

Hasten stared at it.

"This Dip is set, not for antiquity, but—for the future." Wood looked directly into Hasten's face. "Do you understand? The future."

"You're dredging the future? But you can't! It's forbidden by law; you know that!" Hasten drew back. "If the Executive Council knew this they'd break this building apart. You know the dangers. Berkowsky himself demonstrated them in his original thesis."

Hasten paced angrily. "I can't understand you, using a future oriented Dip. When you pull material from the future you automatically introduce new factors into the present; the future is altered—you start a never-ending shift. The more you dip the more new factors are brought in. You create unstable conditions for centuries to come. That's why the law was passed."

Wood nodded. "I know."

"And you still keep dipping?" Hasten gestured at the machine and the technicians. "Stop, for God's sake! Stop before you introduce some lethal element that can't be erased. Why do you keep—"

Wood sagged suddenly. "All right, Hasten, don't lecture us. It's too late; it's already happened. A lethal factor was introduced in our first experiments. We thought we knew what we were doing . . . " He looked up. "And that's why you were brought here. Sit down—you're going to hear all about it."

❖ ❖ ❖

They faced each other across the desk. Wood folded his hands. "I'm going to put it straight on the line. You are considered an expert, *the* expert at Histo-Research. You know more about using a Time Dip than anyone alive; that's why you've been shown our work, our illegal work."

"And you've already got into trouble?"

"Plenty of trouble, and every attempt to meddle further makes it that much worse. Unless we do something, we'll be the most culpable organization in history."

"Please start at the beginning," Hasten said.

"The Dip was authorized by the Political Science Council; they wanted to know the results of some of their decisions. At first we objected, giving Berkowsky's theory; but the idea is hypnotic, you know. We gave in, and the Dip was built—secretly, of course.

"We made our first dredge about one year hence. To protect ourselves against Berkowsky's factor we tried a subterfuge; we actually brought nothing back. This Dip is geared to pick up nothing. No object is scooped; it merely photographs from a high altitude. The film comes back to us and we make enlargements and try to gestalt the conditions.

"Results were all right, at first. No more wars, cities growing, much better looking. Blow-ups of street scenes show many people, well-content, apparently. Pace a little slower.

"Then we went ahead fifty years. Even better: cities on the decrease. People not so dependent on machines. More grass, parks. Same general conditions, peace, happiness, much leisure. Less frenetic waste, hurry.

"We went on, skipping ahead. Of course, with such an indirect viewing method we couldn't be certain of anything, but it all looked fine. We relayed our information to the Council and they went ahead with their planning. And then it happened."

"What, exactly?" Hasten said, leaning forward.

"We decided to revisit a period we had already photographed, about a hundred years hence. We sent out the Dip, got it back with a full reel. The men developed it and we watched the run." Wood paused.

"And?"

"And it wasn't the same. It was different. Everything was changed. War—war and destruction everywhere." Wood shuddered. "We were appalled; we sent the Dip back at once to make absolutely certain."

"And what did you find this time?"

Wood's fists clenched. "Changed again, and for worse! Ruins, vast ruins. People poking around. Ruin and death everywhere. Slag. The *end* of war, the last phase."

"I see," Hasten said, nodding.

"That's not the worst! We conveyed the news to the Council. It ceased all activity and went into a two-week conference; it canceled all ordinances and withdrew every plan formed on the basis of our reports. It was a month before the Council got in touch with us again. The members wanted us to try once more, take one more Dip to the same period. We said no, but they insisted. It could be no worse, they argued.

"So we sent the Dip out again. It came back and we ran the film. Hasten, there are things worse than war. You wouldn't believe what we saw. There was no human life; none at all, not a single human being."

"Everything was destroyed?"

"No! No destruction, cities big and stately, roads, buildings, lakes, fields. But no human life; the cities empty, functioning mechanically, every machine and wire untouched. But no living people."

"What was it?"

"We sent the Dip on ahead, at fifty year leaps. Nothing. Nothing each time. Cities, roads, buildings, but no human life. Everyone dead. Plague, radiation, or what, we don't know. But *something* killed them. Where did it come from? We don't know. It wasn't there at first, not in our original dips.

"Somehow, *we* introduced it, the lethal factor. *We* brought it, with our meddling. It wasn't there when we started; it was done by us, Hasten." Wood stared at him, his face a white mask. "We brought it and now we've got to find what it is and get rid of it."

"How are you going to do that?"

"We've built a Time Car, capable of carrying one human observer into the future. We're sending a man there to see what it is. Photographs don't tell us enough; we have to know more! When did it first appear? How? What were the first signs? *What is it?* Once we know, maybe we can eliminate it, the factor, trace it down and remove it. Someone must go into the future and find out what it was we began. It's the only way."

Woods stood up, and Hasten rose, too.

"You're that person," Wood said. "You're going, the most competent person available. The Time Car is outside, in an open square, carefully guarded." Wood gave a signal. Two soldiers came toward the desk.

"Sir?"

"Come with us," Wood said. "We're going outside to the square; make sure no one follows after us." He turned to Hasten. "Ready?"

Hasten hesitated. "Wait a minute. I'll have to go over your work, study what's been done. Examine the Time Car itself. I can't—"

The two soldiers moved closer, looking to Wood. Wood put his hand on Hasten's shoulder. "I'm sorry," he said, "we have no time to waste; come along with me."

❖ ❖ ❖

All around him blackness moved, swirling toward him and then receding. He sat down on the stool before the bank of controls, wiping the perspiration from his face. He was on his way, for better or worse. Briefly, Wood had outlined the operation of the Time Car. A few moments of instruction, the controls set for him, and then the metal door slammed behind him.

Hasten looked around him. It was cold in the sphere; the air was thin and chilly. He watched the moving dials for a while, but presently the cold began to make him uncomfortable. He went over to the equipment-locker and slid the door back. A jacket, a heavy jacket, and a flash gun. He held the gun for a minute, studying it. And tools, all kinds of tools and equipment. He was just putting the gun away when the dull chugging under him suddenly ceased. For one terrible second he was floating, drifting aimlessly, then the feeling was gone.

Sunlight flowed through the window, spreading out over the floor. He snapped the artificial lights off and went to the window to see. Wood had set the controls for a hundred years hence; bracing himself, he looked out.

A meadow, flowers and grass, rolling off into the distance. Blue sky and wandering clouds. Some animals grazed a long way off, standing together in the shade of a tree. He went to the door and unlocked it, stepping out. Warm sunlight struck him, and he felt better at once. Now he could see the animals were cows.

He stood for a long time at the door, his hands on his hips. Could the plague have been bacterial? Air-carried? If it *were* a plague. He reached up, feeling the protective helmet on his shoulders. Better to keep it on.

He went back and got the gun from the locker. Then he returned to the lip of the sphere, checked the door-lock to be certain it would remain closed during his absence. Only then, Hasten stepped down onto the grass of the meadow. He closed the door and looked around him. Presently he began to walk quickly away from the sphere, toward the top of a long hill that stretched out half a mile away. As he strode along, he examined the click-band on his wrist which would guide him back to the metal sphere, the Time Car, if he could not find the way himself.

He came to the cows, passing by their tree. The cows got up and moved away from him. He noticed something that gave him a sudden chill; their udders were small and wrinkled. Not herd cows.

When he reached the top of the hill he stopped, lifting his glasses from his waist. The earth fell away, mile after mile of it, dry green fields without pattern or design, rolling like waves as far as the eye could see. Nothing else? He turned, sweeping the horizon.

He stiffened, adjusting the sight. Far off to the left, at the very limit of vision, the vague perpendiculars of a city rose up. He lowered the glasses and hitched up his heavy boots. Then he walked down the other side of the hill, taking big steps; he had a long way to go.

❖ ❖ ❖

Hasten had not walked more than half an hour when he saw butter-flies. They rose up suddenly a few yards in front of him, dancing and fluttering in the sunlight. He stopped to rest, watching them. They were all colors, red and blue, with splashes of yellow and green. They were the largest butterflies he had ever seen. Perhaps they had come from some zoo, escaped and bred wild after man left the scene. The butterflies rose higher and higher in the air. They took no notice of him but struck out toward the distant spires of the city; in a moment they were gone.

Hasten started up again. It was hard to imagine the death of man in such circumstances, butterflies and grass and cows in the shade. What a quiet and lovely world was left, without the human race!

Suddenly one last butterfly fluttered up, almost in his face, rising quickly from the grass. He put his arm up automatically, batting at it. The butterfly dashed against his hand. He began to laugh—

Pain made him sick; he fell half to his knees, gasping and retching. He rolled over on his face, hunching himself up, burying his face in the ground. His arm ached, and pain knotted him up; his head swam and he closed his eyes.

When Hasten turned over at last, the butterfly was gone; it had not lingered.

He lay for a time in the grass, then he sat up slowly, getting shakily to his feet. He stripped off his shirt and examined his hand and wrist. The flesh was black, hard and already swelling. He glanced down at it and then at the distant city. The butterflies had gone there . . .

He made his way back to the Time Car.

❖ ❖ ❖

Hasten reached the sphere a little after the sun had begun to drop into evening darkness. The door slid back to his touch and he stepped inside. He dressed his hand and arm with salve from the medicine kit and then sat down on the stool, deep in thought, staring at his arm. A small sting, accidental, in fact. The butterfly had not even noticed. Suppose the whole pack—

He waited until the sun had completely set and it was pitch black outside the sphere. At night all the bees and butterflies disappeared; or at least, those he knew did. Well, he would have to take a chance. His arm still ached dully, throbbing without respite. The salve had done no good; he felt dizzy, and there was a fever taste in his mouth.

Before he went out he opened the locker and brought all the things out. He examined the flash gun but put it aside. A moment later he found what he wanted. A blowtorch, and a flashlight. He put all the other things back and stood up. Now he was ready—if that were the word for it. As ready as he would ever be.

He stepped out into the darkness, flashing the light ahead of him. He walked quickly. It was a dark and lonely night; only a few stars shone above him, and his was the only earthly light. He passed up the hill and down the other side. A grove of trees loomed up, and then he was on a level plain, feeling his way toward the city by the beam of the flashlight.

❖ ❖ ❖

When he reached the city he was very tired. He had gone a long way, and his breath was beginning to come hard. Huge ghostly outlines rose up ahead of him, disappearing above, vanishing into darkness. It was not a large city, apparently, but its design was strange to Hasten, more vertical and slim than he was used to.

He went through the gate. Grass was growing from the stone pavement of the streets. He stopped, looking down. Grass and weeds everywhere; and in the corners, by the buildings were bones, little heaps of bones and dust. He walked on, flashing his light against the sides of the slender buildings. His footsteps echoed hollowly. There was no light except his own.

The buildings began to thin out. Soon he found himself entering a great tangled square, overgrown with bushes and vines. At the far end a building larger than the others rose. He walked toward it, across the empty, desolate square, flashing his light from side to side. He walked up a half-buried step and onto a concrete plaza. All at once he stopped. To his right, another building reared up, catching his attention. His heart thudded. Above the doorway his light made out a word cut expertly into the arch:

Bibliotheca

This was what he wanted, the library. He went up the steps toward the dark entrance. Wood boards gave under his feet. He reached the entrance and found himself facing a heavy wood door with metal handles. When he took hold of the handles the door fell toward him, crashing past him, down the steps and into the darkness. The odor of decay and dust choked him.

He went inside. Spider webs brushed against his helmet as he passed along silent halls. He chose a room at random and entered it. Here were more heaps of dust and gray bits of bones. Low tables and shelves ran along the walls. He went to the shelves and took down a handful of books. They powdered and broke in his hands, showering bits of paper and thread onto him. Had only a century passed since his own time?

❖ ❖ ❖

Hasten sat down at one of the tables and opened one of the books that was in better condition. The words were no language he knew, a Romance language that he knew must be artificial. He turned page after page. At last he took a handful of books at random and moved back toward the door. Suddenly his heart jumped. He went over to the wall, his hands trembling. Newspapers.

He took the brittle, cracking sheets carefully down, holding them to the light. The same language, of course. Bold, black headlines. He managed to roll some of the papers together and add them to his load of books. Then he went through the door, out into the corridor, back the way he had come.

When he stepped out onto the steps cold fresh air struck him, tingling his nose. He looked around at the dim outlines rising up on all sides of the square. Then he walked down and across the square, feeling his way carefully along. He came to the gate of the city, and a moment later he was outside, on the flat plain again, heading back toward the Time Car.

For an endless time he walked, his head bent down, plodding along. Finally fatigue made him stop, swaying back and forth, breathing deeply. He set down his load and looked around him. Far off, at the edge of the horizon, a long streak of gray had appeared, silently coming into existence while he was walking. Dawn. The sun coming up.

A cold wind moved through the air, eddying against him. In the forming gray light the trees and hills were beginning to take shape, a hard, unbending outline. He turned toward the city. Bleak and thin, the shafts of the deserted buildings stuck up. For a moment he watched, fascinated by the first color of day as it struck the shafts and towers. Then the color faded, and a drifting mist moved between him and the city. All at once he bent down and grabbed up his load. He began to walk, hurrying as best he could, chill fear moving through him.

From the city a black speck had leaped up into the sky and was hovering over it.

❖❖❖

After a time, a long time, Hasten looked back. The speck was still there—but it had grown. And it was no longer black; in the clear light of day the speck was beginning to flash, shining with many colors.

He increased his pace; he went down the side of a hill and up another. For a second he paused to snap on his click-band. It spoke loudly; he was not far from the sphere. He waved his arm and the clicks rose and fell. To the right. Wiping the perspiration from his hands he went on.

A few minutes later he looked down from the top of a ridge and saw a gleaming metal sphere resting silently on the grass, dripping with cold dew from the night. The Time Car; sliding and running, he leaped down the hill toward it.

He was just pushing the door open with his shoulder when the first cloud of butterflies appeared at the top of the hill, moving quietly toward him.

He locked the door and set his armload down, flexing his muscles. His hand ached, burning now with an intense pain. He had no time for that—he hurried to the window and peered out. The butterflies were swarming toward the sphere, darting and dancing above him, flashing with color. They began to settle down onto the metal, even onto the window. Abruptly, his gaze was cut off by gleaming bodies, soft and pulpy, their beating wings mashed together. He listened. He could hear them, a muffled, echoing sound that came from all sides of him. The interior of the sphere dimmed into darkness as the butterflies sealed off the window. He lit the artificial lights.

Time passed. He examined the newspapers, uncertain of what to do. Go back? Or ahead? Better jump ahead fifty years or so. The butterflies were dangerous, but perhaps not the real thing, the lethal factor that he was looking for. He looked at his hand. The skin was black and hard, a dead area was increasing. A faint shadow of worry went through him; it was getting worse, not better.

The scratching sound on all sides of him began to annoy him, filling him with an uneasy restlessness. He put down the books and paced back and forth. How could insects, even immense insects such as these, destroy the human race? Surely human beings could combat them. Dusts, poisons, sprays.

A bit of metal, a little particle drifted down onto his sleeve. He brushed it off. A second particle fell, and then some tiny fragments. He leaped, his head jerking up.

A circle was forming above his head. Another circle appeared to the right of it, and then a third. All around him circles were forming in the walls and roof of the sphere. He ran to the control board and closed the safety switch. The board hummed into life. He began to set the indicator panel, working rapidly, frantically. Now pieces of metal were dropping down, a rain of metal fragments onto the floor. Corrosive, some kind of substance exuded from them. Acid? Natural secretion of some sort. A large piece of metal fell; he turned.

Into the sphere the butterflies came, fluttering and dancing toward him. The piece that had fallen was a circle of metal, cut cleanly through. He did not have time even to notice it; he snatched up the blowtorch and snapped it on. The flame sucked and gurgled. As the butterflies came toward him he pressed the handle and held the spout up. The air burst alive with burning particles that rained down all over him, and a furious odor reeked through the sphere.

He closed the last switches. The indicator lights flickered, the floor chugged under him. He threw the main lever. More butterflies were pushing in, crowding each other eagerly, struggling to get through. A second circle of metal crashed to the floor suddenly, emitting a new horde. Hasten cringed, backing away, the blowtorch up, spouting flame. The butterflies came on, more and more of them.

Then sudden silence settled over everything, a quiet so abrupt that he blinked. The endless, insistent scratching had ceased. He was alone, except for a cloud of ashes and particles over the floor and walls, the remains of the butterflies that had got into the sphere. Hasten sat down on the stool, trembling. He was safe, on his way back to his own time; and there was no doubt, no possible doubt that he had found the lethal factor. It was there, in the heap of ashes on the floor, in the circles neatly cut in the hull of the car. Corrosive secretion? He smiled grimly.

His last vision of them, of the swelling horde had told him what he wanted to know. Clutched carefully against the first butterflies through the circles were tools, tiny cutting tools. They had cut their way in, bored through; they had come carrying their own equipment.

He sat down, waiting for the Time Car to complete its journey.

❖ ❖ ❖

Department guards caught hold of him, helping him from the Car. He stepped down unsteadily, leaning against them. "Thanks," he murmured.

Wood hurried up. "Hasten, you're all right?"

He nodded. "Yes. Except my hand."

"Let's get inside at once." They went through the door, into the great chamber. "Sit down." Wood waved his hand impatiently, and a soldier hurried a chair over. "Get him some hot coffee."

Coffee was brought. Hasten sat sipping. At last he pushed the cup away and leaned back.

"Can you tell us now?" Wood asked.

"Yes."

"Fine." Wood sat down across from him. A tape recorder whirred into life and a camera began to photograph Hasten's face as he talked. "Go on. What did you find?"

❖ ❖ ❖

When he had finished the room was silent. None of the guards or technicians spoke.

Wood stood up, trembling. "God. So it's a form of toxic life that got them. I thought it was something like that. But butterflies? And intelligent. Planning attacks. Probably rapid breeding, quick adaptation."

"Maybe the books and newspapers will help us."

"But where did they come from? Mutation of some existing form? Or from some other planet. Maybe space travel brought them in. We've got to find out."

"They attacked only human beings," Hasten said. "They left the cows. Just people."

"Maybe we can stop them." Wood snapped on the vidphone. "I'll have the Council convene an emergency session. We'll give them your description and recommendations. We'll start a program, organize units all over the planet. Now that we know what it is, we have a chance. Thanks to you, Hasten, maybe we can stop them in time!"

The operator appeared and Wood gave the Council's code letter. Hasten watched dully. At last he got to his feet and wandered around the room. His arm throbbed unmercifully. Presently he went back outside, through the doorway into the open square. Some soldiers were examining the Time Car curiously. Hasten watched them without feeling, his mind blank.

"What is it, sir?" one asked.

"That?" Hasten roused himself, going slowly over. "That's a Time Car."

"No, I mean this." The soldier pointed to something on the hull. "This, sir; it wasn't on there when the Car went out."

Hasten's heart stopped beating. He pushed past them, staring up. At first he saw nothing on the metal hull, only the corroded metal surface. Then chill fright rushed through him.

Something small and brown and furry was there, on the surface. He reached out, touching it. A sack, a stiff little brown sack. It was dry, dry and empty. There was nothing in it; it was open at one end. He stared up. All across the hull of the Car were little brown sacks, some still full, but most of them already empty.

Cocoons.

BEYOND THE DOOR

That night at the dinner table he brought it out and set it down beside her plate. Doris stared at it, her hand to her mouth. "My God, what is it?" She looked up at him, bright-eyed.

"Well, open it."

Doris tore the ribbon and paper from the square package with her sharp nails, her bosom rising and falling. Larry stood watching her as she lifted the lid. He lit a cigarette and leaned against the wall.

"A cuckoo clock!" Doris cried. "A real old cuckoo clock like my mother had." She turned the clock over and over. "Just like my mother had, when Pete was still alive." Her eyes sparkled with tears.

"It's made in Germany," Larry said. After a moment he added, "Carl got it for me wholesale. He knows some guy in the clock business. Otherwise I wouldn't have—" He stopped.

Doris made a funny little sound.

"I mean, otherwise, I wouldn't have been able to afford it." He scowled. "What's the matter with you? You've got your clock, haven't you? Isn't that what you want?"

Doris sat holding onto the clock, her fingers pressed against the brown wood.

"Well," Larry said, "what's the matter?"

He watched in amazement as she leaped up and ran from the

room, still clutching the clock. He shook his head. "Never satisfied. They're all that way. Never get enough."

He sat down at the table and finished his meal.

The cuckoo clock was not very large. It was hand-made, however, and there were countless frets on it, little indentations and ornaments scored in the soft wood. Doris sat on the bed drying her eyes and winding the clock. She set the hands by her wristwatch. Presently she carefully moved the hands to two minutes of ten. She carried the clock over to the dresser and propped it up.

Then she sat waiting, her hands twisted together in her lap—waiting for the cuckoo to come out, for the hour to strike.

As she sat she thought about Larry and what he had said. And what she had said, too, for that matter—not that she could be blamed for any of it. After all, she couldn't keep listening to him forever without defending herself; you had to blow your own trumpet in the world.

She touched her handkerchief to her eyes suddenly. Why did he have to say that, about getting it wholesale? Why did he have to spoil it all? If he felt that way he needn't have got it in the first place. She clenched her fists. He was so mean, so damn mean.

But she was glad of the little clock sitting there ticking to itself, with its funny grilled edges and the door. Inside the door was the cuckoo, waiting to come out. Was he listening, his head cocked on one side, listening to hear the clock strike so that he would know to come out?

Did he sleep between hours? Well, she would soon see him: she could ask him. And she would show the clock to Bob. He would love it; Bob loved old things, even old stamps and buttons. Of course, it was a little *awkward*, but Larry had been staying at the office so much, and that helped. If only Larry didn't call up sometimes to—

There was a whirr. The clock shuddered and all at once the door opened. The cuckoo came out, sliding swiftly. He paused and looked around solemnly, scrutinizing her, the room, the furniture.

It was the first time he had seen her, she realized, smiling to herself in pleasure. She stood up, coming toward him shyly. "Go on," she said. "I'm waiting."

The cuckoo opened his bill. He whirred and chirped, quickly, rhythmically. Then, after a moment of contemplation, he retired. And the door snapped shut.

She was delighted. She clapped her hands and spun in a little circle. He was marvelous, perfect! And the way he had looked around, studying her, sizing her up. He liked her; she was certain of it. And she, of course, loved him at once, completely. He was just what she had hoped would come out of the little door.

Doris went to the clock. She bent over the little door, her lips close to the wood. "Do you hear me?" she whispered. "I think you're the most wonderful cuckoo in the world." She paused, embarrassed. "I hope you'll like it here."

Then she went downstairs again, slowly, her head high.

Larry and the cuckoo clock really never got along well from the start. Doris said it was because he didn't wind it right, and it didn't like being only half-wound all the time. Larry turned the job of winding over to her; the cuckoo came out every quarter hour and ran the spring down without remorse, and someone had to be ever after it, winding it up again.

Doris did her best, but she forgot a good deal of the time. Then Larry would throw his newspaper down with an elaborate weary motion and stand up. He would go into the dining-room where the clock was mounted on the wall over the fireplace. He would take the clock down and making sure that he had his thumb over the little door, he would wind it up.

"Why do you put your thumb over the door?" Doris asked once.

"You're supposed to."

She raised an eyebrow. "Are you sure? I wonder if it isn't that you don't want him to come out while you're standing so close."

"Why not?"

"Maybe you're afraid of him."

Larry laughed. He put the clock back on the wall and gingerly removed his thumb. When Doris wasn't looking he examined his thumb.

There was still a trace of the nick cut out of the soft part of it. Who—or what—had pecked at him?

❖ ❖ ❖

One Saturday morning, when Larry was down at the office working over some important special accounts, Bob Chambers came to the front porch and rang the bell.

Doris was taking a quick shower. She dried herself and slipped into her robe. When she opened the door Bob stepped inside, grinning.

"Hi," he said, looking around.

"It's all right. Larry's at the office."

"Fine." Bob gazed at her slim legs below the hem of the robe. "How nice you look today."

She laughed. "Be careful! Maybe I shouldn't let you in after all."

They looked at one another, half amused half frightened. Presently Bob said, "If you want, I'll—"

"No, for God's sake." She caught hold of his sleeve. "Just get out of the doorway so I can close it. Mrs. Peters across the street, you know."

She closed the door. "And I want to show you something," she said. "You haven't seen it."

He was interested. "An antique? Or what?"

She took his arm, leading him toward the dining-room. "You'll love it, Bobby." She stopped wide-eyed. "I hope you will. You must; you must love it. It means so much to me—*he* means so much."

"He?" Bob frowned. "Who is he?"

Doris laughed. "You're jealous! Come on." A moment later they stood before the clock, looking up at it. "He'll come out in a few minutes. Wait until you see him. I know you two will get along fine."

"What does Larry think of him?"

"They don't like each other. Sometimes when Larry's here he won't come out. Larry gets mad if he doesn't come out on time. He says—"

"Says what?"

Doris looked down. "He always says he's been robbed, even if he did get it wholesale." She brightened. "But I know he won't come out because he doesn't like Larry. When I'm here alone he comes right out for me, every fifteen minutes, even though he really only has to come out on the hour."

She gazed up at the clock. "He comes out for me because he wants to. We talk; I tell him things. Of course, I'd like to have him upstairs in my room, but it wouldn't be right."

There was a sound of footsteps on the front porch. They looked at each other, horrified.

Larry pushed the front door open, grunting. He set his briefcase down and took off his hat. Then he saw Bob for the first time.

"Chambers. I'll be damned." His eyes narrowed. "What are you doing here?" He came into the dining-room. Doris drew her robe about her helplessly, backing away.

"I—" Bob began. "That is, we—" He broke off, glancing at Doris. Suddenly the clock began to whirr. The cuckoo came rushing out, bursting into sound. Larry moved toward him.

"Shut that din off," he said. He raised his fist toward the clock. The cuckoo snapped into silence and retreated. The door closed. "That's better." Larry studied Doris and Bob, standing mutely together.

"I came over to look at the clock," Bob said. "Doris told me that it's a rare antique and that—"

"Nuts. I bought it myself." Larry walked up to him. "Get out of here." He turned to Doris. "You too. And take that damn clock with you."

He paused, rubbing his chin. "No. Leave the clock here. It's mine; I bought it and paid for it."

In the weeks that followed after Doris left, Larry and the cuckoo clock got along even worse than before. For one thing, the cuckoo stayed inside most of the time, sometimes even at twelve o'clock when he should have been busiest. And if he did come out at all he usually spoke only once or twice, never the correct number of times. And there was a sullen, uncooperative note in his voice, a jarring sound that made Larry uneasy and a little angry.

But he kept the clock wound, because the house was very still and quiet and it got on his nerves not to hear someone running around, talking and dropping things. And even the whirring of a clock sounded good to him.

But he didn't like the cuckoo at all. And sometimes he spoke to him.

"Listen," he said late one night to the closed little door. "I know you can hear me. I ought to give you back to the Germans—back to the Black Forest." He paced back and forth. "I wonder what they're doing now, the two of them. That young punk with his books and his antiques. A man shouldn't be interested in antiques; that's for women."

He set his jaw. "Isn't that right?"

The clock said nothing. Larry walked up in front of it. "Isn't that right?" he demanded. "Don't you have anything to say?"

He looked at the face of the clock. It was almost eleven, just a few seconds before the hour. "All right. I'll wait until eleven. Then I want to hear what you have to say. You've been pretty quiet the last few weeks since she left."

He grinned wryly. "Maybe you don't like it here since she's gone." He scowled. "Well, I paid for you, and you're coming out whether you like it or not. You hear me?"

Eleven o'clock came. Far off, at the end of town, the great tower clock boomed sleepily to itself. But the little door remained shut. Nothing moved. The minute hand passed on and the cuckoo did not stir. He was someplace inside the clock, beyond the door, silent and remote.

"All right, if that's the way you feel," Larry murmured, his lips twisting. "But it isn't fair. It's your job to come out. We all have to do things we don't like."

He went unhappily into the kitchen and opened the great gleaming refrigerator. As he poured himself a drink he thought about the clock.

There was no doubt about it—the cuckoo should come out, Doris or no Doris. He had always liked her, from the very start. They had got along well, the two of them. Probably he liked Bob too—probably he had seen enough of Bob to get to know him. They would be quite happy together, Bob and Doris and the cuckoo.

Larry finished his drink. He opened the drawer at the sink and took out the hammer. He carried it carefully into the dining-room. The clock was ticking gently to itself on the wall.

"Look," he said, waving the hammer. "You know what I have here? You know what I'm going to do with it? I'm going to start on you-first." He smiled. "Birds of a feather, that's what you are—the three of you."

The room was silent.

"Are you coming out? Or do I have to come in and get you?"

The clock whirred a little.

"I hear you in there. You've got a lot of talking to do, enough for the last three weeks. As I figure it, you owe me—"

The door opened. The cuckoo came out fast, straight at him. Larry was looking down, his brow wrinkled in thought. He glanced up, and the cuckoo caught him squarely in the eye.

Down he went, hammer and chair and everything, hitting the floor with a tremendous crash. For a moment the cuckoo paused, its small body poised rigidly. Then it went back inside its house. The door snapped tight-shut after it.

The man lay on the floor, stretched out grotesquely, his head bent over to one side. Nothing moved or stirred. The room was completely silent, except, of course, for the ticking of the clock.

❖ ❖ ❖

"I see," Doris said, her face tight. Bob put his arm around her, steadying her.

"Doctor," Bob said, "can I ask you something?"

"Of course," the doctor said.

"Is it very easy to break your neck, falling from so low a chair? It wasn't very far to fall. I wonder if it might not have been an accident. Is there any chance it might have been—"

"Suicide?" the doctor rubbed his jaw. "I never heard of anyone committing suicide that way. It was an accident; I'm positive."

"I don't mean suicide," Bob murmured under his breath, looking up at the clock on the wall. "I meant *something else*."

But no one heard him.

JON'S WORLD

Kastner walked around the ship without speaking. He climbed the ramp and entered, disappearing cautiously inside. For a time his outline could be seen, stirring around. He appeared again, his broad face dimly alight.

"Well?" Caleb Ryan said. "What do you think?"

Kastner came down the ramp. "Is it ready to go? Nothing left to work out?"

"It's almost ready. Workmen are finishing up the remaining sections. Relay connections and feed lines. But no major problems exist. None we can predict, at least."

The two men stood together, looking up at the squat metal box with its ports and screens and observation grills. The ship was not lovely. There were no trim lines, no chrome and rexeroid struts to ease the hull into a gradually tapering tear-drop. The ship was square and knobby, with turrets and projections rising up everywhere.

"What will they think when we emerge from that?" Kastner murmured.

"We had no time to beautify it. Of course, if you want to wait another two months—"

"Couldn't you take off a few of the knobs? What are they for? What do they do?"

"Valves. You can examine the plans. They drain off the power load when it peaks too far up. Time travel is going to be dangerous. A vast load is collected as the ship moves back. It has to be leaked off gradually—or we'll be an immense bomb charged with millions of volts."

"I'll take your word on it." Kastner picked up his briefcase. He moved toward one of the exits. League Guards stepped out of his way. "I'll tell the Directors it's almost ready. By the way, I have something to reveal."

"What is it?"

"We've decided who's going along with you."

"Who?"

"I'm going. I've always wanted to know what things were like before the war. You see the history spools, but it isn't the same. I want to *be* there. Walk around. You know, they say there was no ash before the war. The surface was fertile. You could walk for miles without seeing ruins. This I would like to see."

"I didn't know you were interested in the past."

"Oh, yes. My family preserved some illustrated books showing how it was. No wonder USIC wants to get hold of Schonerman's papers. If reconstruction could begin—"

"That's what we all want."

"And maybe we'll get it. I'll see you later."

Ryan watched the plump little businessman depart, his briefcase clutched tightly. The row of League Guards stepped aside for him to pass, filling in behind him as he disappeared through the doorway.

Ryan returned his attention to the ship. So Kastner was to be his companion. USIC—United Synthetic Industries Combine—had held out for equal representation on the trip. One man from the League, one from USIC. USIC had been the source of supply, both commercial and financial, for Project Clock. Without its help the Project would never have got out of the paper stage. Ryan sat down at the bench and sent the blueprints racing through the scanner. They had worked a long time. There was not much left to be done. Only a few finishing touches here and there.

The vidscreen clicked. Ryan halted the scanner and swung to catch the call.

"Ryan."

The League monitor appeared on the screen. The call was coming through League cables. "Emergency call."

Ryan froze. "Put it through."

The monitor faded. After a moment an old face appeared, florid and lined. "Ryan—"

"What's happened?"

"You had better come home. As soon as you can."

"What is it?"

"Jon."

Ryan forced himself to be calm. "Another attack?" His voice was thick.

"Yes."

"Like the others?"

"Exactly like the others."

Ryan's hand jerked to the cut-off switch. "All right. I'll be home at once. Don't let anyone in. Try to keep him quiet. Don't let him out of his room. Double the guard, if necessary."

Ryan broke the circuit. A moment later he was on his way to the roof, toward his inter-city ship parked above him, at the roof field of the building.

❖ ❖ ❖

His inter-city ship rushed above the unending gray ash, automatic grapples guiding it toward City Four. Ryan stared blankly out the port, only half-seeing the sight below.

He was between cities. The surface was wasted, endless heaps of slag and ash as far as the eye could see. Cities rose up like occasional toadstools, separated by miles of gray. Toadstools here and there, towers and buildings, men and women working. Gradually the surface was being reclaimed. Supplies and equipment were being brought down from the Lunar Base.

During the war human beings had left Terra and gone to the moon. Terra was devasted. Nothing but a globe of ruin and ash. Men had come back gradually, when the war was over.

Actually there had been two wars. The first was man against man. The second was man against the claws—complex robots that had been created as a war weapon. The claws had turned on their makers, designing their own new types and equipment.

Ryan's ship began to descend. He was over City Four. Presently the ship came to rest on the roof of his massive private residence at the center of the city. Ryan leaped quickly out and crossed the roof to the lift.

A moment later he entered his quarters and made his way toward Jon's room.

He found the old man watching Jon through the glass side of the room, his face grave. Jon's room was partly in darkness. Jon was sitting on the edge of his bed, his hands clasped tightly together. His eyes were shut. His mouth was open a little, and from time to time his tongue came out, stiff and rigid. .

"How long has he been like that?" Ryan said to the old man beside him.

"About an hour."

"The other attacks followed the same pattern?"

"This is more severe. Each has been more severe."

"No one has seen him but you?"

"Just the two of us. I called you when I was certain. It's almost over. He's coming out of it."

On the other side of the glass Jon stood up and walked away from his bed, his arms folded. His blond hair hung down raggedly in his face. His eyes were still shut. His face was pale and set. His lips twitched.

"He was completely unconscious at first. I had left him alone for awhile. I was in another part of the building. When I came back I found him lying on the floor. He had been reading. The spools were scattered all around him. His face was blue. His breathing was irregular. There were repeated muscular spasms, as before."

"What did you do?"

"I entered the room and carried him to the bed. He was rigid at first, but after a few minutes he began to relax. His body became limp. I tested his pulse. It was very slow. Breathing was coming more easily. And then it began."

"It?"

"The talk."

"Oh." Ryan nodded.

"I wish you could have been here. He talked more than ever before. On and on. Streams of it. Without pause. As if he couldn't stop."

"Was—was it the same talk as before?"

"Exactly the same as it's always been. And his face was lit up. Glowing. As before."

Ryan considered. "Is it all right for me to go into the room?"

"Yes. It's almost over."

Ryan moved to the door. His fingers pressed against the code lock and the door slid back into the wall.

Jon did not notice him as he came quietly into the room. He paced back and forth, eyes shut, his arms wrapped around his body. He swayed a little, rocking from side to side. Ryan came to the center of the room and stopped.

"Jon!"

The boy blinked. His eyes opened. He shook his head rapidly. "Ryan? What—what did you want?"

"Better sit down."

Jon nodded. "Yes. Thank you." He sat down on the bed uncertainly. His eyes were wide and blue. He pushed his hair back out of his face, smiling a little at Ryan.

"How do you feel?"

"I feel all right."

Ryan sat down across from him, drawing a chair over. He crossed his legs, leaning back. For a long time he studied the boy. Neither of them spoke. "Grant says you had a little attack," Ryan said finally.

Jon nodded.

"You're over it now?"

"Oh, yes. How is the time ship coming?"

"Fine."

"You promised I could see it, when it's ready."

"You can. When it's completely done."

"When will that be?"

"Soon. A few more days."

"I want to see it very much. I've been thinking about it. Imagine going into time. You could go back to Greece. You could go back and see Pericles and Xenophon and—and Epictetus. You could go back to Egypt and talk to Ikhnaton." He grinned. "I can't wait to see it."

Ryan shifted. "Jon, do you really think you're well enough to go outside? Maybe—"

"Well enough? What do you mean?"

"Your attacks. You really think you should go out? Are you strong enough?"

Jon's face clouded. "They're not attacks. Not really. I wish you wouldn't call them attacks."

"Not attacks? What are they?"

Jon hesitated. "I—I shouldn't tell you, Ryan. You wouldn't understand."

Ryan stood up. "All right, Jon. If you feel you can't talk to me I'll go back to the lab." He crossed the room to the door. "It's a shame you can't see the ship. I think you'd like it."

Jon followed him plaintively. "Can't I see it?"

"Maybe if I knew more about your—your attacks I'd know whether you're well enough to go out."

Jon's face flickered. Ryan watched him intently. He could see thoughts crossing Jon's mind, written on his features. He struggled inwardly.

"Don't you want to tell me?"

Jon took a deep breath. "They're *visions*."

"What?"

"They're visions." Jon's face was alive with radiance. "I've known it a long time. Grant says they're not, but they are. If you could see them you'd know, too. They're not like anything else. More real than, well, than this." He thumped the wall. "More real than that."

Ryan lit a cigarette slowly. "Go on."

It all came with a rush. "More real than *anything* else! Like looking through a window. A window into another world. A real world. Much more real than this. It makes all this just a shadow world. Only dim shadows. Shapes. Images."

"Shadows of an ultimate reality?"

"Yes! Exactly. The world behind all this." Jon paced back and forth, animated by excitement. "This, all these things. What we see here. Buildings. The sky. The cities. The endless ash. None is quite real. It's so dim and vague! I don't really feel it, not like the other. And it's becoming less real, all the time. The other is growing, Ryan. Growing more and more vivid! Grant told me it's only my imagination. But it's not. It's real. More real than any of these things here, these things in this room."

"Then why can't we all see it?"

"I don't know. I wish you could. You ought to see it, Ryan. It's beautiful. You'd like it, after you got used to it. It takes time to adjust."

Ryan considered. "Tell me," he said at last. "I want to know exactly what you see. Do you always see the same thing?"

"Yes. Always the same. But more intensely."

"What is it? What do you see that's so real?"

Jon did not answer for awhile. He seemed to have withdrawn. Ryan waited, watching his son. What was going on in his mind? What was he thinking? The boy's eyes were shut again. His hands were pressed together, the fingers white. He was off again, off in his private world.

"Go on," Ryan said aloud.

So it was *visions* the boy saw. Visions of ultimate reality. Like the Middle Ages. His own son. There was a grim irony in it. Just when it seemed they had finally licked that proclivity in man, his eternal inability to face reality. His eternal dreaming. Would science never be able to realize its ideal? Would man always go on preferring illusion to reality?

His own son. Retrogression. A thousand years lost. Ghosts and gods and devils and the secret inner world. The world of ultimate reality. All the fables and fictions and metaphysics that man had used for centuries to compensate for his fear, his terror of the world. All the dreams he had made up to hide the truth, the harsh world of reality. Myths, religions, fairy tales. A better land, beyond and above. Paradise. All coming back, reappearing again, and in his own son.

"Go on," Ryan said impatiently. "What do you see?"

"I see fields," Jon said. "Yellow fields as bright as the sun. Fields and parks. Endless parks. Green, mixed in with the yellow. Paths, for people to walk."

"What else?"

"Men and women. In robes. Walking along the paths, among the trees. The air fresh and sweet. The sky bright blue. Birds. Animals. Animals moving through the parks. Butterflies. Oceans. Lapping oceans of clear water."

"No cities?"

"Not like our cities. Not the same. People living in the parks. Little wood houses here and there. Among the trees."

"Roads?"

"Only paths. No ships or anything. Only walking."

"What else do you see?"

"That's all." Jon opened his eyes. His cheeks were flushed. His eyes sparkled and danced. "That's all, Ryan. Parks and yellow fields. Men and women in robes. And so many animals. The wonderful animals."

"How do they live?"

"What?"

"How do the people live? What keeps them alive?"

"They grow things. In the fields."

"Is that all? Don't they build? Don't they have factories?"

"I don't think so."

"An agrarian society. Primitive." Ryan frowned. "No business or commerce."

"They work in the fields. And discuss things."

"Can you *hear* them?"

"Very faintly. Sometimes I can hear them a little, if I listen very hard. I can't make out any words, though."

"What are they discussing?"

"Things."

"What kind of things?"

Jon gestured vaguely. "Great things. The world. The universe."

There was silence. Ryan grunted. He did not say anything. Finally he put out his cigarette. "Jon—"

"Yes?"

"You think what you see is *real*?"

Jon smiled. "I know it's real."

Ryan's gaze was sharp. "What do you mean, real? In what way is this world of yours real?"

"It exists."

"Where does it exist?"

"I don't know."

"Here? Does it exist here?"

"No. It's not here."

"Some place else? A long way off? Some other part of the universe beyond our range of experience?"

"Not another part of the universe. It has nothing to do with space. It's here." Jon waved around him. "Close by. It's very close. I see it all around me."

"Do you see it now?"

"No. It comes and goes."

"It ceases to exist? It only exists sometimes?"

"No, it's always there. But I can't always make contact with it."

"How do you know it's always there?"

"I just know."

"Why can't *I* see it? Why are you the only one who can see it?"

"I don't know." Jon rubbed his forehead wearily. "I don't know why I'm the only one who can see it. I wish you could see it. I wish everybody could see it."

"How can you demonstrate it isn't an hallucination? You have no objective validation of it. You have only your own inner sense, your state of consciousness. How could it be presented for empirical analysis?"

"Maybe it can't. I don't know. I don't care. I don't *want* to present it for empirical analysis."

There was silence. Jon's face was set and grim, his jaw tight. Ryan sighed. Impasse.

"All right, Jon." He moved slowly toward the door. "I'll see you later."

Jon said nothing.

At the door Ryan halted, looking back. "Then your visions are getting stronger, aren't they? Progressively more vivid."

Jon nodded curtly.

Ryan considered awhile. Finally he raised his hand. The door slid away and he passed outside the room, into the hall.

Grant came up to him. "I was watching through the window. He's quite withdrawn, isn't he?"

"It's difficult to talk to him. He seems to believe these attacks are some kind of vision."

"I know. He's told me."

"Why didn't you let me know?"

"I didn't want to alarm you more. I know you've been worried about him."

"The attacks are getting worse. He says they're more vivid. More convincing."

Grant nodded.

Ryan moved along the corridor, deep in thought, Grant a little behind. "It's difficult to be certain of the best course of action. The attacks absorb him more and more. He's beginning to take them seriously. They're usurping the place of the outside world. And in addition—"

"And in addition you're leaving soon."

"I wish we knew more about time travel. A great number of things may happen to us." Ryan rubbed his jaw. "We might not come back. Time is a potent force. No real exploration has been done. We have no idea what we may run into."

He came to the lift and stopped.

"I'll have to make my decision right away. It has to be made before we leave."

"Your decision?"

Ryan entered the lift. "You'll know about it later. Watch Jon constantly from now on. Don't be away from him for even a moment. Do you understand?"

Grant nodded. "I understand. You want to be sure he doesn't leave his room."

"You'll hear from me either tonight or tomorrow." Ryan ascended to the roof and entered his inter-city ship.

As soon as he was in the sky he clicked on the vidscreen and dialed the League Offices. The face of the League Monitor appeared. "Offices."

"Give me the medical center."

The monitor faded. Presently Walter Timmer, the medical director, appeared on the screen. His eyes flickered as he recognized Ryan. "What can I do for you, Caleb?"

"I want you to get out a medical car and a few good men and come over here to City Four."

"Why?"

"It's a matter I discussed with you several months ago. You recall, I think."

Timmer's expression changed. "Your son?"

"I've decided. I can't wait any longer. He's getting worse, and we'll be leaving soon on the time trip. I want it performed before I leave."

"All right." Timmer made a note. "We'll make immediate arrangements here. And we'll send a ship over to pick him up at once."

Ryan hesitated. "You'll do a good job?"

"Of course. We'll have James Pryor perform the actual operation." Timmer reached up to cut the vidscreen circuit. "Don't worry, Caleb. He'll do a good job. Pryor is the best lobotomist the center has."

❖ ❖ ❖

Ryan laid out the map, stretching the corners flat against the table. "This is a time map, drawn up in the form of a space projection. So we can see where we're going."

Kastner peered over his shoulder. "Will we be confined to the one Project—getting Schonerman's papers? Or can we move around?"

"Only the one Project is contemplated. But to be certain of success we should make several stops on this side of Schonerman's continuum. Our time map may be inaccurate, or the drive itself may act with some bias."

The work was finished. All the final sections were put in place.

In a corner of the room Jon sat watching, his face expressionless. Ryan glanced toward him. "How does it look to you?"

"Fine."

The time ship was like some stubby insect, overgrown with warts and knobs. A square box with windows and endless turrets. Not really a ship at all.

"I guess you wish you could come," Kastner said to Jon. "Right?"

Jon nodded faintly.

"How are you feeling?" Ryan asked him.

"Fine."

Ryan studied his son. The boy's color had come back. He had regained most of his original vitality. The visions, of course, no longer existed.

"Maybe you can come next time," Kastner said.

Ryan returned to the map. "Schonerman did most of his work between 2030 and 2037. The results were not put to any use until several years later. The decision to use his work in the war was reached only after long consideration. The Governments seemed to have been aware of the dangers."

"But not sufficiently so."

"No." Ryan hesitated. "And we may be getting ourselves into the same situation."

"How do you mean?"

"Schonerman's discovery of the artificial brain was lost when the last claw was destroyed. None of us have been able to duplicate his work. If we bring his papers we may put society back in jeopardy. We may bring back the claws."

Kastner shook his head. "No. Schonerman's work was not implicitly related to the claws. The development of an artificial brain does not imply lethal usage. Any scientific discovery can be used for destruction. Even the wheel was used in the Assyrian war chariots."

"I suppose so." Ryan glanced up at Kastner. "Are you certain USIC doesn't intend to use Schonerman's work along military lines?"

"USIC is an industrial combine. Not a government."

"It would ensure its advantage for a long time."

"USIC is strong enough as it is."

"Let it go." Ryan rolled up the map. "We can start any minute. I'm anxious to get going. We've worked a long time on this."

"I agree."

Ryan crossed the room to his son. "We're leaving, Jon. We should be back fairly soon. Wish us luck."

Jon nodded. "I wish you luck."

"You're feeling all right?"

"Yes."

"Jon—you feel better now, don't you? Better than before?"

"Yes."

"Aren't you glad they're gone? All the troubles you were having?"

"Yes."

Ryan put his hand awkwardly on the boy's shoulder. "We'll see you later."

Ryan and Kastner made their way up the ramp to the hatch of the time ship. From the corner, Jon watched them silently. A few League Guards lounged at the entrances to the work lab, watching with idle interest.

Ryan paused at the hatch. He called one of the guards over. "Tell Timmer I want him."

The guard went off, pushing through the exit.

"What is it?" Kastner said.

"I have some final instructions to give him."

Kastner shot him a sharp glance. "Final? What's the matter? You think something's going to happen to us?"

"No. Just a precaution."

Timmer came striding in. "You're leaving, Ryan?"

"Everything's ready. There's no reason to hold back any longer."

Timmer came up the ramp. "What did you want me for?"

"This may be unnecessary. But there's always the possibility something might go wrong. In case the ship doesn't reappear according to schedule I've filed with the League members—"

"You want me to name a protector for Jon."

"That's right."

"There's nothing to worry about."

"I know. But I'd feel better. Someone should watch out for him."

They both glanced at the silent, expressionless boy sitting in the corner of the room. Jon stared straight ahead. His face was blank. His eyes were dull, listless. There was nothing there.

"Good luck," Timmer said. He and Ryan shook hands. "I hope everything works out."

Kastner climbed inside the ship, setting down his briefcase. Ryan followed him, lowering the hatch into place and bolting it into position. He sealed the inner lock. A bank of automatic lighting came on. Controlled atmosphere began to hiss into the cabin of the ship.

"Air, light, heat," Kastner said. He peered out the port at the League Guards outside. "It's hard to believe. In a few minutes all this will disappear. This building. These guards. Everything."

Ryan seated himself at the control board of the ship, spreading out the time map. He fastened the map into position, crossing the surface with the cable leads from the board before him. "It's my plan to make several observation stops along the way, so we can view some of the past events relevant to our work."

"The war?"

"Mainly. I'm interested in seeing the claws in actual operation. At one time they were in complete control of Terra, according to the War Office records."

"Let's not get too close, Ryan."

Ryan laughed. "We won't land. We'll make our observations from the air. The only actual contact we'll make will be with Schonerman."

Ryan closed the power circuit. Energy flowed through the ship around them, flooding into the meters and indicators on the control board. Needles jumped, registering the load.

"The main thing we have to watch is our energy peak," Ryan explained. "If we build up too much of a load of time ergs the ship won't be able to come out of the time stream. We'll keep moving back into the past, building up a greater and greater charge."

"An enormous bomb."

"That's right." Ryan adjusted the switches before him. The meter readings changed. "Here we go. Better hang on."

He released the controls. The ship shuddered as it polarized into position, easing into the time flow. The vanes and knobs changed their settings, adjusting themselves to the stress. Relays closed, braking the ship against the current sweeping around them.

"Like the ocean," Ryan murmured. "The most potent energy in the universe. The great dynamic behind all motion. The Prime Mover."

"Maybe this is what they used to mean by God."

Ryan nodded. The ship was vibrating around them. They were in the grip of a giant hand, an immense fist closing silently. They were in motion. Through the port the men and walls had begun to waver, fading out of existence as the ship slipped out of phase with the present, drifting farther and farther into the flow of the time stream.

"It won't be long," Ryan murmured.

All at once the scene beyond the port winked out. There was nothing there. Nothing beyond them.

"We've not phased with any space-time objects," Ryan explained. "We're out of focus with the universe itself. At this moment we exist in non-time. There's no continuum in which we're operating."

"I hope we can get back again." Kastner sat down nervously, his eyes on the blank port. "I feel like the first man who went down in a submarine."

"That was during the American Revolution. The submarine was propelled by a crank which the pilot turned. The other end of the crank was a propeller."

"How could he go very far?"

"He didn't. He cranked his ship under a British frigate and then bored a hole in the frigate's hull."

Kastner glanced up at the hull of the time ship, vibrating and rattling from stress. "What would happen if this ship should break open?"

"We'd be atomized. Dissolved into the stream around us." Ryan lit a cigarette. "We'd become a part of the time flow. We'd move back and forth endlessly, from one end of the universe to the other."

"End?"

"The time ends. Time flows both ways. Right now we're moving back. But energy must move both ways to keep a balance. Otherwise time ergs in vast amounts would collect at one particular continuum and the result would be catastrophic."

"Do you suppose there's some purpose behind all of this? I wonder how the time flow ever got started."

"Your question is meaningless. Questions of purpose have no objective validity. They can't be subjected to any form of empirical investigation."

Kastner lapsed into silence. He picked at his sleeve nervously, watching the port.

Across the time map the cable arms moved, tracing a line from the present back into the past. Ryan studied the motion of the arms. "We're reaching the latter part of the war. The final stages. I'm going to rephase the ship and bring it out of the time flow."

"Then we'll be back in the universe again?"

"Among objects. In a specific continuum."

Ryan gripped the power switch. He took a deep breath. The first great test of the ship had passed. They had entered the time stream without accident. Could they leave it as easily? He opened the switch.

The ship leaped. Kastner staggered, catching hold of the wall support. Outside the port a gray sky twisted and wavered. Adjustments fell into place, leveling the ship in the air. Down below them Terra circled and tilted as the ship gained equilibrium.

Kastner hurried to the port to peer out. They were a few hundred feet above the surface, rushing parallel to the ground. Gray ash stretched out in all directions, broken by the occasional mounds of rubbish. Ruins of towns, buildings, walls. Wrecks of military equipment. Clouds of ash blew across the sky, darkening the sun.

"Is the war still on?" Kastner asked.

"The claws still possess Terra. We should be able to see them."

Ryan raised the time ship, increasing the scope of their view. Kastner scanned the ground. "What if they fire at us?"

"We can always escape into time."

"They might capture the ship and use it to come to the present."

"I doubt it. At this stage in the war the claws were busy fighting among themselves."

To their right ran a winding road, disappearing into the ash and reappearing again later on. Bomb craters gaped here and there, breaking the road up. Something was coming slowly along it.

"There," Kastner said. "On the road. A column of some sort."

Ryan maneuvered the ship. They hung above the road, the two of them peering out. The column was dark brown, a marching file making its way steadily along. Men, a column of men, marching silently through the landscape of ash.

Suddenly Kastner gasped. "They're identical! All of them are the same!"

They were seeing a column of claws. Like lead toys, the robots marched along, tramping through the gray ash. Ryan caught his breath. He had expected such a sight, of course. There were only four types of claws. These he saw now had all been turned out in the same underground plant, from the same dies and stampers. Fifty or sixty robots, shaped like young men, marched calmly along. They moved very slowly. Each had only one leg.

"They must have been fighting among themselves," Kastner murmured.

"No. This type was made this way. The Wounded Soldier Type. Originally they were designed to trick human sentries to gain entrance into regular bunkers."

It was weird, watching the silent column of men, identical men, each the same as the next, plodding along the road. Each soldier supported himself with a crutch. Even the crutches were identical. Kastner opened and closed his mouth in revulsion.

"Not very pleasant, is it?" Ryan said. "We're lucky the human race got away to Luna."

"Didn't any of these follow?"

"A few, but by the time we had identified the four types and were ready for them." Ryan took hold of the power switch. "Let's go on."

"Wait." Kastner raised his hand. "Something's going to happen."

To the right of the road a group of figures were slipping rapidly down the side of a rise, through the ash. Ryan let go of the power switch, watching. The figures were identical. Women. The women, in uniforms and boots, advanced quietly toward the column on the road.

"Another variety," Kastner said.

Suddenly the column of soldiers halted. They scattered, hobbling awkwardly in all directions. Some of them fell, stumbling and dropping their crutches. The women rushed out on the road. They were slender and young, with dark hair and eyes. One of the Wounded Soldiers began to fire. A woman fumbled at her belt. She made a throwing motion.

"What—" Kastner muttered. There was a sudden flash. A cloud of white light rose from the center of the road, billowing in all directions.

"Some kind of concussion bomb," Ryan said.

"Maybe we better get out of here."

Ryan threw the switch. The scene below them began to waver. Abruptly it faded. It winked out.

"Thank God that's over," Kastner said. "So that's what the war was like."

"The second part. The major part. Claw against claw. It's a good thing they started fighting with each other. Good for us, I mean."

"Where to now?"

"We'll make one more observation stop. During the early part of the war. Before claws came into use."

"And then Schonerman?"

Ryan set his jaw. "That's right. One more stop and then Schonerman."

Ryan adjusted the controls. The meters moved slightly. Across the map the cable arms traced their path. "It won't be long," Ryan murmured. He gripped the switch, setting the relays in place. "This time we have to be more careful. There'll be more war activity."

"Maybe we shouldn't even—"

"I want to see. This was man against man. The Soviet region against the United Nations. I'm curious to see what it was like."

"What if we're spotted?"

"We can get away quickly."

Kastner said nothing. Ryan manipulated the controls. Time passed. At the edge of the board Ryan's cigarette burned to an ash. At last he straightened up.

"Here we go. Get set." He opened the switch.

Below them green and brown plains stretched out, pocked with bomb craters. Part of a city swept past. It was burning. Towering columns of smoke rose up, drifting into the sky. Along the roads black dots moved, vehicles and people streaming away.

"A bombing," Kastner said. "Recent."

The city fell behind. They were over open country. Military trucks rushed along. Most of the land was still intact. They could see a few farmers working the fields. The farmers dropped down as the time ship moved over them.

Ryan studied the sky. "Watch out."

"Air craft?"

"I'm not sure where we are. I don't know the location of the sides in this part of the war. We may be over UN territory, or Soviet territory." Ryan held on tight to the switch.

From the blue sky two dots appeared. The dots grew. Ryan watched them intently. Beside him Kastner gave a nervous grunt. "Ryan, we better—"

The dots separated. Ryan's hand closed over the power switch. He yanked it closed. As the scene dissolved the dots swept past. Then there was nothing but grayness outside.

In their ears the roar of the two planes still echoed.

"That was close," Kastner said.

"Very. They didn't waste any time."

"I hope you don't want to stop any more."

"No. No more observation stops. The Project itself comes next. We're close to Schonerman's time area. I can begin to slow down the velocity of the ship. This is going to be critical."

"Critical?"

"There are going to be problems getting to Schonerman. We must hit his continuum exactly, both in space as well as time. He may be guarded. In any case they won't give us much time to explain who we are." Ryan tapped the time map. "And there's always the chance the information given here is incorrect."

"How long before we rephase with a continuum? Schonerman's continuum?"

Ryan looked at his wristwatch. "About five or ten minutes. Get ready to leave the ship. Part of this is going to be on foot."

❖ ❖ ❖

It was night. There was no sound, only unending silence. Kastner strained to hear, his ear against the hull of the ship. "Nothing."

"No. I don't hear anything either." Carefully, Ryan unbolted the hatch, sliding the locks back. He pushed the hatch open, his gun gripped tight. He peered out into the darkness.

The air was fresh and cold. Full of smells of growing things. Trees and flowers. He took a deep breath. He could see nothing. It was pitch black. Far off, a long way off, a cricket chirruped.

"Hear that?" Ryan said.

"What is it?"

"A beetle." Ryan stepped gingerly down. The ground was soft underfoot. He was beginning to adjust to the darkness. Above him a few stars glinted. He could make out trees, a field of trees. And beyond the trees a high fence.

Kastner stepped down beside him. "What now?"

"Keep your voice down." Ryan indicated the fence. "We're going that way. Some kind of building."

They crossed the field to the fence. At the fence Ryan aimed his gun, setting the charge at minimum. The fence charred and sank, the wire glowed red.

Ryan and Kastner stepped over the fence. The side of the building rose, concrete and iron. Ryan nodded to Kastner. "We'll have to move quickly. And low."

He crouched, taking a breath. Then he ran, bent over, Kastner beside him. They crossed the ground to the building. A window loomed up in front of them. Then a door. Ryan threw his weight against the door.

The door opened. Ryan fell inside, staggering. He caught a quick glimpse of startled faces, men leaping to their feet.

Ryan fired, sweeping the interior of the room with his gun. Flame rushed out, crackling around him. Kastner fired past his shoulder. Shapes moved in the flame, dim outlines falling and rolling.

The flames died. Ryan advanced, stepping over charred heaps on the floor. A barracks. Bunks, remains of a table. An overturned lamp and radio.

By the rays of the lamp Ryan studied a battle map pinned on the wall. He traced the map with his finger, deep in thought.

"Are we far?" Kastner asked, standing by the door with his gun ready.

"No. Only a few miles."

"How do we get there?"

"We'll move the time ship. It's safer. We're lucky. It might have been on the other side of the world."

"Will there be many guards?"

"I'll tell you the facts when we get there." Ryan moved to the door. "Come on. Someone may have seen us."

Kastner grabbed up a handful of newspapers from the remains of the table. "I'll bring these. Maybe they'll tell us something."

"Good idea."

❖ ❖ ❖

Ryan set the ship down in a hollow between two hills. He spread the newspapers out, studying them intently. "We're earlier than I thought. By a few months. Assuming these are new." He fingered the newsprint. "Not turned yellow. Probably only a day or so old."

"What is the date?"

"Autumn, 2030. September 21."

Kastner peered out the port. "The sun is going to be coming up soon. The sky is beginning to turn gray."

"We'll have to work fast."

"I'm a little uncertain. What am I supposed to do?"

"Schonerman is in a small village beyond this hill. We're in the United States. In Kansas. This area is surrounded by troops, a circle of pillboxes and dugouts. We're inside the periphery. Schonerman is virtually unknown at this continuum. His research has never been published. At this time he's working as part of a large Government research project."

"Then he's not especially protected."

"Only later on, when his work has been turned over to the Government will he be protected day and night. Kept in an underground laboratory and never let up to the surface. The Government's most valuable research worker. But right now—"

"How will we know him?"

Ryan handed Kastner a sheaf of photographs. "This is Schonerman. All the pictures that survived up to our own time."

Kastner studied the pictures. Schonerman was a small man with horn-rimmed glasses. He smiled feebly at the camera, a thin nervous man with a prominent forehead. His hands were slender, the fingers long and tapered. In one photograph he sat at his desk, a pipe beside him, his thin chest covered by a sleeveless wool sweater. In another he sat with his legs crossed, a tabby cat in his lap, a mug of beer in front of him. An old German enamel mug with hunting scenes and Gothic letters.

"So that's the man who invented the claws. Or did the research work."

"That's the man who worked out the principles for the first workable artificial brain."

"Did he know they were going to use his work to make the claws?"

"Not at first. According to reports, Schonerman first learned about it only when the initial batch of claws was released. The United Nations were losing the war. The Soviets gained an original advantage, due to their opening surprise attacks. The claws were hailed as a triumph of Western development. For a time they seemed to have turned the tide of the war."

"And then—"

"And then the claws began to manufacture their own varieties and attack Soviets and Westerners alike. The only humans that survived were those at the UN base on Luna. A few dozen million."

"It was a good thing the claws finally turned on each other."

"Schonerman saw the whole development of his work to the last stages. They say he became greatly embittered."

Kastner passed the pictures back. "And you say he's not especially well guarded?"

"Not at this continuum. No more than any other research worker. He's young. In this continuum he's only twenty-five. Remember that."

"Where'll we find him?"

"The Government Project is located in what was once a school house. Most of the work is done on the surface. No big underground development has begun yet. The research workers have barracks about a quarter mile from their labs." Ryan glanced at his watch. "Our best chance is to nab him as he begins work at his bench in the lab."

"Not in the barracks?"

"The papers are all in the lab. The Government doesn't allow any written work to be taken out. Each worker is searched as he leaves."

Ryan touched his coat gingerly. "We have to be careful. Schonerman must not be harmed. We only want his papers."

"We won't use our blasters?"

"No. We don't dare take the chance of injuring him."

"His papers will definitely be at his bench?"

"He's not allowed to remove them for any reason. We know exactly where we'll find what we want. There's only one place the papers can be."

"Their security precautions play right into our hands."

"Exactly," Ryan murmured.

Ryan and Kastner slipped down the hillside, running between the trees. The ground was hard and cold underfoot. They emerged at the edge of the town. A few people were already up, moving slowly along the street. The town had not been bombed. There was no damage, as yet. The windows of the stores had been boarded up and huge arrows pointed to the underground shelters.

"What do they have on?" Kastner said. "Some of them have something on their faces."

"Bacteria masks. Come on." Ryan gripped his blast pistol as he and Kastner made their way through the town. None of the people paid any attention to them.

"Just two more uniformed people," Kastner said.

"Our main hope is surprise. We're inside the wall of defense. The sky is patrolled against Soviet craft. No Soviet agents could be landed here. And in any case, this is a minor research lab, in the center of the United States. There would be no reason for Soviet agents to come here."

"But there will be guards."

"Everything is guarded. All science. All kinds of research work."

The school house loomed up ahead of them. A few men were milling around the doorway. Ryan's heart constricted. Was Schonerman one of them?

The men were going inside, one by one. A guard in helmet and uniform was checking their badges. A few of the men wore bacteria masks, only their eyes visible. Would he recognize Schonerman? What if he wore a mask? Fear gripped Ryan suddenly. In a mask Schonerman would look like anyone else.

Ryan slipped his blast pistol away, motioning Kastner to do the same. His fingers closed over the lining of his coat pocket. Sleep-gas crystals. No one this early would have been immunized against sleep-gas. It had not been developed until a year or so later. The gas would put everyone for several hundred feet around into varying periods of sleep. It was a tricky and unpredictable weapon—but perfect for this situation.

"I'm ready," Kastner murmured.

"Wait. We have to wait for *him*."

They waited. The sun rose, warming the cold sky. More research workers appeared, filing up the path and inside the building. They puffed white clouds of frozen moisture and slapped their hands together. Ryan began to become nervous. One of the guards was watching him and Kastner. If they became suspicious—

A small man in a heavy overcoat and horn-rimmed glasses came up the path, hurrying toward the building.

Ryan tensed. Schonerman! Schonerman flashed his badge to the guard. He stamped his feet and went inside the building, stripping off his mittens. It was over in a second. A brisk young man, hurrying to get to his work. To his papers.

"Come on," Ryan said.

He and Kastner moved forward. Ryan pulled the gas crystals loosed from the lining of his pocket. The crystals were cold and hard in his hand. Like diamonds. The guard was watching them coming, his gun alert. His face was set. Studying them. He had never seen them before. Ryan, watching the guard's face, could read his thoughts without trouble.

Ryan and Kastner halted at the doorway. "We're from the FBI," Ryan said calmly.

"Identify yourselves." The guard did not move.

"Here are our credentials," Ryan said. He drew his hand out from his coat pocket. And crushed the gas crystals in his fist.

The guard sagged. His face relaxed. Limply, his body slid to the ground. The gas spread. Kastner stepped through the door, peering around, his eyes bright.

The building was small. Lab benches and equipment stretched out on all sides of them. The workers lay where they had been standing, inert heaps on the floor, their arms and legs out, their mouths open.

"Quick." Ryan passed Kastner, hurrying across the lab. At the far end of the room Schonerman lay slumped over his bench, his head resting against the metal surface. His glasses had fallen off. His eyes were open, staring. He had taken his papers out of the drawer. The padlock and key were still on the bench. The papers were under his head and between his hands.

Kastner ran to Schonerman and snatched the papers up, stuffing them into his briefcase.

"Get them all!"

"I have them all." Kastner pulled open the drawer. He grabbed the remaining papers in the drawer. "Every one of them."

"Let's go. The gas will dissipate rapidly."

They ran back outside. A few sprawled bodies lay across the entrance, workers who had come into the area.

"Hurry."

They ran through the town, along the single main street. People gaped at them in astonishment. Kastner gasped for breath, holding on tight to his briefcase as he ran. "I'm—winded."

"Don't stop."

They reached the edge of the town and started up the hillside. Ryan ran between the trees, his body bent forward, not looking back. Some of the workers would be reviving. And other guards would be coming into the area. It would not be long before the alarm would be out.

Behind them a siren whirred into life.

"Here they come." Ryan paused at the top of the hill, waiting for Kastner. Behind them men were swelling rapidly into the street, coming up out of underground bunkers. More sirens wailed, a dismal echoing sound.

"Down!" Ryan ran down the hillside toward the time ship, sliding and slipping on the dry earth. Kastner hurried after him, sobbing for breath. They could hear orders being shouted. Soldiers swarming up the hillside after them.

Ryan reached the ship. He grabbed Kastner and pulled him inside. "Get the hatch shut. Get it closed!"

Ryan ran to the control board. Kastner dropped his briefcase and tugged at the rim of the hatch. At the top of the hill a line of soldiers appeared. They made their way down the hillside, aiming and firing as they ran.

"Get down," Ryan barked. Shells crashed against the hull of the ship. "Down!"

Kastner fired back with his blast pistol. A wave of flame rolled up the hillside at the soldiers. The hatch came shut with a bang. Kastner spun the bolts and slid the inner lock into place. "Ready. All ready."

Ryan threw the power switch. Outside, the remaining soldiers fought through the flame to the side of the ship. Ryan could see their faces through the port, seared and scorched by the blast.

One man raised his gun awkwardly. Most of them were down, rolling and struggling to rise. As the scene dimmed and faded he saw one of them crawling to his knees. The man's clothing was on fire. Smoke billowed from him, from his arms and shoulders. His face was contorted with pain. He reached out, toward the ship, reaching up at Ryan, his hands shaking, his body bent.

Suddenly Ryan froze.

He was still staring fixedly when the scene winked out and there was nothing. Nothing at all. The meters changed reading. Across the time map the arms moved calmly, tracing their lines.

In the last moment Ryan had looked directly into the man's face. The pain-contorted face. The features had been twisted, screwed up out of shape. And the horn-rimmed glasses were gone. But there was no doubt—It was Schonerman.

Ryan sat down. He ran a shaking hand through his hair.

"You're certain?" Kastner said.

"Yes. He must have come out of the sleep very quickly. It reacts differently on each person. And he was at the far end of the room. He must have come out of it and followed after us."

"Was he badly injured?"

"I don't know."

Kastner opened his briefcase. "Anyhow, we have the papers."

Ryan nodded, only half hearing. Schonerman injured, blasted, his clothing on fire. That had not been part of the plan.

But more important—*had it been part of history?*

For the first time the ramification of what they had done was beginning to emerge in his mind. Their own concern had been to obtain Schonerman's papers, so that USIC could make use of the artificial brain. Properly used, Schonerman's discovery could have great value in aiding the restoration of demolished Terra. Armies of worker-robots replanting and rebuilding. A mechanical army to make Terra fertile again. Robots could do in a generation what humans would toil at for years. Terra could be reborn.

But in returning to the past had they introduced new factors? Had a new past been created? Had some kind of balance been upset?

Ryan stood up and paced back and forth.

"What is it?" Kastner said. "We got the papers."

"I know."

"USIC will be pleased. The League can expect aid from now on. Whatever it wants. This will set up USIC forever. After all, USIC will manufacture the robots. Worker-robots. The end of human labor. Machines instead of men to work the ground."

Ryan nodded. "Fine."

"Then what's wrong?"

"I'm worried about our continuum."

"What are you worried about?"

Ryan crossed to the control board and studied the time map. The ship was moving back toward the present, the arms tracing a path back. "I'm worried about new factors we may have introduced into past continuums. There's no record of Schonerman being injured. There's no record of this event. It may have set a different causal chain into motion."

"Like what?"

"I don't know. But I intend to find out. We're going to make a stop right away and discover what new factors we've set into motion."

Ryan moved the ship into a continuum immediately following the Schonerman incident. It was early October, a little over a week later. He landed the ship in a farmer's field outside of Des Moines, Iowa, at sunset. A cold autumn night with the ground hard and brittle underfoot.

Ryan and Kastner walked into town, Kastner holding tightly onto his briefcase. Des Moines had been bombed by Russian guided missiles. Most of the industrial sections were gone. Only military men and construction workers still remained in the city. The civilian population had been evacuated.

Animals roamed around the deserted streets, looking for food. Glass and debris lay everywhere. The city was cold and desolate. The streets were gutted and wrecked from the fires following the bombing. The autumn air was heavy with the decaying smells of vast heaps of rubble and bodies mixed together in mounds at intersections and open lots.

From a boarded-up newsstand Ryan stole a copy of a news magazine, *Week Review*. The magazine was damp and covered with mold.

Kastner put it into his briefcase and they returned to the time ship. Occasional soldiers passed them, moving weapons and equipment out of the city. No one challenged them.

They reached the time ship and entered, locking the hatch behind them. The fields around them were deserted. The farm building had been burned down, and the crops were withered and dead. In the driveway the remains of a ruined automobile lay on its side, a charred wreck. A group of ugly pigs nosed around the remains of the farmhouse, searching for something to eat.

Ryan sat down, opened the magazine. He studied it for a long time, turning the damp pages slowly.

"What do you see?" Kastner asked.

"All about the war. It's still in the opening stages. Soviet guided missiles dropping down. American disc bombs showering all over Russia."

"Any mention of Schonerman?"

"Nothing I can find. Too much else going on." Ryan went on studying the magazine. Finally, on one of the back pages, he found what he was looking for. A small item, only a paragraph long.

SOVIET AGENTS SURPRISED

A group of Soviet agents, attempting to demolish a Government research station at Harristown, Kansas, were fired on by guards and quickly routed. The agents escaped, after attempting to slip past the guards into the work offices of the station. Passing themselves off as FBI men, the Soviet agents tried to gain entry as the early morning shift was beginning work. Alert guards intercepted them and gave chase. No damage was done to the research labs or equipment. Two guards and one worker were killed in the encounter. The names of the guards

❖ ❖ ❖

Ryan clutched the magazine.

"What is it?" Kastner hurried over.

Ryan read the rest of the article. He laid down the magazine, pushing it slowly toward Kastner.

"What is it?" Kastner searched the page.

"Schonerman died. Killed by the blast. We killed him. We've changed the past."

Ryan stood up and walked to the port. He lit a cigarette, some of his composure returning. "We set up new factors and started a new line of events. There's no telling where it will end."

"What do you mean?"

"Someone else may discover the artificial brain. Maybe the shift will rectify itself. The time flow will resume its regular course."

"Why should it?"

"I don't know. As it stands, we killed him and stole his papers. There's no way the Government can get hold of his work. They won't even know it ever existed. Unless someone else does the same work, covers the same material—"

"How will we know?"

"We'll have to take more looks. It's the only way to find out."

❖ ❖ ❖

Ryan selected the year 2051.

In 2051 the first claws had begun to appear. The Soviets had almost won the war. The UN was beginning to bring out the claws in the last desperate attempt to turn the tide of the war.

Ryan landed the time ship at the top of a ridge. Below them a level plain stretched out, criss-crossed with ruins and barbed wire and the remains of weapons.

Kastner unscrewed the hatch and stepped gingerly out onto the ground.

"Be careful," Ryan said. "Remember the claws."

Kastner drew his blast gun. "I'll remember."

"At this stage they were small. About a foot long. Metal. They hid down in the ash. The humanoid types hadn't come into existence, yet."

The sun was high in the sky. It was about noon. The air was warm and thick. Clouds of ash rolled across the ground, blown by the wind.

Suddenly Kastner tensed. "Look. What's that? Coming along the road."

A truck bumped slowly toward them, a heavy brown truck, loaded with soldiers. The truck made its way along the road to the base of the ridge. Ryan drew his blast gun. He and Kastner stood ready.

The truck stopped. Some of the soldiers leaped down and started up the side of the ridge, striding through the ash.

"Get set," Ryan murmured.

The soldiers reached them, halted a few feet away. Ryan and Kastner stood silently, their blast guns up.

One of the soldiers laughed. "Put them away. Don't you know the war's over?"

"*Over?*"

The soldiers relaxed. Their leader, a big man with a red face, wiped sweat from his forehead and pushed his way up to Ryan. His uniform was ragged and dirty. He wore boots, split and caked with ash. "That war's been over for a week. Come on! There's a lot to do. We'll take you on back."

"Back?"

"We're rounding up all the outposts. You were cut off? No communications?"

"No," Ryan said.

"Be months before everyone knows the war's over. Come along. No time to stand here jawing."

Ryan shifted. "Tell me. You say the war is really over? But—"

"Good thing, too. We couldn't have lasted much longer." The

officer tapped his belt. "You don't by any chance have a cigarette, do you?"

Ryan brought out his pack slowly. He took the cigarettes from it and handed them to the officer, crumpling the pack carefully and restoring it to his pocket.

"Thanks." The officer passed the cigarettes around to his men. They lit up. "Yes, it's a good thing. We were almost finished."

Kastner's mouth opened. "The claws. What about the claws?"

The officer scowled. "What?"

"Why did the war end so—so suddenly?"

"Counter-revolution in the Soviet Union. We had been dropping agents and material for months. Never thought anything would come of it, though. They were a lot weaker than anyone realized."

"Then the war's really ended?"

"Of course." The officer grabbed Ryan by the arm. "Let's go. We have work to do. We're trying to clear this god damn ash away and get things planted."

"Planted? Crops?"

"Of course. What would *you* plant?"

Ryan pulled away. "Let me get this straight. The war is over. No more fighting. And you know nothing about any claws? Any kind of weapon called claws?"

The officer's face wrinkled. "What do you mean?"

"Mechanical killers. Robots. As a weapon."

The circle of soldiers drew back a little. "What the hell is he talking about?"

"You better explain," the officer said, his face suddenly hard. "What's this about claws?"

"No weapon was ever developed along those lines?" Kastner asked.

There was silence. Finally one of the soldiers grunted. "I think I know what he means. He means Dowling's mine."

Ryan turned. "What?"

"An English physicist. He's been experimenting with artificial mines, self-governing. Robot mines. But the mines couldn't repair themselves. So the Government abandoned the project and increased its propaganda work instead."

"That's why the war's over," the officer said. He started off. "Let's go."

The soldiers trailed after him, down the side of the ridge.

"Coming?" The officer halted, looking back at Ryan and Kastner.

"We'll be along later," Ryan said. "We have to get our equipment together."

"All right. The camp is down the road about half a mile. There's a settlement there. People coming back from the moon."

"From the moon?"

"We had started moving units to Luna, but now there isn't any need. Maybe it's a good thing. Who the hell wants to leave Terra?"

"Thanks for the cigarettes," one the soldiers called back. The soldiers piled in the back of the truck. The officer slid behind the wheel. The truck started up and continued on its way, rumbling along the road.

Ryan and Kastner watched it go.

"Then Schonerman's death was never balanced," Ryan murmured. "A whole new past—"

"I wonder how far the change carries. I wonder if it carries up to our own time."

"There's only one way to find out."

Kastner nodded. "I want to know right away. The sooner the better. Let's get started."

Ryan nodded, deep in thought. "The sooner the better."

They entered the time ship. Kastner sat down with his briefcase. Ryan adjusted the controls. Outside the port the scene winked out of existence. They were in the time flow again, moving toward the present.

Ryan's face was grim. "I can't believe it. The whole structure of the past changed. An entire new chain set in motion. Expanding through every continuum. Altering more and more of our stream."

"Then it won't be our present, when we get back. There's no telling how different it will be. All stemming from Schonerman's death. A whole new history set in motion from one incident."

"Not from Schonerman's death," Ryan corrected.

"What do you mean?"

"Not from his death but from the loss of his papers. Because Schonerman died the Government didn't obtain a successful methodology by which they could build an artificial brain. Therefore the claws never came into existence."

"It's the same thing."

"Is it?"

Kastner looked up quickly. "Explain."

"Schonerman's death is of no importance. The loss of his papers to the Government is the determining factor." Ryan pointed at Kastner's briefcase. "Where are the papers? In there. We have them."

Kastner nodded. "That's true."

"We can restore the situation by moving back into the past and delivering the papers to some agency of the Government. Schonerman is unimportant. It's his papers that matter."

Ryan's hand moved toward the power switch.

"Wait!" Kastner said. "Don't we want to see the present? We should see what changes carry down to our own time."

Ryan hesitated. "True."

"Then we can decided what we want to do. Whether we want to restore the papers."

"All right. We'll continue to the present and then make up our minds."

The fingers crossing the time map had returned almost to their original position. Ryan studied them for a long time, his hand on the power switch. Kastner held on tightly to the briefcase, his arms wrapped around it, the heavy leather bundle resting in his lap.

"We're almost there," Ryan said.

"To our own time?"

"In another few moments." Ryan stood up, gripping the switch. "I wonder what we'll see."

"Probably very little we'll recognize."

Ryan took a deep breath, feeling the cold metal under his fingers. How different would their world be? Would they recognize anything? Had they swept everything familiar out of existence?

A vast chain had been started in motion. A tidal wave moving through time, altering each continuum, echoing down through all the ages to come. The second part of the war had never happened. Before the claws could be invented the war had ended. The concept of the artificial brain had never been transformed into workable practice. The most potent engine of war had never come into existence. Human energies had turned from war to rebuilding of the planet.

Around Ryan the meters and dials vibrated. In a few seconds they would be back. What would Terra be like? Would anything be the same?

The Fifty Cities. Probably they would not exist. Jon, his son, sitting quietly in his room reading. USIC. The Government. The League and its labs and offices, its buildings and roof fields and guards. The whole complicated social structure. Would it all be gone without a trace? Probably.

And what would he find instead?

"We'll know in a minute," Ryan murmured.

"It won't be long," Kastner got to his feet and moved to the port. "I want to see it. It should be a very unfamiliar world."

Ryan threw the power switch. The ship jerked, pulling out of the time flow. Outside the port something drifted and turned, as the ship righted itself. Automatic gravity controls slipped into place. The ship was rushing above the surface of the ground.

Kastner gasped.

"What do you see?" Ryan demanded, adjusting the velocity of the ship. "What's out there?"

Kastner said nothing.

"What do you see?"

After a long time Kastner turned away from the port. "Very interesting. Look for yourself."

"What's out there?"

Kastner sat down slowly, picking up his briefcase. "This opens up a whole new line of thought."

Ryan made his way to the port and gazed out. Below the ship lay Terra. But not the Terra they had left.

Fields, endless yellow fields. And parks. Parks and yellow fields. Squares of green among the yellow, as far as the eye could see. Nothing else.

"No cities," Ryan said thickly.

"No. Don't you remember? The people are all out in the fields. Or walking in the parks. Discussing the nature of the universe."

"This is what Jon saw."

"Your son was extremely accurate."

Ryan moved back to the controls, his face blank. His mind was numb. He sat down and adjusted the landing grapples. The ship sank lower and lower until it was coasting over the flat fields. Men and women glanced up at the ship, startled. Men and women in robes.

They passed over a park. A herd of animals rushed frantically away. Some kind of deer.

This was the world his son had seen. This was his vision. Fields and parks and men and women in long flowing robes. Walking along the paths. Discussing the problems of the universe.

And the other world, his world, no longer existed. The League was gone. His whole life's work destroyed. In this world it did not exist. Jon. His son. Snuffed out. He would never see him again. His work, his son, everything he had known had winked out of existence.

"We have to go back," Ryan said suddenly.

Kastner blinked. "Beg pardon?"

"We have to take the papers back to the continuum where they belong. We can't recreate the situation exactly, but we can place the papers in the Government's hands. That will restore all the relevant factors."

"Are you serious?"

Ryan stood up unsteadily, moving toward Kastner. "Give me the papers. This is a very serious situation. We must work quickly. Things have to be put back in place."

Kastner stepped back, whipping out his blaster. Ryan lunged. His shoulder caught Kastner, bowling the little businessman over. The blaster skidded across the floor of the ship, clattering against the wall. The papers fluttered in all directions.

"You damn fool!" Ryan grabbed at the papers, dropping down to his knees.

Kastner chased after the blaster. He scooped it up, his round face set with owlish determination. Ryan saw him out of the corner of his eye. For a moment the temptation to laugh almost overcame him. Kastner's face was flushed, his cheeks burning red. He fumbled with the blaster, trying to aim it.

"Kastner, for God's sake—"

The little businessman's fingers tightened around the trigger. Abrupt fear chilled Ryan. He scrambled to his feet. The blaster roared, flame crackling across the time ship. Ryan leaped out of the way, singed by the trail of fire.

Schonerman's papers flared up, glowing where they lay scattered over the floor. For a brief second they burned. Then the glow died out, flickering into charred ash. The thin acrid smell of the blast drifted to Ryan, tickling his nose and making his eyes water.

"Sorry," Kastner murmured. He laid the blaster down on the control board. "Don't you think you better get us down? We're quite close to the surface."

Ryan moved mechanically to the control board. After a moment he took his seat and began to adjust the controls, decreasing the velocity of the ship. He said nothing.

"I'm beginning to understand about Jon," Kastner murmured. "He must have had some kind of parallel time sense. Awareness of other possible futures. As work progressed on the time ship his visions increased, didn't they? Every day his visions become more real. Every day the time ship became more actual."

Ryan nodded.

"This opens up whole new lines of speculation. The mystical visions of medieval saints. Perhaps they were of other futures, other time flows. Visions of hell would be worse time flows. Visions of heaven would be better time flows. Ours must stand some place in the middle. And the vision of the eternal unchanging world. Perhaps that's an awareness of non-time. Not another world but this world, seen outside of time. We'll have to think more about that, too."

The ship landed, coming to rest at the edge of one of the parks. Kastner crossed to the port and gazed out at the trees beyond the ship.

"In the books my family saved there were some pictures of trees," he said thoughtfully. "These trees here, by us. They're pepper trees. Those over there are what they call evergreen trees. They stay that way all year around. That's why the name."

Kastner picked up his briefcase, gripping it tightly. He moved toward the hatch.

"Let's go find some of the people. So we can begin discussing things. Metaphysical things." He grinned at Ryan. "I always did like metaphysical things."

PROGENY

Ed Doyle hurried. He caught a surface car, waved fifty credits in the robot driver's face, mopped his florid face with a red pocket-handkerchief, unfastened his collar, perspired and licked his lips and swallowed piteously all the way to the hospital.

The surface car slid up to a smooth halt before the great white-domed hospital building. Ed leaped out and bounded up the steps three at a time, pushing through the visitors and convalescent patients standing on the broad terrace. He threw his weight against the door and emerged in the lobby, astonishing the attendants and persons of importance moving about their tasks.

"Where?" Ed demanded, gazing around, his feet wide apart, his fists clenched, his chest rising and falling. His breath came hoarsely, like an animal's. Silence fell over the lobby. Everyone turned toward him, pausing in their work. "Where?" Ed demanded again. "Where is she? *They?*"

It was fortunate Janet had been delivered of a child on this of all days. Proxima Centauri was a long way from Terra and the service was bad. Anticipating the birth of his child, Ed had left Proxima some weeks before. He had just arrived in the city. While stowing his suitcase in the luggage tread at the station the message had been handed to him by a robot courier: *Los Angeles Central Hospital. At once.*

Ed hurried, and fast. As he hurried he couldn't help feeling pleased he had hit the day exactly right, almost to the hour. It was a good feeling. He had felt it before, during years of business dealings in the "colonies," the frontier, the fringe of Terran civilization where the streets were still lit by electric lights and doors opened by hand.

That was going to be hard to get used to. Ed turned toward the door behind him, feeling suddenly foolish. He had shoved it open, ignoring the eye. The door was just now closing, sliding slowly back in place. He calmed down a little, putting his handkerchief away in his coat pocket. The hospital attendants were resuming their work, picking up their activities where they had left off. One attendant, a strapping late-model robot, coasted over to Ed and halted.

The robot balanced his noteboard expertly, his photocell eyes appraising Ed's flushed features. "May I inquire whom you are looking for, sir? Whom do you wish to find?"

"My wife."

"Her name, sir?"

"Janet. Janet Doyle. She's just had a child."

The robot consulted his board. "This way, sir." He coasted off down the passage.

Ed followed nervously. "Is she okay? Did I get here in time?" His anxiety was returning.

"She is quite well, sir." The robot raised his metal arm and a side door slid back. "In here, sir."

Janet, in a chic blue-mesh suit, was sitting before a mahogany desk, a cigarette between her fingers, her slim legs crossed, talking rapidly. On the other side of the desk a well-dressed doctor sat listening.

"Janet!" Ed said, entering the room.

"Hi, Ed." She glanced up at him. "You just now get in?"

"Sure. It's—it's all over? You—I mean, it's *happened*?"

Janet laughed, her even white teeth sparkling. "Of course. Come in and sit. This is Doctor Bish."

"Hello, Doc." Ed sat down nervously across from them. "Then it's all over?"

"The event has happened," Doctor Bish said. His voice was thin and metallic. Ed realized with a sudden shock that the doctor was a robot. A top-level robot, made in humanoid form, not like the ordinary metal-limbed workers. It had fooled him—he had been away so long. Doctor Bish appeared plump and well fed, with kindly features and eyeglasses. His large fleshy hands rested on the desk, a ring on one finger. Pinstripe suit and necktie. Diamond tie clasp. Nails carefully manicured. Hair black and evenly parted.

But his voice had given him away. They never seemed to be able to get a really human sound into the voice. The compressed air and whirling disc system seemed to fall short. Otherwise, it was very convincing.

"I understand you've been situated near Proxima, Mr. Doyle," Doctor Bish said pleasantly.

Ed nodded. "Yeah."

"Quite a long way, isn't it? I've never been out there. I have always wanted to go. Is it true they're almost ready to push on to Sirius?"

"Look, doc—"

"Ed, don't be impatient." Janet stubbed out her cigarette, glancing reprovingly up at him. She hadn't changed in six months. Small blond face, red mouth, cold eyes like little blue rocks. And now, her perfect figure back again. "They're bringing him here. It takes a few minutes. They have to wash him off and put drops in his eyes and take a wave shot of his brain."

"*He?* Then it's a boy?"

"Of course. Don't you remember? You were with me when I had the shots. We agreed at the time. You haven't changed your mind, have you?"

"Too late to change your mind now, Mr. Doyle," Doctor Bish's toneless voice came, high-pitched and calm. "Your wife has decided to call him Peter."

"Peter." Ed nodded, a little dazed. "That's right. We did decide, didn't we? Peter." He let the word roll around in his mind. "Yeah. That's fine. I like it."

The wall suddenly faded, turning from opaque to transparent. Ed spun quickly. They were looking into a brightly lit room, filled with hospital equipment and white-clad attendant robots. One of the robots was moving toward them, pushing a cart. On the cart was a container, a big metal pot.

Ed's breathing increased. He felt a wave of dizziness. He went up to the transparent wall and stood gazing at the metal pot on the cart.

Doctor Bish rose. "Don't you want to see, too, Mrs. Doyle?"

"Of course." Janet crossed to the wall and stood beside Ed. She watched critically, her arms folded.

Doctor Bish made a signal. The attendant reached into the pot and lifted out a wire tray, gripping the handles with his magnetic clamps. On the tray, dripping through the wire, was Peter Doyle, still wet from his bath, his eyes wide with astonishment. He was pink all over, except for a fringe of hair on the top of his head, and his great blue eyes. He was little and wrinkled and toothless, like an ancient withered sage.

"Golly," Ed said.

Doctor Bish made a second signal. The wall slid back. The attendant robot advanced into the room, holding his dripping tray out. Doctor Bish removed Peter from the tray and held him up for inspection. He turned him around and around, studying him from every angle.

"He looks fine," he said at last.

"What was the result of the wave photo?" Janet asked.

"Result was good. Excellent tendencies indicated. Very promising. High development of the—" The doctor broke off. "What is it, Mr. Doyle?"

Ed was holding out his hands. "Let me have him, doc. I want to hold him." He grinned from ear to ear. "Let's see how heavy he is. He sure looks big."

Doctor Bish's mouth fell open in horror. He and Janet gaped.

"Ed!" Janet exclaimed sharply. "What's the matter with you?"

"Good heavens, Mr. Doyle," the doctor murmured.

Ed blinked. "What?"

"If I had thought you had any such thing in mind—" Doctor Bish quickly returned Peter to the attendant. The attendant rushed Peter from the room, back to the metal pot. The cart and robot and pot hurriedly vanished, and the wall banged back in place.

Janet grabbed Ed's arm angrily. "Good Lord, Ed! Have you lost your mind? Come on. Let's get out of here before you do something else."

"But—"

"Come on." Janet smiled nervously at Doctor Bish. "We'll run along now, doctor. Thanks so much for everything. Don't pay any attention to him. He's been out there so long, you know."

"I understand," Doctor Bish said smoothly. He had regained his poise. "I trust we'll hear from you later, Mrs. Doyle."

Janet pulled Ed out into the hall. "Ed, what's the matter with you? I've never been so embarrassed in all my life." Two spots of red glowed in Janet's cheeks. "I could have kicked you."

"But what—"

"You know we aren't allowed to touch him. What do you want to do, ruin his whole life?"

"But—"

"Come on." They hurried outside the hospital, on to the terrace. Warm sunlight streamed down on them. "There's no telling what harm you've done. He may already be hopelessly warped. If he grows up all warped and—and neurotic and emotional, it'll be your fault."

Suddenly Ed remembered. He sagged, his features drooping with misery. "That's right. I forgot. Only robots can come near the children. I'm sorry, Jan. I got carried away. I hope I didn't do anything they can't fix."

"How *could* you forget?"

"It's so different out at Prox." Ed waved to a surface car, crestfallen and abashed. The driver drew up in front of them. "Jan, I'm sorry as hell. I really am. I was all excited. Let's go have a cup of coffee some place and talk. I want to know what the doctor said."

Ed had a cup of coffee and Janet sipped at a brandy frappé. The Nymphite Room was pitch black except for a vague light oozing up from the table between them. The table diffused a pale illumination that spread over everything, a ghostly radiation seemingly without source. A robot waitress moved back and forth soundlessly with a tray of drinks. Recorded music played softly in the back of the room.

"Go on," Ed said.

"Go on?" Janet slipped her jacket off and laid it over the back of her chair. In the pale light her breasts glowed faintly. "There's not much to tell. Everything went all right. It didn't take long. I chatted with Doctor Bish most of the time."

"I'm glad I got here."

"How was your trip?"

"Fine."

"Is the service getting any better? Does it still take as long as it did?"

"About the same."

"I can't see why you want to go all the way out there. It's so—so cut off from things. What do you find out there? Are plumbing fixtures really that much in demand?"

"They need them. Frontier area. Everyone wants the refinements." Ed gestured vaguely. "What did he tell you about Peter? What's he going to be like? Can he tell? I guess it's too soon."

"He was going to tell me when you started acting the way you did. I'll call him on the vidphone when we get home. His wave pattern should be good. He comes from the best eugenic stock."

Ed grunted. "On your side, at least."

"How long are you going to be here?"

"I don't know. Not long. I'll have to go back. I'd sure like to see him again, before I go." He glanced up hopefully at his wife. "Do you think I can?"

"I suppose."

"How long will he have to stay there?"

"At the hospital? Not long. A few days."

Ed hesitated. "I didn't mean at the hospital, exactly. I mean with *them*. How long before we can have him? How long before we can bring him home?"

There was silence. Janet finished her brandy. She leaned back, lighting a cigarette. Smoke drifted across to Ed, blending with the pale light. "Ed, I don't think you understand. You've been out there so long. A lot has happened since you were a child. New methods, new techniques. They've found so many things they didn't know. They're making progress, for the first time. They know what to do. They're developing a real methodology for dealing with children. For the growth period. Attitude development. Training." She smiled brightly at Ed. "I've been reading all about it."

"How long before we get him?"

"In a few days he'll be released from the hospital. He'll go to a child guidance center. He'll be tested and studied. They'll determine his various capacities and his latent abilities. The direction his development seems to be taking."

"And then?"

"Then he's put in the proper educational division. So he'll get the right training. Ed, you know, I think he's really going to be something! I could tell by the way Doctor Bish looked. He was studying the wave pattern charts when I came in. He had a look on his face. How can I describe it?" She searched for the word. "Well, almost—almost a greedy look. Real excitement. They take so much interest in what they're doing. He—"

"Don't say he. Say it."

"Ed, really! What's got into you?"

"Nothing." Ed glared sullenly down. "Go on."

"They make sure he's trained in the right direction. All the time he's there ability tests are given. Then, when he's about nine, he'll be transferred to—"

"Nine! You mean nine *years*?"

"Of course."

"But when do we get him?"

"Ed, I thought you knew about this. Do I have to go over the whole thing?"

"My God, Jan! We can't wait nine years!" Ed jerked himself upright. "I never heard of such a thing. Nine years? Why, he'll be half grown up then."

"That's the point." Janet leaned towards him, resting her bare elbow against the table. "As long as he's growing he has to be with them. Not with us. Afterwards, when he's finished growing, when he's no longer so plastic, then we can be with him all we want."

"Afterwards? When he's eighteen?" Ed leaped up, pushing his chair back. "I'm going down there and get him."

"Sit down, Ed." Janet gazed up calmly, one supple arm thrown lightly over the back of her chair. "Sit down and act like an adult for a change."

"Doesn't it matter to you? Don't you care?"

"Of course I care." Janet shrugged. "But it's necessary. Otherwise he won't develop correctly. It's for *his* good. Not ours. He doesn't exist for us. Do you want him to have conflicts?"

Ed moved away from the table. "I'll see you later."

"Where are you going?"

"Just around. I can't stand this kind of place. It bothers me. I'll see you later." Ed pushed across the room to the door. The door opened and he found himself on the shiny noonday street. Hot sunlight beat down on him. He blinked, adjusting himself to the blinding light. People streamed around him. People and noise. He moved with them.

He was dazed. He had known, of course. It was there in the back of his mind. The new developments in child care. But it had been abstract, general. Nothing to do with him. With *his* child.

He calmed himself, as he walked along. He was getting all upset about nothing. Janet was right, of course. It was for Peter's good. Peter didn't exist for them, like a dog or cat. A pet to have around the house. He was a human being, with his own life. The training was for him, not for them. It was to develop him, his abilities, his powers. He was to be molded, realized, brought out.

Naturally, robots could do the best job. Robots could train him scientifically, according to a rational technique. Not according to emotional whim. Robots didn't get angry. Robots didn't nag and whine. They didn't spank a child or yell at him. They didn't give conflicting orders. They didn't quarrel among themselves or use the child for their own ends. And there could be no *Oedipus Complex*, with only robots around.

No complexes at all. It had been discovered long ago that neurosis could be traced to childhood training. To the way parents brought up the child. The inhibitions he was taught, the manners, the lessons, the punishments, the rewards. Neuroses, complexes, warped development, all stemmed from the subjective relationship existing between the child and the parent. If perhaps the parent could be eliminated as a factor . . .

Parents could never become objective about their children. It was always a biased, emotional projection the parent held toward the child. Inevitably, the parent's view was distorted. No parent could be a fit instructor for his child.

Robots could study the child, analyze his needs, his wants, test his abilities and interests. Robots would not try to force the child to fit a certain mold. The child would be trained along his own lines; wherever scientific study indicated his interest and need lay.

Ed came to the corner. Traffic whirred past him. He stepped absently forward.

A clang and crash. Bars dropped in front of him, stopping him. A robot safety control.

"Sir, be more careful!" the strident voice came, close by him.

"Sorry." Ed stepped back. The control bars lifted. He waited for the lights to change. It was for Peter's own good. Robots could train him right. Later on, when he was out of growth stage, when he was not so pliant, so responsive—"It's better for him," Ed murmured. He said it again, half aloud. Some people glanced at him and he colored. Of course it was better for him. No doubt about it.

Eighteen. He couldn't be with his son until he was eighteen. Practically grown up.

The lights changed. Deep in thought, Ed crossed the street with the other pedestrians, keeping carefully inside the safety lane. It was best for Peter. But eighteen years was a long time.

"A hell of a long time," Ed murmured, frowning. "Too damn long a time."

❖ ❖ ❖

Doctor 2g-Y Bish carefully studied the man standing in front of him. His relays and memory banks clicked, narrowing down the image identification, flashing a variety of comparison possibilities past the scanner.

"I recall you, sir," Doctor Bish said at last. "You're the man from Proxima. From the colonies. Doyle, Edward Doyle. Let's see. It was some time ago. It must have been—"

"Nine years ago," Ed Doyle said grimly. "Exactly nine years ago, practically to the day."

Doctor Bish folded his hands. "Sit down, Mr. Doyle. What can I do for you? How is Mrs. Doyle? Very engaging wife, as I recall. We had a delightful conversation during her delivery. How—"

"Doctor Bish, do you know where my son is?"

Doctor Bish considered, tapping his fingers on the desk top, the polished mahogany surface. He closed his eyes slightly, gazing off into the distance. "Yes. Yes, I know where your son is, Mr. Doyle."

Ed Doyle relaxed. "Fine." He nodded, letting his breath out in relief.

"I know exactly where your son is. I placed him in the Los Angeles Biological Research Station about a year ago. He's undergoing specialized training there. Your son, Mr. Doyle, has shown exceptional ability. He is, shall I say, one of the few, the very few we have found with real possibilities."

"Can I see him?"

"See him? How do you mean?"

Doyle controlled himself with an effort. "I think the term is clear."

Doctor Bish rubbed his chin. His photocell brain whirred, operating at maximum velocity. Switches routed power surges, building up loads and leaping gaps rapidly, as he contemplated the man before him. "You wish to *view* him? That's one meaning of the term. Or do you wish to talk to him? Sometimes the term is used to cover a more direct contact. It's a loose word."

"I want to talk to him."

"I see." Bish slowly drew some forms from the dispenser on his desk. "There are a few routine papers that have to be filled out first, of course. Just how long did you want to speak to him?"

Ed Doyle gazed steadily into Doctor Bish's bland face. "I want to talk to him several hours. *Alone.*"

"Alone?"

"No robots around."

Doctor Bish said nothing. He stroked the papers he held, creasing the edges with his nail. "Mr. Doyle," he said carefully, "I wonder if you're in a proper emotional state to visit your son. You have recently come in from the colonies?"

"I left Proxima three weeks ago."

"Then you have just arrived here in Los Angeles?"

"That's right."

"And you've come to see your son? Or have you other business?"

"I came for my son."

"Mr. Doyle, Peter is at a very critical stage. He has just recently been transferred to the Biology Station for his higher training. Up to now his training has been general. What we call the non-differentiated stage. Recently he has entered a new period. Within the last six months Peter has begun advanced work along his specific line, that of organic chemistry. He will—"

"What does Peter think about it?"

Bish frowned. "I don't understand, sir."

"How does *he* feel? Is it what he wants?"

"Mr. Doyle, your son has the possibility of becoming one of the world's finest bio-chemists. In all the time we have worked with human beings, in their training and development, we have never come across a more alert and integrated faculty for the assimilation of data, construction of theory, formulation of material, than that which your son possesses. All tests indicate he will rapidly rise to the top of his chosen field. He is still only a child, Mr. Doyle, but it is the children who must be trained."

Doyle stood up. "Tell me where I can find him. I'll talk to him for two hours and then the rest is up to him."

"The rest?"

Doyle clamped his jaw shut. He shoved his hands in his pockets. His face was flushed and set, grim with determination. In the nine years he had grown much heavier, more stocky and florid. His thinning hair had turned iron-gray. His clothes were dumpy and unpressed. He looked stubborn.

Doctor Bish sighed. "All right, Mr. Doyle. Here are your papers. The law allows you to observe your boy whenever you make proper application. Since he is out of his non-differentiated stage, you may also speak to him for a period of ninety minutes."

"Alone?"

"You can take him away from the Station grounds for that length of time." Doctor Bish pushed the papers over to Doyle. "Fill these out, and I'll have Peter brought here."

He looked up steadily at the man standing before him.

"I hope you'll remember that any emotional experience at this crucial stage may do much to inhibit his development. He has chosen his field, Mr. Doyle. He must be permitted to grow along his selected lines, unhindered by situational blocks. Peter has been in contact with out technical staff throughout his entire training period. He is not accustomed to contact with other human beings. So please be careful."

Doyle said nothing. He grabbed up the papers and plucked out his fountain pen.

He hardly recognized his son when the two robot attendants brought him out of the massive concrete Station building and deposited him a few yards from Ed's parked surface car.

Ed pushed the door open. "Pete!" His heart was thumping heavily, painfully. He watched his son come toward the car, frowning in the bright sunlight. It was late afternoon, about four. A faint breeze blew across the parking lot, rustling a few papers and bits of debris.

Peter stood slim and straight. His eyes were large, deep brown, like Ed's. His hair was light, almost blond. More like Janet's. He had Ed's jaw, though, the firm line, clean and well chiseled. Ed grinned at him. Nine years it had been. Nine years since the robot attendant had lifted the rack up from the conveyor pot to show him the little wrinkled baby, red as a boiled lobster.

Peter had grown. He was not a baby any longer. He was a young boy, straight and proud, with firm features and wide, clear eyes.

"Pete," Ed said. "How the hell are you?"

The boy stopped by the door of the car. He gazed at Ed calmly. His eyes flickered, taking in the car, the robot driver, the heavy set man in the rumpled tweed suit grinning nervously at him.

"Get in. Get inside." Ed moved over. "Come on. We have places to go."

The boy was looking at him again. Suddenly Ed was conscious of his baggy suit, his unshined shoes, his gray stubbled chin. He flushed, yanking out his red pocket-handkerchief and mopping his forehead uneasily. "I just got off the ship, Pete. From Proxima. I haven't had time to change. I'm a little dusty. Long trip."

Peter nodded. "4.3 light years, isn't it?"

"Takes three weeks. Get in. Don't you want to get in?"

Peter slid in beside him. Ed slammed the door.

"Let's go." The car started up. "Drive—" Ed peered out the window. "Drive up there. By the hill. Out of town." He turned to Pete. "I hate big cities. I can't get used to them."

"There are no large cities in the colonies, are there?" Pete murmured. "You're unused to urban living."

Ed settled back. His heart had begun to slow down to its normal beat. "No, as a matter of fact it's the other way around, Pete."

"How do you mean?"

"I went to Prox *because* I couldn't stand cities."

Peter said nothing. The surface car was climbing, going up a steel highway into the hills. The Station, huge and impressive, spread out like a heap of cement bricks directly below them. A few cars moved along the road, but not many. Most transportation was by air, now. Surface cars had begun to disappear.

The road leveled off. They moved along the ridge of the hills. Trees and bushes rose on both sides of them. "It's nice up here," Ed said.

"Yes."

"How—how have you been? I haven't seen you for a long time. Just once. Just after you were born."

"I know. Your visit is listed in the records."

"You been getting along all right?"

"Yes. Quite well."

"They treating you all right?"

"Of course."

After a while Ed leaned forward. "Stop here," he said to the robot driver.

The car slowed down, pulling over to the side of the road. "Sir, there is nothing—"

"This is fine. Let us out. We'll walk from here."

The car stopped. The door slid reluctantly open. Ed stepped quickly out of the car, on to the pavement. Peter got out slowly after him, puzzled. "Where are we?"

"No place." Ed slammed the door. "Go on back to town," he said to the driver. "We won't need you."

The car drove off. Ed walked to the side of the road. Peter came after him. The hill dropped away, falling down to the beginnings of the city below. A vast panorama stretched out, the great metropolis in the late afternoon sun. Ed took a deep breath, throwing his arms out. He took off his coat and tossed it over his shoulder.

"Come on." He started down the hillside. "Here we go."

"Where?"

"For a walk. Let's get off this damn road."

They climbed down the side of the hill, walking carefully, holding on to the grass and roots jutting out from the soil. Finally they came to a level place by a big sycamore tree. Ed threw himself down on the ground, grunting and wiping sweat from his neck.

"Here. Let's sit here."

Peter sat down carefully, a little way off. Ed's blue shirt was stained with sweat. He unfastened his tie and loosened his collar. Presently he searched through his coat pockets. He brought out his pipe and tobacco.

Peter watched him fill the pipe and light it with a big sulphur match. "What's that?" he murmured.

"This? My pipe." Ed grinned, sucking at the pipe. "Haven't you ever seen a pipe?"

"No."

"This is a good pipe. I got this when I first went out to Proxima. That was a long time ago. Pete. It was twenty-five years ago. I was just nineteen, then. Only about twice as old as you."

He put his tobacco away and leaned back, his heavy face serious, preoccupied.

"Just nineteen. I went out there as a plumber. Repair and sales, when I could make a sale. Terran Plumbing. One of those big ads you used to see. Unlimited opportunities. Virgin lands. Make a million. Gold in the streets." Ed laughed.

"How did you make out?"

"Not bad. Not bad at all. I own my own line, now, you know. I service the whole Proxima system. We do repairing, maintenance, building, construction. I've got six hundred people working for me. It took a long time. It didn't come easy."

"No."

"Hungry?"

Peter turned. "What?"

"Are you hungry?" Ed pulled a brown paper parcel from his coat and unwrapped it. "I still have a couple of sandwiches from the trip. When I come in from Prox I bring some food along with me. I don't like to buy in the diner. They skin you." He held out the parcel. "Want one?"

"No thank you."

Ed took a sandwich and began to eat. He ate nervously, glancing at his son. Peter sat silently, a short distance off, staring ahead without expression. His smooth handsome face was blank.

"Everything all right?" Ed said.

"Yes."

"You're not cold, are you?"

"No."

"You don't want to catch cold."

A squirrel crossed in front of them, hurrying toward the sycamore tree. Ed threw it a piece of his sandwich. The squirrel ran off a way, then came back slowly. It scolded at them, standing up on its hind feet, its great gray tail flowing out behind it.

Ed laughed. "Look at him. Ever see a squirrel before?"

"I don't think so."

The squirrel ran off with the piece of sandwich. It disappeared among the brush and bushes.

"Squirrels don't exist out around Prox," Ed said.

"No."

"It's good to come back to Terra once in a while. See some of the old things. They're going, though."

"Going?"

"Away. Destroyed. Terra is always changing." Ed waved around at the hillside. "This will be gone, some day. They'll cut down the trees. Then they'll level it. Some day they'll carve the whole range up and carry it off. Use it for fill, some place along the coast."

"That's beyond our scope," Peter said.

"What?"

"I don't receive that type of material. I think Doctor Bish told you. I'm working with bio-chemistry."

"I know," Ed murmured. "Say, how the hell did you ever get mixed up with that stuff? Bio-chemistry?"

"The tests showed that my abilities lie along those lines."

"You enjoy what you're doing?"

"What a strange thing to ask. Of course I enjoy what I'm doing. It's the work I'm fitted for."

"It seems funny as hell to me, starting a nine year old kid off on something like that."

"Why?"

"My God, Pete. When I was nine I was bumming around town. In school sometimes, outside mostly, wandering here and there. Playing. Reading. Sneaking into the rocket launching yards all the time." He considered. "Doing all sorts of things. When I was sixteen I hopped over to Mars. I stayed there a while. Worked as a hasher. I went on to Ganymede. Ganymede was all sewed up tight. Nothing doing there. From Ganymede I went out to Prox. Got a work-away all the way out. Big freighter."

"You stayed at Proxima?"

"I sure did. I found what I wanted. Nice place, out there. Now we're starting on to Sirius, you know." Ed's chest swelled. "I've got an outlet in the Sirius system. Little retail and service place."

"Sirius is 8.8 light years from Sol."

"It's a long way. Seven weeks from here. Rough grind. Meteor swarms. Keeps things hot all the way out."

"I can imagine."

"You know what I thought I might do?" Ed turned toward his son, his face alive with hope and enthusiasm. "I've been thinking it over. I thought maybe I'd go out there. To Sirius. It's a fine little place we have. I drew up the plans myself. Special design to fit with the characteristics of the system."

Peter nodded.

"Pete—"

"Yes?"

"Do you think maybe you'd be interested? Like to hop out to Sirius and take a look? It's a good place. Four clean planets. Never touched. Lots of room. Miles and miles of room. Cliffs and mountains. Oceans. Nobody around. Just a few colonists, families, some construction. Wide, level plains."

"How do you mean, interested?"

"In going all the way out." Ed's face was pale. His mouth twitched nervously. "I thought maybe you'd like to come along and see how things are. It's a lot like Prox was, twenty-five years ago. It's good and clean out there. No cities."

Peter smiled.

"Why are you smiling?"

"No reason." Peter stood up abruptly. "If we have to walk back to the Station we'd better start. Don't you think? It's getting late."

"Sure." Ed struggled to his feet. "Sure, but—"

"When are you going to be back in the Sol system again?"

"Back?" Ed followed after his son. Peter climbed up the hill toward the road. "Slow down, will you?"

Peter slowed down. Ed caught up with him.

"I don't know when I'll be back. I don't come here very often. No ties. Not since Jan and I separated. As a matter of fact I came here this time to—"

"This way." Peter started down the road.

Ed hurried along beside him, fastening his tie and putting his coat on, gasping for breath. "Peter, what do you say? You want to hop out to Sirius with me? Take a look? It's a nice place out there. We could work together. The two of us. If you want."

"But I already have my work."

"That stuff? That damn chemistry stuff?"

Peter smiled again.

Ed scowled, his face dark red. "Why are you smiling?" he demanded. His son did not answer. "What's the matter? What's so damn funny?"

"Nothing," Peter said. "Don't become excited. We have a long walk down." He increased his pace slightly, his supple body swinging in long, even strides. "It's getting late. We have to hurry."

❖ ❖ ❖

Doctor Bish examined his wristwatch, pushing back his pin-striped coat sleeve. "I'm glad you're back."

"He sent the surface car away," Peter murmured. "We had to walk down the hill on foot."

It was dark outside. The Station lights were coming on automatically, along the rows of buildings and laboratories.

Doctor Bish rose from his desk. "Sign this, Peter. Bottom of this form."

Peter signed. "What is it?"

"Certifies you saw him in accord with the provisions of the law. We didn't try to obstruct you in any way."

Peter handed the paper back. Bish filed it away with the others. Peter moved toward the door of the doctor's office. "I'll go. Down to the cafeteria for dinner."

"You haven't eaten?"

"No."

Doctor Bish folded his arms, studying the boy. "Well?" he said. "What do you think of him? This is the first time you've seen your father. It must have been strange for you. You've been around us so much, in all your training and work."

"It was—unusual."

"Did you gain any impressions? Was there anything you particularly noticed."

"He was very emotional. There was a distinct bias through everything he said and did. A distortion present, virtually uniform."

"Anything else?"

Peter hesitated, lingering at the door. He broke into a smile. "One other thing."

"What was it?"

"I noticed—" Peter laughed. "I noticed a distinct odor about him. A constant pungent smell, all the time I was with him."

"I'm afraid that's true of all of them," Doctor Bish said. "Certain skin glands. Waste products thrown off from the blood. You'll get used to it, after you've been around them more."

"Do I have to be around them?"

"They're your own race. How else can you work with them? Your whole training is designed with that in mind. When we've taught you all we can, then you will—"

"It reminded me of something. The pungent odor. I kept thinking about it, all the time I was with him. Trying to place it."

"Can you identify it now?"

Peter reflected. He thought hard, concentrating deeply. His small face wrinkled up. Doctor Bish waited patiently by his desk, arms folded. The automatic heating system clicked on for the night, warming the room with a soft glow that drifted gently around them.

"I know!" Peter exclaimed suddenly.

"What was it?"

"The animals in the biology lab. It was the same smell. The same smell as the experimental animals."

They glanced at each other, the robot doctor and the promising young boy. Both of them smiled, a secret, private smile. A smile of complete understanding.

"I believe I know what you mean," Doctor Bish said. "In fact, I know *exactly* what you mean."

OF WITHERED APPLES

Something was tapping on the window. Blowing up against the pane, again and again. Carried by the wind. Tapping faintly, insistently.

Lori, sitting on the couch, pretended not to hear. She gripped her book tightly and turned a page. The tapping came again, louder and more imperative. It could not be ignored.

"Darn!" Lori said, throwing her book down on the coffee table and hurrying to the window. She grasped the heavy brass handles and lifted.

For a moment the window resisted. Then, with a protesting groan, it reluctantly rose. Cold autumn air rushed into the room. The bit of leaf ceased tapping and swirled against the woman's throat, dancing to the floor.

Lori picked the leaf up. It was old and brown. Her heart skipped a beat as she slipped the leaf into the pocket of her jeans. Against her loins the leaf cut and tingled, a little hard point piercing her smooth skin and sending exciting shivers up and down her spine. She stood at the open window a moment, sniffing the air. The air was full of the presence of trees and rocks, of great boulders and remote places. It was time—time to go again. She touched the leaf. She was *wanted*.

Quickly Lori left the big living room, hurrying through the hall into the dining room. The dining room was empty. A few chords of laughter drifted from the kitchen. Lori pushed the kitchen door open. "Steve?"

Her husband and his father were sitting around the kitchen table, smoking their cigars and drinking steaming black coffee. "What is it?" Steve demanded, frowning at his young wife. "Ed and I are in the middle of business."

"I—I want to ask you something."

The two men gazed at her, brown-haired Steven, his dark eyes full of the stubborn dignity of New England men, and his father, silent and withdrawn in *her* presence. Ed Patterson scarcely noticed her. He rustled through a sheaf of feed bills, his broad back turned toward her.

"What is it?" Steve demanded impatiently. "What do you want? Can't it wait?"

"I have to go," Lori blurted.

"Go where?"

"Outside." Anxiety flooded over her. "This is the last time. I promise. I won't go again, after this. Okay?" She tried to smile, but her heart was pounding too hard. "Please let me, Steve."

"Where does she go?" Ed rumbled.

Steve grunted in annoyance. "Up in the hills. Some old abandoned place up there."

Ed's gray eyes flickered. "Abandoned farm?"

"Yes. You know it?"

"The old Rickley farm. Rickley moved away years ago. Couldn't get anything to grow, not up there. Ground's all rocks. Bad soil. A lot of clay and stones. The place is all overgrown, tumbled down."

"What kind of farm was it?"

"Orchard. Fruit orchard. Never yielded a damn thing. Thin old trees. Waste of effort."

Steve looked at his pocket watch. "You'll be back in time to fix dinner?"

"Yes!" Lori moved toward the door. "Then I can go?"

Steve's face twisted as he made up his mind. Lori waited impatiently, scarcely breathing. She had never got used to Vermont men and their slow, deliberate way. Boston people were quite different. And her group had been more the college youths, dances and talk, and late laughter.

"Why do you go up there?" Steve grumbled.

"Don't ask me, Steve. Just let me go. This is the last time." She writhed in agony. She clenched her fists. "Please!"

Steve looked out the window. The cold autumn wind swirled through the trees. "All right. But it's going to snow. I don't see why you want to—"

Lori ran to get her coat from the closet. "I'll be back to fix dinner!" she shouted joyfully. She hurried to the front porch, buttoning her coat, her heart racing. Her cheeks were flushed a deep, excited red as she closed the door behind her, her blood pounding in her veins.

Cold wind whipped against her, rumpling her hair, plucking at her body. She took a deep breath of the wind and started down the steps.

She walked rapidly onto the field, toward the bleak line of hills beyond. Except for the wind there was no sound. She patted her pocket. The dry leaf broke and dug hungrily into her.

"I'm coming . . . " she whispered, a little awed and frightened. "I'm on my way . . . "

❖ ❖ ❖

Higher and higher the woman climbed. She passed through a deep cleft between two rocky ridges. Huge roots from old stumps spurted out on all sides. She followed a dried-up creek bed, winding and turning.

After a time low mists began to blow about her. At the top of the ridge she halted, breathing deeply, looking back the way she had come.

A few drops of rain stirred the leaves around her. Again the wind moved through the great dead trees along the ridge. Lori turned and started on, her head down, hands in her coat pockets.

She was on a rocky field, overgrown with weeds and dead grass. After a time she came to a ruined fence, broken and rotting. She stepped over it. She passed a tumbled-down well, half filled with stones and earth.

Her heart beat quickly, fluttering with nervous excitement. She was almost there. She passed the remains of a building, sagging timbers and broken glass, a few ruined pieces of furniture strewn nearby. An old automobile tire caked and cracked. Some damp rags heaped over rusty, bent bedsprings.

And there it was—directly ahead.

Along the edge of the field was a grove of ancient trees. Lifeless trees, withered and dead, their thin, blackened stalks rising up leaflessly. Broken sticks stuck in the hard ground. Row after row of dead trees, some bent and leaning, torn loose from the rocky soil by the unending wind.

Lori crossed the field to the trees, her lungs laboring painfully. The wind surged against her without respite, whipping the foul-smelling mists into her nostrils and face. Her smooth skin was damp and shiny with the mist. She coughed and hurried on, stepping over the rocks and clods of earth, trembling with fear and anticipation.

She circled around the grove of trees, almost to the edge of the ridge. Carefully, she stepped among the sliding heaps of rocks. Then—

She stopped, rigid. Her chest rose and fell with the effort of breathing. "I came," she gasped.

For a long time she gazed at the withered old apple tree. She could not take her eyes from it. The sight of the ancient tree fascinated and repelled her. It was the only one alive, the only tree of all the grove still living. All the others were dead, dried-up. They had lost the struggle. But this tree still clung to life.

The tree was hard and barren. Only a few dark leaves hung from it—and some withered apples, dried and seasoned by the wind and mists. They had stayed there, on the branches, forgotten and abandoned. The ground around the tree was cracked and bleak. Stones and decayed heaps of old leaves in ragged clumps.

"I came," Lori said again. She took the leaf from her pocket and held it cautiously out. "This tapped at the window. I knew when I heard it." She smiled mischievously, her red lips curling. "It tapped and tapped, trying to get in. I ignored it. It was so—so impetuous. It annoyed me."

The tree swayed ominously. Its gnarled branches rubbed together. Something in the sound made Lori pull away. Terror rushed through her. She hurried back along the ridge, scrambling frantically out of reach.

"Don't," she whispered. "*Please.*"

The wind ceased. The tree became silent. For a long time Lori watched it apprehensively.

Night was coming. The sky was darkening rapidly. A burst of frigid wind struck her, half turning her around. She shuddered, bracing herself against it, pulling her long coat around her. Far below, the floor of the valley was disappearing into shadow, into the vast cloud of night.

In the darkening mists the tree was stern and menacing, more ominous than usual. A few leaves blew from it, drifting and swirling with the wind. A leaf blew past her and she tried to catch it. The leaf escaped, dancing back toward the tree. Lori followed a little way and then stopped, gasping and laughing.

"No," she said firmly, her hands on her hips. "I won't."

There was silence. Suddenly the heaps of decayed leaves blew up in a furious circle around the tree. They quieted down, settling back.

"No," Lori said. "I'm not afraid of you. You can't hurt me." But her heart was hammering with fear. She moved back farther away.

The tree remained silent. Its wiry branches were motionless.

Lori regained her courage. "This is the last time I can come," she said. "Steve says I can't come any more. He doesn't like it."

She waited, but the tree did not respond.

"They're sitting in the kitchen. The two of them. Smoking cigars and drinking coffee. Adding up feed bills." She wrinkled her nose. "That's all they ever do. Add and subtract feed bills. Figure and figure. Profit and loss. Government taxes. Depreciation on the equipment."

The tree did not stir.

Lori shivered. A little more rain fell, big icy drops that slid down her cheeks, down the back of her neck and inside her heavy coat.

She moved closer to the tree. "I won't be back. I won't see you again. This is the last time. I wanted to tell you . . . ."

The tree moved. Its branches whipped into sudden life. Lori felt something hard and thin cut across her shoulder. Something caught her around the waist, tugging her forward.

She struggled desperately, trying to pull herself free. Suddenly the tree released her. She stumbled back, laughing and trembling with fear. "No!" she gasped. "You can't have me!" She hurried to the edge of the ridge. "You'll never get me again. Understand? And I'm not afraid of you!"

She stood, waiting and watching, trembling with cold and fear. Suddenly she turned and fled, down the side of the ridge, sliding and falling on the loose stones. Blind terror gripped her. She ran on and on, down the steep slope, grabbing at roots and weeds—

Something rolled beside her shoe. Something small and hard. She bent down and picked it up.

It was a little dried apple.

Lori gazed back up the slope at the tree. The tree was almost lost in the swirling mists. It stood, jutting up against the black sky, a hard unmoving pillar.

Lori put the apple in her coat pocket and continued down the side of the hill. When she reached the floor of the valley she took the apple out of her pocket.

It was late. A deep hunger began to gnaw inside her. She thought suddenly of dinner, the warm kitchen, the white tablecloth. Steaming stew and biscuits.

As she walked she nibbled on the little apple.

❖ ❖ ❖

Lori sat up in bed, the covers falling away from her. The house was dark and silent. A few night noises sounded faintly, far off. It was past midnight. Beside her Steven slept quietly, turned over on his side.

What had wakened her? Lori pushed her dark hair back out of her eyes, shaking her head. What—

A spasm of pain burst loose inside her. She gasped and put her hand to her stomach. For a time she wrestled silently, jaws locked, swaying back and forth.

The pain went away. Lori sank back. She cried out, a faint, thin cry. "Steve—"

Steven stirred. He turned over a little, grunting in his sleep.

The pain came again. Harder. She fell forward on her face, writhing in agony. The pain ripped at her, tearing at her belly. She screamed, a shrill wail of fear and pain.

Steve sat up. "For God's sake—" He rubbed his eyes and snapped on the lamp. "What the hell—"

Lori lay on her side, gasping and moaning, her eyes staring, knotted fists pressed into her stomach. The pain twisted and seared, devouring her, eating into her.

"Lori!" Steven grated. "What is it?"

She screamed. Again and again. Until the house rocked with echoes. She slid from the bed, onto the floor, her body writhing and jerking, her face unrecognizable.

Ed came hurrying into the room, pulling his bathrobe around him. "What's going on?"

The two men stared helplessly down at the woman on the floor.

"Good God," Ed said. He closed his eyes.

❖❖❖

The day was cold and dark. Snow fell silently over the streets and houses, over the red brick county hospital building. Doctor Blair walked slowly up the gravel path to his Ford car. He slid inside and turned the ignition key. The motor leaped alive, and he let the brake out.

"I'll call you later," Doctor Blair said. "There are certain particulars."

"I know," Steve muttered. He was still dazed. His face was gray and puffy from lack of sleep.

"I left some sedatives for you. Try to get a little rest."

"You think," Steve asked suddenly, "if we had called you earlier—"

"No." Blair glanced up at him sympathetically. "I don't. In a thing like that, there's not much chance. Not after it's burst."

"Then it *was* appendicitis?"

Blair nodded. "Yes."

"If we hadn't been so damn far out," Steve said bitterly. "Stuck out in the country. No hospital. Nothing. Miles from town. And we didn't realize at first—"

"Well, it's over now." The upright Ford moved forward a little. All at once a thought came to the Doctor. "One more thing."

"What is it?" Steve said dully.

Blair hesitated. "Post mortems—very unfortunate. I don't think there's any reason for one in this case. I'm certain in my own mind. . . . But I wanted to ask—"

"What is it?"

"Is there anything the girl might have swallowed? Did she put things in her mouth? Needles—while she was sewing? Pins, coins, anything like that? Seeds? Did she ever eat watermelon? Sometimes the appendix—"

"No."

Steve shook his head wearily. "I don't know."

"It was just a thought." Doctor Blair drove slowly off down the narrow tree-lined street, leaving two dark streaks, two soiled lines that marred the packed, glistening snow.

❖ ❖ ❖

Spring came, warm and sunny. The ground turned black and rich. Overhead the sun shone, a hot white orb, full of strength.

"Stop here," Steve murmured.

Ed Patterson brought the car to a halt at the side of the street. He turned off the motor. The two men sat in silence, neither of them speaking.

At the end of the street children were playing. A high school boy was mowing a lawn, pushing the machine over wet grass. The street was dark in the shade of the great trees growing along each side.

"Nice," Ed said.

Steve nodded without answering. Moodily, he watched a young girl walking by, a shopping bag under her arm. The girl climbed the stairs of a porch and disappeared into an old-fashioned yellow house.

Steve pushed the car door open. "Come on. Let's get it over with."

Ed lifted the wreath of flowers from the back seat and put them in his son's lap. "You'll have to carry it. It's your job."

"All right." Steve grabbed the flowers and stepped out onto the pavement.

The two men walked up the street together, silent and thoughtful.

"It's been seven or eight months, now," Steve said abruptly.

"At least." Ed lit the cigar as they walked along, puffing clouds of gray smoke around them. "Maybe a little more."

"I never should have brought her up here. She lived in town all her life. She didn't know anything about the country."

"It would have happened anyhow."

"If we had been closer to a hospital—"

"The doctor said it wouldn't have made any difference. Even if we'd called him right away instead of waiting until morning." They came to the corner and turned. "And as you know—"

"Forget it," Steve said, suddenly tense.

The sounds of the children had fallen behind them. The houses had thinned out. Their footsteps rang out against the pavement as they walked along.

"We're almost there," Steve said.

They came to a rise. Beyond the rise was a heavy brass fence, running the length of a small field. A green field, neat and even. With carefully placed plaques of white marble criss-crossing it.

"Here we are," Steve said tightly.

"They keep it nice."

"Can we get in from this side?"

"We can try." Ed started along the brass fence, looking for a gate.

Suddenly Steve halted, grunting. He stared across the field, his face white. "*Look.*"

"What is it?" Ed took off his glasses to see. "What are you looking at?"

"I was right." Steve's voice was low and indistinct. "I thought there was something. Last time we were here . . . I saw . . . You see it?"

"I'm not sure. I see the tree, if that's what you mean."

In the center of the neat green field the little apple tree rose proudly. Its bright leaves sparkled in the warm sunlight. The young tree was strong and very healthy. It swayed confidently with the wind, its supple trunk moist with sweet spring sap.

"They're *red*," Steve said softly. "They're already red. How the hell can they be red? It's only April. How the hell can they be red so soon?"

"I don't know," Ed said. "I don't know anything about apples." A strange chill moved through him. But graveyards always made him uncomfortable. "Maybe we ought to go."

"Her cheeks were that color," Steve said, his voice low. "When she had been running. Remember?"

The two men gazed uneasily at the little apple tree, its shiny red fruit glistening in the spring sunlight, branches moving gently with the wind.

"I remember, all right," Ed said grimly. "Come on." He took his son's arm insistently, the wreath of flowers forgotten. "Come on, Steve. Let's get out of here."

ADJUSTMENT TEAM

It was bright morning. The sun shone down on the damp lawns and sidewalks, reflecting off the sparkling parked cars. The Clerk came walking hurriedly, leafing through his instructions, flipping pages and frowning. He stopped in front of the small green stucco house for a moment, and then turned up the walk, entering the back yard.

The dog was asleep inside his shed, his back turned to the world. Only his thick tail showed.

"For heaven's sake," the Clerk exclaimed, hands on his hips. He tapped his mechanical pencil noisily against his clipboard. "Wake up, you in there."

The dog stirred. He came slowly out of his shed, head first, blinking and yawning in the morning sunlight. "Oh, it's you. Already?" He yawned again.

"Big doings." The Clerk ran his expert finger down the traffic-control sheet. "They're adjusting Sector T137 this morning. Starting at exactly nine o'clock." He glanced at his pocket watch. "Three hour alteration. Will finish by noon."

"T137? That's not far from here."

The Clerk's thin lips twisted with contempt. "Indeed. You're showing astonishing perspicacity, my black-haired friend. Maybe you can divine why I'm here."

"We overlap with T137."

"Exactly. Elements from this Sector are involved. We must make sure they're properly placed when the adjustment begins." The Clerk glanced toward the small green stucco house. "Your particular task concerns the man in there. He is employed by a business establishment lying within Sector T137. It's essential that he be there before nine o'clock."

The dog studied the house. The shades had been let up. The kitchen light was on. Beyond the lace curtains dim shapes could be seen, stirring around the table. A man and woman. They were drinking coffee.

"There they are," the dog murmured. "The man, you say? He's not going to be harmed, is he?"

"Of course not. But he must be at his office early. Usually he doesn't leave until after nine. Today he must leave at eight-thirty. He must be within Sector T137 before the process begins, or he won't be altered to coincide with the new adjustment."

The dog sighed. "That means I have to summon."

"Correct." The Clerk checked his instruction sheet. "You're to summon at precisely eight-fifteen. You've got that? Eight-fifteen. No later."

"What will an eight-fifteen summons bring?"

The Clerk flipped open his instruction book, examining the code columns. "It will bring A Friend with a Car. To drive him to work early." He closed the book and folded his arms, preparing to wait. "That way he'll get to his office almost an hour ahead of time. Which is vital."

"Vital," the dog murmured. He lay down, half inside his shed. His eyes closed. "Vital."

"Wake up! This must be done exactly on time. If you summon too soon or too late—"

The dog nodded sleepily. "I know. I'll do it right. I *always* do it right."

❖ ❖ ❖

Ed Fletcher poured more cream in his coffee. He sighed, leaning back in his chair. Behind him the oven hissed softly, filling the kitchen with warm fumes. The yellow overhead light beamed down.

"Another roll?" Ruth asked.

"I'm full." Ed sipped his coffee. "You can have it."

"Have to go." Ruth got to her feet, unfastening her robe. "Time to go to work."

"Already?"

"Sure. You lucky bum! Wish I could sit around." Ruth moved toward the bathroom, running her fingers through her long black hair. "When you work for the Government you start early."

"But you get off early," Ed pointed out. He unfolded the *Chronicle*, examining the sporting green. "Well, have a good time today. Don't type any wrong words, any double-entendres."

The bathroom door closed, as Ruth shed her robe and began dressing.

Ed yawned and glanced up at the clock over the sink. Plenty of time. Not even eight. He sipped more coffee and then rubbed his stubbled chin. He would have to shave. He shrugged lazily. Ten minutes, maybe.

Ruth came bustling out in her nylon slip, hurrying into the bedroom. "I'm late." She rushed rapidly around, getting into her blouse and skirt, her stockings, her little white shoes. Finally she bent over and kissed him. "Good-bye, honey. I'll do the shopping tonight."

"Good-bye." Ed lowered his newspaper and put his arm around his wife's trim waist, hugging her affectionately. "You smell nice. Don't flirt with the boss."

Ruth ran out the front door, clattering down the steps. He heard the click of her heels diminish down the sidewalk.

She was gone. The house was silent. He was alone.

Ed got to his feet, pushing his chair back. He wandered lazily into the bathroom, and got his razor down. Eight-ten. He washed his face, rubbing it down with shaving cream, and began to shave. He shaved leisurely. He had plenty of time.

❖ ❖ ❖

The Clerk bent over his round pocket watch, licking his lips nervously. Sweat stood out on his forehead. The second hand ticked on. Eight-fourteen. Almost time.

"Get ready!" the Clerk snapped. He tensed, his small body rigid. "Ten seconds to go!"

"*Time!*" the Clerk cried.

Nothing happened.

The Clerk turned, eyes wide with horror. From the little shed a thick black tail showed. The dog had gone back to sleep.

"TIME!" the Clerk shrieked. He kicked wildly at the furry rump. "In the name of God—"

The dog stirred. He thumped around hastily, backing out of the shed. "My goodness." Embarrassed, he made his way quickly to the fence. Standing up on his hind paws, he opened his mouth wide. "Woof!" he summoned. He glanced apologetically at the Clerk. "I beg your pardon. I can't understand how—"

The Clerk gazed fixedly down at his watch. Cold terror knotted his stomach. The hands showed eight-sixteen. "You failed," he grated. "You failed! You miserable flea-bitten rag-bag of a wornout old mutt! You failed!"

The dog dropped and came anxiously back. "I failed, you say? You mean the summons time was—?"

"You summoned too late." The Clerk put his watch away slowly, a glazed expression on his face. "You summoned too late. We won't get A Friend with a Car. There's no telling what will come instead. I'm afraid to see what eight-sixteen brings."

"I hope he'll be in Sector T137 in time."

"He won't," the Clerk wailed. "He won't be there. We've made a mistake. We've made things go wrong!"

❖ ❖ ❖

Ed was rinsing the shaving cream from his face when the muffled sound of the dog's bark echoed through the silent house.

"Damn," Ed muttered. "Wake up the whole block." He dried his face, listening. Was somebody coming?

A vibration. Then—

The doorbell rang.

Ed came out of the bathroom. Who could it be? Had Ruth forgotten something? He tossed on a white shirt and opened the front door.

A bright young man, face bland and eager, beamed happily at him. "Good morning, sir." He tipped his hat. "I'm sorry to bother you so early—"

"What do you want?"

"I'm from the Federal Life Insurance Company. I'm here to see you about—"

Ed pushed the door closed. "Don't want any. I'm in a rush. Have to get to work."

"Your wife said this was the only time I could catch you." The young man picked up his briefcase, easing the door open again. "She especially asked me to come this early. We don't usually begin our work at this time, but since she asked me, I made a special note about it."

"OK." Sighing wearily, Ed admitted the young man. "You can explain your policy while I get dressed."

The young man opened his briefcase on the couch, laying out heaps of pamphlets and illustrated folders. "I'd like to show you some of these figures, if I may. It's of great importance to you and your family to—"

Ed found himself sitting down, going over the pamphlets. He purchased a ten-thousand-dollar policy on his own life and then eased the young man out. He looked at the clock. Practically nine-thirty!

"Damn." He'd be late to work. He finished fastening his tie, grabbed his coat, turned off the oven and the lights, dumped the dishes in the sink, and ran out on the porch.

As he hurried toward the bus stop he was cursing inwardly. Life insurance salesmen. Why did the jerk have to come just as he was getting ready to leave?

Ed groaned. No telling what the consequences would be, getting to the office late. He wouldn't get there until almost ten. He set himself in anticipation. A sixth sense told him he was in for it. Something bad. It was the wrong day to be late.

If only the salesman hadn't come.

Ed hopped off the bus a block from his office. He began walking rapidly. The huge clock in front of Stein's Jewelry Store told him it was almost ten.

His heart sank. Old Douglas would give him hell for sure. He could see it now. Douglas puffing and blowing, red-faced, waving his thick finger at him; Miss Evans, smiling behind her typewriter; Jackie, the office boy, grinning and snickering; Earl Hendricks; Joe and Tom; Mary, dark-eyed, full bosom and long lashes. All of them, kidding him the whole rest of the day.

He came to the corner and stopped for the light. On the other side of the street rose a big white concrete building, the towering column of steel and cement, girders and glass windows—the office building. Ed flinched. Maybe he could say the elevator got stuck. Somewhere between the second and third floor.

The street light changed. Nobody else was crossing. Ed crossed alone. He hopped up on the curb on the far side—

And stopped, rigid.

The sun had winked off. One moment it was beaming down. Then it was gone. Ed looked up sharply. Gray clouds swirled above him. Huge, formless clouds. Nothing more. An ominous, thick haze that made everything waver and dim. Uneasy chills plucked at him. *What was it?*

He advanced cautiously, feeling his way through the mist. Everything was silent. No sounds—not even the traffic sounds. Ed peered frantically around, trying to see through the rolling haze. No people. No cars. No sun. Nothing.

The office building loomed up ahead, ghostly. It was an indistinct gray. He put out his hand uncertainly—

A section of the building fell away. It rained down, a torrent of particles. Like sand. Ed gaped foolishly. A cascade of gray debris, spilling around his feet. And where he had touched the building, a jagged cavity yawned—an ugly pit marring the concrete.

Dazed, he made his way to the front steps. He mounted them. The steps gave way underfoot. His feet sank down. He was wading through shifting sand, weak, rotted stuff that broke under his weight.

He got into the lobby. The lobby was dim and obscure. The overhead lights flickered feebly in the gloom. An unearthly pall hung over everything.

He spied the cigar stand. The seller leaned silently, resting on the counter, toothpick between his teeth, his face vacant. *And gray.* He was gray all over.

"Hey," Ed croaked. "What's going on?"

The seller did not answer. Ed reached out toward him. His hand touched the seller's gray arm—and passed right through.

"Good God," Ed said.

The seller's arm came loose. It fell to the lobby floor, disintegrating into fragments. Bits of gray fiber. Like dust. Ed's senses reeled.

"Help!" he shouted, finding his voice.

No answer. He peered around. A few shapes stood here and there: a man reading a newspaper, two women waiting at the elevator.

Ed made his way over to the man. He reached out and touched him.

The man slowly collapsed. He settled into a heap, a loose pile of gray ash. Dust. Particles. The two women dissolved when he touched them. Silently. They made no sound as they broke apart.

Ed found the stairs. He grabbed hold of the banister and climbed. The stairs collapsed under him. He hurried faster. Behind him lay a broken path—his footprints clearly visible in the concrete. Clouds of ash blew around him as he reached the second floor.

He gazed down the silent corridor. He saw more clouds of ash. He heard no sound. There was just darkness—rolling darkness.

He climbed unsteadily to the third floor. Once, his shoe broke completely through the stair. For a sickening second he hung, poised over a yawning hole that looked down into a bottomless nothing.

Then he climbed on, and emerged in front of his own office: DOUGLAS AND BLAKE, REAL ESTATE.

The hall was dim, gloomy with clouds of ash. The overhead lights flickered fitfully. He reached for the door handle. The handle came off in his hand. He dropped it and dug his fingernails into the door. The plate glass crashed past him, breaking into bits. He tore the door open and stepped over it, into the office.

Miss Evans sat at her typewriter, fingers resting quietly on the keys. She did not move. She was gray, her hair, her skin, her clothing. She was without color. Ed touched her. His fingers went through her shoulder, into dry flakiness.

He drew back, sickened. Miss Evans did not stir.

He moved on. He pushed against a desk. The desk collapsed into rotting dust. Earl Hendricks stood by the water cooler, a cup in his hand. He was a gray statue, unmoving. Nothing stirred. No sound. No life. The whole office was gray dust—without life or motion.

Ed found himself out in the corridor again. He shook his head, dazed. What did it mean? Was he going out of his mind? Was he—?

A sound.

Ed turned, peering into the gray mist. A creature was coming, hurrying rapidly. A man—a man in a white robe. Behind him others came. Men in white, with equipment. They were lugging complex machinery.

"Hey—" Ed gasped weakly.

The men stopped. Their mouths opened. Their eyes popped.

"Look!"

"Something's gone wrong!"

"One still charged."

"Get the de-energizer."

"We can't proceed until—"

The men came toward Ed, moving around him. One lugged a long hose with some sort of nozzle. A portable cart came wheeling up. Instructions were rapidly shouted.

Ed broke out of his paralysis. Fear swept over him. Panic. Something hideous was happening. He had to get out. Warn people. Get away.

He turned and ran, back down the stairs. The stairs collapsed under him. He fell half a flight, rolling in heaps of dry ash. He got to his feet and hurried on, down to the ground floor.

The lobby was lost in the clouds of gray ash. He pushed blindly through, toward the door. Behind him, the white-clad men were coming, dragging their equipment and shouting to each other, hurrying quickly after him.

He reached the sidewalk. Behind him the office building wavered and sagged, sinking to one side, torrents of ash raining down in heaps. He raced toward the corner, the men just behind him. Gray cloud swirled around him. He groped his way across the street, hands outstretched. He gained the opposite curb—

The sun winked on. Warm yellow sunlight streamed down on him. Cars honked. Traffic lights changed. On all sides men and women in bright spring clothes hurried and pushed: shoppers, a blue-clad cop, salesmen with briefcases. Stores, windows, signs . . . noisy cars moving up and down the street . . .

And overhead was the bright sun and familiar blue sky.

Ed halted, gasping for breath. He turned and looked back the way he had come. Across the street was the office building—as it had always been. Firm and distinct. Concrete and glass and steel.

He stepped back a pace and collided with a hurrying citizen. "Hey," the man grunted. "Watch it."

"Sorry." Ed shook his head, trying to clear it. From where he stood, the office building looked like always, big and solemn and substantial, rising up imposingly on the other side of the street.

But a minute ago—

Maybe he was out of his mind. He had seen the building crumbling into dust. Building—and people. They had fallen into gray clouds of dust. And the men in white—they had chased him. Men in white robes, shouting orders, wheeling complex equipment.

He was out of his mind. There was no other explanation. Weakly, Ed turned and stumbled along the sidewalk, his mind reeling. He moved blindly, without purpose, lost in a haze of confusion and terror.

❖ ❖ ❖

The Clerk was brought into the top-level Administrative chambers and told to wait.

He paced back and forth nervously, clasping and wringing his hands in an agony of apprehension. He took off his glasses and wiped them shakily. ·

Lord. All the trouble and grief. And it wasn't his fault. But he would have to take the rap. It was his responsibility to get the Summoners routed out and their instructions followed. The miserable flea-infested Summoner had gone back to sleep—and *he* would have to answer for it.

The doors opened. "All right," a voice murmured, preoccupied. It was a tired, care-worn voice. The Clerk trembled and entered slowly, sweat dripping down his neck into his celluloid collar.

The Old Man glanced up, laying aside his book. He studied the Clerk calmly, his faded blue eyes mild—a deep, ancient mildness that made the Clerk tremble even more. He took out his handkerchief and mopped his brow.

"I understand there was a mistake," the Old Man murmured. "In connection with Sector T137. Something to do with an element from an adjoining area."

"That's right." The Clerk's voice was faint and husky. "Very unfortunate."

"What exactly occurred?"

"I started out this morning with my instruction sheets. The material relating to T137 had top priority, of course. I served notice on the Summoner in my area that an eight-fifteen summons was required."

"Did the Summoner understand the urgency?"

"Yes, sir." The Clerk hesitated. "But—

"But what?"

The Clerk twisted miserably. "While my back was turned the Summoner crawled back in his shed and went to sleep. I was occupied, checking the exact time with my watch. I called the moment—but there was no response."

"You called at eight-fifteen exactly?"

"Yes, sir! Exactly eight-fifteen. But the Summoner was asleep. By the time I managed to arouse him it was eight-*sixteen*. He summoned, but instead of A Friend with a Car we got—A Life Insurance Salesman." The Clerk's face screwed up with disgust. "The Salesman kept the element there until almost nine-thirty. Therefore he was late to work instead of early."

For a moment the Old Man was silent. "Then the element was not within T137 when the adjustment began."

"No. He arrived about ten o'clock."

"During the middle of the adjustment." The Old Man got to his feet and paced slowly back and forth, face grim, hands behind his back. His long robe flowed out behind him. "A serious matter. During a Sector Adjustment all related elements from other Sectors must be included. Otherwise, their orientations remain out of phase. When this element entered T137 the adjustment had been in progress fifty minutes. The element encountered the Sector at its most de-energized stage. He wandered about until one of the adjustment teams met him."

"Did they catch him?"

"Unfortunately, no. He fled, out of the Sector. Into a nearby fully energized area."

"What—what then?"

The Old Man stopped pacing, his lined face grim. He ran a heavy hand through his long white hair. "We do not know. We lost contact with him. We will reestablish contact soon, of course. But for the moment he is out of control."

"What are you going to do?"

"He must be contacted and contained. He must be brought up here. There's no other solution."

"Up *here!*"

"It is too late to de-energize him. By the time he is regained he will have told others. To wipe his mind clean would only complicate matters. Usual methods will not suffice. I must deal with this problem myself."

"I hope he's located quickly," the Clerk said.

"He will be. Every Watcher is alerted. Every Watcher and every Summoner." The Old Man's eyes twinkled. "Even the Clerks, although we hesitate to count on them."

The Clerk flushed. "I'll be glad when this thing is over," he muttered.

❖ ❖ ❖

Ruth came tripping down the stairs and out of the building, into the hot noonday sun. She lit a cigarette and hurried along the walk, her small bosom rising and falling as she breathed in the spring air.

"Ruth." Ed stepped up behind her.

"Ed!" She spun, gasping in astonishment. "What are you doing away from—?"

"Come on." Ed grabbed her arm, pulling her along. "Let's keep moving."

"But what—?"

"I'll tell you later." Ed's face was pale and grim. "Let's go where we can talk. In private."

"I was going down to have lunch at Louie's. We can talk there." Ruth hurried along breathlessly. "What is it? What's happened? You look so strange. And why aren't you at work? Did you—did you get fired?"

They crossed the street and entered a small restaurant. Men and women milled around, getting their lunch. Ed found a table in the back, secluded in a corner. "Here." He sat down abruptly. "This will do." She slid into the other chair.

Ed ordered a cup of coffee. Ruth had salad and creamed tuna on toast, coffee and peach pie. Silently, Ed watched her as she ate, his face dark and moody.

"Please tell me," Ruth begged him.

"You really want to know?"

"Of course I want to know!" Ruth put her small hand anxiously on his. "I'm your wife."

"Something happened today. This morning. I was late to work. A damn insurance man came by and held me up. I was half an hour late."

Ruth caught her breath. "Douglas fired you."

"No." Ed ripped a paper napkin slowly into bits. He stuffed the bits in the half-empty water glass. "I was worried as hell. I got off the bus and hurried down the street. I noticed it when I stepped up on the curb in front of the office."

"Noticed what?"

Ed told her. The whole works. Everything.

When he had finished, Ruth sat back, her face white, hands trembling. "I see," she murmured. "No wonder you're upset." She drank a little cold coffee, the cup rattling against the saucer. "What a terrible thing."

Ed leaned intently toward his wife. "Ruth. Do you think I'm going crazy?"

Ruth's red lips twisted. "I don't know what to say. It's so strange . . . "

"Yeah. Strange is hardly the word for it. I poked my hands right through them. Like they were clay. Old dry clay. Dust. Dust figures." Ed lit a cigarette from Ruth's pack. "When I got out I looked back and there it was. The office building. Like always."

"You were afraid Mr. Douglas would bawl you out, weren't you?"

"Sure. I was afraid—and guilty." Ed's eyes flickered. "I know what you're thinking. I was late and I couldn't face him. So I had some sort of protective psychotic fit. Retreat from reality." He stubbed the cigarette out savagely. "Ruth, I've been wandering around town since. Two and a half hours. Sure, I'm afraid. I'm afraid like hell to go back."

"Of Douglas?"

"No! The men in white." Ed shuddered. "God. Chasing me. With their damn hoses and—and equipment."

Ruth was silent. Finally she looked up at her husband, her dark eyes bright. "You have to go back, Ed."

"Back? Why?"

"To prove something."

"Prove what?"

"Prove it's all right." Ruth's hand pressed against his. "You have to, Ed. You have to go back and face it. To show yourself there's nothing to be afraid of."

"The hell with it! After what I saw? Listen, Ruth. I saw the fabric of reality split open. I saw—*behind*. Underneath. I saw what was really there. And I don't want to go back. I don't want to see dust people again. Ever."

Ruth's eyes were fixed intently on him. "I'll go back with you," she said.

"For God's sake."

"For *your* sake. For your sanity. So you'll know." Ruth got abruptly to her feet, pulling her coat around her. "Come on, Ed. I'll go with you. We'll go up there together. To the office of Douglas and Blake, Real Estate. I'll even go in with you to see Mr. Douglas."

Ed got up slowly, staring hard at his wife. "You think I blacked out.

Cold feet. Couldn't face the boss." His voice was low and strained. "Don't you?"

Ruth was already threading her way toward the cashier. "Come on. You'll see. It'll all be there. Just like it always was."

"OK," Ed said. He followed her slowly. "We'll go back there—and see which of us is right."

They crossed the street together, Ruth holding on tight to Ed's arm. Ahead of them was the building, the towering structure of concrete and metal and glass.

"There it is," Ruth said. "See?"

There it was, all right. The big building rose up, firm and solid, glittering in the early afternoon sun, its windows sparkling brightly.

Ed and Ruth stepped up onto the curb. Ed tensed himself, his body rigid. He winced as his foot touched the pavement—

But nothing happened: the street noises continued; cars, people hurrying past; a kid selling papers. There were sounds, smells, the noise of a city in the middle of the day. And overhead was the sun and the bright blue sky.

"See?" Ruth said. "I was right."

They walked up the front steps, into the lobby. Behind the cigar stand the seller stood, arms folded, listening to the ball game. "Hi, Mr. Fletcher," he called to Ed. His face lit up good-naturedly. "Who's the dame? Your wife know about this?"

Ed laughed unsteadily. They passed on toward the elevator. Four or five businessmen stood waiting. They were middle-aged men, well dressed, waiting impatiently in a bunch. "Hey, Fletcher," one said. "Where you been all day? Douglas is yelling his head off."

"Hello, Earl," Ed muttered. He gripped Ruth's arm. "Been a little sick."

The elevator came. They got in. The elevator rose. "Hi, Ed," the elevator operator said. "Who's the good-looking gal? Why don't you introduce her around?"

Ed grinned mechanically. "My wife."

The elevator let them off at the third floor. Ed and Ruth got out, heading toward the glass door of Douglas and Blake, Real Estate.

Ed halted, breathing shallowly. "Wait." He licked his lips. "I—"

Ruth waited calmly as Ed wiped his forehead and neck with his handkerchief. "All right now?"

"Yeah." Ed moved forward. He pulled open the glass door.

Miss Evans glanced up, ceasing her typing. "Ed Fletcher! Where on earth have you been?"

"I've been sick. Hello, Tom."

Tom glanced up from his work. "Hi, Ed. Say, Douglas is yelling for your scalp. Where have you been?"

"I know." Ed turned wearily to Ruth. "I guess I better go in and face the music."

Ruth squeezed his arm. "You'll be all right. I know." She smiled, a relieved flash of white teeth and red lips. "OK? Call me if you need me."

"Sure." Ed kissed her briefly on the mouth. "Thanks, honey. Thanks a lot. I don't know what the hell went wrong with me. I guess it's over."

"Forget it. So long." Ruth skipped back out of the office, the door closing after her. Ed listened to her race down the hall to the elevator.

"Nice little gal," Jackie said appreciatively.

"Yeah." Ed nodded, straightening his necktie. He moved unhappily toward the inner office, steeling himself. Well, he had to face it. Ruth was right. But he was going to have a hell of a time explaining it to the boss. He could see Douglas now, thick red wattles, big bull roar, face distorted with rage—

Ed stopped abruptly at the entrance to the inner office. He froze rigid. The inner office—it was *changed*.

The hackles of his neck rose. Cold fear gripped him, clutching at his windpipe. The inner office was different. He turned his head slowly, taking in the sight: the desks, chairs, fixtures, file cabinets, pictures.

Changes. Little changes. Subtle. Ed closed his eyes and opened them slowly. He was alert, breathing rapidly, his pulse racing. It was changed, all right. No doubt about it.

"What's the matter, Ed?" Tom asked. The staff watched him curiously, pausing in their work.

Ed said nothing. He advanced slowly into the inner office. The office had been *gone over*. He could tell. Things had been altered. Rearranged. Nothing obvious—nothing he could put his finger on. But he could tell.

Joe Kent greeted him uneasily. "What's the matter, Ed? You look like a wild dog. Is something—?"

Ed studied Joe. He was different. Not the same. What was it?

Joe's face. It was a little fuller. His shirt was blue-striped. Joe never wore blue stripes. Ed examined Joe's desk. He saw papers and accounts. The desk—it was too far to the right. And it was bigger. It wasn't the same desk.

The picture on the wall. It wasn't the same. It was a different picture entirely. And the things on top of the file cabinet—some were new, others were gone.

He looked back through the door. Now that he thought about it, Miss Evans' hair was different, done a different way. And it was lighter.

In here, Mary, filing her nails, over by the window—she was taller, fuller. Her purse, lying on the desk in front of her—a red purse, red knit.

"You always . . . have that purse?" Ed demanded.

Mary glanced up. "What?"

"That purse. You always have that?"

Mary laughed. She smoothed her skirt coyly around her shapely thighs, her long lashes blinking modestly. "Why, Mr. Fletcher. What do you mean?"

Ed turned away. *He knew.* Even if she didn't. She had been redone—changed: her purse, her clothes, her figure, everything about her.

None of them knew—but him. His mind spun dizzily. They were all changed. All of them were different. They had all been remolded, recast. Subtly—but it was there.

The wastebasket. It was smaller, not the same. The window shades—white, not ivory. The wallpaper was not the same pattern. The lighting fixtures . . .

Endless, subtle changes.

Ed made his way back to the inner office. He lifted his hand and knocked on Douglas' door.

"Come in."

Ed pushed the door open. Nathan Douglas looked up impatiently. "Mr. Douglas—" Ed began. He came into the room unsteadily—and stopped.

Douglas was not the same. Not at all. His whole office was changed: the rugs, the drapes. The desk was oak, not mahogany. And Douglas himself . . . .

Douglas was younger, thinner. His hair, brown. His skin not so red. His face smoother. No wrinkles. Chin reshaped. Eyes green, not black. He was a different man. But still Douglas—a different Douglas. A different version!

"What is it?" Douglas demanded impatiently. "Oh, it's you, Fletcher. Where were you this morning?"

Ed backed out. Fast.

He slammed the door and hurried back through the inner office. Tom and Miss Evans glanced up, startled. Ed passed them by, grabbing the hall door open.

"Hey!" Tom called. "What—?"

Ed hurried down the hall. Terror leaped through him. He had to hurry. He had *seen*. There wasn't much time. He came to the elevator and stabbed the button.

No time.

He ran to the stairs and started down. He reached the second floor. His terror grew. It was a matter of seconds.

Seconds!

The public phone. Ed ran into the phone booth. He dragged the door shut after him. Wildly, he dropped a dime in the slot and dialed. He had to call the police. He held the receiver to his ear, his heart pounding.

Warn them. Changes. Somebody tampering with reality. Altering it. He had been right. The white-clad men . . . their equipment . . . going through the building.

"Hello!" Ed shouted hoarsely. There was no answer. No hum. Nothing.

Ed peered frantically out the door.

And he sagged, defeated. Slowly he hung up the telephone receiver.

He was no longer on the second floor. The phone booth was rising, leaving the second floor behind, carrying him up, faster and faster. It rose floor by floor, moving silently, swiftly.

The phone booth passed through the ceiling of the building and out into the bright sunlight. It gained speed. The ground fell away below. Buildings and streets were getting smaller each moment. Tiny specks hurried along, far below, cars and people, dwindling rapidly.

Clouds drifted between him and the earth. Ed shut his eyes, dizzy with fright. He held on desperately to the door handles of the phone booth.

Faster and faster the phone booth climbed. The earth was rapidly being left behind, far below.

Ed peered up wildly. *Where?* Where was he going? Where was it taking him?

He stood gripping the door handles, waiting.

❖ ❖ ❖

The Clerk nodded curtly. "That's him, all right. The element in question."

Ed Fletcher looked around him. He was in a huge chamber. The edges fell away into indistinct shadows. In front of him stood a man with notes and ledgers under his arm, peering at him through steel-rimmed glasses. He was a nervous little man, sharp-eyed, with celluloid collar, blue serge suit, vest, watch chain. He wore black shiny shoes.

And beyond him—

An old man sat quietly, in an immense modern chair. He watched Fletcher calmly, his blue eyes mild and tired. A strange thrill shot through Fletcher. It was not fear. Rather it was a vibration, rattling his bones—a deep sense of awe, tinged with fascination.

"Where—what is this place?" he asked faintly. He was still dazed from his quick ascent.

"Don't ask questions!" the nervous little man snapped angrily, tapping his pencil against his ledgers. "You're here to answer, not ask."

The Old Man moved a little. He raised his hand. "I will speak to the element alone," he murmured. His voice was low. It vibrated and rumbled through the chamber. Again the waver of fascinated awe swept Ed.

"Alone?" The little fellow backed away, gathering his books and papers in his arms. "Of course." He glanced hostilely at Ed Fletcher. "I'm glad he's finally in custody. All the work and trouble just for—"

He disappeared through a door. The door closed softly behind him. Ed and the Old Man were alone.

"Please sit down," the Old Man said.

Ed found a seat. He sat down awkwardly, nervously. He got out his cigarettes and then put them away again.

"What's wrong?" the Old Man asked.

"I'm just beginning to understand."

"Understand what?"

"That I'm dead."

The Old Man smiled briefly. "Dead? No, you're not dead. You're . . . visiting. An unusual event, but necessitated by circumstances." He leaned toward Ed. "Mr. Fletcher, you have got yourself involved with something."

"Yeah," Ed agreed. "I wish I knew what it was. Or how it happened."

"It was not your fault. You were a victim of a clerical error. A mistake was made—not by you. But involving you."

"What mistake?" Ed rubbed his forehead wearily. "I—I got in on something. I saw *through*. I saw something I wasn't supposed to see."

The Old Man nodded. "That's right. You saw something you were not supposed to see—something few elements have been aware of, let alone witnessed."

"Elements?"

"An official term. Let it pass. A mistake was made, but we hope to rectify it. It is my hope that—"

"Those people," Ed interrupted "Heaps of dry ash. And gray. Like they were dead. Only it was everything: the stairs and walls and floor. No color or life."

"That Sector had been temporarily de-energized. So the adjustment team could enter and effect changes."

"Changes." Ed nodded. "That's right. When I went back later, everything was alive again. But not the same. It was all different."

"The adjustment was complete by noon. The team finished its work and re-energized the Sector."

"I see," Ed muttered.

"You were supposed to have been in the Sector when the adjustment began. Because of an error you were not. You came into the Sector late—during the adjustment itself. You fled, and when you returned it was over. You saw, and you should not have seen. Instead of a witness you should have been part of the adjustment. Like the others, you should have undergone changes."

Sweat came out on Ed Fletcher's head. He wiped it away. His stomach turned over. Weakly, he cleared his throat. "I get the picture." His voice was almost inaudible. A chilling premonition moved through him. "I was supposed to be changed like the others. But I guess something went wrong."

"Something went wrong. An error occurred. And now a serious problem exists. You have seen these things. You know a great deal. And you are not coordinated with the new configuration."

"Gosh," Ed muttered. "Well, I won't tell anybody." Cold sweat poured off him. "You can count on that. I'm as good as changed."

"You have already told someone," the Old Man said coldly.

"Me?" Ed blinked. "Who?"

"Your wife."

Ed trembled. The color drained from his face, leaving it sickly white. "That's right. I did."

"Your wife knows." The Old Man's face twisted angrily. "A woman. Of all the things to tell—"

"I didn't know." Ed retreated, panic leaping through him. "But I know *now*. You can count on me. Consider me changed."

The ancient blue eyes bored keenly into him, peering far into his depths. "And you were going to call the police. You wanted to inform the authorities."

"But I didn't know *who* was doing the changing."

"Now you know. The natural process must be supplemented— adjusted here and there. Corrections must be made. We are fully licensed to make such corrections. Our adjustment teams perform vital work."

Ed plucked up a measure of courage. "This particular adjustment. Douglas. The office. What was it for? I'm sure it was some worthwhile purpose."

The Old Man waved his hand. Behind him in the shadows an immense map glowed into existence. Ed caught his breath. The edges of the map faded off in obscurity. He saw an infinite web of detailed sections, a network of squares and ruled lines. Each square was marked. Some glowed with a blue light. The lights altered constantly.

"The Sector Board," the Old Man said. He sighed wearily. "A staggering job. Sometimes we wonder how we can go on another period. But it must be done. For the good of all. For *your* good."

"The change. In our—our Sector."

"Your office deals in real estate. The old Douglas was a shrewd man, but rapidly becoming infirm. His physical health was waning. In a few days Douglas will be offered a chance to purchase a large unimproved forest area in western Canada. It will require most of his assets. The older, less virile Douglas would have hesitated. It is imperative he not hesitate. He must purchase the area and clear the land at once. Only a younger man—a younger Douglas—would undertake this.

"When the land is cleared, certain anthropological remains will be discovered. They have already been placed there. Douglas will lease his land to the Canadian Government for scientific study. The remains found there will cause international excitement in learned circles.

"A chain of events will be set in motion. Men from numerous countries will come to Canada to examine the remains. Soviet, Polish, and Czech scientists will make the journey.

"The chain of events will draw these scientists together for the first time in years. National research will be temporarily forgotten in the excitement of these nonnational discoveries. One of the leading Soviet scientists will make friends with a Belgian scientist. Before they depart they will agree to correspond—without the knowledge of their governments, of course.

"The circle will widen. Other scientists on both sides will be drawn in. A society will be founded. More and more educated men will transfer an increasing amount of time to this international society. Purely national research will suffer a slight but extremely critical eclipse. The war tension will somewhat wane.

"This alteration is vital. And it is dependent on the purchase and clearing of the section of wilderness in Canada. The old Douglas would not have dared take the risk. But the altered Douglas, and his altered, more youthful staff, will pursue this work with wholehearted enthusiasm. And from this, the vital chain of widening events will come about. The beneficiaries will be *you*. Our methods may seem strange and indirect. Even incomprehensible. But I assure you we know what we're doing."

"I know that now," Ed said.

"So you do. You know a great deal. Much too much. No element should possess such knowledge. I should perhaps call an adjustment team in here . . . "

A picture formed in Ed's mind: swirling gray clouds, gray men and women. He shuddered. "Look," he croaked. "I'll do anything. Anything at all. Only don't de-energize me." Sweat ran down his face. "OK?"

The Old Man pondered. "Perhaps some alternative could be found. There is another possibility . . . "

"What?" Ed asked eagerly. "What is it?"

The Old Man spoke slowly, thoughtfully. "If I allow you to return, you will swear never to speak of the matter? Will you swear not to reveal to anyone the things you saw? The things you know?"

"Sure!" Ed gasped eagerly, blinding relief flooding over him. "I swear!"

"Your wife. She must know nothing more. She must think it was only a passing psychological fit—retreat from reality."

"She thinks that already."

"She must continue to."

Ed set his jaw firmly. "I'll see that she continues to think it was a mental aberration. She'll never know what really happened."

"You are certain you can keep the truth from her?"

"Sure," Ed said confidently. "I know I can."

"All right." The Old Man nodded slowly. "I will send you back. But you must tell no one." He swelled visibly. "Remember: you will eventually come back to me—everyone does, in the end—and your fate will not be enviable."

"I won't tell her," Ed said, sweating. "I promise. You have my word on that. I can handle Ruth. Don't give it a second thought."

❖ ❖ ❖

Ed arrived home at sunset.

He blinked, dazed from the rapid descent. For a moment he stood on the pavement, regaining his balance and catching his breath. Then he walked quickly up the path.

He pushed the door open and entered the little green stucco house.

"Ed!" Ruth came flying, face distorted with tears. She threw her arms around him, hugging him tight. "Where the hell have you been?"

"Been?" Ed murmured. "At the office, of course."

Ruth pulled back abruptly. "No, you haven't."

Vague tendrils of alarm plucked at Ed. "Of course I have. Where else—?"

"I called Douglas about three. He said you left. You walked out, practically as soon as I turned my back. Eddie—"

Ed patted her nervously. "Take it easy, honey." He began unbuttoning his coat. "Everything's OK. Understand? Things are perfectly all right."

Ruth sat down on the arm of the couch. She blew her nose, dabbing at her eyes. "If you knew how much I've worried." She put her handkerchief away and folded her arms. "I want to know where you were."

Uneasily, Ed hung his coat in the closet. He came over and kissed her. Her lips were ice cold. "I'll tell you all about it. But what do you say we have something to eat? I'm starved."

Ruth studied him intently. She got down from the arm of the couch. "I'll change and fix dinner."

She hurried into the bedroom and slipped off her shoes and nylons.

Ed followed her. "I didn't mean to worry you," he said carefully. "After you left me today I realized you were right."

"Oh?" Ruth unfastened her blouse and skirt, arranging them over a hanger. "Right about what?"

"About me." He manufactured a grin and made it glow across his face. "About . . . what happened."

Ruth hung her slip over the hanger. She studied her husband intently as she struggled into her tight-fitting jeans. "Go on."

The moment had come. It was now or never. Ed Fletcher braced himself and chose his words carefully. "I realized," he stated, "that the whole darn thing was in my mind. You were right, Ruth. Completely right. And I even realize what caused it."

Ruth rolled her cotton T-shirt down and tucked it in her jeans. "What was the cause?"

"Overwork."

"Overwork?"

"I need a vacation. I haven't had a vacation in years. My mind isn't on the job. I've been daydreaming." He said it firmly, but his heart was in his mouth. "I need to get away. To the mountains. Bass fishing. Or—" He searched his mind frantically. "Or—"

Ruth came toward him ominously. "Ed!" she said sharply. "Look at me!"

"What's the matter?" Panic shot through him. "Why are you looking at me like that?"

"*Where were you this afternoon?*"

Ed's grin faded. "I told you. I went for a walk. Didn't I tell you? A walk. To think things over."

"Don't lie to me, Eddie Fletcher! I can tell when you're lying!" Fresh tears welled up in Ruth's eyes. Her breasts rose and fell excitedly under her cotton shirt. "Admit it! You didn't go for a walk!"

Ed stammered weakly. Sweat poured off him. He sagged helplessly against the door. "What do you mean?"

Ruth's black eyes flashed with anger. "Come on! I want to

know where you were! Tell me! I have a right to know. What really happened?"

Ed retreated in terror, his resolve melting like wax. It was going all wrong. "Honest. I went out for a—"

"Tell me!" Ruth's sharp fingernails dug into his arm. "I want to know where you were—and who you were with!"

Ed opened his mouth. He tried to grin, but his face failed to respond. "I don't know what you mean."

"You know what I mean. Who were you with? Where did you go? Tell me! I'll find out sooner or later."

There was no way out. He was licked—and he knew it. He couldn't keep it from her. Desperately he stalled, praying for time. If he could only distract her get her mind on something else. If she would only let up, even for a second. He could invent something—a better story. Time—he needed more time. "Ruth, you've got to—"

Suddenly there was a sound: the bark of a dog, echoing through the dark house.

Ruth let go, cocking her head alertly. "That was Dobbie. I think somebody's coming."

The doorbell rang.

"You stay here. I'll be right back." Ruth ran out of the room, to the front door. "Darn it." She pulled the front door open.

"Good evening!" The young man stepped quickly inside, loaded down with objects, grinning broadly at Ruth. "I'm from the Sweep-Rite Vacuum Cleaner Company."

Ruth scowled impatiently. "Really, we're about to sit down at the table."

"Oh, this will only take a moment." The young man set down the vacuum cleaner and its attachments with a metallic crash. Rapidly, he unrolled a long illustrated banner, showing the vacuum cleaner in action. "Now, if you'll just hold this while I plug in the cleaner—"

He bustled happily about, unplugging the TV set, plugging in the cleaner, pushing the chairs out of his way.

"I'll show you the drape scraper first." He attached a hose and nozzle to the big gleaming tank. "Now, if you'll just sit down I'll demonstrate each of these easy-to-use attachments." His happy voice rose over the roar of the cleaner. "You'll notice—"

❖❖❖

Ed Fletcher sat down on the bed. He groped in his pocket until he found his cigarettes. Shakily he lit one and leaned back against the wall, weak with relief.

He gazed up, a look of gratitude on his face. "Thanks," he said softly. "I think we'll make it—after all. Thanks a lot."

JAMES P. CROW

"You're a nasty little—*human being*," the newly-formed Z Type robot shrilled peevishly.

Donnie flushed and slunk away. It was true. He was a human being, a human child. And there was nothing science could do. He was stuck with it. A human being in a robot's world.

He wished he were dead. He wished he lay under the grass and the worms were eating him up and crawling through him and devouring his brain, his poor miserable human's brain. The Z-236r, his robot companion, wouldn't have anybody to play with and it would be sorry.

"Where are you going?" Z-236r demanded.

"Home."

"Sissy."

Donnie didn't reply. He gathered up his set of fourth dimensional chess, stuffed it in his pocket, and walked off between the rows of ecarda trees, toward the human quarter. Behind him, Z236r stood gleaming in the late afternoon sun, a pale tower of metal and plastic.

"See if I care," Z-236r shouted sullenly. "Who wants to play with a human being, anyhow? Go on home. You—you smell."

Donnie said nothing. But he hunched over a little more. And his chin sank lower against his chest.

❖❖❖

"Well, it happened," Edgar Parks said gloomily to his wife, across the kitchen table.

Grace looked quickly up. "It?"

"Donnie learned his place today. He told me while I was changing my clothes. One of the new robots he was playing with. Called him a human being. Poor kid. Why the hell do they have to rub it in? Why can't they let us alone?"

"So that's why he didn't want any dinner. He's in his room. I knew something had happened." Grace touched her husband's hand. "He'll get over it. We all have to learn the hard way. He's strong. He'll snap back."

Ed Parks got up from the table and moved into the living room of his modest five-room dwelling unit, located in the section of the city set aside for humans. He didn't feel like eating. "Robots." He clenched his fists futilely. "I'd like to get hold of one of them. Just once. Get my hands into their guts. Rip out handfuls of wire and parts. Just once before I die."

"Maybe you'll get your chance."

"No. No, it'll never come to that. Anyhow, humans wouldn't be able to run things without robots. It's true, honey. Humans haven't got the integration to maintain a society. The Lists prove that twice a year. Let's face it. Humans are inferior to robots. But it's their damn holding it up to us! Like today with Donnie. Holding it up to our faces. I don't mind being a robot's body servant. It's a good job. Pays well and the work is light. But when my kid gets told he's—"

Ed broke off. Donnie had come out of his room slowly, into the living room. "Hi, Dad."

"Hi, son." Ed thumped the boy gently on the back. "How you doing? Want to take in a show tonight?"

Humans entertained nightly on the vid-screens. Humans made good entertainers. That was one area the robots couldn't compete in. Human beings painted and wrote and danced and sang and acted for the amusement of robots. They cooked better, too, but robots didn't eat. Human beings had their place. They were understood and wanted: as body servants, entertainers, clerks, gardeners, construction workers, repairmen, odd-jobbers and factory workers.

But when it came to something like civic control coordinator or traffic supervisor for the usone tapes that fed energy into the planet's twelve hydrosystems—

❖ ❖ ❖

"Dad," Donnie said, "can I ask you something?"

"Sure." Ed sat down on the couch with a sigh. He leaned back and crossed his legs. "What is it?"

Donnie sat quietly beside him, his little round face serious. "Dad, I want to ask you about the Lists."

"Oh, yeah." Ed rubbed his jaw. "That's right. Lists in a few weeks. Time to start boning up for your entry. We'll get out some of the sample tests and go over them. Maybe between the two of us we can get you ready for Class Twenty."

"Listen." Donnie leaned close to his father, his voice low and intense. "Dad, how many humans have ever passed their Lists?"

Ed got up abruptly and paced around the room, filling his pipe and frowning. "Well, son, that's hard to say. I mean, humans don't have access to the C-Bank records. So I can't check to see. The law says any human who gets a score in the top forty per cent is eligible for classification with a gradual upward gradation according to subsequent showing. I don't know how many humans have been able to—"

"Has *any* human ever passed his List?"

Ed swallowed nervously. "Gosh, kid. I don't know. I mean, I don't honestly know of any, when you put it like that. Maybe not. The Lists have been conducted only three hundred years. Before that the Government was reactionary and forbade humans to compete with robots. Nowdays, we have a liberal Government and we can compete on the Lists and if we get high enough scores . . . " His voice wavered and faded. "No, kid," he said miserably. "No human ever passed a List. We're—just—not—smart enough."

The room was silent. Donnie nodded faintly, expressionless. Ed didn't look at him. He concentrated on his pipe, hands shaking.

"It's not so bad," Ed said huskily. "I have a good job. I'm body servant to a hell of a fine N Type robot. I get big tips at Christmas and Easter. It gives me time off when I'm sick." He cleared his throat noisily. "It's not so bad."

Grace was standing at the door. Now she came into the room, eyes bright. "No, not bad. Not at all. You open doors for it, bring its instruments to it, make calls for it, run errands for it, oil it, repair it, sing to it, talk to it, scan tapes for it—"

"Shut up," Ed muttered irritably. "What the hell should I do? Quit? Maybe I should mow lawns like John Hollister and Pete Klein. At least my robot calls me by name. Like a living thing. It calls me Ed."

"Will a human ever pass a List?" Donnie asked.

"Yes," Grace said sharply.

Ed nodded. "Sure, kid. Of course. Someday maybe humans and robots will live together in equality. There's an Equality Party among the robots. Holds ten seats in the Congress. They think humans should be admitted without Lists. Since it's obvious—" He broke off. "I mean, since no humans have ever been able to pass their Lists so far—"

"Donnie," Grace said fiercely, bending down over her son. "Listen to me. I want you to pay attention. Nobody knows this. The robots don't talk about it. Humans don't know. But it's true."

"What is it?"

"I know of a human being who—who's classified. He passed his Lists. Ten years ago. And he's gone up. He's up to Class Two. Someday he'll be Class One. Do you hear? A human being. And he's going up."

Donnie's face showed doubt. "Really?" The doubt turned to wistful hope. "Class Two? No kidding?"

"It's just a story," Ed grunted. "I've heard that all my life."

"It's true! I heard two robots talking about it when I was cleaning up one of the Engineering Units. They stopped when they noticed me."

"What's his name?" Donnie asked, wide-eyed.

"James P. Crow," Grace said proudly.

"Strange name," Ed murmured.

"That's his name. I know. It's not a story. It's true! And sometime, someday, he'll be on the top level. On the Supreme Council."

❖ ❖ ❖

Bob McIntyre lowered his voice. "Yeah, it's true, all right. James P. Crow is his name."

"It's not a legend?" Ed demanded eagerly.

"There really is such a human. And he's Class Two. Gone all the way up. Passed his Lists like *that*." McIntyre snapped his fingers. "The robs hush it up, but it's a fact. And the news is spreading. More and more humans know."

The two men had stopped by the service entrance of the enormous Structural Research Building. Robot officials moved busily in and out through the main doors, at the front of the building. Robot planners who guided Terran society with skill and efficiency.

Robots ran Earth. It had always been that way. The history tapes said so. Humans had been invented during the Total War of the Eleventh Millibar. All types of weapons had been tested and used; humans were one of many. The War had utterly wrecked society. For decades after, anarchy and ruin lay everywhere. Only gradually had society reformed under the patient guidance of robots. Humans had been useful in the reconstruction. But why they had originally been made, what they had been used for, how they had served in the War—all knowledge had perished in the hydrogen bomb blasts. The historians had to fill in with conjecture. They did so.

"Why such a strange name?" Ed asked.

McIntyre shrugged. "All I know is he's sub-Advisor to the Northern Security Conference. And in line for the Council when he makes Class One."

"What do the robs think?"

"They don't like it. But there's nothing they can do. The law says they have to let a human hold a job if he's qualified. They never thought a human would be qualified, of course. But this Crow passed his Lists."

"It certainly is strange. A human, smarter than the robs. I wonder why."

"He was an ordinary repairman. A mechanic, fixing machinery and designing circuits. Unclassified, of course. Then suddenly he passed his first List. Entered Class Twenty. He rose the next bi-annual to Class Nineteen. They had to put him to work." McIntyre chuckled. "Too damn bad, isn't it? They have to sit with a human being."

"How do they react?"

"Some quit. Walk out, rather than sit with a human. But most stay. A lot of robs are decent. They try hard."

"I'd sure like to meet this fellow Crow."

McIntyre frowned. "Well—"

"What is it?"

"I understand he doesn't like to be seen with humans too much."

"Why not?" Ed bristled. "What's wrong with humans? Is he too high and mighty, sitting up there with robots—"

"It's not that." There was a strange look in McIntyre's eyes. A yearning, distant look. "It's not just that, Ed. He's up to something. Something important. I shouldn't be saying. But it's big. Big as hell."

"What is it?"

"I can't say. But wait until he gets on the Council. Wait." McIntyre's eyes were feverish. "It's so big it'll shake the world. The stars and the sun'll shake."

"What is it?"

"I don't know. But Crow's got something up his sleeve. Something incredibly big. We're all waiting for it. Waiting for the day . . . "

❖ ❖ ❖

James P. Crow sat at his polished mahogany desk, thinking. That wasn't his real name, of course. He had taken it after the first experiments, grinning to himself as he did so. Nobody would ever know what it meant; it would remain a private joke, personal and unannounced. But it was a good joke nonetheless. Biting and appropriate.

He was a small man. Irish-German. A little lean light-skinned man with blue eyes and sandy hair that fell down in his face and had to be brushed back. He wore unpressed baggy pants and rolled-up sleeves. He was nervous, highstrung. He smoked all day and drank black coffee and usually couldn't sleep at night. But there was a lot on his mind.

A hell of a lot. Crow got abruptly to his feet and paced over to the vidsender. "Send in the Commissioner of Colonies," he ordered.

The Commissioner's metal and plastic body pushed through the door, into the office. An R Type robot, patient and efficient. "You wished to—" It broke off, seeing a human. For a second its pale eye lens flickered doubtfully. A faint sheen of distaste spread across its features. "You wished to see me?"

Crow had seen that expression before. Endless times. He was used to it—almost. The surprise, and then the lofty withdrawal, the cold, clipped formality. He was "*Mister* Crow." Not Jim. The law made them address him as an equal. It hurt some of them more than others. Some showed it without restraint. This one held its feelings back a trifle; Crow was its official superior.

"Yes, I wished to see you," Crow said calmly. "I want your report. Why hasn't it come in?"

The robot stalled, still lofty and withdrawn. "Such a report takes time. We're doing the best we can."

"I want it within two weeks. No later."

The robot struggled with itself, life-long prejudices versus the requirements of Governmental codes. "All right, *sir*. The report will be ready in two weeks." It moved out of the office. The door formed behind it.

Crow let his breath out with a rush. Doing the best they could? Hardly. Not to please a human being. Even if he was at Advisory Level, Class Two. They all dragged their feet, all the way down the line. Little things here and there.

His door melted and a robot wheeled quickly into the office. "I say there, Crow. Got a minute?"

"Of course." Crow grinned. "Come in and sit down. I'm always glad to talk to you."

The robot dumped some papers on Crow's desk. "Tapes and such. Business trifles." It eyed Crow intently. "You look upset. Anything happen?"

"A report I want. Overdue. Somebody taking its time."

L-87t grunted. "Same old stuff. By the way . . . We're having a meeting tonight. Want to come over and make a speech? Should have a good turn out."

"Meeting?"

"Party meeting. Equality." L-87t made a quick sign with its right gripper, a sort of half-arc in the air. The Equality sign. "We'd be glad to have you, Jim. Want to come?"

"No. I'd like to, but I have things to do."

"Oh." The robot moved toward the door. "All right. Thanks anyhow." It lingered at the door. "You'd give us a shot in the arm, you know. Living proof of our contention that a human being is the equal of a robot and should be afforded such recognition."

Crow smiled faintly. "But a human isn't the equal of a robot."

L-87t sputtered indignantly. "What are you saying? Aren't you the living proof? Look at your List scores. Perfect. Not a mistake. And in a couple of weeks you'll be Class One. Highest there is."

Crow shook his head. "Sorry. A human isn't the equal of a robot anymore than he's the equal of a stove. Or a diesel motor. Or a snowplow. There are a lot of things a human can't do. Let's face facts."

L-87t was baffled. "But—"

"I mean it. You're ignoring reality. Humans and robots are completely different. We humans can sing, act, write plays, stories, operas, paint, design sets, flower gardens, buildings, cook delicious meals, make love, scratch sonnets on menus—and robots can't. But robots can build elaborate cities and machines that function perfectly, work for days without rest, think without emotional interruption, gestalt complex data without a time lag.

"Humans excel in some fields, robots in others. Humans have highly developed emotions and feelings. Esthetic awareness. We're sensitive to colors and sounds and textures and soft music mixed with wine. All very fine things. Worthwhile. But realms totally beyond robots. Robots are purely intellectual. Which is fine, too. Both realms are fine. Emotional humans, sensitive to art and music and drama. Robots who think and plan and design machinery. But that doesn't mean we're both the same."

L-87t shook its head sadly. "I don't understand you, Jim. Don't you want to help your race?"

"Of course. But realistically. Not by ignoring facts and making an illusionary assertion that men and robots are interchangeable. Identical elements."

A curious look slid across L-87t's eye lens. "What's your solution, then?"

Crow clamped his jaw tight. "Stick around another few weeks and maybe you'll see."

❖ ❖ ❖

Crow headed out of the Terran Security Building and along the street. Around him robots streamed, bright hulls of metal and plastic and d/n fluid. Except for body servants, humans never came to this area. This was the managerial section of the city, the core, the nucleus, where the planning and organization went on. From this area the life of the city was controlled. Robots were everywhere. In the surface cars, on the moving ramps, the balconies, entering buildings, streaming out, standing in pale glowing knots here and there like Roman Senators, talking and discussing business.

A few greeted him, faintly, formally, with a nod of their metal heads. And then turned their backs. Most robots ignored him or pulled aside to avoid contact. Sometimes a clump of talking robots would become abruptly silent, as Crow pushed past. Robot eye lenses fixed on him, solemn and half astonished. They noticed his arm color, Class Two. Surprise and indignation. And after he had passed, a quick angry buzz of resentment. Backward glances at him as he threaded his way toward the human quarter.

A pair of humans stood in front of the Domestic Control Offices, armed with pruning shears and rakes. Gardeners, weeding and watering the lawns of the big public building. They watched Crow pass with excited stares. One waved nervously at him, feverish and hopeful. A menial human waving at the only human ever to reach classification.

Crow waved back briefly.

The two humans' eyes grew wide with awe and reverence. They were still looking after him when he turned the corner at the main intersection and mixed with the business crowds shopping at the trans-planet marts.

Goods from the wealthy colonies of Venus and Mars and Ganymede filled the open-air marts. Robots drifted in swarms, sampling and pricing and discussing and gossiping. A few humans were visible, mostly household servants in charge of maintenance, stocking up on supplies. Crow edged his way through and beyond the marts. He was approaching the human quarter of the city. He could smell it already. The faint pungent scent of humans.

The robots, of course, were odorless. In a world of odorless machines the human scent stood out in bold relief. The human quarter was a section of the city once prosperous. Humans had moved in and property values had dropped. Gradually the houses had been abandoned by robots and now humans exclusively lived there. Crow, in spite of his position, was obliged to live in the human quarter. His house, a uniform five-room dwelling, identical with all the others, was located to the rear of the quarter. One house of many.

He held his hand up to the front door and the door melted. Crow entered quickly and the door reformed. He glanced at his watch. Plenty of time. An hour before he was due back at his desk.

He rubbed his hands. It was always a thrilling moment to come here, to his personal quarters, where he had grown up, lived as an ordinary unclassified human being—before he had come across *it* and begun his meteoric ascent into the upper-class regions.

❖❖❖

Crow passed through the small silent house, to the work shed in back. He unlocked the bolted doors and slid them aside. The shed was hot and dry. He clicked off the alarm system. Complex tangles of bells and wires that were really unnecessary: robots never entered the human section, and humans seldom stole from each other.

Locking the doors behind him, Crow seated himself before a bank of machinery assembled in the center of the shed. He snapped on the power and the machinery hummed into life. Dials and meters swing into activity. Lights glowed.

Before him, a square window of gray faded to light pink and shimmered slightly. The Window. Crow's pulse throbbed painfully. He flicked a key. The Window clouded and showed a scene. He slid a tape scanner before the Window and activated it. The scanner clicked as the Window gained shape. Forms moved, dim forms that wavered and hesitated. He steadied the picture.

Two robots were standing behind a table. They moved quickly, jerkily. He slowed them down. The two robots were handling something. Crow increased the power of the image and the objects bloated up, to be caught by the scanning lens and preserved on tape.

The robots were sorting Lists. Class One Lists. Grading and dividing them into groups. Several hundred packets of questions and answers. Before the table a restless crowd waited, eager robots waiting to hear their scores. Crow speeded the image up. The two robots leaped into activity, tossing and arranging Lists in a blur of energy. Then the master Class One List was held up—

The List. Crow caught it in the Window, dropping the velocity to zero. The List was held, fixed tight like a specimen on a slide. The tape scanner hummed away, recording the question and answers.

He felt no guilt. No sting of conscience at using a Time Window to see the results of future Lists. He had been doing it ten years, all the way up from the bottom, from unclassified up to the top List, to Class One. He had never kidded himself. Without advance sight of the answers he could never have passed. He would still be unclassified, at the bottom of the pile, along with the great undifferentiated mass of humans.

The Lists were geared to robot minds. Made up by robots, phased to a robot culture. A culture which was alien to humans, to which humans had to make difficult adjustment. No wonder only robots passed their Lists.

Crow wiped the scene from the Window and threw the scanner aside. He sent the Window back into time, spinning back through the centuries into the past. He never tired of seeing the early days, the days before the Total War wrecked human society and destroyed all human tradition. The days when man lived without robots.

He fiddled with the dials, capturing a moment. The Window showed robots building up their post-war society, swarming over their ruined planet, erecting vast cities and buildings, clearing away the debris. With humans as slaves. Second-class servant citizens.

He saw the Total War, the rain of death from the sky. The blossoming pale funnels of destruction. He saw man's society dissolve into radioactive particles. All human knowledge and culture lost in the chaos.

And once again, he caught his favorite of all scenes. A scene he had examined repeatedly, enjoying with acute satisfaction this unique sight. A scene of human beings in an undersurface lab, in the early days of the war. Designing and building the first robots, the original A Type robots, four centuries before.

❖ ❖ ❖

Ed Parks walked home slowly, holding his son's hand. Donnie gazed down at the ground. He said nothing. His eyes were red and puffy. He was pale with misery.

"I'm sorry, Dad," he muttered.

Ed's grip tightened. "It's okay, kid. You did your best. Don't worry about it. Maybe next time. We'll get started practicing sooner." He cursed under his breath. "Those lousy metal tubs. Damn soul-less heaps of tin!"

It was evening. The sun was setting. The two of them climbed the porch steps slowly and entered the house. Grace met them at the door. "No luck?" She studied their faces. "I can see. Same old story."

"Same old story," Ed said bitterly. "He didn't have a chance. Hopeless."

From the dining room came a murmur of sound. Voices, men and women.

"Who's in there?" Ed demanded irritably. "Do we have to have company? For God's sake, today of all days—"

"Come on." Grace pulled him toward the kitchen. "Some news. Maybe it'll make you feel better. Come along, Donnie. This will interest you, too."

Ed and Donnie entered the kitchen. It was full of people. Bob McIntyre and his wife Pat. John Hollister and his wife Joan and their two daughters. Pete Klein and Rose Klein. Neighbors, Nat Johnson and Tim Davis and Barbara Stanley. An eager murmur buzzed through the room. Everybody was grouped around the table, excited and nervous. Sandwiches and beer bottles were piled up in heaps. The men and women were laughing and grinning happily, eyes bright with agitation.

"What's up?" Ed grumbled. "Why the party?"

Bob McIntyre clapped him on the shoulder. "How you doing, Ed? We've got news." He rattled a public news tape. "Get ready. Brace yourself."

"Read it to him," Pete Klein said excitedly.

"Go on! Read it!" They all grouped around McIntyre. "Let's hear it again!"

McIntyre's face was alive with emotion. "Well, Ed. This is it. He made it. He's there."

"Who? Who made what?"

"Crow. Jim Crow. He made Class One." The tape spool trembled in McIntyre's hand. "He's been named to the Supreme Council. Understand? He's in. A human being. A member of the supreme governing body of the planet."

"Gosh," Donnie said, awed.

"Now what?" Ed asked. "What's he going to do?"

McIntyre grinned shakily. "We'll know, soon. He's got something. We know. We can feel it. And we should start seeing it in action—any time, now."

❖ ❖ ❖

Crow strode briskly into the Council Chamber, his portfolio under his arm. He wore a slick new suit. His hair was combed. His shoes were shined. "Good day," he said politely.

The five robots regarded him with mixed feelings. They were old, over a century old. The powerful N Type that had dominated the social scene since its construction. And an incredibly ancient D Type, almost three centuries old. As Crow advanced toward his seat the five robots stepped away, leaving a wide path for him.

"You," one of the N Types said. "You are the new Council member?"

"That's right." Crow took his seat. "Care to examine my credentials?"

"Please."

Crow passed over the card plate given him by the Lists Committee. The five robots studied it intently. Finally they passed it back.

"It appears to be in order," the D admitted reluctantly.

"Of course." Crow unzipped his portfolio. "I wish to begin work at once. There's quite a lot of material to cover. I have some reports and tapes you'll find worth your while."

The robots took their places slowly, eyes still on Jim Crow. "This is incredible," the D said. "Are you serious? Can you really expect to sit with us?"

"Of course," Crow snapped. "Let's forego this and get down to business."

One of the N Types leaned toward him, massive and contemptuous, its patina-encrusted hull glinting dully. "Mr. Crow," it said icily. "You must understand this is utterly impossible. In spite of the legal ruling and your technical right to sit on this—"

Crow smiled calmly back. "I suggest you check my Listing scoring. You'll discover I've made no errors in all twenty Lists. A perfect score. To my knowledge, none of you has achieved a perfect score. Therefore, according to the Governmental ruling contained in the official Lists Committee decree, I'm your superior."

The word fell like a bomb shell. The five robots slumped down in their seats, stricken. Their eye lenses flickered uneasily. A worried hum rose in pitch, filling the chamber.

"Let's see," an N murmured, extending its gripper. Crow tossed his List sheets over and the five robots each scanned them rapidly.

"It's true," the D stated. "Incredible. No robot has ever achieved a perfect score. This human outranks us, according to our own laws."

"Now," Crow said. "Let's get down to business." He spread out his tapes and reports. "I won't waste any time. I have a proposal to make. An important proposal bearing on the most critical problem of this society."

"What problem is that?" an X asked apprehensively.

Crow was tense. "The problem of humans. Humans occupying an inferior position in a robot world. Menials in an alien culture. Servants of robots."

Silence.

The five robots sat frozen. It had happened. The thing they had feared. Crow sat back in his chair, lighting a cigarette. The robots watched each motion, his hands, the cigarette, the smoke, the match as he ground it out underfoot. The moment had come.

"What do you propose?" the D asked at last, with metallic dignity. "What is this proposal of yours?"

"I propose you robots evacuate Earth at once. Pack up and leave. Emigrate to the colonies. Ganymede, Mars, Venus. Leave Earth to us humans."

The robots got instantly up. "Incredible! We built this world. This is our world! Earth belongs to us. It has always belonged to us."

"*Has it?*" Crow said grimly.

An uneasy chill moved through the robots. They hesitated, strangely alarmed. "Of course," the D murmured.

Crow reached toward his heap of tapes and reports. The robots watched his movement with fear. "What is that?" an N demanded nervously. "What do you have there?"

"Tapes," Crow said.

"What kind of tapes?"

"History tapes." Crow signalled and a gray-clad human servant hurried into the chamber with a tape scanner. "Thanks," Crow said.

The human started out. "Wait. You might like to stay and watch this, my friend."

The servant's eyes bulged. He found a place in the back and stood trembling and watching.

"Highly irregular," the D protested. "What are you doing? What is this?"

"Watch." Crow snapped on the scanner, feeding the first tape into it. In the air, in the center of the Council table, a three-dimensional image formed. "Keep your eyes on this. You'll remember this moment for a long time."

The image hardened. They were looking into the Time Window. A scene from the Total War was in motion. Men, human technicians, working frantically in an undersurface lab. Assembling something. Assembling—

The human servant squawked wildly. "An A! It's a Type A robot! They're making it!"

The five Council robots buzzed in consternation. "Get that servant out of here!" the D ordered.

The scene changed. It showed the first robots, the original Type A, rising to the surface to fight the war. Other early robots appeared, snaking through the ruins and ash, approaching warily. The robots clashed. Bursts of white light. Gleaming clouds of particles.

"Robots were originally designed as soldiers," Crow explained. "Then more advanced types were produced to act as technicians and lab workers and machinists."

The scene showed an undersurface factory. Rows of robots worked presses and stampers. The robots worked rapidly, efficiently—supervised by human foremen.

"These tapes are fake!" an N cried angrily. "Do you expect us to believe this?"

A new scene formed. Robots, more advanced, types more complex and elaborate. Taking over more and more economic and industrial functions as humans were destroyed by the War.

"At first robots were simple," Crow explained. "They served simple needs. Then, as the War progressed, more advanced types were created. Finally, humans were making Types D and E. Equal to humans—and in conceptual faculties, superior to humans."

"This is insane!" an N stated. "Robots evolved. The early types were simple because they were original stages, primitive forms that gave rise to more complex forms. The laws of evolution fully explain this process."

A new scene formed. The last stages of the War. Robots fighting men. Robots eventually winning. The complete chaos of the latter years. Endless wastes of rolling ash and radioactive particles. Miles of ruin.

"All cultural records were destroyed," Crow said. "Robots emerged masters without knowing how or why, or in what manner they came into being. But now you see the facts. Robots were created as human tools. During the war they got out of hand."

He snapped off the tape scanner. The image faded. The five robots sat in stunned silence.

Crow folded his arms. "Well? What do you say?" He jerked his thumb at the human servant crouching in the rear of the chamber, dazed and astonished. "Now you know and now he knows. What do you imagine he's thinking? I can tell you. He's thinking—"

"How did you get these tapes?" the D demanded. "They can't be genuines. They must be fakes."

"Why weren't they found by our archeologists?" an N shouted shrilly.

"I took them personally," Crow said.

"*You* took them? What do you mean?"

"Through a Time Window." Crow tossed a thick package onto the table. "Here are the schematics. You can build a Time Window yourself if you want."

"A time machine." The D snatched up the package and leafed through the contents. "You saw into the past." Dawning realization showed on its ancient face. "Then—"

"He saw ahead!" an N searched wildly. "Into the future! That explains his perfect Lists. He scanned them in advance."

Crow rattled his papers impatiently. "You've heard my proposal. You've seen the tapes. If you vote down the proposal I'll release the tapes publicly. And the schematics. Every human in the world will know the true story of his origin, and of yours."

"So?" an N said nervously. "We can handle humans. If there's an uprising we'll put it down."

"Will you?" Crow got suddenly to his feet, his face hard. "Consider. Civil war raging over the whole planet. Men on one side, centuries of pent-up hatred. On the other side robots suddenly deprived of their myth. Knowing they were originally mechanical tools. Are you sure you'll come out on top this time? Are you positive?"

The robots were silent.

"If you'll evacuate Earth I'll suppress the tapes. The two races can go on, each with its own culture and society. Humans here on Earth. Robots on the colonies. Neither one master. Neither one slave."

The five robots hesitated, angry and resentful. "But we worked centuries to build up this planet! It won't make sense. Our leaving. What'll we say? What'll we give as our reason?"

Crow smiled harshly. "You can say Earth isn't adequate for the great original master race."

There was silence. The four Type N robots looked at each other nervously, drawing together in a whispered huddle. The massive D sat silent, its archaic brass eye lens fixed intently on Crow, a baffled, defeated expression on its face.

Calmly, Jim Crow waited.

❖ ❖ ❖

"Can I shake your hand?" L-87t asked timidly. "I'll be going soon. I'm in one of the first loads."

Crow stuck out his hand briefly and L-87t shook, a little embarrassed.

"I hope it works out," L-87t ventured. "Vid us from time to time. Keep us posted."

Outside the Council Buildings the blaring voices of the street speakers were beginning to disturb the late afternoon gloom. All up and down the city the speakers roared out their message, the Council Directive.

Men, scurrying home from work, paused to listen. In the uniform houses in the human quarter men and women glanced up, pausing in their routine of living, curious and attentive. Everywhere, in all cities of Earth, robots and human beings ceased their activities and looked up as the Government speakers roared into life.

"This is to announce that the Supreme Council has decreed the rich colony planets Venus, Mars, and Ganymede, are to be set aside exclusively for the use of robots. No humans will be permitted outside of Earth. In order to take advantage of the superior resources and living conditions of these colonies, all robots now on Earth are to be transferred to the colony of their choice.

"The Supreme Council has decided that Earth is no fit place for robots. Its wasted and still partly-devastated condition renders it unworthy of the robot race. All robots are to be conveyed to their new homes in the colonies as quickly as adequate transportation can be arranged.

"In no case can humans enter the colony areas. The colonies are exclusively for the use of robots. The human population will be permitted to remain on Earth.

"This is to announce that the Supreme Council has decreed that the rich colony planets of Venus—"

Crow moved away from the window, satisfied.

He returned to his desk and continued assembling papers and reports in neat piles, glancing at them briefly as he classified them and laid them aside.

"I hope you humans will get along all right," L-87t repeated. Crow continued checking the heaps of top-level reports, marking them with his writing stick. Working rapidly, with absorbed attention, deep in his work. He scarcely noticed the robot lingering at the door. "Can you give me some idea of the government you'll set up?"

Crow glanced up impatiently. "What?"

"Your form of government. How will your society be ruled, now that you've maneuvered us off Earth? What sort of government will take place of our Supreme Council and Congress?"

Crow didn't answer. He had already returned to his work. There was a strange granite cast to his face, a peculiar hardness L-87t had never seen.

"Who'll run things?" L-87t asked. "Who'll be the Government now that we're gone? You said yourself humans show no ability to manage a complex modern society. Can you find a human capable of keeping the wheels turning? Is there a human being capable of leading mankind?"

Crow smiled thinly. And continued working.

SOUVENIR

"Here we go, sir," the robot pilot said. The words startled Rogers and made him look up sharply. He tensed his body and adjusted the trace web inside his coat as the bubble ship started dropping, swiftly and silently, toward the planet's surface.

This—his heart caught—was Williamson's World. The legendary lost planet—found, after three centuries. By accident, of course. This blue and green planet, the holy grail of the Galactic System, had been almost miraculously discovered by a routine charting mission.

Frank Williamson had been the first Terran to develop an outer-space drive—the first to hop off from the Solar System toward the universe beyond. He had never come back. He—his world, his colony—had never been found. There had been endless rumors, false leads, fake legends—and nothing more.

"I'm receiving field clearance." The robot pilot raised the gain on the control speaker, and clicked to attention.

"Field ready," came a ghostly voice from below. "Remember, your drive mechanism is unfamiliar to us. How much run is required? Emergency brake-walls are up."

Rogers smiled. He could hear the pilot telling them that no run would be required. Not with this ship. The brake-walls could be lowered with perfect safety.

Three hundred years! It had taken a long time to find Williamson's World. Many authorities had given him up. Some believed he had never landed, had died out in space. Perhaps there was *no* Williamson's World. Certainly there had been no real clues, nothing tangible to go on. Frank Williamson and three families had utterly disappeared in the trackless void, never to be heard from again.

Until now . . .

The young man met him at the field. He was thin and red-haired and dressed in a colorful suit of bright material. "You're from the Galactic Relay Center?" he asked.

"That's right," Rogers said huskily. "I'm Edward Rogers."

The young man held out his hand. Rogers shook it awkwardly. "My name is Williamson," the young man said. "Gene Williamson."

The name thundered in Rogers' ears. "Are you—"

The young man nodded, his gaze enigmatical. "I'm his great-great-great-great-grandson. His tomb is here. You may see it, if you wish."

"I almost expected to see him. He's—well, almost a god-figure to us. The first man to break out of the Solar System."

"He means a lot to us, too," the young man said. "He brought us here. They searched a long time before they found a planet that was habitable." Williamson waved at the city stretched out beyond the field. "This one proved satisfactory. It's the System's tenth planet."

❖ ❖ ❖

Rogers' eyes began to shine. Williamson's World. Under his feet. He stamped hard as they walked down the ramp together, away from the field. How many men in the Galaxy had dreamed of striding down a landing ramp onto Williamson's World with a young descendant of Frank Williamson beside them?

"They'll all want to come here," Williamson said, as if aware of his thoughts. "Throw rubbish around and break off the flowers. Pick up handfuls of dirt to take back." He laughed a little nervously. "The Relay will control them, of course."

"Of course," Rogers assured him.

At the ramp-end Rogers stopped short. For the first time he saw the city.

"What's wrong?" Gene Williamson asked, with a faint trace of amusement.

They had been cut off, of course. Isolated—so perhaps it wasn't so surprising. It was a wonder they weren't living in caves, eating raw meat. But Williamson had always symbolized progress—development. He had been a man *ahead* of other men.

True, his space-drive by modern standards had been primitive, a curiosity. But the concept remained unaltered; Williamson the pioneer, and inventor. The man who built.

Yet the city was nothing more than a village, with a few dozen houses, and some public buildings and industrial units at its perimeter. Beyond the city stretched green fields, hills, and broad prairies. Surface vehicles crawled leisurely along the narrow streets and most of the citizens walked on foot. An incredible anachronism it seemed, dragged up from the past.

"I'm accustomed to the uniform Galactic culture," Rogers said. "Relay keeps the technocratic and ideological level constant throughout. It's hard to adjust to such a radically different social stage. But you've been cut off."

"Cut off?" asked Williamson.

"From Relay. You've had to develop without help."

In front of them a surface vehicle crept to a halt. The driver opened the doors manually.

"Now that I recall these factors, I can adjust," Rogers assured him.

"On the contrary," Williamson said, entering the vehicle. "We've been receiving your Relay coordinates for over a century." He motioned Rogers to get in beside him.

Rogers was puzzled. "I don't understand. You mean you hooked onto the web and yet made no attempt to—"

"We receive your coordinates," Gene Williamson said, "but our citizens are not interested in using them."

The surface vehicle hurried along the highway, past the rim of an immense red hill. Soon the city lay behind them—a faintly glowing place reflecting the rays of the sun. Bushes and plants appeared along the highway. The sheer side of the cliff rose, a towering wall of deep red sandstone; ragged, untouched.

"Nice evening," Williamson said.

Rogers nodded in disturbed agreement.

Williamson rolled down the window. Cool air blew into the car. A few gnatlike insects followed. Far off, two tiny figures were plowing a field—a man and a huge lumbering beast.

When will we be there?" Rogers asked.

"Soon. Most of us live away from the cities. We live in the country—in isolated self-sufficient farm units. They're modeled on the manors of the Middle Ages."

"Then you maintain only the most rudimentary subsistence level. How many people live on each farm?"

"Perhaps a hundred men and women."

"A hundred people can't manage anything more complex than weaving and dyeing and paper pressing."

"We have special industrial units—manufacturing systems. This vehicle is a good example of what we can turn out. We have communication and sewage and medical agencies. We have technological advantages equal to Terra's."

"Terra of the twenty-first century," Rogers protested. "But that was three hundred years ago. You're purposely maintaining an archaic culture in the face of the Relay coordinates. It doesn't make any sense."

"Maybe we prefer it."

"But you're not free to prefer an inferior cultural stage. Every culture has to keep pace with the general trend. Relay makes actual a uniformity of development. It integrates the valid factors and rejects the rest."

They were approaching the farm, Gene Williamson's "manor." It consisted of a few simple buildings clustered together in a valley, to the side of the highway, surrounded by fields and pastures. The surface vehicle turned down a narrow side road and spiralled cautiously toward the floor of the valley. The air became darker. Cold wind blew into the car, and the driver clicked his headlights on.

"No robots?" Rogers asked.

"No," Williamson replied. "We do all our own work"

"You're making a purely arbitrary distinction," Rogers pointed out. "A robot is a machine. You don't dispense with machines as such. This car is a machine."

"True," Williamson acknowledged.

"The machine is a development of the tool," Rogers went on. "The axe is a simple machine. A stick becomes a tool, a simple machine, in the hands of a man reaching for something. A machine is merely a multi-element tool that increases the power ratio. Man is the tool-making animal. The history of man is the history of tools into machines, greater and more efficient functioning elements. If you reject machinery you reject man's essential key."

"Here we are," Williamson said. The vehicle came to a halt and the driver opened the doors for them.

Three or four huge wooden buildings loomed up in the darkness. A few dim shapes moved around—human shapes.

"Dinner's ready," Williamson said, sniffing. "I can smell it."

They entered the main building. Several men and women were sitting at a long rough table. Plates and dishes had been set in front of them. They were waiting for Williamson.

"This is Edward Rogers," Williamson announced. The people studied Rogers curiously, then turned back to their food.

"Sit down," a dark-eyed girl urged. "By me."

They made a place for him near the end of the table. Rogers started forward, but Williamson restrained him. "Not there. You're *my* guest. You're expected to sit with me."

The girl and her companions laughed. Rogers sat down awkwardly by Williamson. The bench was rough and hard under him. He examined a hand-made wooden drinking cup. The food was piled in huge wooden bowls. There was a stew and a salad and great loaves of bread.

"We could be back in the fourteenth century," Rogers said.

"Yes," Williamson agreed. "Manor life goes back to Roman times and to the classical world. The Gauls. Britons."

"These people here. Are they—"

Williamson nodded. "My family. We're divided up into small units arranged according to the traditional patriarch basis. I'm the oldest male and titular head."

The people were eating rapidly, intent on their food—boiled meat, vegetables, scooped up with hunks of bread and butter and washed down with milk. The room was lit by fluorescent lighting.

"Incredible," Rogers murmured. "You're still using electric power."

"Oh, yes. There are plenty of waterfalls on this planet. The vehicle was electric. It was run by a storage battery."

"Why are there no older men?" Rogers saw several dried-up old women, but Williamson was the oldest man. And he couldn't have been over thirty.

"The fighting," Williamson replied, with an expressive gesture.

"Fighting?"

"Clan wars between families are a major part of our culture." Williamson nodded toward the long table. "We don't live long."

Rogers was stunned. "Clan wars? But—"

"We have pennants, and emblems—like the old Scottish tribes."

He touched a bright ribbon on his sleeve, the representation of a bird. "There are emblems and colors for each family and we fight over them. The Williamson family no longer controls this planet. There is no central agency, now. For a major issue we have the plebiscite—a vote by all the clans. Each family on the planet has a vote."

"Like the American Indians."

Williamson nodded. "It's a tribal system. In time we'll be distinct tribes, I suppose. We still retain a common language, but we're breaking up—decentralizing. And each family to its own ways, its own customs and manners."

"Just what do you fight for?"

Williamson shrugged. "Some real things like land and women. Some imaginary. Prestige for instance. When honor is at stake we have an official semi-annual public battle. A man from each family takes part. The best warrior and his weapons."

"Like the medieval joust."

"We've drawn from all traditions. Human tradition as a whole."

"Does each family have its separate deity?"

Williamson laughed. "No. We worship in common a vague animism. A sense of the general positive vitality of the universal process." He held up a loaf of bread. "Thanks for all this."

"Which you grew yourselves."

"On a planet provided for us." Williamson ate his bread thoughtfully. "The old records say the ship was almost finished. Fuel just about gone—one dead, arid waste after another. If this planet hadn't turned up, the whole expedition would have perished."

❖ ❖ ❖

"Cigar?" Williamson said, when the empty bowls had been pushed back.

"Thanks." Rogers accepted a cigar noncommittally. Williamson lit his own, and settled back against the wall.

"How long are you staying?" he asked presently.

"Not long," Rogers answered.

"There's a bed fixed up for you," Williamson said. "We retire early, but there'll be some kind of dancing, also singing and dramatic acts. We devote a lot of time to staging, and producing drama."

"You place an emphasis on psychological release?"

"We enjoy making and doing things, if that's what you mean."

Rogers stared about him. The walls were covered with murals painted directly on the rough wood. "So I see," he said. "You grind your own colors from clay and berries?"

"Not quite," Williamson replied. "We have a big pigment industry. Tomorrow I'll show you our kiln where we fire our own things. Some of our best work is with fabrics and screen processes."

"Interesting. A decentralized society, moving gradually back into primitive tribalism. A society that voluntarily rejects the advanced technocratic and cultural products of the Galaxy, and thus deliberately withdraws from contact with the rest of mankind."

"From the uniform Relay-controlled society only," Williamson insisted.

"Do you know why Relay maintains a uniform level for all worlds?" Rogers asked. "I'll tell you. There are two reasons. First, the body of knowledge which men have amassed doesn't permit duplication of experiment. There's no time."

"When a discovery has been made it's absurd to repeat it on countless planets throughout the universe. Information gained on any of the thousand worlds is flashed to Relay Center and then out again to the whole Galaxy. Relay studies and selects experiences and co-ordinates them into a rational, functional system without contradictions. Relay orders the total experience of mankind into a coherent structure."

"And the second reason?"

"If uniform culture is maintained, controlled from a central source, there won't be war."

"True," Williamson admitted.

"We've abolished war. It's as simple as that. We have a homogeneous culture like that of ancient Rome—a common culture for all mankind which we maintain throughout the Galaxy. Each planet is as involved in it as any other. There are no backwaters of culture to breed envy and hatred."

"Such as this."

Rogers let out his breath slowly. "Yes—you've confronted us with a strange situation. We've searched for Williamson's World for three centurie We've wanted it, dreamed of finding it. It has seemed like Prester John's Empire—a fabulous world, cut off from the rest of humanity. Maybe not real at all. Frank Williamson might have crashed."

"But he didn't."

"He didn't, and Williamson's World is alive with a culture of its own. Deliberately set apart, with its own way of life, its own standards. Now contact has been made, and our dream has come true. The people of the Galaxy will soon be informed that Williamson's World has been found. We can now restore the first colony outside the Solar System to its rightful place in the Galactic culture."

Rogers reached into his coat, and brought out a metal packet. He unfastened the packet and laid a clean, crisp document on the table.

"What's this?" Williamson asked.

"The Articles of Incorporation. For you to sign, so that Williamson's World can become a part of the Galactic culture."

Williamson and the rest of the people in the room fell silent. They gazed down at the document, none of them speaking.

"Well?" Rogers said. He was tense. He pushed the document toward Williamson. "Here it is."

Williamson shook his head. "Sorry." He pushed the document firmly back toward Rogers. "We've already taken a plebiscite. I hate to disappoint you, but we've already decided not to join. That's our *final* decision."

❖ ❖ ❖

The Class-One battleship assumed an orbit outside the gravity belt of Williamson's World.

Commander Ferris contacted the Relay Center. "We're here. What next?"

"Send down a wiring team. Report back to me as soon as it has made surface contact."

Ten minutes later Corporal Pete Matson was dropped overboard in a pressurized gravity suit. He drifted slowly toward the blue and green globe beneath, turning and twisting as he neared the surface of the planet.

Matson landed and bounced a couple of times. He got shakily to his feet. He seemed to be at the edge of a forest. In the shadow of the huge trees he removed his crash helmet. Holding his blast rifle tightly he made his way forward, cautiously advancing among the trees.

His earphones clicked. "Any sign of activity?"

"None, Commander," he signaled back.

"There's what appears to be a village to your right. You may run into some one. Keep moving, and watch out. The rest of the team is dropping, now. Instructions will follow from your Relay web."

"I'll watch out," Matson promised, cradling his blast rifle. He sighted it experimentally at a distant hill and squeezed the trigger. The hill disintegrated into dust, a rising column of waste particles.

Matson climbed a long ridge and shielded his eyes to peer around him.

He could see the village. It was small, like a country town on Terra. It looked interesting. For a moment he hesitated. Then he stepped quickly down from the ridge and headed toward the village, moving rapidly, his supple body alert.

Above him, from the Class-One battleship, three more of the team were already falling, clutching their guns and tumbling gently toward the surface of the planet . . .

❖❖❖

Rogers folded up the Incorporation papers and returned them slowly to his coat. "You understand what you're doing?" he asked.

The room was deathly silent. Williamson nodded. "Of course. We're refusing to join your Relay system."

Rogers' fingers touched the trace web. The web warmed into life. "I'm sorry to hear that," he said.

"Does it surprise you?"

"Not exactly. Relay submitted our scout's report to the computers. There was always the possibility you'd refuse. I was given instructions in case of such an event."

"What are your instructions?"

Rogers examined his wristwatch. "To inform you that you have six hours to join us—or be blasted out of the universe." He got abruptly to his feet. "I'm sorry this had to happen. Williamson's World is one of our most precious legends. But nothing must destroy the unity of the Galaxy."

Williamson had risen. His face was ash white, the color of death. They faced each other defiantly.

"We'll fight," Williamson said quietly. His fingers knotted together violently, clenching and unclenching.

"That's unimportant. You've received Relay coordinates on weapons development. You know what our war fleet has."

The other people sat quietly at their places, staring rigidly down at their empty plates. No one moved.

"Is it necessary?" Williamson said harshly.

"Cultural variation must be avoided if the Galaxy is to have peace," Rogers replied firmly.

"You'd destroy us to avoid war?"

"We'd destroy anything to avoid war. We can't permit our society to degenerate into bickering provinces, forever quarreling and fighting—like your clans. We're stable because we lack the very concept of variation. Uniformity must be preserved and separation must be discouraged. The idea itself must remain unknown."

Williamson was thoughtful. "Do you think you can keep the idea unknown? There are so many semantic correlatives, hints, verbal leads. Even if you blast us, it may arise somewhere else."

"We'll take that chance." Rogers moved toward the door. "I'll return to my ship and wait there. I suggest you take another vote. Maybe knowing how far we're prepared to go will change the results."

"I doubt it."

Rogers' web whispered suddenly. "This is North at Relay."

Rogers fingered the web in acknowledgment.

"A Class-One battleship is in your area. A team has already been landed. Keep your ship grounded until it can fall back. I've ordered the team to lay out its fission-mine terminals."

Rogers said nothing. His fingers tightened around the web convulsively.

"What's wrong?" Williamson asked.

"Nothing." Rogers pushed the door open. "I'm in a hurry to return to my ship. Let's go."

❖ ❖ ❖

Commander Ferris contacted Rogers as soon as his ship had left Williamson's World.

"North tells me you've already informed them," Ferris said.

"That's right. He also contacted your team directly. Had it prepare to attack."

"So I'm informed. How much time did you offer them?"

"Six hours."

"Do you think they'll give in?"

"I don't know," Rogers said. "I hope so. But I doubt it."

Williamson's World turned slowly in the viewscreen with its green and blue forest, rivers and oceans. Terra might have looked that way, once. He could see the Class-One battleship, a great silvery globe moving slowly in its orbit around the planet.

The legendary world had been found and contacted. Now it would be destroyed. He had tried to prevent it, but without success. He couldn't prevent the inevitable.

If Williamson's World refused to join the Galactic culture its destruction became a necessity—grim, axiomatic. It was either Williamson's World or the Galaxy. To preserve the greater, the lesser had to be sacrificed.

He made himself as comfortable as possible by the viewscreen, and waited.

At the end of six hours a line of black dots rose from the planet and headed slowly toward the Class-One battleship. He recognized them for what they were—old-fashioned jet-driven rocket ships. A formation of antiquated war vessels, rising up to give battle.

The planet had not changed its mind. It was going to fight. It was willing to be destroyed, rather than give up its way of life.

The black dots grew swiftly larger, became roaring blazing metal disks puffing awkwardly along. A pathetic sight. Rogers felt strangely moved, watching the jet-driven ships divide up for the contact. The Class-One battleship had secured its orbit, and was swinging in a lazy, efficient arc. Its banks of energy tubes were slowly rising, lining up to meet the attack.

Suddenly the formation of the ancient rocketships dived. They rumbled over the Class-One, firing jerkily. The Class-One's tubes followed their path. They began to reform clumsily, gaining distance for a second try, and another run.

A tongue of colorless energy flicked out. The attackers vanished.

Commander Ferris contacted Rogers. "The poor tragic fools." His heavy face was gray. "Attacking us with those things."

"Any damage?"

"None whatever." Ferris wiped his forehead shakily. "No damage to me at all."

"What next?" Rogers asked stonily.

"I've declined the mine operation and passed it back to Relay. They'll have to do it. The impulse should already be—"

Below them, the green and blue globe shuddered convulsively. Soundlessly, effortlessly, it flew apart. Fragments rose, bits of debris and the planet dissolved in a cloud of white flame, a blazing mass of incandescent fire. For an instant it remained a miniature sun, lighting up the void. Then it faded into ash.

The screens of Rogers' ship hummed into life, as the debris struck. Particles rained against them, and were instantly disintegrated.

"Well," Ferris said. "It's over. North will report the original scout mistaken. Williamson's World wasn't found. The legend will remain a legend."

Rogers continued to watch until the last bits of debris had ceased flying, and only a vague, discolored shadow remained. The screens clicked off automatically. To his right, the Class-One battleship picked up speed and headed toward the Riga System.

Williamson's World was gone. The Galactic Relay culture had been preserved. The idea, the concept of a separate culture with its own ways, its own customs, had been disposed of in the most effective possible way.

"Good job," the Relay trace web whispered. North was pleased. "The fission mines were perfectly placed. Nothing remains."

"No," Rogers agreed. "Nothing remains."

❖❖❖

Corporal Pete Matson pushed the front door open, grinning from ear to ear. "Hi, honey! Surprise!"

"Pete!" Gloria Matson came running, throwing her arms around her husband. "What are you doing home? Pete—"

"Special leave. Forty-eight hours." Pete tossed down his suitcase triumphantly. "Hi there, kid."

His son greeted him shyly. "Hello."

Pete squatted down and opened his suitcase. "How have things been going? How's school?"

"He's had another cold," Gloria said. "He's almost over it. But what happened? Why did they—"

"Military secret." Pete fumbled in his suitcase. "Here." He held something out to his son. "I brought you something. A souvenir."

He handed his son a hand-made wooden drinking cup. The boy took it shyly and turned it around, curious and puzzled. "What's a—a *souvenir?*"

Matson struggled to express the difficult concept. "Well, it's something that reminds you of a different place. Something you don't have, where you are. You know." Matson tapped the cup. "That's to drink out of. It's sure not like our plastic cups, is it?"

"No," the child said.

"Look at this, Gloria." Pete shook out a great folded cloth from his suitcase, printed with multi-colored designs. "Picked this up cheap. You can make a skirt out of it. What do you say? Ever seen anything like it?"

"No," Gloria said, awed. "I haven't." She took the cloth and fingered it reverently.

Pete Matson beamed, as his wife and child stood clutching the souvenirs he had brought them, reminders of his excursions to distant places. Foreign lands.

"Gee," his son whispered, turning the cup around and around. A strange light glowed in his eyes. "Thanks a lot, Dad. For the—*souvenir.*"

The strange light grew.

STORY NOTES

BEYOND LIES THE WUB

First published in *Planet Stories*, July 1952. "My first published story," wrote Dick for its appearance in the short story anthology *First Voyages*, "in the most lurid all pulp magazines on the stands at the time, *Planet Stories*. As I carried four copies into the record store where I worked, a customer gazed at me and them, with dismay, and said, 'Phil, you *read* that kind of stuff?' I had to admit I not only read it, I wrote it." Dick was at the time working not for Berkeley's Art Music Company, which had been a second home for him in his adolescence, but for the more upscale Tupper and Reed, which had an older, more respectable clientele that might indeed have been horrified at Dick's choice of reading matter. (Tupper and Reed lasted as a music store into the 2000s, when it was replaced with all due irony by a "Used Computers" shop.) *Planet Stories*, then edited by Jack O'Sullivan, specialized in what frequent contributor Leigh Brackett proudly called "space opera," which she defined in 1974 as "the folk-tale, the hero-tale of our particular niche in history." According to historian Thomas Clareson (in his entry on *Planet Stories* in the definitive reference book on the field, Marshall B. Tymn and Mike Ashley's *Science Fiction, Fantasy, and Weird Fiction Magazines*), the reader knew what to expect on picking a copy up: "Strange Adventures on Other Worlds," to quote its subhead. Published from 1939 to 1955, the magazine showcased space adventures by Brackett and others, including a Brackett-Ray Bradbury contribution, "Lorelei of the Red Mist" (1946). Bradbury also published two stories of what would become his classic *The Martian Chronicles* in *Planet Stories*, "The Million Year Picnic" (1946) and "Mars is Heaven" (1948). The term "hero-tale" thus allows for some elasticity, for how else to explain the distinctly non-heroic space farers in "Beyond Lies the Wub"? In his introduction to the story published in *First Voyages*, Dick wrote "The idea I wanted to get down on paper had to do with the definition of 'human.' The dramatic way I trapped the idea was to present ourselves, the literal humans, and then an alien lifeform that exhibits the deeper traits that I associate with humanity: not a biped with an enlarged cortex—a forked radish that thinks, to paraphrase the old saying—but an organism that is human in terms of soul." At least the wub is interested in human folklore, pursuing a discussion of "the role of Odysseus in the myths" despite every effort made to silence him.

THE GUN

Planet Stories, September 1952. The cover of this issue features a leggy, ray-gun wielding damsel illustrating Poul Anderson's novella "The Star Plunderer." Phil Dick didn't leave a record of what the folk at Tupper and Reed thought of this issue. "The Gun" was the second of five stories Dick placed at *Planet Stories* during his early career in what Thomas Clareson avers was the magazine's major contribution to the field in its final years. Clareson singles out "The Infinites" (May 1953) and "James P. Crow" (May 1954) for special mention. But "The Gun" is worth notice as well. One of Dick's more intriguing notions is that of self-repairing wartime machinery that carries on the endless struggle long after the human civilization that created them has died. "The Gun" introduces this concept, which he would further develop in stories like "Autofac" (1955) and "Pay for the Printer" (1956). By the time of this later story once perfect copies have begun to degenerate, a trope that adds to the air of seediness and despair in such later novels as *A Maze of Death* (1970). More generally "The Gun" can thus be seen as fitting into an even more significant theme, that of eternal multiplication and duplication of human souls, as in such masterpieces as "Upon the Dull Earth" (1954) and *The Three Stigmata of Palmer Eldritch* (1965).

THE SKULL

If, September 1952. A topless, one-eyed goddess emerges from a machine before an audience of leering scientists on the cover of this issue of this magazine. The story illustrated isn't "The Skull" (unmentioned on the cover) but instead "Shock Treatment" by Stanley Mullen. But *If*, unlike *Planet Stories*, was near the beginning of a long, successful run that lasted from 1952 until 1974, when it was absorbed into the lower circulation, higher prestige *Galaxy*. Philip K. Dick would go on to publish 13 stories in its pages. The September issue, the magazine's fourth, was the last edited by the magazine's founder, Paul Fairman. Fairman nonetheless set the tone for the magazine's entire run, seeing science fiction as "entertainment and escape," with the science in the stories he published just a "background... based on tangible gimmicks with at least a pseudo-scientific basis under them" (*If*, July 1952). "The Skull" meets these criteria in a rather dark tale whose basic theme is that of the Christ story... or of James Cameron's first *Terminator* film! Discussing other science fiction authors with me in 1981, Dick noted this tale's similarities with Michael Moorcock's acclaimed "Behold the Man" (1966), also about a time traveler who inadvertently founds a religion. "It's a dumb idea. It's evident by the third word that the guy himself is going to turn out to be the Savior. And I wrote that once, in a story called 'The Skull.' It was about a guy sent back in time to kill the Savior. And he's given the Savior's skull. And he goes back in time, and he's standing there getting ready to walk out into that world, in the costume of that time period, and he's holding the skull, and he suddenly sees that it's his own skull. He realizes that *he* is the Savior." Dick allowed that his story (the details of which he's reordered) is subtler than Moorcock's, as "just by being back there, he missed the time, he got there after the guy had been killed" and thus is responsible for his "resurrection" as well. One of Dick's most carefully worked-out early stories, its success stems from a grimly realistic setting meticulously built up from details like a room that is "warm and close from the heat of the little kerosene heater in the corner." Dick's first published fiction set on the planet Earth, it's also one of his least known works, never reprinted after first publication until its appearance in *The Collected Stories* in 1987—and now here.

MR. SPACESHIP

Imagination, January 1953. This was the first of eleven stories Philip Dick published in this magazine, including (in 1953 alone) "Piper in the Woods," "Paycheck," "The Cosmic Poachers," "The Impossible Planet" and "Project: Earth." Published from 1950-58, *Imagination* was edited for its entire run by William L. Hamling, a former fan. Hamling deliberately aimed the magazine for younger readers, promoting it with many lurid "BEM" ("bug-eyed monsters") covers, whose appropriateness was the subject of many anguished letters from readers. ("The salesgirl in the drugstore raises one eyebrow and lifts a corner of her upper lip in a well-bred sneer as she glances at the cover," complained one letter in the December 1954 issue.) Joe Sanders, in the Tymn-Ashley anthology *Science Fiction, Fantasy, and Weird Fiction Magazines*, considers most of the journal's output at once routine and melodramatic (with stories titled "Compete or Die!" and "Bring Back My Brain!"). *Imagination* had one of the strongest personalities of any 1950s science fiction pulp, with a chatty letter column personifying the journal as "Madge." "What did it signify, the coming to life of metal and plastic?" asks this story, in a line that could be an epigraph for much of Philip Dick's work. Human and machine merge into one in this little-known tale, again one not reprinted in Dick's lifetime. Dick's story antedates some better known work which used the same idea, listed in Peter Nicholls' *The Science Fiction Encyclopedia* as Thomas Scortia's "Sea Change" (1956), Cordwainer Smith's "Three to a Given Star" (1965) and Anne McCaffrey's *The Ship Who Sang* (1969). The toneless mechanical voice of "Mr. Spaceship" will return as the endless drone over the radio in "What the Dead Men Say" (1964), or on the telephone in *Ubik* (1969).

PIPER IN THE WOODS

Imagination, February 1953. In this magazine's November issue editor William Hamling will define what he seeks from his writers as "Well-plotted yarns with a fast pace. Dissertations into sociology, technology, and sadism are not our meat. Unless they are an afterthought to a darn good story! And even then keep the philosophizing to a minimum." This may be the most philosophical of any of Dick's sales to this journal. The defense mechanism against foreign absorption the residents of this planet develop—convincing their human visitors that they are, of all things, *plants*—is another example of Dick's interest in how the very weak can use the imagination to defeat, outwit and outlast the very strong. "Beyond Lies the Wub" introduces this theme, which will recur in many different stories over the next three decades—as late as 1980's "Chains of Air, Web of Aether," for example. Dick displays an intimate knowledge of psychiatric jargon in this story—"Primitive identification and projection," muses Dr. Harris when first confronted with his unusual patient. Not for the last time in this author's work, institutional psychology is seen as an instrument of social control, Harris being tasked not with his charge's happiness but rather with the efficiency of a military operation.

THE VARIABLE MAN

Space Science Fiction, September 1953. Technically, this novella was first published in the British edition of the same name of this magazine (in its July 1953 issue). Both journals were in fact the same magazine, the British edition a reprint of the American original, in both nations a short-lived (eight issues) digest-sized magazine edited by Lester del Rey. Del Rey, who would publish much of Dick's subsequent fiction, would later establish in his history of the field, *The World of Science Fiction* (1979), that 1953 was the peak year of the magazine boom, with 36 separate titles. "Many editors knew nothing of the field and cared even less," he would write. Del Rey was an obvious exception, which may be why "The Variable Man" is a standout among Dick's earliest fiction. In it he introduces one of his favorite stock characters, the practical mechanic who can fix anything, whose descendents would be trapped in the nightmare worlds of *Ubik* or *A Maze of Death* but here is actually able to outsmart the overly specialized lords of a future dystopia. Thomas Cole's lineage can be traced to a common figure in 19th century American literature, the Yankee peddler, previously employed in another tale of time travel Dick probably knew, Mark Twain's *A Connecticut Yankee in King Arthur's Court* (1889). Twain's hero uses his mastery of practical mechanics to defeat authoritarian rule in a way not dissimilar to Cole, who however remains an innocent abroad, and not a sharper. The character of Johnny Dooit, a mechanic who easily assembles a sandboat that can travel the Deadly Desert in L. Frank Baum's *The Road to Oz* (1909), may be another antecedent. It's characteristic of Dick's science fiction to have his "deadly desert" be the atomic-blasted ruins of New York.

THE CRYSTAL CRYPT

Planet Stories, January 1954. This is the last story in this volume drawn from the fifteen stories Dick wrote and sold prior to becoming a client of the Scott Meredith Literary Agency in July 1952. Philip Dick first discovered the world of science fiction pulps when he (according to a 1968 "Self-Portrait") was looking for *Popular Science*, and found *Stirring Science Stories* by mistake.

I was most amazed. Stories about science? At once I recognized the magic which I had found, in earlier times, in Oz books—this magic now coupled not with magic wands, but with science, and set in the future . . . My view became magic equals science . . . and science (of the future) equals magic.

This minor story reads like a spy thriller, set against a sci-fi backdrop of interplanetary war. Once again deception plays a key part in both offense and defence. Most of Dick's work is however more Day of Wrath than Bond, James Bond. "The Crystal Crypt" is an exception to this rule, proving that Dick could have written more conventional material, if only he had wanted to. But the bizarre nature of the science used here—shrinking an entire city—points to the fantastic nature of the whole enterprise. Indeed, Dick's inspiration here seems to come less from *Stirring Science Stories* and more from one of L. Frank Baum's Oz books. Dick is known to have devoured them as a child. If one sees these visitors to Mars waving their wand and miniaturizing The City as something akin to the Nome King miniaturizing The Emerald City and attempting to steal it away, it puts one in a more receptive mood . . .

MEDDLER

Reaching the Scott Meredith Literary Agency (hereinafter, SMLA) on July 24, 1952, "Meddler" was published in *Future*, October 1954. *Future Fiction* had begun during the first science fiction boom of the prewar era (1939-43), shut down, and been revived during the postwar boom of 1950. It lasted in different formats until 1960. Editor Robert W. Lowndes had been a member of the key group of prewar New York City science fiction fans and writers that have come to be known as "the Futurians," a group including future genre great Cyril Kornbluth, illustrator Hannes Bok, and Donald Wollheim, the future publisher of many of Dick's paperback originals for Ace. Lowndes returned as editor during the magazine's revival in 1950, the least expensive SF magazine then on for sale for a mere 15 cents a copy. With very little money to work with—contributor Robert Silverberg once referred to the magazine as "esteemed but impoverished"—Lowndes is seen by historian Mike Ashley (in the Tymn-Ashley anthology *Science Fiction, Fantasy, and Weird Fiction Magazines*) as "an alchemist in the SF field, forever attempting to convert lead into gold." Dick eventually published three stories in *Future*, including the original version of "Vulcan's Hammer" (1956), which he later expanded into a novel. In 1980 he contributed this story note to a reprinting of "Meddler" in the Mark Hurst-edited anthology *The Golden Man (Berkley)*: "Within the beautiful lurks the ugly; you can see in this rather crude story the germ of my whole theme that nothing is what it seems. This story should be read as a trial run on my part; I was just beginning to grasp that obvious form and latent form are not the same thing. As Heraclitus said in fragment 54: 'Latent structure is master of obvious structure,' and out of this comes the later more sophisticated Platonic dualism between the phenomenal world and the real but invisible realm of forms lying behind it. I may be reading too much into this simple-minded early story, but at least I was beginning to see in a dim way what I later saw so clearly; in fragment 123, Heraclitus said, 'The nature of things is in the habit of concealing itself,' and therein lies it all."

BEYOND THE DOOR
Submitted as "The Cuckoo Clock." Reached SMLA August 29, 1952, published in *Fantastic Universe*, January 1954. Dick's writing skills appreciably improve in the course of the non-stop creativity of these months. Dick uses just a few lines to sum up how a husband spoils the effect of a present by his careless words in the opening page of this effort ("Doris made a funny little sound"). Dick's agents at Scott Meredith made occasional attempts to break their client out of the science fiction market, and thought well enough of this story to submit it to *Esquire* and *Today's Woman* before finally placing it with *Fantastic Universe*, in an issue edited during her three-month tenure

by Beatrice Jones. Dick would ultimately publish seven of his stories in *Fantastic Universe*, including the now famous (because filmed by Steven Spielberg) "The Minority Report" (1956). The magazine, founded by Leo Margulies in 1953, lasted until 1960 under different editors and changing directions. Its offerings at the time Dick wrote for it were very eclectic, ranging from new "Conan the Barbarian" stories completed from Robert E. Howard fragments, to major work by Isaac Asimov and Algis Budrys, as well as the contributions of new authors like Harlan Ellison. "Beyond the Door" is an early example of a form Dick will make quite a specialty of in later work—sharp sour portraits of bad marriages. One can't see it finding a home at either the all-male *Esquire*, or with the editor of *Today's Woman*, for precisely that reason!

JON'S WORLD

Submitted as "Jon." Reached SMLA October 21, 1952, published in the anthology *Time to Come* (New York: Farrar Straus & Young, 1954), edited by August Derleth. This was Dick's first hardcover publication. Derleth (1909-71) was closely associated with the legendary horror author H.P. Lovecraft, and had co-founded Arkham House to publish Lovecraft's works. He edited many books and wrote a great deal of fantasy himself, as well as a series of Sherlock Holmes pastiches featuring as their hero one "Solar Pons." Other contributors to *Time to Come* included Isaac Asimov and Arthur C. Clarke. "Jon's World" was written directly after, and is in many ways is a sequel to one of Dick's best known stories, "Second Variety" (which reached SMLA on October 3 and was the last thing Dick wrote before "Jon's World"). In this story we see the world of the "claws"—four varieties of android soldiers passing themselves off as human—from above, as Kastner and Ryan fly over them in their time ship. In "Second Variety" (which would first see print in *Space Science Fiction* in 1954) we see the claws in action, as they use human empathy as their weapon against humanity. The claws of "Second

Variety" are the direct ancestors of the soulless androids we find in much of Dick's fiction, most famously *Do Androids Dream of Electric Sheep?* (1968). "Jon's World" is another story, coming from a completely different direction, of empathy denied and destroyed. The wonderful child Jon is an early example of a Dickian mystic who perceives another, better world and as such is a precursor of no less than the Philip K. Dick/Horselover Fat of *VALIS* (1981). Dick's harsh critique of psychiatric therapy here is in line with modern thought, which condemns lobotomies, but at the time Dick wrote this story the procedure was still quite common.

PROGENY

Reached SMLA on Nov. 3, 1952, published in *If,* November 1954. The magazine's publisher, James L. Quinn, was editing the magazine at this time; after losing two strong editors, he took command himself. Evc Wulff was his Associate Editor, and the pair emphasized what they called "variety and diversity" until the next change of management, in 1958. The Quinn-Wulff years saw *If* publish such signature work of Dick's as "The Golden Man" (1954) and "Captive Market" (1955). "Progeny" is just as good, but is usually perceived as a satire of the vogue for the behaviorist psychology of B.F. Skinner and his notorious "Skinner Box," the lightproof, soundproof "operant conditioning chambers" invented for use in studying the behavior of lab animals under different stimuli (pellets, electric shocks). Dick was however coming off of the powerful "Jon's World," which dealt with themes very close to him; it's easy to see "Progeny" flowing naturally from his sympathetic portrait of the mystical boy Jon. Here the boy is spiritually "lobotomized" by his conditioning. The autobiographical aspects of the author's grappling with the effects of institutionalized psychology in his own life are overtly treated here—his mother Dorothy had attempted to raise him using behaviorist precepts very similar to those used here, as she explained to her son in a 1975 letter:

(T)hat was the period when pediatricians and all the books about infant care were under the influence of behaviorist psychology. The idea was that the infant was a healthy animal that could be cared for physically and left alone . . . Cuddling, rocking, kissing were frowned on; the baby must wait a rigid 4 hours for his feeding; if he began to cry for food 20 minutes before the time you let him cry; you never picked him up when he cried . . . Pediatricians made an ignorant young mother feel that to violate any of the rules would cause irreparable damage to the child.

Dorothy Dick Hudner's assertions are fully backed up by a look at the pediatric literature of the time, and it's easy to read off the rest of the story as allegory (the boy's initials are "P.D." and the story's father is, like Dick's father, a traveling businessman who disappeared from his life for many years). But "Progeny" wouldn't work as well as it does if a reader needed to know anything about Philip K. Dick to enjoy it. That is the art of fiction.

OF WITHERED APPLES

This was one of Dick's early fantasies that the author had submitted to many magazines in 1951-52 in a vain effort to place it. Submitted to Meredith on January 26, 1953, it finally saw print in the last of the four issues of *Cosmos Science Fiction and Fantasy*, July 1954. There's quite a story here! *Cosmos* (1953-4) carried work by some of the field's top names—Arthur C. Clarke, Poul Anderson, Jack Vance, Gordon Dickson, Algys Budrys—all of whom were clients of Scott Meredith's. Its official editor, L.B. Cole, was a front for Laurence Janifer, an SMLA employee. As Janifer explained to Mike Ashley in 1986,

Scott began to make arrangements for the packaging of magazines of various sorts. The policy was set by mutual agreement between Scott and the publishers, but it wasn't much of a policy. We were to pay low rates (about a cent a word), not to get *too* damn experimental, and draw our material either from stories written for *Cosmos* by clients of the agency, including me, or from the backlog of stories which we had at the agency and hadn't sold to higher-pay markets . . . no writers except agency writers could be considered.

Dick's "The Great C" was in the magazine's first issue (a year after he had submitted it to SMLA) as well as this evidently unsalable work. "Of Withered Apples" is a tart souvenir from Dick's earliest days as an aspiring writer, and it's good *Cosmos* existed, for it otherwise would probably be lost. Dick's 1954 masterpiece "Upon the Dull Earth" is a point-for-point reworking of this story, down to the young woman fatally drawn to a fearsome nature. It's only too bad Dick may never have heard of the elaborate lengths the agency went to cover its tracks. According to Janifer (who told his story in the Tymn-Ashley *Science Fiction, Fantasy, and Weird Fiction Magazines*) SMLA "hired an empty office and a spare phone line booked in the name of the relevant aliases" to prevent anyone from learning the real identity of the magazine's editor. One wonders if Ernest Lehman worked for the agency as well, for this exact setup was used in his screenplay for Hitchcock's *North by Northwest* (1959) by the U.S. Government to create the spy, George Kaplan, who isn't there.

ADJUSTMENT TEAM

Reached SMLA February 11, 1953, published in *Orbit Science Fiction*, September-October 1954. Like *Cosmos*, *Orbit Science Fiction* was edited by a professional using a front, and like *Cosmos*, *Orbit* only lasted a few issues—five, in this case. It was begun by a publisher seeking to cash in on the sf boom of the era; his editor of record (Jules Saltman) did the layouts and other editorial work, but knew nothing of science fiction. The experienced fan turned book publisher Donald Wollheim, who would shortly begin buying Dick's original manuscripts for publication at his new company, Ace Books, was asked in to anonymously select and edit each issue's stories. In addition to this classic, *Orbit* also published "Tony and the Beetles" (1953) and "The Last of the Masters" (1954). "Ol' Don Wollheim," Dick told me in 1981, "saved science fiction when it was dying" thanks to his perseverance during a market slump in the late 1950s. He also told me that he'd had no contact with Wollheim before his agent sent him his novel manuscript for *Solar Lottery* in 1954, so Dick probably didn't know, or wasn't aware of, Wollheim's purchase of these three early tales. "Adjustment Team" is a key early work of Dick's, moving his "ash world" theme away from a far future Earth or from a faraway planet, and locating it in the contemporary U.S. This bold move anticipates much of Dick's future work.

JAMES P. CROW

Reached SMLA March 17, 1953, published in *Planet Stories*, May 1954. "James P. Crow" is an overt commentary on civil rights, a theme Dick would return to many times over the course of his career. Racial issues pop up in such disparate later work as *Eye in the Sky* (1958), *The Crack in Space* (1966), and *Flow My Tears, the Policeman Said* (1974). This particular story was published, by happy chance, right at the time of the U.S. Supreme Court's "Brown v. Board of Education" decision. In an interesting essay sf veteran Algis Budrys has discussed the many "Nonliterary Influences in Science Fiction" which included, in the 1950s, extensive rewritings undertaken by pulp science fiction magazine editors to among other things force conservative social mores onto stories. There would be "no villainous Anglo-Saxons," for example. If *Planet Stories* editors Malcolm Reiss or Jack O'Sullivan were at all inclined to censor this story for political reasons, the fact that it was about humans vs. robots rather than blacks vs. whites probably would have let the story go untouched. Dick would go on to use this story's device of rigged tests as a device to prevent the rise of humans in his 1970 novel *Our Friends from Frolix 8* (1970).

SOUVENIR

Reached SMLA March 26, 1953, published in *Fantastic Universe*, October 1954. Publisher Leo Marguiles, editing this magazine by the time this story was published, had first caught notice editing space adventures at his *Thrilling Wonder Stories* in the later 1930s. Dick told Paul Williams in the 1970s how as a boy he passed from the Oz books and *Stirring Science Stories* to the pulp adventure fiction of magazines like *Thrilling Wonder Stories*.

I thought that was keen. Manly Wade Wellman and Robert Moore Williams. Wrote 'em all. Every damn story. And you know what they were about? . . . They were looking at Mars and it cracks open, and instead of being all red , underneath it was all green. These big hinges open up and it's all green and there's a bunch of horrible people coming at you with guns . . . I thought, "Well, this is really awful. But on the other hand, there is something exciting about going to other planets . . . "

The device Dick uses here of "isolated self-sufficient farm-units . . . modeled on the manors of the Middle Ages," is taken up and used in many novels of the 1960s, such as the vast tracts ruled over by isolated humans in novels like *The Penultimate Truth* (1964).